# 183 Reasons

## THE NEWFOUND LAKE SERIES
# ALANNA GRACE

First e-book edition October 2023

First paperback edition October 2023

*Book cover and interior design by SGA Books*

*Photograph © Luke Gram for Stocksy via Adobe Stock*

*Editing by Plumfield Editing*

ISBN-13 (paperback): 979-8-9883296-0-2

ISBN-13 (e-book): 979-8-9883296-1-9

www.alannagraceauthor.com

*To Ruth Cardello and Jennifer Sommersby, who both gave me the courage to begin this journey and have believed in me from the start.*

*We never know where the road will take us; we just have to be brave enough to follow the path.*

# 1

*Sofia*

The local meteorologist estimated today's high to reach ninety degrees. The humidity and direction of the mountain breeze will determine whether the cabin will transform into a sauna. Luckily, I dressed for the weather in my comfy sneakers and no-show socks, a loose tee tucked into blue jean cutoffs. This outfit screams summer, and I love it. My shorts might be just a little too short, but who knows me here? A peek of ass cheek poking out from under the frayed edging never hurt anyone.

And it's always my favorite time of year when I get to box up my teaching clothes and trade out that summer wardrobe!

Finding everything I need at Raubuchon's is a cinch; pumping myself up to clean for half the day will take a little more effort. As the cashier rings up my purchase, the older gentleman bagging gives me a soft smile and, with the kindest eyes, says, "Welcome to town."

Meriden is a small place where everyone knows who the locals are, who the summer people are, and who is just plain lost. Despite having spent the summers of my childhood and fewer weekends than I would've liked during my adolescence here, I don't fit neatly into one category.

Because I have more cleaning supplies than a maid service, I have to stash these items in the bed of my truck so they won't fly out as I drive. I hoist all five feet two inches of myself onto the back tire, one foot on the wheel and one foot leaning on the shopping cart. I grab the hair elastic off my wrist and throw my long hair into a loose ponytail.

I continue to maneuver the bags into the truck, my shorts creeping higher and higher. As I do my last squat to grab the final bag, I catch a baseball hat in my peripheral view coming toward me. I freeze, staying in my squat, ass cheeks dipping low while I whip my head to my left and notice a man who stops me dead in my tracks.

His downward gaze is glued to my ass cheeks, exposed for viewing pleasure. I promptly reposition, his eyes forced to meet mine, and jump off my back tire. My keys, phone, debit card, and license fall under my truck. My cheeks burn with embarrassment as I scramble through the dirt, trying to collect everything. I stand up to regain composure. He hasn't moved an inch.

Damn, he is attractive. He is wearing fitted blue jeans, dirty work boots, a once-white local brewery shirt, and shaggy blond hair tucked under his backward Red Sox hat. His eyes, his freaking eyes. They are a green you rarely get a glimpse of, resembling flecks of emerald. His cheeks are the brightest shade of red. He saw more of me than I'd intended.

In one smooth motion, he lifts his arms, removes his hat, and finger-combs his hair, revealing a six-pack under his shirt. His mouth curves into a grin when he witnesses my attention traveling to his stomach. He smirks, pulls his hat back on, and tucks his hands into both pockets, thumbs resting on top of his jeans. I wipe the rapidly drying mud on my palms onto my already tanned thighs and tug at my shorts as much as possible while holding his gaze.

*What is going on?* I'm at the hardware store, prepping to spend the day cleaning, and I am fanning the flames of heat erupting between my legs.

"Hi, I didn't mean to stare, but you rarely spot such a sweet view at the hardware store. I'm Jackson. You must be new to town." His stare is intense and breathtaking, and he holds out his hand.

"Yes, I am, and apparently it's obvious. I'm Solia." Shocked I can string coherent sentences together, I extend my hand.

"It's a small town. If I'd seen you around, I would've remembered," he confesses, flashing a boyish smile that will also be hard to forget. "Well, welcome to town. Maybe I'll bump into you again?" He gives a soft laugh and walks toward the store's entrance, but not before glancing back to catch me staring at his tight ass as he saunters away.

*I guess we're even now.*

Not exactly how I expected my first Meriden interaction to go. When I pulled off exit 23 into New Hampshire today, meeting a hot guy was at the very bottom of my list.

Driving out of the hardware store lot, I open the windows, crank the music, and remind myself that I left every poor excuse of a man behind. I am a force to be reckoned with. I always wanted to be this girl—independent, fearless, taking charge of my life.

Today, I am that girl.

I inhale the fresh mountain air of my new hometown. I won't let myself dwell on Jackson's downright sexiness. I will not let myself think twice about walking into the store to find him.

Onward to the cabin.

If you'd asked me where I'd be at twenty-six, I wouldn't have guessed I'd be driving solo in a beat-up pickup truck, venturing out of my comfort zone, and starting fresh. I finally read the writing on the wall. Sure, I was trading one small town for another, but there had to be more to life than what I was doing.

I've always been a type A personality, the girl everyone thought had her shit together. I was checking off my life goals one by one, like a contestant in a race. Live in a small town near where I grew up: Check! Get a job and earn a living as an elementary school teacher: Check! Lease an apartment: Check!

Find the man of my dreams: Nada!

I didn't think that was too much to ask for. I am an outgoing, adventurous, goal-oriented person. I take care of myself and the people in my life.

Growing up in a small town has its disadvantages, but it has more pros than cons. The community is one big, supportive family. Staying close to family was important, so I rented a furnished apartment in town. I filled each room with things I love—indoor plants in every spot they'd fit, whimsical chimes in a few of the windows, and memories of the people I love most. A picture of my parents, taken during their last trip to Florida, rested on the side table in the living room. A picture of my brother, his wife, and their two kids sat in a frame beside them.

I had a few throwbacks from college alongside recent pictures of Mia, my best friend, and me. People often mistake us for sisters, both blue-eyed, with long, brown hair, and small button noses. But of course, there is the height difference. Mia is a lengthy five foot seven, plus her hair is pin-straight and tame compared to mine. While she may not be my actual sister, she's the closest thing I'll ever have to one.

My parents recently helped paint my bedroom a washout white, and I'd purchased new curtains and a comforter. Two wooden shelves by my bed held pictures of Kyle and me. My favorite was the one with our backs to the ocean as the sun set below the horizon at Camp Cronan. Kyle wore the blue bathing suit I bought for him—I knew it would fit him amazingly. I had on my favorite blue bikini and my beach waves blew in the breeze. We both squinted and smiled, my head tilted to Kyle to meet his gaze. We had such a great day.

I had convinced myself things were going great.

My teaching career started in a neighboring town. I taught second grade and the kids were amazing, but the hours as a new teacher were taking a toll. Quitting was never an option; I continued to work hard and trudge through. However, our enrollment declined after a new charter school opened in town. Because of low numbers, a second-grade classroom would be cut. Being the lowest on the seniority list, I was officially laid off at the end of the school year.

In the meantime, I was enjoying my exciting whirlwind romance. Kyle and the phrase "the love of my life" became synonymous, or so I thought. We had just celebrated our seven-month anniversary at Whispering Dunes, a beautiful seaside restaurant on Ocean Drive in Narragansett. Things were an absolute dream—until I received a text later that night.

> MIA
>
> Are you sitting down? I'm not sure how to tell you, but I just came across Kyle's profile when I was swiping through the dating app.
> Apparently, he is still on the market.

It was a punch to the gut I didn't foresee. Of course, I searched for him, and there he was, single and ready to fuck. Not needing another second to process, I drove over to his place and told him exactly what I thought of him. I have too much self-respect to deal with his bullshit.

I'd be lying if I didn't say the whole situation lowered my

self-esteem a couple notches. I spent the next week replaying our entire relationship over and over, tossing countless tissue boxes in the garbage. This was the third relationship that had gone up in flames in the past few years. It was time to wave the white flag and hang up the towel. The guys around here just plain sucked.

However, I'm certain I deserve better. Mia picked me up off the ground and reminded me what a catch I am. Thankfully, I grew up as an athlete and love exercise. I consider myself fashionable and choose styles that highlight my assets. My hair is naturally wavy and shades of light brown, and I keep it long and healthy. And goddamn it, I've got great boobs. So many women want bigger boobs, smaller boobs, or perkier boobs. They won't always stay this way, but I'll keep my full C cup, thank you very much.

My family is amazing; I am supported and loved. My mom's attempt to lift my spirits always comes in the form of sugar. A dozen blueberry muffins one day, magic cookie bars the next. My dad, who stays up to date on pop culture, texts me about the latest dating app or articles detailing a newly married couple who met online. He's aware the chances of me meeting someone teaching at an elementary school are slim to none. Being from a rural area, pretty much every guy in town was in your preschool class or the one next to it, and there were only so many new arrivals to the dating pool. "Everyone meets this way now" is Dad's signature saying. He wants me to be happy, but after the shit show I just experienced, I can't bring myself to swipe to find love.

Honestly, love is the last thing I need right now. I need to focus and zoom in on the other aspects of my crumbling world.

A week before school ended, my parents came over for our traditional Sunday night family dinner. These dinners had been a party of four until Kyle and I split up. Now we're back to the three of us.

To show my parents that I had my shit together, despite my breakup, I cleaned my place and planned out a decent meal. I tied up my hair into a messy bun, threw on a pair of old joggers, and got to work making dinner. I'd have enough time to get ready after I cooked. I made my mother's favorite meal and my father's latest dessert.

Despite telling them to come at five, they arrived at four and told me they had news to share. With dinner in the oven, they video-called my older brother and informed us of their plans to sell the family's New Hampshire cabin. The upkeep was too much for them, and no one was going up there as much as before. They wanted the freedom to travel whenever and wherever without having to arrange for the cabin to be taken care of. My laissez-faire brother accepted the news and was hopeful they would spend more time in North Carolina with him and his family. While change is good, especially for my aging parents, selling the cabin was a hard no for me.

After the call ended and the news had sunk in, my heart felt heavy, an awful lot like heartbreak. My life had become a giant dumpster fire.

Our family's cabin is the dream of log cabin living. Resembling the Lincoln Log cabins I built as a kid, this place sits on top of a gorgeous sloping hill in the middle of the woods, with a forested marsh extending for countless acres as the front view and various sky-high evergreen trees as the backdrop. Standing on the front porch, I can hear the rustling of leaves as the wind dances by and the chirping of songbirds high up in the pines. And on a calm day, the stillness of everything is in perfect harmony.

This cabin holds endless memories and stories from my childhood, which is why I couldn't fathom my parents selling it.

It's not that they aren't interested in the cabin anymore; it's simply too much. A place that brought them so much joy has become a headache. Too remote, too much upkeep, and too isolated for their new hopes of a busier social circle and more months of sunshine.

There are certain places where you spend time that touch your soul in a way words can't explain. Places that calm you to the core and make you stop and truly cherish what's around you. The air fills your lungs, the water calms your thoughts, and peace surrounds you. That's what this cabin and lake are to me.

Some people will never understand, but if you've been lucky enough to spend time there, you just might. Losing this place couldn't happen. I wouldn't let it happen.

After they left that night, I did a lot of thinking and soul-searching, as well as deleting of contacts. Kyle sent several groveling messages attempting to explain the error of his ways. Delete contact. Delete all the exes. I knew what I needed to do —a fresh start was the answer. Losing the cabin would be equal to losing a part of me, part of my soul and future memories. It didn't occur to me how important it was until I was faced with losing it. I had to persuade my parents to let me have it.

I made my decision and wanted nothing more than to start fresh—a clean slate, an unmarked trail. I grew up summering on the shores of Newfound Lake. Lazy days filled with sunshine, sand, the wind blowing through my hair, surrounded by the beauty of the mountains.

I didn't have it figured out, but there was no better time than now. The dumpster fire was blazing, and I wasn't sticking around to watch it burn.

I no longer had a job, and the lease on my apartment was up next month. I'd need a job in the Meriden area, a better vehicle for the mountain winters, and to figure out how in the world I would maintain the cabin on my own.

After countless text messages, phone calls, and late-night dinners, my persistence paid off. Saying I had my parents' support would be an exaggeration. They spouted the laundry list of reasons why this was too big of an undertaking. They didn't think I could handle being alone in the woods, when I was used to having them a few miles away and many friends within a mile's radius. I'd be trading neighbors and small-town comforts for a cabin with absolute solitude within an even smaller town. Sure, that'll take some getting used to. I'll have to order and stack wood for the woodstove, the cabin's primary heat source—when the most I'd ever had to do before was press the up arrow on the thermostat.

The cabin sits on a private road with zero street lights; therefore, I'll have to arrange the plowing during the winter. And there's no weekly trash service. I'll have to stay on top of shoveling the wrap-around deck and front porch to avoid sagging from the weight of the snow, as winter storms in the Lakes Region can be relentless. They reminded me to rake and dispose of the fall leaves, mow the grass, and clean the house, a space five times bigger than I'm used to. I would need to be prepared for anything since there aren't any big-box stores to run to at ten o'clock at night. Everything in Meriden closes by eight (or earlier).

My parents think I'm being too nostalgic, and quite frankly, they (or I should say my mother) don't think I have what it takes. Mom, the biggest naysayer of the two, reminded me my cabin memories were of summer sunshine when everything was handled in the background, relieving me from ever having to think about what is required to live up here year-round. Hence, the expiration date on the deal.

Their deal? I have until the end of the summer. Two and a half months to learn to live in the middle of nowhere and figure out how to maintain the cabin to keep them from selling it. If I can't figure it out, the For Sale sign goes up Labor Day weekend.

If I find what I'm searching for, they will move forward with their other plans, and I will stay in my mountain retreat.

So here I am, writing a new chapter to my story. I'm not sure if it'll have a happy ending, but I'm going to give it my best shot.

# 2

*Sofia*

As I cruise through town, a warm breeze circulates through the truck. I inhale deeply, the clean mountain air reassuring me I am home. The sun shines high above as it always does toward the end of June. Meriden is a nostalgic New England town with quaint shops lining Main Street. Among the storefronts are a mom-and-pop bookstore, a fudge factory, and of course, a post office, library, and fire station. Every location opens and closes at the same time, and each has a lamppost out front that holds potted summer flowers. This is small-town perfection.

People stroll both sides with paper bags swinging from their wrists as they push their strollers or hold the hand of a loved one. In summer, the locals come out of their snowy bungalows, finished with hibernation and ready to socialize, mingle, and enjoy the majestic beauty around them. The population quadruples this time of year as visitors vacation on Newfound Lake. Meriden, nestled in a beautiful mountain range and surrounded by countless lakes, lures nature lovers from every corner of the country, generation after generation.

Visitors and locals pack the streets today. People search for parking spots at the Christianson's Country Store, hoping to grab today's special to enjoy later on the shores. Moms and dads head into Small Mart for an extra fishing pole or water tube for the kids to enjoy while they relax on the pontoon boat. It's strange to experience this as an adult because my memories of this town are from my childhood. Taking in my surroundings reminds me of just how ready I am to make fresh memories.

Anticipation and freedom tingle through my veins as I turn my F-150 onto Chasm Drive. Trading in my SUV for this used pickup was the right move. Getting around safely is my number one priority. Being snowed in sounds fabulous, but navigating Chasm Drive for supply runs during the winter will be a necessity.

The tires bump against the rocky hill, and the cabin comes into focus. I have a list a mile long of things to figure out and work through, but living here fills me with excitement, and the hard work will be worth it.

The sun beams through the trees without a breeze, but I'll be damned if I turn on the cabin's air conditioning. Trying to keep bills to a minimum is my goal. I plan to combat the heat with lemonade and cool showers. If I'm lucky, the lake breeze will sneak through the trees from time to time.

Unpacking is simple, and I am ready to begin my cleaning spree. On the counter, I line up the products and everything else I need. I tell the speaker to crank the music, open every window and door, and pull my T-shirt over my head, revealing my black sports bra. The fewer clothes, the better. It's hot as hell.

For the next several hours, I hustle from room to room, singing along while dusting, vacuuming, washing and changing sheets, and scrubbing toilets. You name it, I clean it. Three trash bags later, I have two spotless bathrooms, two bedrooms ready to be slept in, one kitchen organized to be cooked in, and one spotless living room. The only thing not done is the loft, but it will require more attention, and really, I want to make sure the second bedroom is in top shape for Mia's first visit, whenever she can get her butt up here.

Three hours and four '90s hip-hop playlists later, I am a sweaty mess. This place is as clean as it is ever going to be. I'm proud of the work I've done; cleaning can be crossed off the list. I'll make this cabin mine in no time. But right now, I have to shower. Even I find myself offensive.

Living out here definitely has its advantages, and no neighbors is at the top of the list. I walk out of the sliding glass doors onto the deck where the midday sun beats heavily on the planks. While I love the summer heat, my skin is baking. I let the music continue, pull my ponytail elastic out so my hair tumbles free, and tug my tight sports bra over my head, exposing my breasts to the sizzling mountain air. I undo my sneakers, slide my blue jeans off, and toss everything into the corner. I can do that here. It is sensual and freeing to stand outside naked with the scorching sun penetrating my skin, sweat dripping.

The next song on the playlist pounds through the windows and vibrates off the trees. I am living my best life, hair loose, jamming to the beat, singing along so loud my lungs hurt. This is what I wanted—freedom, experiences, living every day to the fullest. I drop my ass low, lower than I would dare on a dance floor in a dark club. I bend in half, one hand on the deck plank near my foot, and I twerk, glistening breasts bouncing, creating tiny pools on the deck, as I belt out the lyrics. As my head hangs upside down between my legs, I recognize two work boots on the deck behind me.

I swing upright so fast, staring straight into the face of the man from the hardware store, scream louder than I was singing, hurdle the three deck steps, and slam through the first door available, which happens to be the outdoor shower.

Oh my god, oh my god. What the hell just happened? I can't think straight. The music is still blaring, and I look through the tiny slats of the outdoor shower to spot Jackson's backward Red Sox hat, his body hunched over in laughter.

"Stop the music! Stop!" Finally, my voice weasels through and the playlist stops. What am I supposed to do now? What is he doing here? Every nerve ending in my body is shot; I didn't hear or see him.

He clears his throat and walks across the deck and toward the shower.

"Listen, I am so sorry to have shown up unannounced. I didn't mean to scare you and certainly didn't mean to interrupt you. When I was getting into my truck to leave the supply store, I spotted your debit card in the mud, so I took it inside in case you returned looking for it. When I gave it to Gerry, he told me your family owned the cabin at the end of this road. I did a couple of errands in Plymouth and figured I'd swing by and return it on my way back to town."

Jackson takes a deep breath, and I watch through the shower slats as he nervously sways back and forth. "I'll leave your card on the deck and go."

My heart pounds in my chest and a tsunami of humiliation crashes through me.

"I'm sorry again. I don't know what else to say, so I guess I'll see you around. I apologize for repeating, but we rarely get views this hot in Meriden, never mind twice in one day, so I'll consider myself lucky." He isn't aware I'm staring at him through the wooden shower planks, eating up his sweet smile, his sincerity, but mostly, the bulge filling the front of his jeans.

I remain absolutely quiet, because what should I say? *No*

*problem, thanks for returning my card. Stop by anytime?* I don't usually sing at the top of my lungs and twerk on the deck for the birds. Ugh, I cannot come to terms with the fact I was just caught, butt-ass naked, at what I thought was the most remote cabin, by the sexy man in work boots from the hardware store.

Solitude: Uncheck!

When I hear his truck reverse and drive up the rocky dirt road, I breathe a sigh of relief. Blood returns to my head and the panic begins to subside. Wait until Mia hears this one.

For now, I still need to shower. No music, no singing, no distractions, just the sound of water and the birds. If anyone drives up, I'll hear it. I'll have to figure out how to handle Jackson the next time I run into him. I also need to figure out who the hell Gerry is and how he knows my address.

First, though, I need to relax, wash off the built-up sweat and grime, and make some dinner.

There is nothing that holds a flame to an outdoor shower with the sun setting, the cool breeze, and the protection of the trees. Standing in awe of my surroundings, my breathing again under control, my thoughts drift back to Jackson's excitement between the shower boards. Although I am mortified as hell he witnessed my junk bouncing in the air, I am damn happy I have been working out over the past few months. My ass is the firmest it's been in years (thank you, Peloton), and I just got waxed before leaving. So there's that. It was obvious he was turned on by what he saw.

We have hot guys where I'm from, and I've had hot guys check me out before, but there is something different about Jackson.

I haven't been in town for one full day, and already I've managed to showcase my ass to the hardware store, drop my belongings in the mud, and get caught twerking naked on my back deck by a man I met hours earlier.

I shut off the shower and the realization that I don't have a damn towel sets in. Nothing left to do but laugh at this point. Everything living in these woods has gotten familiar with me on an intimate level rather quickly, so walking back into the cabin stark naked is the least of my worries.

# 3

Jackson

Holy hell. This morning when I walked through the hardware store parking lot, a surge of testosterone ripped through me. A woman leaning over the side of her truck was wearing the shortest shorts I'd ever seen. I've spent my entire life in Meriden, and I've never been so caught off guard. In a small town, you recognize every backside around, and this one was definitely new. The best thing was, she was oblivious to how much she was showing off.

I stood behind her before I even comprehended what I was doing. Clearly, I'm out of practice because she totally caught me staring at her stunning curves. She bounced off the truck tire and shimmied her shorts back into place, and I was stunned when she faced me. She's a knockout, and I, for once, was at a loss for words.

From her toned, tanned legs to her slender curves and her engulfing blue eyes, she had me panting. I must've looked like a complete idiot standing there, but no way in hell could I have walked on by. Call it gravitational pull—whatever it was, I felt it immediately. As soon as we started talking, a connection zinged through me. Loose strands falling from the pile of hair knotted on top of her head blew in the breeze, and I wanted those wisps against my chest. She was undeniably sexy in her fitted T-shirt and short jean shorts, and the pickup truck put me in overdrive.

Not wanting to make a complete ass out of myself, I told her I hoped to see her again. But my mind reeled with images of her without shorts on, the shape of her body underneath the sheets. The dirty things I wanted to do to her are unspeakable. I walked away and didn't dare turn to look back, but I'm pretty sure I felt her checking me out.

As I left the store, I spotted a debit card in the mud next to where Solia had been parked. I figured it must be hers and so I went back inside to leave it with Gerry. I didn't expect him to know who she was or where she lived. Even though my day was jam-packed with errands and a never-ending list of farm chores, I figured this was as good a reason as any to see her again. I could certainly make time for those ass cheeks—I mean, returning that woman's debit card.

I pull up to the address Gerry gave me and hear music blaring from the side deck. I make my way around the cabin and am pleasantly surprised to see the lady of the house has lost her clothes somewhere between the hardware store and the deck. Her long, thick hair, freed from its bun, flies about her head as she dances, truly in the zone. She drops her hand to the deck and starts twerking in my direction. I almost lose it—I envision riding up behind her and sliding into home plate.

Then, she spots me and her face immediately reddens. I freeze, and the referee calls the out. The slam of the shower door brings me back to the present and I'm standing here with a hard-on. I eventually mutter something about Gerry and the debit card, but she doesn't respond. She must be more humiliated than I am, so I apologize, trying to make the situation less awkward.

When she still doesn't acknowledge me, I assume I should leave.

I get back to my truck and spot myself grinning ear to ear in the rearview mirror, and there's more to it than catching Solia on the deck in her birthday suit. I can't remember the last time I felt this present. I've been moping around this town with my head in a storm cloud for the past nine months, and this is the first time in a very long time that I've smiled this big.

Anyone in Meriden would say I went from being one of the town bachelors to someone they felt sorry for. Women used to see a hardworking farmer with muscles—at least, that's what I've been told. Now they see a tragedy.

Sometimes when bad things happen, the world changes their perception of a person. Everything I was before vanished that day. When they see me now, they see Trinity, and there is nothing I can do to alter that reality. Instead of trying, I keep to myself. Working at the family orchard every day provides me with more than enough to keep busy, and luckily, the drama in Shannon's life is currently front and center.

I love my sister, but I'm as excited as she is about her divorce being finalized. Getting rid of Richard has been a long time coming. The damn asshole needs to sign the papers and get this thing over with. I'm not sure what pleasure he's getting from dragging out this saga. She deserves a medal for putting up with him for the last four years. Thankfully, they didn't start a family, so she can walk away with a clean slate. Thinking of others and putting herself last had to stop. One can only put up with a drunk for so long before it exacts a toll.

Rich tried to get sober more than once, but Shannon reached her breaking point. Hopefully, we get word he signed soon and she'll finally be free. Richard's taking this pretty hard. Thankfully, her soon-to-be ex-husband accepted a job in the next town over. I'm hoping she can find some peace along the shores of Newfound during the rest of her summer vacation before she returns to the classroom in September.

I spend the day at the orchard using the flail mower to trim the overgrown grass but can't get Solia off my mind. Fields need tending, but I can't focus for the first time in forever. I do as much as I can manage, but at the end of the day, I'm not ready to go home.

I ease down Main Street and think how many times I've traveled this road on autopilot, never remembering how I got from point A to point B. But tonight is different. I have a renewed view of this little town. I turn on West Shore Road as the crimson sun dips behind Mount Cardigan, turning the clouds a deep burnt orange, appearing to set the mountaintops ablaze.

My grandparents never lost sight of the magic within this place; their lives began here and will end here. Newfound is a permanent part of their souls. I always thought my life would mirror theirs, that Earl and Sylvia's shoes were mine to fill.

But last Labor Day weekend, the magic of this place dissolved.

Life has taught me sometimes your path will take a sudden sharp turn, leading you in the opposite direction, whether you see it coming or not. A few months ago, I decided to move to New York in the fall. I still remember the shock I felt three years ago when my parents announced they were leaving New Hampshire for upstate New York to pursue hard cider production. My father's ambition to expand the family business couldn't be squashed.

And no one could deny the potential of this latest venture. The popularity of hard cider has exploded in the last decade, especially from independent breweries. It's now the most popular drink among twenty- to thirty-year-olds. Using the apples from our orchard, my father now helms East Coast

Cider, one of the most lucrative, independently owned hard cider breweries in New England.

After the past nine months, it's best to trade in a tractor for a clipboard.

I'm going to hold on tight to the last bits of happiness Meriden offers because I'm not sure how New York will compare. I can always visit. My family will still be here. But I've committed to my father, and this move is happening.

Instead of heading home, I make a pit stop at the Binn. My buddies continually harass me to meet them for a beer after work, and I keep standing them up. Not because I don't want to see them, but because our group will never be whole again. Nights at the Binn were once a regular occurrence for us, the five hardworking townies the locals expected to see enjoying a few beers and horsing around. But since last September …

The guys have been relentless, texting before every get-together, and each time they ask, I come up with an even more outrageous excuse than the last. They know I'm full of shit, but no one has the balls to call me out on it.

As I step inside, wooden barn doors swinging behind me, I take in the familiar sight of my bar, my neighbors. Old, rustic lanterns burning low hang from the exposed beams, giving the place that cozy dive-bar vibe. Wooden tables are tucked in each alcove, and Tom Petty flows through the invisible sound system. Behind the bar, Cindy fills a pint for me before I even make it across the room. My wooden stool is mid-swing as Jay, Ryan, and Tyler turn their heads in unison.

"No shit, look what the cat dragged in." Jay's smile says it all. He looks equal parts surprised and proud. "We knew you couldn't stay away forever. Happy you're here, man."

Ryan and Tyler both nod and grin. I see sadness flicker briefly before parting to make room for joy.

Cindy slides a pint across the oak bar. "You hungry? Or are we just drinking?"

"I'll have my usual."

My friends look at one another, and my response stuns them into silence.

"You got it. Mike, grab the man a steak and cheese, hold the mushroom." She turns her head to the line cook who's worked here for more years than we can count. Some things never change.

"Bro, it's good to see you here. Why tonight?" Tyler asks as he slides his stool toward me.

Ryan clears his throat and steps closer to Tyler. "Dude, enjoy it? Who cares what finally got his ass in here. Let's skip the heavy talk and shoot the shit."

I shake my head in relief, thankful that Ryan stepped in, wanting nothing more than to let loose. Certainly not as loose as the scene I witnessed earlier, which won't stop playing in my mind, but loose enough to smile and enjoy the company of others. The laughter that erupted from me earlier reignited a spark, a tiny little flame that makes me stop and wonder ... maybe not all hope is lost.

Three hours and three pints later, my stomach aches from the jokes, the roasts, and the "remember when" stories. I can't think of a time when I didn't have my boys around—we've been together forever. I've always understood how lucky I am to have these guys, to be sure that when shit hits the fan, I can count on them. And damn, I've missed these nights. I am thankful Ryan has been sober for two years and can drive my drunk ass home. It won't be the first time we leave a truck in the Binn lot.

The ride home is quiet except for the low hum of half rock, half static of the local radio station. Thank you, mountains, for your beauty, but solid radio reception? Forget it.

"Seriously, Jackson, I am stoked you came out tonight. I was worried we'd never be together again. Listen, you've gone through a lot, but she'd want you to be happy again. Even though you're not ready today, someday you will be. Don't forget that. I'll come over in the morning to take you back to your truck. We could grab breakfast?"

Ryan's tires meet the dirt driveway of my condo complex, and I slowly slide out when the truck stops. "Sounds good. Thanks for the ride, man."

I usually leave my front door unlocked, so there is no reason to search for keys. Once inside, I toss my hat on the coffee table, turn off the porch light for the night, yank my T-shirt over my head, and plop on the couch. Not having the energy to climb the stairs, I grab the blanket that rests along the edge, kick off my boots, and get comfortable.

As the tide of exhaustion washes over me, the events of the day flood back. The vision of her balancing on the tire between the carriage and truck, hoisting those bags over the side of the bed. Man, she set my blood to pumping at that moment. Solia is just plain sexy without even trying, and that's without mentioning what I saw at the cabin. Such a woman has the ultimate power to derail a man and has me questioning every plan I have in place.

# 4

_Sofia_

I had the best sleep ever last night. Nothing compares to the lilac-scented breeze coming off the mountains and the sound of the birds waking as the sun finds its way over the ridge. Rolling to my right, I have a perfect view from my bedroom windows of the sun rising above the mountain ridge and the trees, and I take a minute to be present, truly appreciating where I am. I can make this work and be happy here. There isn't a chance I can be lonely in my mountainside escape, right?

After a few more quiet moments, I slide into my slippers, thinking of how many times my mother must have gone through this same motion every morning she spent here. Sometimes apples don't fall far from the tree. Walking into the small kitchen, I brew coffee—the stronger, the better—and make my way to the front porch. I have a list a mile long to accomplish today, but I can soak up a little more vitamin D before I begin.

I hear my phone ringing from inside. Running to catch it, I see it's my mother on FaceTime.

"Hi, Mom."

"How are you doing, honey? You didn't call to tell us you arrived."

"I'm good. I haven't been here for more than a day, so not too much can go wrong in that amount of time." My mom is always over the top, but I'll rationalize she's being protective.

"I listened when you said this is what you want, but don't get used to us checking in on you too often. We aren't a hop, skip, or a stone's throw away, so this will be an adjustment."

"I don't need you to. And I know where you are if I need you. I can do this, Mom. Remember, you and Dad agreed to give me the summer to prove I've got this. You're ready to move and sell the cabin, but I'm not ready to let this place go. It's a win-win in my book. I'll find a new job, have a place I love, and you and Dad can move on and the cabin can remain in the family."

"Sure, sweetie, that's fine. OK, I just wanted you to hear my voice. Try to get out and make some new friends. Oh, and don't forget the trash will start to smell. I'm sure it's warm there. And don't forget to pick up a town dump pass."

"OK, Mom. I won't forget. Thanks for checking in."

"Love you. The trash, Solia, don't forget."

"Mom! I won't, jeez, have some faith."

"All right, all right, have a good day."

"Bye, Mom."

This is the first time in my life that we'll be separated by a couple hundred miles. I would never admit it to my parents, but it will take some getting used to. Driving to their house in a few minutes is something I have always taken for granted. But I need to grow the fuck up and carve my own path. Most people my age don't live two miles from where they grew up. For god's sake, my brother moved fourteen hours away, so a mere three-hour car ride is nothing.

As soon as I hang up, I run through my mental checklist of the things I have to get done today. I need to go to the market and go back to the hardware store to figure out who the hell Gerry is and how he was able to recite my address off the top of his head. I also need to ask where to get my season pass for the local beach and find a place to store my kayak and paddleboard by the lake. Oh, and the town dump pass. I can't forget the freaking dump pass. How glamorous. If I can get these tasks done today, I will be well on my way to an epic summer. And if my mother will take a few steps back, I'll be even better off.

When I'm finally motivated to get a move on, my phone blows up. I swear if it's my mother again, I'm going to lose it. Thankfully, it's Mia. We keep in constant contact, and we are due for a quick chat. During the school year, she and I would have our morning "conference calls" on our drive to school, each of us equally adoring our students and dreading what the day may bring. When school lets out for summer, our routine calls naturally fall apart. Sometimes finding a rhythm proves difficult, but every time we text or call, we pick up right where we left off.

MIA

Hey, stranger, met any hot guys yet?

SOLIA

I'm not here for love! I'm here to … what do they call it? Find myself, be one with nature.

Whatever you say! But sound the mating call into the woods, for god's sake. There's bound to be some small-town hotties in those woods somewhere.

No problem. I'll round them up when you come to visit. BTW, when are you coming???

I have to finish some stupid professional development thing this week and then I'm free for the summer. The weekend after the Fourth?

> How about the weekend of the Fourth?

Sorry, I can't. Steve and I have plans. 😔

> Seriously, you are still keeping this going? I thought if he didn't drop to the knee by April, you were outta there?

IDK, there are some things he is fantastic at. Plus I'm too young to get married.

> Seriously shallow.

If you'd find me a mountain man, I'd be a little more motivated.

> I'll try my best. TTYL.

K. 💚

I quickly scan the weather app that says the sun will deliver another scorcher today. From my bureau drawer, I select a royal blue V-neck tank top and blue jean cutoffs, paired with some cute sandals. I toss my sleep shorts and tank on the bed and dress for the day, tying my Meriden Shores hoodie around my waist because the market is an icebox.

I grab my belt bag and double-check the contents are zipped up. I learned my lesson yesterday; my cards need to stay out of the mud. I double-step the long staircase, reach the driveway, and notice the steam burning off the mountains. This is the kind of day I yearned for as a kid. Hot and sticky so I could sit by the lake, legs hanging out of a plastic tube, ankles crossed on the swim line, and a book balanced on my lap. Even though I'm adulting these days, I need to make time for that. I'll get to the swim line later once I handle my grown-up to-do list.

After the market, my next stop is the hardware store. I need to fix a few of the deck boards. Therefore, a hammer, nails, sandpaper, and a drill are on my list. Driving into town, I notice the locals getting their morning steps in, going to work, picking up supplies for the day, or heading into Billy's for breakfast.

Approaching Raubuchon Hardware, I'm surprised by how busy it is. The parking lot looks almost at capacity, and customers flood in and out. Taking the only open spot in the back row, I slide out of my truck and head in.

I scan the aisles looking for the various items on my list as well as the man from yesterday. As I squeeze through the crowds, everyone is as friendly as I expected. People don't ignore each other around here. If you make eye contact with someone, you say hello or ask how they're doing. That's the way it is in small towns.

It takes me ten minutes to locate everything I need and then I head to check out.

Eyeing which register looks the least busy, I spot the older gentleman who welcomed me to town yesterday. He tucks his maroon T-shirt bearing the store's logo into baggy jeans held up by navy suspenders and then heads to register three to bag supplies. I remember the fluffy gray mop of hair. This has to be Gerry, the man who so thoughtfully gave Jackson my address so he could return my card. *Who the hell is this guy?*

"You're back, young lady?" Gerry takes my items one by one and places them in a large paper bag.

"Sure am. By the way, a man named Jackson returned something that belonged to me yesterday. He mentioned you told him where to find me. As I'm sure you'd expect, I'm more than concerned. I didn't think I'd ever seen you before yesterday, so how is it you know my name and where I live, and why are you giving random men directions to my house?" I don't care if I sound aggressive. Gerry's facial muscles transition from slack to taut, and he appears slightly terrified when I finish speaking.

"Well, dear, I can certainly imagine that you're finding this situation a little strange. I hope I didn't cause you any alarm. At my age, sometimes we don't think through what we say before we say it. Plus, Jackson is as good as they come. He's family to me, and when I say you can trust him, you have my word on that."

He takes hold of one of my bags and walks toward the exit. I grab the rest and follow him. Just before walking out of the store, he pulls a flyer off the bulletin board that hangs to the right of the doors.

Once outside, I walk a few steps in front of him and lead him to my truck. As he places the bags into the back, I thank him, and he takes a gigantic sigh. "I blew my cover, Solia. I've been ringing out your father at these registers for more summers than I can count, though I haven't seen you since you were this tall." He puts his hand out, indicating waist high. "I'm thinking you had better places to be than the hardware store with your pops. Upon agreeing to the deal with the cabin, your father called me. I knew it was you the minute you appeared. I can spot an Anderson when I see one. I wasn't supposed to mention it to you. They asked me to keep a close eye on you. Your old man wants to make sure his little girl has someone looking out for her."

Gerry's expression pleads for forgiveness. "My name's Gerry, but I'm guessing Jackson already told you?" He politely shakes my hand while giving me a wide smile that reminds me of my grandfather. I miss that smile. Seeing Gerry's makes me happy.

The puzzle pieces match up. Of course, my father would reach out to an old friend from Meriden to keep tabs on me; his worry is understandable. He's stated many times that although he loves me, he doubts I'm tough enough to brave the elements in these parts. Having his daughter alone in the woods without a friend nearby keeps him up at night.

"Don't worry, Gerry, your secret is under lock and key. I appreciate you looking out for me. I can always use a friend around here."

"Solia, I appreciate that. Do you have a pen in that truck of yours?"

Opening the driver's side door, I find one.

"I'm going to write the store number on the back of this flyer here. You can put it on your fridge and call me anytime you need anything." He hands me the page.

"Sounds great. You are my first official friend here in Meriden. Though I assume this hardware store isn't open twenty-four hours a day."

"Correct, but when the store closes, calls get rerouted to my home. So, you always have a direct line to me, young lady." He smiles and tucks his thumbs behind his suspenders.

"Thanks again. How did you end up as the hardware store's twenty-four-hour customer service representative?" There must be younger, more energetic workers better suited for this role. I mean, Gerry has to be pushing eighty.

"Oh, dear, I own this joint. There is no one more in charge than me."

"Ah, that makes sense. I appreciate you very much and will call if I ever need anything." I take my flyer newly decorated with my first emergency contact in Meriden, step up on the running board, and pull myself into the driver's seat. As I close my door, I open the window. "Thanks again, Gerry."

The old man taps the side of my truck twice and nods. "Also, that might be worth checking out. You might have a grand time and meet some friends. Everyone needs friends. I sure hope to see you there." His energy makes me smile once again as he turns and shuffles toward the store.

I quickly place the paper on the seat, flipping it to scan the opposite side. Christianson's Orchard and Farm Festival, hosted by Raubuchon Hardware, celebrating its anniversary. The first of the three events will be held at ten a.m. on June 25.

*Why not?*

I slide my cell out of my pocket and enter the date and time into my calendar. Meeting new people and getting acquainted with my lakeside neighbors will be a good thing. At least Gerry will be there.

Last stop, Meriden Recycle and Waste Center, otherwise known as the town dump. I follow the street signs to the outskirts of town since GPS and cell service are so damn spotty. I can smell I'm going in the correct direction before I have visual confirmation. I can't say I've ever had the pleasure of visiting before today as this is something my father took care of.

I need my hands to drive; otherwise, I'd hold my nose. I park in the small dirt lot near a ten-foot pile of pallets. Scanning the entrance, I spot a small brown building the size of a closet near what appears to be the official entrance. Chin tucked to my chest, I try to breathe through my mouth and continuously swallow to keep the vomit from escaping.

"Hey there, sweetie. How can I be of service?"

Walking out of the wooden shack is a plump man dressed in a dark blue jumpsuit and black boots, work goggles resting on his head. He has a name tag on his chest, but he's too far for me to read it.

"Hi." With every step, the smell intensifies.

"I'm Wayne," he says as he extends his hand.

I scan the piles of garbage in the distance and then the splatter of mystery substances on his thighs, and I inch my hand toward his, holding my breath. "I'm Solia. I was hoping to get a dump pass. I was told I could get one here."

"Sure thing. Come right over to the office."

I expect to follow him to a building somewhere, but instead, we head to the tiny shack. "Come on in," Wayne says as he steps into the four-by-four office. I peek inside—it has just enough space for a folding chair and a wooden shelf with papers scattered everywhere.

I linger outside the opening to the "office," and Wayne sticks his head back out and says, "Watch your step. It's a dump in here, but it's a dump out there too. Ha-ha, I love that joke. Get it?"

"I sure do, Wayne. I sure do." I cross my arms over my stomach and lean on the doorframe but then think better of it and stand up straight.

Wayne shuffles through a pile and pulls out a sheet of stickers and a clipboard. "Here we are. Just fill out your name and address, and I'll assign you a number."

I scribble my info on the sheet and push the clipboard back. "All set."

"The lady is in a hurry. All right, let's see." He squints and looks over my sheet. The seconds crawl by.

"Is everything OK?" I ask.

"Sure is. Let me just write the pass number next to this here form. OK, so you're going to take this sticker and place it on the bottom left of your front windshield. On the inside, of course. When you arrive at the facility, you drive up to the gate, and someone will be there to flag you in. Depending on what you have, you drive to the container you need."

"Depending on what I have? I'm only bringing trash."

"There are all kinds of trash. There's your regular household trash, recycling, mattress area, grass clippings, leaves, outside-type trash, and electronics. I'm missing one, but you get the idea."

"What happens when I drive to the one I need? How does the trash get out of the truck?"

Wayne laughs and coughs deep and junky. "Sorry, excuse me. That's when you put your truck in park, get out of the truck, get your trash, and throw it in the container."

Staring at him blankly, it dawns on me how stupid my question was. "Got it, sorry, I thought someone took it."

"Nope, it's all you, honey. Anything else?"

"No, that's all. Thanks, Wayne."

"Sure thing. Oh, and when you come back, you may want to wear shoes you don't care to get caked up with … stuff. You never know what you might encounter around here." He looks at my feet and breaks into another coughing fit as I hightail it back to my truck.

I slam the door, crank the AC, and take several deep breaths. Even though I only went as far as the office, I feel like a film of dirt coats my skin, and the smell of garbage is suffocating. I'll have to figure something out; I can't be doing this every time I have a full trash can.

Sure, I'll miss my family and friends, but I'm convinced I'll miss my trash man even more.

# 5

*Jackson*

The Christianson's Orchard and Farm Festival was Shannon's brainchild. Although she has practically nothing to do with the farm, she helps out when she's around in the summer, and my grandparents latched on to the idea. Our orchard is part of the historical landscape of Meriden and has been in the family for almost two centuries. We agreed it deserves to be celebrated—and what a fun way to kick off the summer.

Deep down, everyone is slightly worried the orchard's legacy will end because I'm leaving. Always the educator, Shannon came up with the festival as a way of reminding us of the history and importance of the orchard. Given the age of both my grandparents, we agree to help with everything that's needed, and they aren't afraid to take advantage of this. When Shannon shared her vision for this event, my grandparents ran with it. They created list after list, and then assigned task after task to me. Thankfully, most of our farmhands have worked for the family for decades, so we can count on them. On top of planting, monitoring, weeding, and harvesting, I've had to add event planning and delegation to my list of responsibilities.

Although it's a race to the finish, everybody at Christianson's is celebrating the success of getting the store and farm ready for our very first festival.

"Jackson, I put the handbaskets next to the barn and cleaned the carts for checkout near the register. Greg dropped off the cider doughnuts and coffee. They left those with your grandmother."

"Thanks, Lucas. Can you ask Brynn to see if Sylvia needs help with the doughnuts and setting up the milk and sugar?" We are lucky to have snagged Brynn for the summer. She just finished her freshman year at Plymouth State. Greg met her one day at the country store and hired her. Bringing her over to the orchard for the summer was the best decision we've made in a while. My grandmother loves her, she's a quick learner, and she has endless energy.

"Yeah, no problem. I'm going to set up the cornhole games on the lawn and put the cardboard apples on those two maple trees. Families with little kids will have fun doing that. It'll keep them busy for a little while, anyway."

"I agree. Are you doing that slingshot squash thing you mentioned?"

"Don't worry! I set it up on the other side of the barn. I figure we don't want squash being slung into the customers, so it's set farther away and the slingshots will face the woods."

"Smart thinking. Shannon told me she planned on being around this area if anyone needs anything. Last night, I hooked the hay wagon to the older tractor, so it's ready to pull throughout the orchard. With the weather being so nice, we should expect a sizable crowd."

Lucas hoists the massive wooden cornhole games under his arms, making them look light as paper. "Don't sweat it, Jackson. We have everything covered. It'll come together. We thought of everything we could."

He's right. Shannon had the vision, and the community will love it.

Each year we have regulars who visit the orchard. Some live a street away, while others make it a point to drive a hundred miles to get here. My family is always grateful for the support, even more so this year because the future of our farm is a little unstable.

With an hour to spare, my grandparents, along with the staff, stand under the barn overhang, admiring the orchard. Everything looks fantastic. The scent of apple doughnuts and freshly brewed coffee fills the air. Looking at my grandparents' faces, seeing their arms linked, holding each other tight as they take in the scene makes everything worthwhile.

My grandparents took ownership of the orchard over seventy years ago, five years after their marriage, after the passing of Grandpa Earl's parents. Their story is one for the ages. They lived and were separated through hard times and war, but their love for each other is simply too strong to be broken, their bond beyond admirable. Even after almost eighty years, they're still crazy in love. I hope to find my soulmate someday.

"Are you going to clean yourself up a little? Even though you don't plan on sticking around forever, the least you could do is shower," Shannon says, walking closer to me.

I peek at my watch and sigh—twenty minutes until people arrive. Glancing at my ever-bossy sister, I salute and head to the house.

My grandparents' white farmhouse, built over two hundred and fifty years ago, sits in front of the barn. Having been through its share of renovations and upgrades, no one would ever mistake it for a new build, but it certainly looks years younger than its true age. Even though I only lived here briefly after my parents moved to New York, my grandparents still maintain my bedroom as if I might return one day. The same

183 Reasons · 37


full-size bed sits up against the left-hand wall with my red buffalo-plaid comforter. My six-drawer bureau rests along the back wall, storing a few clothes perfect for an event such as today.

Sitting on the edge of my bed, I unlace my work boots, pull my sweaty T-shirt over my head, and throw it in the corner, along with my jeans and boxer briefs. I hop into the shower and quickly shave, not a nick in sight. I pull jeans from the bureau and the blue Mt. Washington T-shirt my grandmother gave me. It's snug, but she'll smile seeing me wear it. Work boots back on, I head out the door.

Shannon appears just as I make my way out the back of the house, ready to give me the rundown of the day's events. "I moved the rocking chairs from the porch and put them under the awning by the barn for Grandma and Grandpa. They won't admit it, but they are exhausted. The nonstop talk and prep for this event have wiped them out. I told the staff to come to us if they need anything. I'll keep checking on them, and you just oversee the farm area. Everything is taken care of. I want them to enjoy the day and be surrounded by love."

"I agree. Besides, everything is under control. I want you to enjoy this day too. The summer is your vacation time, remember."

"I will, but honestly, planning this has been the best thing for me. It has taken my mind off everything. Being down in the dumps all summer is pathetic. I've been effective and useful, and Grandma and Grandpa are proud to see everyone come together. I hope we get a good turnout."

"You'll be okay, Shan. You're through the worst of it. Everyone says there's a grieving process throughout divorce, and hopefully you won't run into Richard around town anytime soon. Before long, you'll be out meeting new people … heck, anything could happen this summer."

"Hey, don't put me out in the social scene just yet. I'm not officially single. He still needs to sign the papers. Let's just enjoy what we've done here."

She makes her way to the barn, and I go check on my grandparents. Just as Shannon hoped, they're rocking away, enjoying some apple cider as cars and trucks pull into the lot. As soon as I'm close enough to my grandmother, I see a smile form on her face, lighting up as she spots me wearing the gifted T-shirt.

I bend between them. "You should be very proud of this place. People love it here, and today is going to be perfect. I'll be over on the tractor, but if you need anything, Shannon is in the barn and everyone else is out working too. Just ask. I'll come by soon. OK?"

"Don't you give us a second thought, dear. We'll be right here, rocking away. These doughnuts are fantastic. Who made them?"

"Pretty sure Greg did. I'll tell him."

My grandpa sets his cider on the barrel next to his rocker and drops his hand onto my knee while his other hand holds Grandma's. "Things are just as they should be, Jackson. We are so proud of this place and everything you've done to help us along. We are going to enjoy the day. Don't worry about us."

I squeeze his hand, stand up, and give him a nod. I'm fortunate to have them. A small part of me aches when I think about leaving at the end of the summer.

As a result of our limited parking, cars squeeze in where they can, and vehicles start to line both sides of the street. I spot my parents' friends, the O'Briens, the Hendersons, and the Smiths. Shannon's friend, Nora, and her family are pulling in too.

I round the barn and follow the worn dirt trail to my rusty red tractor, climbing into the cab. Key turned, I give the engine a minute to warm up and get the gas flowing. This tractor and I go way back to the days I spent riding through these fields on my dad's lap, memorizing the lay of the land, and learning the responsibilities of the farm. I've spent my whole life maintaining this land, the map of these fields forever ingrained in my mind. This farm and the surrounding acreage are filled with memories, my secrets, and will forever be a part of me. Next to the pine trees to the west, I had my first kiss. In the fields to the north, I got caught drinking my first beer, and the back field is where I cried after losing my first love.

The morning moves quickly, people coming and going. As I travel through the orchard, I wave at the families, watching them walk through the fields as they admire the trees, the branches sprouting young apple fruit for our chosen varieties—Gala, McIntosh, Honeycrisp, and great cider apples, the Winesap. They pause to read the fun-fact wooden signs we've stuck in the ground along the way. Below, I see families piling into the wagon for a hayride and kids enjoying the lawn games. Laughter echoes from every corner, and the warmth of friends and neighbors fills the air.

A couple chores and hours later, I park the tractor and walk to the barn to check on my grandparents, despite their insistence not to. On approach, I spot a familiar pickup pulling into the drive. I stop and lean against the porch post. The truck stops, and I immediately recognize the legs that slide out on the driver's side and onto the running boards. Solia. For the third time in two weeks, I'm a little lost for words as a flush of heat courses through my body. I have the advantage of seeing her without being seen, so I take in every inch and determine she's more beautiful today than I remembered.

Those jean shorts—damn. Taking her time strolling to the barn, she grabs a band off her wrist, gathers her long, wavy hair, and pulls it into a ponytail. Staring at her, I'm unaware of anything else around me, removed from the scene, an outsider looking in. I can't help but notice that her muscular stomach shows when she reaches to tighten her hair.

Mesmerized by the sight of her, I snap back to reality when I hear a man behind me clearing his throat.

"Gerry! Hey, buddy! I didn't notice you there."

"I can't imagine why, son. It wouldn't be because of the sweet young lady in the driveway, would it?" Gerry smirks.

I can't pretend I don't know he's referring to Solia, so I shrug and lean into the post, turn my hat backward, and smile in her direction. Sweat forms on my palms, and she has my full attention.

# 6

*Solia*

As the new girl, I need to weave myself into the fabric of Meriden. I am determined to make this work and prove to my parents that I am capable of much more than simply surviving here. Anyone from a small town can validate that the connection you build with friends and community is the special ingredient to belonging. My goal is to spend a couple hours, meet more people, and enjoy being outside. All through the summers I spent here growing up, I don't remember ever visiting Christianson's Apple Orchard, so now is the perfect time.

The sun bakes my skin, its heat beading sweat on the back of my neck. Getting out of my truck, I pull my hair up and look toward the barn in front of me. As I get closer, my gaze focuses on the attached porch, and I am suddenly stopped dead in my tracks. *How can it be that the only two people I've met since arriving are standing next to each other under the porch staring my way?*

Immediately, I notice every inch of my body—each inch that Jackson has already seen. I don't think either of us blinks for a whole minute. If I were to dream up a hot, small-town guy, he would be my fantasy. His shirt is tight, and I imagine his muscles under my fingertips as my hands dip below the cotton. This man is desirable, and the sight of him makes my stomach flutter.

As I near the porch, I stare at his muscular hands resting in his pockets. He leans against the post, and his fitted jeans hug strong, tight legs. To finish it off, he's wearing his freaking sexy work boots. Boots I wish he'd left at my doorstep.

*What is going on with me?* I don't think I've ever been so turned on meeting a man in my life. I couldn't tell you his full name but desperately want to be screaming it from under my sheets.

"Hello there, Solia."

I refocus on the man standing next to Jackson, breaking free of my steamy daydream, and register the man speaking is Gerry. I continue up the path.

Jackson lifts his right hand and waves with a smirk, making me question if he is a witness to the scenes playing out in my mind.

"Why am I suddenly under the impression that you orchestrated a setup here today?" I glare at Gerry, but I can't help my smile.

This man is beyond sweet; his energy is magnetic. "Did you encourage Jackson to be here? Did my father put you up to playing matchmaker?"

Gerry smiles as I laugh in embarrassment.

"Hey, Solia. Don't blame old Gerry here. My family owns and operates this orchard. Gerry is basically family. I'm just here earning a living in the best place around. It wouldn't be a celebration without Gerry and the rest of the locals."

"Your family owns the orchard? I had no idea. Beautiful doesn't do it justice—this place is breathtaking. It's my first time here. I may have visited as a kid, but I'd remember."

Gerry attempts to hide his grin, but I am even more convinced he has something up his sleeve.

Muscles, a pickup, a face chiseled at angles made for a magazine shoot, and to top it off, Jackson runs an orchard. Damn.

His relationship with Gerry is beyond adorable and reminds me so much of my family back home. Being a small-town girl from New England, there is nothing steamier than a hometown hottie who rides a tractor and gets muddy on the daily. I'm a huge believer in signs, but I didn't expect someone to catch my attention this soon. However, I'm not opposed to a little fun if love finds me. My thoughts sizzle at the possibility of Jackson seeing me naked under different circumstances …

"Me, playing matchmaker? I wouldn't dream of it! But my boy Jackson here," Gerry says, grabbing hold of Jackson's shoulder, "would surely love to give a new lady in town a tour of the farm on his tractor. Right, J?"

Jackson's face turns bright red and appears momentarily frozen. Then he stands up straight and does that thing where he lifts his backward-facing hat, brushes his fingers through his hair, and returns the hat to his head. Must be a nervous habit. Without missing a beat, he reaches his hand out to me. "Of course, Gerry. If Solia is up for a tractor ride, she can hop on mine."

Riding his tractor isn't the only thing I am envisioning riding at the moment, but I'll take it. "Sure," I utter, the only word I can manage, and without thinking, I grab hold of Jackson's hand.

It's just a hand, but somehow when our fingers intertwine, an electrical pulse radiates throughout my body. I'm unsure if he is experiencing what I am, but if he is, this is one ride I'll never forget.

We walk behind the barn where a giant red tractor sits parked in the dirt. He must sense my hesitation when he surveys my white sneakers and laughs. I have to laugh along with him when I look at my poor choice of shoes, yet again. First the dump and now here. *What was I thinking, showing up to a farm with these on?*

He holds his chin, grinning in amusement, and bends into a low squat. I take the hint and climb onto his back. I wrap my legs around his trim waist and lock my arms around his broad shoulders and neck. His body rubbing against mine increases the cadence of my heartbeat with every step. I don't care if mud covers my sneakers; I would have just thrown them in the wash. But I'm willing to pretend if it means I get to hold on to Jackson's ripped body.

"I'm going to have to warn you, my two-seater is out of commission at the moment, so you will have to ride on my lap for a tour." He has his arms wrapped around my shins tightly and squeezes them.

Thank god he can't see my expression because my jaw practically drops. "Of course, I don't mind! Yeah, yeah, I'm good, no problem. You are giving me my first official tour of an apple orchard, so I'll sit wherever you need me to." I cringe as the words stumble out of my mouth.

We approach the tractor backward so I can place my feet on the side rail. While Jackson pulls himself up into the cab, I adjust my shorts and wonder if they were made for tractor rides. I arrange my shirt and yank my ponytail a little tighter. Nerves tingle throughout my body as I envision sitting on Jackson's lap.

"Hop on up, cutie." He pats his thick, muscular thighs. I grab hold of his arm, swing one leg over his lap, and shimmy as far back as I can, my body warming against his core. It's tighter in here than I imagined.

The tractor's engine roars to life. A few visitors turn their heads in our direction, and Jackson gives them a friendly wave.

One couple says something to each other and then throw a smile and nod our way.

The tractor tires tear through the mud, and we make our way up and into the fields. A vast expanse of apple trees come into view, planted in neat rows that continue as far as the eye can see. We maintain silence while Jackson heads toward a line of trees far from the clusters of people enjoying their stroll through the farm.

"How long has your family owned this land?"

"Two hundred years. It's hard to wrap my head around sometimes, but it's part of Meriden's history," he says, straightening his shoulders.

"Wow, that's incredible. It's breathtaking."

He doesn't respond, focused on guiding the tractor. I take in our surroundings as Jackson navigates the lane between the apple trees, and it's a straight-up fact we are both acutely aware of every bump, divot, and hole the tractor tires encounter. With every heave forward and dip of the rig, Jackson keeps one hand on the wheel and the other alternating between the gearshift and my waist, pulling me closer each time.

I'm unsure whether he comprehends that I'm aware of his rock-hard excitement under me. Nevertheless, with every thrust and tug closer to him, my attention wanes from the view and focuses on the pulsing between my thighs.

We continue this way for at least fifteen minutes until we're at the top of a hill overlooking the entire orchard. When the tractor stops, Jackson kills the engine and puts both his hands on my waist to lift me. He then leads me to the grass. As we walk, he explains the varieties of the trees, slowly growing heavy with baby apples, and the months of the growing and picking seasons. Despite being interested in this information, it's hard to concentrate while standing within kissing distance of Jackson.

"Come on, I want to show you something."

He guides me to the hill's peak where an awe-inspiring panoramic view awaits. You can see the entire valley, crystal clear lakes, and mountain ridges. If you told me this was the top of the world, I'd believe you. The view conjures emotions deep within from the sheer beauty of Mother Nature.

"Solia, I don't know what you're doing here or why we continue to run into each other, but I'm happy you are. I saw more of you than I know of you." He laughs, and the temperature of my face skyrockets. As I cover my cheeks, he seizes my wrists, guides them behind my back, and holds them there. His eyes lock onto mine, fire burning in them.

He steps closer and tilts his head until his breath hovers above my lips. "We don't know each other well, but I've wanted to kiss you since the first moment I saw you." I nod and instinctively let the world turn dark as he leans in. The softness and urgency of his mouth on mine holds a sweetness I didn't anticipate craving. He starts with a gentle kiss but within seconds, the fire ignites. He releases my wrists and puts his hands on the back of my thighs, hoisting me into the air, while I wrap both my legs around his waist. His tongue slides into my mouth, and I experience the most sensual, intimate kiss of my life.

I reach for his hat and toss it into the grass. His sexy, wavy hair is loose, and I comb through it, front to back, and weave my fingers together around the base of his neck. The kiss grows harder and faster, and he lifts and pulls me into him as tight as possible. He rubs the back of my thighs, and it takes everything in me not to moan in response.

Hearing the radio static behind us, I'm forced out of the heat and intensity. The kiss slows, and my feet are the only part of me to return to earth. Jackson has me wanting more than he's given me. The heat in my body won't be regulating anytime soon.

# 7

*Jackson*

*What the hell am I doing? I want to take this woman right here in the field.*

I want this woman in my arms, on my lips. I want her to tell me she's experiencing the blazing flames I'm struggling to contain. Without even considering the fact that I met Solia mere days ago, already she has me forgetting everything else. I am drawn to her in a way I can't stop or ignore or explain.

Holding her against me, pressing into her, a yearning surges that I didn't think possible. I don't want to stop. My hands find their way to the edge of her cut-off jeans, I explore the fringe with my fingertips, and as I walk to the tractor and lean her against the cab, I hear the radio beeping before transmitting a message.

"Hey, Jackson. We're a little swamped here and could use another set of hands." Shannon's voice rings out loud and clear, and it's obvious she needs a response. Fantastic timing.

The groan of disappointment vibrates through my chest, and Solia's smile forms against my lips as she pulls away. Forcing my hands to leave her body is like separating a strip of

Velcro. I want to keep them right where they are and continue to explore every inch of her.

"You need to answer that?"

"Yeah, that's my sister Shannon. She helps out on the weekends and during major events. If she's asking for help, I need to go." As if sensing my frustration, Solia drops her shoulders, and her level of disappointment seems equal to mine. This woman has set my world off its axis.

I loosen my grip and lower her to the ground. My lips meet her forehead and I kiss her gently. There is no doubt I have to see this woman again. Leaving it to fate is not something I will risk. "Are you free later on to grab ice cream or something downtown?"

*I'm not thinking this through. What am I doing?* The shoulder devil and angel war with each other:

*"You can't start something knowing you're leaving."*

*"Sure you can. This won't be anything serious. You deserve a little fun. Look at what you've gone through. You're not going to marry this girl, for god's sake. Take her out, see what happens."*

*"Are you ready for this? You've been hiding from the world for almost a year. Why would you think it's a good idea to travel this road if it's a dead end? You've made your decision, you've made promises—you are leaving in a couple months."*

*"Screw that. This girl is magic. Let her cast her spell and see what happens. It will help the weeks pass by, and no one will get hurt."*

"I'd love that," she says, snapping me back to reality.

"Great. I'll pick you up at six?"

"Perfect."

I can tell by her smile and the blush of her cheeks she's pleased I asked. Satisfied I put myself out there, I'll pretend I'm just a normal guy, asking out a beautiful woman on a date. She's the first person in as long as I can remember who isn't aware of my past, of the devastation involved. She isn't from this town, she hasn't been overrun with town shenanigans, and she doesn't see what everyone else does when they look at me. I forgot how much I needed a woman to want me, to see and experience who I am without the pain and loss. Everyone in this town can recite my story, and while they empathize, for once, it's amazing to let the sun shine on my face.

I take a few steps back, and she follows me to the tractor. She climbs up and settles onto my lap. I can't help but remember what's under her jean shorts—the curves, the way her body moves. Solia has my alignment off course, veering into the breakdown lane. I want to unwrap this gift, touch what's inside, and treasure every inch.

Once I rev the tractor's engine, I concentrate on the descending tracks leading back to the barn. The crowd has certainly grown since we left. Families are scattered everywhere, children running through the fields, smiles abundant. It's precisely the environment my family strives to provide for this community. Every homegrown business is rooted in this type of pride. As if Solia could sense my emotion, she spread her legs wider, squeezing her calves against my lower legs, possibly to keep from tilting forward. Whatever the reason, I'm rock-hard, ready, and struggling to focus.

Pulling the tractor against the barn, I turn off the engine. Solia loosens her grip and climbs off. I take an extra beat to make things less noticeable and then she undoes her hair and lets her soft, brown waves fall to her shoulders as she glances back at me.

"I'd call a crowd this size a success."

Shannon appears in my peripheral vision, and her eyes practically pop out of their sockets. "Oh, hey, Jackson. Sorry, I didn't—I could've had Lucas bring them."

She's stunned to see this beautiful woman, or any woman, for that matter, climb off my lap. I'm not surprised by her shock and awe. Today I surprised myself. Shannon squints at me, and it's a perfect buzzkill.

"This is Solia. She's new to town, and I was giving her a tour of the farm."

"Oh, that's great. Hi, Solia. I'm Shannon, Jackson's sister. Welcome to town. What brings you to our corner of the world?" Shannon hands me a pair of work gloves and points to the line of people waiting for the tractor.

Solia smiles in my direction, probably realizing I'm not sure what her response will be since we've exchanged but a few words.

"I came here for a fresh start, a chance to be in a place that captured my heart years ago. My family owns a cabin on the other side of the lake, and I'm trying to stop them from selling it. So far, it's been pretty great. I should check out the rest of the place. I'll see you later, Jackson. I'm sure you both have so much to do. Thank you for the tour, and it's nice to meet you, Shannon."

Shannon looks from me to Solia and back with an expression only a brother could understand. Hope and promise linger in the air between us.

"Hold up, Solia. I'll walk with you and show you around. Bye, brother."

My mouth has been wired shut, so I wave like an idiot and say nothing. I want to tell Shannon to get lost, grab Solia by the waist, and find a spot in the fields isolated from the crowds where I can show Solia how badly I want her.

Watching her from behind, her hips swaying as she walks away from me, is torture. Shannon leads her toward the barn, and I climb up onto the tractor.

*What have I gotten myself into?*

God only knows what dirt my sister will pry out of this woman.

As I restart the engine, Shannon turns her head and glances my way with a smile and a thumbs-up, unseen by Solia.

I return her smile. My sister only wants to see me happy again.

Six o'clock can't come fast enough.

∾

I park my truck on a side road, and we start toward the center of town.

"You want to walk a bit?" Most of the shops close up at eight, and visitors seem to be taking advantage of the later hours. Small crowds linger along the sidewalks, people entering and exiting the Brown Bean, our newest coffee slash dessert shop, and Alejandro's Mexican Restaurant.

"Sure."

We stroll inches apart, and my heart skips beats. I'd forgotten how the proximity and smell of a woman can give me butterflies. I stuff my hands into my pockets, questioning whether to reach for hers.

"Have you been downtown since arriving?" I ask as I accidentally brush against her waist to avoid walking into a fire hydrant.

Solia looks at me and smiles. "I haven't. It's funny to hear you call this downtown. When we were little, we'd drive into town for the week, my brother and I in the back seat. When we'd turn the bend onto Main Street, my dad would say, 'We're here! Don't blink, or you'll miss downtown!'"

"So true. And it hasn't gotten any bigger, still as quaint as you remember it, I'm sure. Are you hungry?"

"Always! What are you in the mood for?"

I take this opportunity to reach for Solia's hand, smiling as her fingers slip between mine.

"You read my mind." She tilts her head to the sky, winks, and gives my hand a little squeeze.

"We could do ice cream, fudge, or Mexican food. Dessert or dinner?"

"Is that place that makes the insane peanut butter fudge still here?"

"Newfound Sweets? Sure is."

We cross along the painted lines to where the connected brick buildings begin. Arranged in a horseshoe, each building has a steel lamppost outside and a wooden chair holding its front door open.

"Is it still in the same spot?" Solia asks.

"Yes. The businesses on each side have changed a few times. Newfound Brewery is on one side."

"Impressive! Meriden getting in on the brewery bandwagon."

"It's popular with everyone, especially the locals. You can order a flight of their different beers or individual pints. You can even take a six-pack home with you."

"I'm more of a cider or wine girl, but I'll definitely check it out." Solia freezes on the sidewalk in front of the shop on our right. "You've got to be kidding me. This place is still here?" She's pointing to the wooden, horizontal sign hanging on the building: Newfound Gifts. "My brother and I used to love coming here when we were little. The man who owned it was always so friendly. He had this turtle living in the back of the store—she was famous around here. I remember taking a picture with her and being so excited because he hung it on the Wall of Fame."

I release my hand from hers and wrap my arm around her shoulders. "Oh, you are going to love this!" She follows my lead up the three concrete steps and through the front door.

"Hey there, folks, come on in," a man's voice calls from somewhere in the back.

Solia lights up as she scans the interior. Treasures fill the room from floor to ceiling. Chimes of every color hang in the windows, puzzles and children's toys occupy one whole section, and bookshelves line the walls. A gigantic statue of a turtle sits in the middle—it has to be eight feet tall.

"No way! The turtle! I have to take a picture." She pulls her phone out of her leggings pocket and gives it to me, pressing her hands together in prayer. "Please, pretty please."

Her adorableness is so attractive. She stands with one arm on the turtle, sporting a smile from ear to ear. "Say cheese!" I take a couple shots, and she skips back to me.

"I can't wait to send these to my parents. They're going to get a kick out of this."

"You're going to love this even more." I walk with her to the back of the store where George sits on a stool behind the wooden desk with an old cash register on top. I haven't seen him in years. His tired expression and hunched posture surprise me.

"Hey, George. This is Solia, although you met her a long time ago." Solia's eyes widen, and she gives George the biggest grin.

"Hi, George. Are you the same George from twenty years ago? I used to visit this store during the summers."

"The one and only. Here to see Diane?"

"No. Way! She's still here? She must be a hundred years old!"

"Fifty-four, to be exact. She even has a series of books featuring her. Come on, I'll take you back. Jackson, it's been too long. The last time I saw you here was when you were shopping for a gift for …"

Thankfully, Solia's squeal curtails George's sentence before he can finish. Her hands covering her mouth, she practically skips to the room behind George. I adore her childlike excitement.

She spends the next fifteen minutes taking selfies with Diane the turtle while George explains what Diane's been up to the last fifteen or so years. They search the Wall of Fame for Solia's old photo, and when they find it—a very young Solia grinning next to Diane—her shriek of excitement is worth every bit of torture listening to George's turtle stories.

"Come back anytime. Diane always loves company," George says as we make our way out of the shop.

"Thanks, George. See you soon." I follow Solia out the door. "I'm not sure how much Diane enjoys visits, but I'm happy you enjoyed seeing her."

"That was awesome. It's amazing they're both still here. I stepped back in time for a few minutes back there. And see? I've been part of Meriden all these years, just hanging around in George's shop." She laughs.

"Let's keep it going. Fudge awaits." The sun is setting, allowing dusk to settle in. Solia wraps her arm in mine, and there is nowhere I'd rather be.

The jingle of bells overhead announces our entry into Newfound Sweets. Walking toward the showcase, I put my arm around Solia's shoulders and she squeezes in close to me, inspecting the selection. "Coffee fudge, white chocolate … each flavor looks tastier than the next. I'm not sure I can pick just one," she says.

"Let's each pick one to eat now and take one home."

"Still difficult, but better. I'll do peanut butter and then the second one, white chocolate."

"Great minds think alike. I was going to do white chocolate."

"Aww, we can't do that. You pick two different ones, and we'll share," she says and begins pointing to other possibilities.

The clerk steps through the swinging door behind the counter and approaches the display. "Hi, guys, what can I get you?"

"We'll take one each of the peanut butter, white chocolate, dark chocolate, and hazelnut."

"Coming right up." She collects our pieces and places them in a small white cardboard box.

"Let's sit out here," Solia says, pointing to a small wrought iron table and chairs outside the shop.

I hand her the peanut butter fudge and take my hazelnut out of the box. "Cheers to a blast from the past." We each take a bite and I'm instantly thankful we stopped in. It's been a long time since I've enjoyed this treat.

"Now, I want a bite of yours," she says as she extends her piece to me. I lean in and take a nibble. "Good, right? My turn."

I hold the hazelnut fudge to her lips and watch her teeth sink into the piece. "Mmm, so good." A smudge of chocolate sticks to the corner of her mouth. I want nothing more than to kiss it away, but instead, I use my thumb. "Thanks," she says as she crosses her legs and pulls her chair in closer. "So, everything went OK today at the orchard? It's beautiful over there."

"It is, isn't it? Everything went as planned, no snags. Everyone seemed happy with the outcome."

"Your grandparents are adorable."

"They are. They're the best. Speaking of family, you mentioned yours wants to sell the cabin. What's up with that?" I lean closer and rest my elbow on the table.

"The short version is they're ready for a change. They are tired of driving up in the winter, dealing with the shoveling and plowing. The expense and time the upkeep requires have taken a toll on them. My brother moved to North Carolina, so they're thinking of going south a couple months of the year. It's easier for them to sell than to maintain it. I couldn't let it happen."

"I can see where you're coming from. The cabin and

property are special, but maintaining everything is a lot of work."

"It will be worth it, and I can handle it. My father has faith in me. My mother is a different story." Solia sits back and crosses her arms.

"Oh, no doubt. I'm sure you can. You're off to a great start." We sit in silence for a few moments, watching people walk along the sidewalks as the shops begin to close their doors.

"Do you own trash cans?"

"I'm sorry, what?" I search her expression for understanding. "Yes, I own trash cans. Is that important to you?"

"Yeah, that came out weird. It's just, the cabin's on a private road, and I had to go to the town dump the other day. I was just wondering if that's something you do."

I throw my head back in laughter. "So you met Wayne? He's a good guy. No, I don't live on a private road. I have trash pickup."

"Nice. It really stinks."

"The dump or taking your trash to the dump?"

"Both, actually. But I'll survive."

"They sell nose plugs at Small Mart," I say as I reach for her hand.

"Seriously, it's dreadful."

We leave the other two fudge pieces in the box and stroll back in the direction of the truck. "I'm glad we got together tonight. I wasn't expecting this," she says.

"What do you mean?"

"Meeting someone wasn't on my radar. I haven't had the best luck lately, and honestly, I'd pretty much crossed men out of the picture for a bit."

"Ouch." I lift my fist to my chest. "That doesn't sound good."

Laughing at my dramatic response, she takes my fist,

uncoils my fingers, and folds her hand into mine. "I said for a bit, not forever. I don't blame every man for the losers I wasted time on." Her hand squeezes mine. "I'm happy I ran into you, as awkward as it may have been."

"I'd call it memorable and inspiring," I say, coughing to hide my laughter.

"Go ahead and laugh. It was pretty damn funny. I never thought someone would show up, and I'm in the middle of nowhere. I die inside every time I picture how ridiculous I must have looked."

"I wouldn't use the word *ridiculous* … *sexy*, *hot*—those words come to mind. Do you want me to continue? Sorry, but I'm not unhappy I got tickets to the show." I crack up. She teasingly bumps her shoulder into my side.

"Let's go, farmer boy. You have an early morning tomorrow, right?"

"Sure do. Up with the roosters." I open the passenger door for her and head to the driver's side.

"I don't think I've ever met a real-life farmer." She shifts sideways in her seat and stares at my profile.

"You make us sound like such an enigma. I'm sure you have and didn't know. We're chameleons. We blend in sometimes."

"Possibly, but I'm sure they weren't as handsome as you," she says, and I grin. If I'm being honest with myself, I want her to want me. Meeting Solia has been anything but ordinary, and I want to see her again.

"Are you free on Saturday?" I ask.

"What do you have in mind?"

"If you're free, I'll think of something."

"Well then, I'm free. Surprise me. Actually, showing up at the cabin unexpectedly the other day was slightly embarrassing, so at least tell me what time."

"How's eleven a.m.?" I love how playful she is. A woman who can take a joke as well as dish one out turns me on.

We pull into her driveway, and I'm thankful for high beams. The cabin is in complete darkness, the only lights the stars in the sky. "This is a beautiful spot you have. It's so quiet, so peaceful. You must love it."

"I do. It's too special to lose. I wish I would remember to flip a few switches before leaving. Lions, tigers, and bears, oh my. No doubt creatures lurk in the shadows."

"Come on, I'll walk with you. I'll leave my truck running so the lights stay on." I open her door and reach for her hand. "I had a great time tonight."

Her head swivels left to right with each step as we ascend the long front staircase. She peers deep into the woods. "I did too," she says as she opens her door and reaches in. Inside and out, the house illuminates, and Solia takes a deep breath. "That's better." She giggles. "Thanks for the escort. The night creatures stayed put."

"Good, I'm glad." I lean in and gently kiss her cheek. "See you soon?"

She hesitates and looks at the front door, slightly ajar. "Yes, soon. Wait! The fudge!"

"Right, hang on." I run down the stairs, grab the box out of the truck, and double-step it back toward Solia. "You can have these."

"No way, we agreed to share." She opens the box, hands me the white chocolate, and takes the dark chocolate. "Ready?" We each take a bite and then feed each other the remainder. With one hand on the screen door, I am heedful of her eyes concentrating on mine. Her front teeth bite her bottom lip and a slight smile forms. If she's trying to tease me, she's doing a hell of a job. Every fiber of my being wants to scoop her up and carry her inside.

But the knot tightening in my stomach nags for my

attention. Solia is irresistible, but I am not an asshole. If I walk through her cabin door, I know what will happen, and I won't be another loser on her list. I fight the fire burning inside and hold myself back.

"Good night, Solia."

"Good night, Jackson." Her lips press tightly together, facial muscles tightening, and she turns to walk inside.

I toss my head back, look at the stars, and wonder why things work out the way they do. Sometimes I wonder if God laughs at the plans we try to make.

# 8

*Sofia*

Tractors and a certain sexy farmer infiltrate my dreams. I came to New Hampshire with a list of goals, and finding a man was not one of them. Men have burned me too many times. While I can't control my dreams at night, my daydreams I can attempt to stop. I need to get things done and tear my focus away from wanting to see Jackson again.

There was something about the way he left last night. I can't quite put my finger on it, but I sensed his hesitation. His energy changed—his demeanor shifted. One minute he was examining my lips, and the next, he was saying goodbye.

I grab my phone, hoping Mia can talk sense into me.

"Hey, sorry, it's early."

Hearing the sleepiness in her voice, there's no denying that I woke her. "Yeah, it is. What's going on?"

"What's up is, I spent half the night getting undressed on a tractor by a guy I just met. This is not what I came here for."

"Wait! Back the hell up. Who? What tractor? This is amazing. I want details now."

"Dreams, Mia. I dreamt of the tractor thing for hours."

"Damn."

"I met this guy right after I arrived. I'll spare you the details, but let's just say he accidentally saw me dancing naked on the deck. And we fed each other fudge."

"Holy shit! Now, this is what I'm talking about. Get it, girl! Is he hot?"

"Yes, Mia, he's fucking gorgeous, muscles from head to toe, and he's a farmer. But I have the worst track record. You've been an eyewitness to every train wreck. He asked me to go out Saturday, and I said yes before thinking it through. I came here to learn to love myself and all that wholesome bullshit. I haven't been here for ten minutes, and I've already found a guy to drool over. What if he's just another prick? I don't get that vibe from him, but I'm pretty certain my radar is broken."

"Solia, get a hold of yourself. You are so dramatic. I'm pretty sure this guy only asked you on a date. You aren't accepting a proposal. Just enjoy it. You are a beautiful, single sex siren living in the mountains. Let the farmer in the dell mow your fields! Why not? Live your life!"

"Oh my god, Mia. Seriously. I called you to help talk me out of this. I should be making friends, watching the stars, and swimming in the lake. Not ogling over the first guy I run into."

"Yeah, and you can do those things, naked, with your sexy farmer. Let his muscles show you what's up in the bedroom while you are at it. Seriously, Solia, not everything has to be so serious. Google him, make sure he's not a psycho, and take him for a ride. But remember to tell me every detail. Can I go back to bed now?"

"Sure, great, thanks for the pep talk. I'll call you later."

I'm not exactly sure what I thought Mia was going to tell me. Although I wanted her to screw my head on straight, she's right. I never let loose—why can't I just have fun and see what happens? No one is making promises or getting in deep. As usual, I'm overthinking things.

Even the good parts of my past relationships are less than

memorable. I don't remember ever experiencing such an instant wish to be undressed by someone as I did upon meeting Jackson. This guy is fire. He lights the end of every nerve in my body, and even if I wanted to say no, there is no way in hell I could resist him.

Trying desperately to stuff my visions of us on Jackson's tractor to the back of my brain, I grab the list I made a few days ago to focus on staying busy and productive today.

My first stop is the post office to file a change of address and check on the P.O. box since my cabin is too far out of town for mail delivery.

I then head to the sleepy Meriden Town Library to request a new card because I'm an old-school kind of reader.

Next, I go to town hall to apply for a beach pass. If I want to leave my car parked by the lake, I'll need a sticker on my windshield. Things have changed over the years as more and more vacationers have discovered the secret of Newfound Lake. In an effort to maintain order and allow property owners access, the town only issues parking stickers to residents (for a five-dollar fee). My cabin is close enough to walk to the shore, but if I decide to bring a kayak, paddleboard, or multiple coolers, a sticker will come in handy.

School is the next location on the list. I'd like to meet the principal and dig a little to see if they're hiring for the fall. My résumé and references have already been uploaded onto the staffing site, but things can get overlooked, especially in the summer. Meriden Elementary is one level, constructed in the shape of a *U*. The play yard is in the center, complete with a brightly colored jungle gym and a few scattered picnic tables. The classroom windows still have student art taped to them from the previous school year.

I loop around back and see a handful of cars in the lot. My guess is they belong to the janitors, principal, and a few teachers wrapping things up before they can officially start their summer. I park and ring the bell at the front door.

A voice crackles through the exterior speaker. "Hello, can I help you?"

"Hi, yes, my name is Solia Anderson. I sent in an application last month and was just stopping by to introduce myself and check on things."

"Oh, sure, sure, I remember that name. Come on in."

After an ear-piercing buzz, I pull the red steel door and wait for the second steel door to unlock.

"Hi, Solia. I'm the principal here, Christine Smith." She takes a sip of the iced coffee in her hand.

"Nice to meet you. I apologize for showing up unannounced, but I figured it couldn't hurt."

"Certainly not. I remember seeing your name come across my desk. I've done the hiring I need to do, but we are desperate for substitutes. They are so hard to come by these days."

I run my tongue along my teeth and try to buy myself a few seconds. "I was hoping for a permanent position, but I will keep it in mind." The pitch of my voice lowers after each word.

Mrs. Smith rests a hand on my shoulder. "I completely understand, but listen, I've been working with the superintendent to post a building substitute position for this school. This would be full time, but this person will move around the building to wherever he or she is needed. Would that be of any interest?"

"I would be willing to give it some thought. I'll continue to look for a permanent spot, but in the meantime, will you keep me in mind in case the posting is cleared with administration?"

"I certainly will. Thank you for stopping by. You should hear from me soon."

The conversation didn't go in the direction I'd hoped. The

last thing I want to do is hop from one room to the next every single day. I didn't even ask for the pay scale; from my experience, that would've sent me running. But with no other options in sight, I have to be open to other possibilities. Paying my bills is not something I can avoid. Starting in September, I need a steady cash stream to support myself.

Widening my job search is in order.

The last stop on my list is Stable Farm—my father mentioned he's ordered firewood from them in the past. Seems absurd to order firewood when I just lived through the first official day of summer. However, Dad swears this is the best time of year to get a couple cords of green wood. I remember my father repeatedly explaining to me that since green wood is still wet, it is much cheaper than seasoned wood, which has dried out completely over a year or so and is ready to burn. He taught me to buy cheap in the summer, stack it, cover it with a tarp, and it will be ready to burn come winter.

I pull off Ragged Highway and travel the long winding road lined with fields of wildflowers stretching toward the sun. I forgot just how vibrant these flowers can grow out here in the country. Years ago, I tried to grow them at home, but they ended up being another meal for the hungry deer in my yard.

The plots of wildflowers guide me to the left, and I spot a quaint farmhouse in the field on my right. A wooden sign directs me to the Stable Farm. I park my truck and walk toward the woman working behind the farm stand.

She sees me approaching and waves. She reminds me of my mother—petite, her brown hair cut just above her shoulders, and warm brown eyes framed with stylish glasses.

"Hey, young lady, how can I help you?" Her smile is welcoming.

"I'm here to order two cords of wood to Chasm Drive."

"Sure thing, hon. Are you staying in that beautiful log cabin on the hill?"

I sometimes need reminding of how small a small town can be. "I am. It's my family's cabin. I moved in last week."

"No kidding. I'm Janice—I remember your folks. Your father used to buy wood from us, and I saw your family at the lake in the summer a few times. I never would've recognized you all grown and mature. How are they doing these days?"

"Nice to meet you, Janice. I'm Solia. They're well, heading to more sunshine and living near my brother and his family for a while." I extend my hand, which she shakes in welcome.

"That's great. Good for them. I'm glad to see that beautiful log cabin stay in the family. That's the way it should be."

"I agree, but my parents haven't sealed the deal yet. We agreed to a summer trial. They aren't sure I'll be happy here, that I'll be able to enjoy it and still work through the tough winters, but I'm going to show them I'll be fine. Better than fine."

"Good for you. It isn't easy here in the mountains. The snow can be difficult, but there's nothing that can replace the peace and tranquility it provides. As long as you embrace the locals, you'll do all right. It's that kind of community around here. Supportive and always willing to lend a hand, as long as you pay it forward. At least that's what I've learned through the years." Janice's love for this town is palpable.

"Absolutely, that is exactly what I'm looking for. I've met a few new people and am looking for a teaching job for the fall."

"No one should mess with a woman who's got a plan. You're on your way. OK, today is Thursday. I can get your wood to you on Saturday around eight a.m. If I remember correctly, they keep the wood racks out back. But you've got that house sitting on a big hill, right?"

"Yes. You've got an excellent memory."

"How's this? I'll have my son, Ryan, and a few of his buddies come to unload and stack it for you."

"Oh, you don't have to do that. I can work on it little by little."

"Consider it my welcome-to-town gift. Plus, I still enjoy bossing my son around every now and then. He and his friends are always in for a workout."

"If you insist. Thank you. That's very kind. Your farm is beautiful, by the way. I'll be back soon for fresh veggies."

"Sounds good, Solia. We got all kinds, and corn will be ready toward the end of summer. I'm biased, but it's the best around."

I take off back to the cabin, satisfied with how much I accomplished. Before getting out of the truck, I text my parents a quick hello and tell them I met Janice. I leave out the part about her offering to have my wood stacked. No need to inform them I don't plan on stacking it myself or that the local elementary school is a dead end. If my mother senses I'm getting off easy, I'll never hear the end of it. I hit Send and a pang of uncertainty creeps into the back of my mind.

*If I don't find a full-time job, there is no way I can support myself.*

Deep breaths. I'll figure it out. I have time.

I haven't even been to the lake yet, and there's still a couple hours of daylight left. I climb the stairs to the cabin, grab a quick PB&J, change into my bathing suit and cover-up, and snatch a tube from the garage. Using the beach sticker isn't in the cards today. I'll enjoy the walk.

At the end of Chasm Drive, I cross a narrow street and then meet the sand. People are scattered along the shoreline, but it's quiet, just the way I remember it. I set my stuff on the sand, I don't have to worry my belongings will disappear. People around here look out for one another. I toss my cover-up onto the beach, drag the tube into the water, and paddle out.

The water in Newfound Lake is far superior to any other in my opinion; people brag and say they have the best lake, but there is no cleaner, more beautiful lake than ours here in Meriden. Locals want to keep this gem hidden from the rest of the world, and I don't blame them. Part of the allure of this location is its remote setting wedged between two powerful mountain ranges.

The sun is strong, hovering above the mountains in the west. I glide to the swim rope, lace my feet around the line, and gaze across the water. I could stay here forever.

Watercraft zoom around the lake. Pontoon boats loaded with families cruise the outskirts, while others in speedboats tow children on tubes. The bass from boat speakers vibrate faintly through the air. Jet Skis fly by, sending a wave toward shore, tilting my tube enough that I have to grip the handles for dear life. Toward the left side of the lake, I catch the sight of a white pontoon boat decorated with streamers around the tower bimini and a poster board duct-taped to the side. I lean forward, pull my sunglasses to the end of my nose, and read the sign.

*No way, they still do this? The ice cream boat!*

Here in Newfound, you'll never see an ice cream truck, but you will see the ice cream boat. It's the best thing ever. When we were kids, we'd hear the jingle in the distance and we'd hit the shore running. Every kid made a beeline to their parents for money that we then had to keep dry after grabbing a tube, sprinting into the water, and heading toward the boat. The swim line would fill with kids, like moths to a flame. The ice cream boat would stop outside the swim line and shut off the motor; it was fair game after that. Minutes later, nothing but tubes as far as the eye could see, kids floating within the swim line licking their melting ice cream. Those were the days.

Traveling through that time machine, I'm ten years old again. I unwrap my feet from the rope and start backstroking as speedily as I can. My money is inside my phone case, on my towel, on shore. Looking out at the boat and back to the sand,

I'm certain I can make it. I can already taste the vanilla ice cream and sweet hot fudge melting in my mouth. The ice cream boat used to add chocolate sprinkles and double cherries —I hope they still do.

A couple of kids are already halfway to the swim line. *Damn it, they're going to get there before me.* I double-time it, sweat dripping down my chest. My butt hits the sandy lake bottom, scratching the back of my legs. I'm in a foot of water, a twenty-six-year-old idiot in a tube. Directly in front of me sits an older couple. The woman points my way, giggling, and her assumed husband waves. *I'm so glad I'm providing amusement.*

Keeping my feet planted in the sand, I lean forward to get out of the tube. I've managed to wedge my ass in the tube so well, I fall forward on my knees, hands in the sand, and my butt sails into the air, still inside the tube. An eruption of laughter from my fans echoes loud and clear. Luckily, I lean up and force the tube off my rear end.

I take a bow, my fans clap, and I dart to retrieve my money. My phone is wrapped up in my towel, so I remove the phone case and grab a ten-dollar bill. There's still time—I can deal with being last. I stand, money in hand, and immediately spot a black pickup cruising the lake road.

Jackson.

I freeze, sand digging into the soles of my feet. Vehicles have to drive at a snail's pace on this road. I should wait and say hello. *But damn it, I want ice cream.* I've got enough time for both. I walk up to the tree on the side of the road, wishing he'd get here quicker. As the truck approaches, I spot a woman on the passenger's side, and I step out of view. I'm certain it's Jackson's pickup, and I'd recognize that backward hat and grin a mile away.

Pressing my body against the tree trunk, I look at the woman inside the cab as they slowly roll by. Her white teeth gleam as she smiles and tosses her hair in the breeze. All I can see of Jackson is the lid of his hat from behind. The exhaust from the truck takes the wind out of my sails. The truck passes the tree, and through the back window, I spot them high-fiving each other.

*What the fuck?* You've got to be kidding me. I knew there was something off the other night. How is it I constantly attract assholes? Seriously.

Tears run off my cheeks, dripping into the sand, as I throw myself on my crumpled towel. I gaze out into the crystal-blue lake to the sound of the ice cream boat honking and kids cheering and waving. Taking every ounce of strength I have, I raise my arm and wave as I watch the boat travel by with my ice cream sundae still aboard.

# 9

Jackson

Finally, Friday night arrives. My grandparents are getting too old to manage any of the physical requirements of the orchard, so each year, I find myself taking on more and more responsibility. My body aches from working the fields, cleaning and maintaining the machinery, and loading and boxing countless crates of vegetables of every variety for delivery. Our vegetable side hustle has expanded over the years, thanks to the new greenhouse. The crates go to local markets, a few travel many miles to restaurants and bakeries, and several ship farther distances.

But right now, my muscles are sore, I need a shower, and my bed is calling my name. I unscrew the cap to my water bottle and chug a huge gulp. Looking left across the field, I spot Brynn leaning against the side of my truck. Tightening the cap, I quicken my pace.

"Hey, Brynn, what's going on?"

"Hey, Jackson, I hate catching you at the end of a long day, but as you can see, I've got a little problem." Brynn lifts her chin in the direction of her Toyota Camry parked a few yards away. I scan the car from left to right and spot the front deflated tire.

"Ahh, you got yourself a flat. Let's see what we can do."

"I dropped off a box of pastries to your grandparents. Greg figured they'd enjoy them. When I was on my way here, the car wasn't driving straight unless I tugged the wheel to the left. I'm a little nervous to drive home. AAA said they'd be here in a bit. A bit can mean many things—twenty minutes or three hours—it's a toss-up. I'm supposed to meet my parents for dinner at their place, so I was wondering if you'd give me a ride? If not, no worries."

"No, I don't mind. Hop in. Where do they live?"

"Tenney Mountain. They bought one of the chalets on the mountainside years ago."

"Well, that's easy."

As we approach the four-way intersection by the lake, the road is blocked off. A cruiser is parked perpendicular to the street, and the officer signals people to detour to the left.

"Yikes, a logging truck is stopped on the other side. Hope everything is OK." Brynn leans her head out the window to get a better view.

"We can just take the lake road and get back on at the end." I veer left and slow to around fifteen miles per hour because little ones never look both ways on this road; they see the walk and run full speed.

"So, what are you doing tonight?" Brynn asks.

"Honestly, sleeping. I'm spent. You? Hitting a local bar?"

"I wish! I turn twenty-one in three weeks!"

I lean over and give her a high five. "A member of the drinking class. Good for you. I'll have to remember to buy you a drink when I see you out."

We turn left off the lake road and Tenney Mountain is a few miles on the left.

"Are you sure you don't need me to do anything with your car?"

"Thanks, Jackson, but my dad will take care of it. I'm still in college, so I can get away with being helpless."

I throw my hands in the air. "Work it while you can, Brynn. You'll be on your own soon enough. See you Monday."

"Bye, Jackson! Thanks again!"

I watch to make sure she's inside safe and then head home for the night. First stop: shower.

I've got one foot under the water and one on the bath mat when a text comes through. Lunging over to the counter, I straddle to check the message.

RYAN

Bud, you free tomorrow morning?

JACKSON

That depends.

My mom signed us up for a two-cord delivery and stacking.

What time?

Eight. Shouldn't take us more than a couple hours.

Yeah, no problem. Swing by and get me.

Sure. Jay's coming too.

I'd never refuse because I have no excuse. I'll have to hope that after a few hours of sleep, it will seem less unappealing.

∿

The next morning, my alarm clock goes off at seven forty-five. Glad I set it because I would've slept until noon. I throw on a pair of dirty jeans and a clean T-shirt and put my hat on backward. I run downstairs, brush my teeth, and slide into my boots. Ryan's no fool—he wouldn't show up without my coffee after asking me to work on my day off. I grab the one muffin left in the container my grandmother gave me. She can't help it. The woman needs to make sure I'm fed at all times. I will never convince her otherwise.

I hear Ryan's truck tires rumble over the pothole in my driveway. When I open the door, a wave of heat hits me in the face. We've had four or five days straight in the nineties. We will get a workout this morning.

"What's up, Jackson?"

Jay nods from the middle of the truck's front bench seat. He's the least friendly of us in the morning.

I reach into the tray on Jay's lap and grab my coffee—large, bold, skim milk, two sugars—ready to get this over with. I tip the cup toward Ryan, guy code for *thank you*.

We ride in silence and let the coffee do its job. They stacked the wood high in the back of the truck. If done correctly, we can knock this out in a couple of hours. When Ryan signals to turn right on Chasm Drive, I nearly spit out my mouthful of coffee.

"What the hell, dude? You good?" Ryan asks.

"Why are we on this road?"

"This is the address my mom gave me. She said there's a new lady in town who needs two cords. Hence the overflowing pile of wood behind you."

"Yeah, I got that, we're stacking wood. No one told me we were stacking wood here."

"And that matters because …?" Ryan looks at me like I'm certifiable.

"It doesn't. It's just I thought you said it was somewhere else," I say, avoiding their stares by looking out the side window.

Out of hundreds of homes in this area, we are delivering and stacking wood at Solia's cabin. What are the chances of this?

Ryan pulls into the driveway, just as I did a week ago, does a three-point turn, and backs up as close as he can to the hill near the rear of the house.

We pile out of the truck, coffees in hand. Ryan hits the button and the bed starts moving, dumping the wood for us to move to the bottom of the hill.

"It's hot as balls out here." The sweat is already running off Jay's face. He pulls his shirt over his head, followed by Ryan doing the same.

We've been friends for years, and if I sit here with my coffee and my shirt on in this heat, they'll razz me to no end. I take off my hat first and then pull the shirt up and over my head, tossing it into the truck cab.

I pull my hair back, replacing my hat on my head, and glance at the north-facing, floor-to-ceiling windows. Just as I look, I see a silhouette. Solia moves a little closer, and I trail her body to where they meet a pair of barely there cotton sleep shorts, followed by a pale pink tank outlining her breasts. Her hair is parted in the middle, falling to her shoulders in the sexiest, sleepiest way. As I take in the full length of her, I hold my stare, and I can tell she wasn't expecting to see me, just as much as I was not expecting to be here. She lifts her hand and grabs hold of the cord hanging in the window and slowly closes the blind.

*That was odd.*

What seemed ten minutes must have been two in reality. The beeping of the truck bed slamming back into place refocuses my mind. Jay and Ryan clearly witnessed the window scene, and Jay watches for my next move. "We've got a resident hottie in the cabin, twelve o'clock."

"Come on, man, let's get done what we came here to do." I try to derail Jay's attention from Solia.

Ryan stays at the bottom of the hill tossing the wood to Jay who is at the top behind the house. Jay then tosses the logs to me to stack in rows, filling each rack.

If anyone has ever stacked wood, they can vouch for the fact it's exhausting and a complete and total body workout. Within fifteen minutes, sweat drips off my face, down my chest, to the waistband of my boxers that extend slightly above my jeans. I forgot to throw on a belt.

Just as I catch the latest log coming at me, Solia appears on the deck. Noticing she changed into a fitted T-shirt and running shorts, I stand still and soak in the view. Leaned against the house in a runner's stance, she appears to be gearing up to pounce over the railing.

"I had no idea you were part of a wood-stacking crew. Just what don't you do?" She is flirting with me. It's beyond hot.

"I honestly had no idea I was coming here this morning. I'm as blindsided as you. I would've warned you this time. Wouldn't want the three of us interrupting another dance party." I wink. "These are my childhood buddies. You must've met Janice? That is Ryan's mom. She's an exceptional woman, but sometimes I get roped into stacking wood for her. Had I known it was for you, I would've offered myself."

"I appreciate the help, but honestly, I'm all set." She ices over, her expression stoic. "Listen, even though we only met days ago, I want to be clear that I'm not into seeing guys who are already hooking up with other chicks. It's not my style, and I have zero energy for this type of bullshit."

I drop the log in my arms and walk toward the deck. "Whoa. Solia, I'm not sure what you mean, but I'm not seeing anyone. I'm as single as they come." I scratch the back of my head and wait for a response.

She places both hands on the deck rail and leans forward. "I was at the lake yesterday and just happened to be standing by the road when you drove by." Her face hardens and she crosses her arms over her chest.

I stretch my back, both hands on my knees, and laugh. "Solia, that was Brynn. She's a college kid we hired from Plymouth State to work at the store this summer. She was at the orchard and had a flat tire, so I gave her a ride to her parents' house a few miles away." I straighten and look directly at her and watch the blood drain from her face. She covers her cheeks with both hands and shakes her head.

"Oh my god, you must think I'm such a psycho. I swear I'm not usually so presumptuous. I assumed … obviously I assumed … shit, sorry. What came over me? I really fucked this up. I was looking forward to our date today, and when I saw you drive by, I immediately felt I missed a red flag. I assumed the worst, and that wasn't fair to you. I'm sorry." She pouts her lips and tips her head to the side.

"Get over here, crazy one. You don't need to apologize, but it is nice to know you are looking forward to today."

She comes off the deck and walks over to our assembly line and tries to join.

Jay stops the next toss when he spots Solia. He looks at me and raises a brow as if to say, "What have we got here?"

I walk with Solia so I can introduce her. "Hey, guys, this is Solia. We met the other day. Ryan, she's the one who met your mom."

Both men appear too stunned to speak. I'm sure it has more to do with the fact that she's drop-dead gorgeous than that I already met her. They both offer goofy smiles and say hello.

"I'm ready to help."

"No way. My mother gave me explicit instructions. This is a gift from her, and we are happy to stack it. We'll be done in no time." It doesn't go unnoticed that Ryan is giving her the once-over while he speaks.

"Thank you so much. Seriously, it's very sweet of you, but am I just supposed to watch while you three sweat, moving wood for the next however many hours?"

I speak up, a ping of jealousy piercing my heart. Secretly not wanting any of her attention going toward my two friends, I clear my throat louder than necessary. "We'll finish in no time. Do whatever you need to do. We've got this."

"If you say so. I'll see you later, Jackson." Solia smiles and heads back into the house.

Without saying a word, I can almost read the guys' minds and predict exactly what is coming next. There is no way to avoid the onslaught of questions.

# 10

*Solia*

SOLIA

You'll never guess what is going on outside my window.

MIA

Well???

Three sweat-drenched hot guys in my backyard stacking two cords of wood.

FaceTime me right now.

No way, you won't be able to control yourself. I was going to call you later. One of these guys is the hot farmer.

Dish it.

I'll fill you in when you come for the weekend, but me and the farmer have our first official date in a couple hours.

Is wood stacking a kind of foreplay out there?

> Hahaha, no. I had no warning, no idea he was coming this morning to do this. My dad's friend ended up being the woman I ordered the wood from. Her son, Ryan, and his two friends are the muscle she offered.

Nice. Muscles? Tattoos? Big, strong hands? Snap a pic.

> Let's just say, mine is tall, tan, and looks chiseled from stone. The sweat is literally dripping through the crevices of his six-pack and into his briefs. Fitted jeans. Work boots. Hat backward. Dying . . .

Name?

> Jackson. Remind me to tell you the story of how I acted like a jealous freak.

Seriously, Solia. You must have it bad. You're not the jealous type. Any eye candy for me?

> What has gotten into me? Are you still taken?

Nope, I ended it. It was a long time coming. You knew it, I knew it. I am as free as a bird and ready to get dirty.

> You are too much, but I'll need details. I guess you'll just have to get your butt here and see if steamy backwoods guys are your thing. But I will say they don't make men like these where we're from.

K, how's the weekend after the Fourth?

> I was hoping you'd say the actual weekend of the Fourth, but sure, that works.

> Seriously, I'm proud of you, Solia. You are way braver than me doing your thing out there. You deserve to smile. Have fun with Jackson! Way too much fun.

> Thanks! I'll text you later.

Setting my phone on the ledge, I lean against the window facing the backyard. These men are on a mission, slinging wood as if they're throwing pillows across a room. With each catch, I swoon over Jackson's defined biceps. Every time he places the wood on the rack, he squats low, accentuating his solid backside, and when he stands, his abs uncoil and the sweat flows. What is this man doing to me? If I stay to watch, I'm not sure I'll be able to control myself.

I take an indoor shower, despite my preference for the outdoor stall on the deck, but since the boys are out there, that seems inappropriate. After, I throw on a pair of shorts and a simple tee, walk around the porch, and admire Jackson. I take in one more tall drink of his muscle-ripped body and head to my truck.

There are just a few things I need to take care of. First stop, the post office. I'm not sure if I'll receive my first utility bill via the mail or online. I'm hell-bent on paying everything the minute it comes in. The last thing I need is a reason for my parents to say "I told you so."

The Meriden Post Office resembles every other small-town New England post office, I imagine. It's a quaint white building with a black metal roof and an American flag in the corner. To the right of the entrance is the queue to speak with a postal worker, and straight ahead, lining the hallway, are rows of post office boxes. I search, and sure enough, inside box 1115, the electric bill sits atop a few other envelopes. I'll take care of these later. Right now, I need to grab a few additional things from the market.

Unsure what Jackson has in mind for today, I want to be prepared with a few options at the cabin in case we hang out there for a bit. Thickets Market is a family-owned shop that comes in handy when you need basics. Pulling into a front spot, I open the truck door and note how the sun is already wearing on the pavement. It's getting hotter by the minute.

An older gentleman holds the door open for me as I approach the store.

"Hello there. Have a great day."

"You too, thank you." People are just so nice around here. Others could learn manners from the locals.

I speed-walk back and forth through the aisles, choosing a six-pack of summer ale, a bottle of white wine, crackers, cheese, the ingredients for s'mores, and a bottle of SPF50 sunscreen. I am confident the contents of my basket comprise the perfect survival kit for whatever this date may bring.

∼

Climbing the hill up Chasm Drive, I can't stop the images of Jackson running through my mind. He's all mine today, and spending the day with him fills me with a giddy nervousness I haven't felt in so long. Coming from a small town, everyone knows everyone and their backstories. And if you don't, your cousin or friend does. Living in another small town and only knowing the area and not the people is not what I am used to. With Jackson, I'm curious, excited, and hopeful. I can't wait to see what the day has in store for me.

Mia's voice resonates in my head, telling me to have fun, relax, and not take everything so seriously. A quick peek at the dashboard shows it's ten thirty. My driveway is vacant, which means the boys are done.

I run up the stairs to the door and stop to catch my breath. My shaking legs signal how anxious I am for this date. I throw the mail on the small island and make a mental note to go through it later. As the white envelopes go flying, I see the return addresses of Meriden Elementary, the Town of Meriden, and Green Breeze Enterprises. No need to waste a second dealing with any of this right now. Twenty-eight minutes to get ready. I just need to decide which bathing suit will be best!

From underneath my pile of suits strewn over the bed, I hear my phone pinging.

MOM

Hi, honey, hope everything is going well. FYI, we forwarded the utility bills to the PO box. I want you to face the reality of what you're getting into. I think the electric bill is due soon. Don't be late.

SOLIA

Yes, Mom. It's all set.

Oh, good. I figured you did. And Dad and I sat and made a list to approximate the yearly costs. We should have given you the list before you left. Do you want me to send it to you?

Yeah, Ma. That would be fantastic.

She's unbelievable. I toss my phone onto the bed instead of staring at the bubble while she types.

I strip and tie the bikini-top strings behind my back and use the tip of my nose to tap my screen.

You're going to need a job as soon as possible. I'm not sure how well you saved your money before now. We just want you to understand what you're getting into. Taxes, $3900/year; elec/heat, $2600/year; internet, $91/month; cable (if you keep it), $75/month; plowing last year, $900; Terminix, $400/year; chimney cleaning (every other year), $250/year; wood, one cord, $300/year . . . that's all I can think of for now. Dad and I have to figure out what other maintenance needs to be done that you won't think of. I'll send you that list soon. Have a great day, honey.

Thanks, Mom.

My mind races and my palms sweat. How the fuck am I going to pull this off? I've got truck payments, the rest of my student loans, and no freaking job in sight. Shit.

Deep breaths.

# 11

*Jackson*

Seeing Solia this morning set a fire inside me that needs to be tamed. She is invading my every thought. Flashbacks of her legs wrapped around my waist, her soft lips melding into mine, are driving me wild.

Back at my condo, I change into my black swim trunks and a clean white T-shirt. I already packed my black hiking bag with a couple beach towels and a change of clothes. I preordered from the store, thinking I could swing by my grandparents', check on them, and get lunch. Despite hearing Shannon's voice echoing in my head, *"They're fine, I'll handle the weekends this summer. You go have a life and enjoy it,"* she's made it transparent I don't *need* to check on them—I want to.

Since school is out for summer, Shannon has time to herself. She needs it. I would lose my mind dealing with twenty-eight second graders daily, but Shannon seems to enjoy it. Dedication is one thing, but she has never-ending patience. Instead of isolating herself on an island for a month, she steps up for the family. Our grandparents are aging; it's a reality the two of us can't avoid. She loves Earl and Sylvia and wants to spend as much time with them as possible.

I enjoy seeing more of Shannon in the summer, but she doesn't hide the fact she wants me to date again. Seeing me at my worst has strengthened our bond, and she's managed to keep me afloat.

We didn't always gel growing up, but since our parents embarked on their new adventure in New York, we've been forced to rely on each other. She has her life, and I have mine, but having her right around the corner puts my mind at ease. I don't think I've ever told her that. I should.

Christianson's Country Store sits on Main Street, diagonal to the laundromat and mechanic shop. My grandparents saw the potential when the old Victorian home went on the market years ago. Back then, my parents were still living in the area. Together, with the help of family and dedicated staff, they turned the house into a store and sandwich shop, and it was a success from the start.

The location is perfect and central to the traffic that flows through the town every summer. Families can easily swing by, order lunch, and head to the lake for the day. Vacationers stop in for local maple syrup, a package of homemade goat soap from Sandy's farm, or a sandwich to go before heading to the lake or home. We offer a bit of everything, and since I grew up here, the store is a second home.

As I pull into the dirt lot, I spot Shannon's truck. The store is jamming as usual for a summer Saturday morning.

I greet Ted, who works the front register each day, and his wife, Alison, who helps customers find what they need among the aisles.

"Hey, Alison. Where are the two lovebirds?"

"Their usual spot, of course. Where else?"

Through the aisle and past the wall of refrigerated units filled with local pasteurized and raw milk, eggs, and cheeses, I take a step up, leading me into the sandwich shop where visitors are transported into a cozy farmhouse. There are bookshelves tucked into a few of the alcoves. Antique signs and unique treasures hang from the cathedral ceiling, placed meticulously around the space to allow them to be discovered and enjoyed. Mismatched tables and chairs are scattered around the floor with weathered checkerboards, tic-tac-toe, and chessboards for customers to play while eating their breakfast or lunch inside.

As expected, my grandparents sit at the corner table, each with their signature cup by their side, his black coffee and her green tea. Despite being in the middle of an intense word search, they both look up and flash smiles and call me over to join.

"What are you doing here on a Saturday morning, son? Shannon's here and has everything covered," Grandpa Earl shouts louder than necessary, causing people to turn and smile. We need to figure out hearing aids soon.

"I know, I know, Grandpa. I am picking up my lunch order and wanted to see how you both were doing."

My grandmother throws a sneaky grin in my grandfather's direction. "Remember, Earl, I told you Jackson ordered two sandwiches to go from—the guy, the man at the counter. He told us this morning. Jackson is supposed to come in around ten thirty to get them. I told you that." She reaches for my grandfather's hand and squeezes tight.

"Greg, Sylvia. The man's name is Greg. And yes, yes, you did. I just forgot for a minute. Did you say two sandwiches?"

With a laugh and a wink my way, my grandmother explains that yes, she said two. "Well, I'll be damned. Who's the second one for? What aren't you telling us, Jackson? You can't keep a secret in this town for more than a hot minute, so who's eating the second one?"

I can't even pretend that my grandfather isn't correct. I would prefer to keep my life private, but in Meriden, word travels as fast as lightning. "The second one is for Solia,

Grandpa. Remember the woman you met at the orchard the other day? The one Gerry had me give a tour of the fields to in my tractor. I'm taking her to Sculptured Falls and if all goes well, dinner."

"Hot damn, good for you. I'm happy for you, son. You need love in your life. No one knows that better than your grandmother and me. Right, Sylvia?"

"Earl, let the boy be. No use jumping the gun when he just met the girl. You go get your sandwiches and enjoy your day. You deserve it. We'll be fine here. We already have Shannon and the rest of the crew checking on us more than we need. You show that girl a good time, and you leave your grandpa to me … spouting advice about love on a first date. Jeez, Earl." Her laugh is contagious. She pats Grandpa's hand and smiles at me. "Get going, you don't want to be late. Ladies don't appreciate tardiness."

These two are too much, but I don't take their wisdom for granted. Having them in my life is beyond a blessing. Without them, Shannon, and the rest of this town, I would not have survived losing Trinity.

"Hey, Greg, how's it going?"

"Busy as ever, but that's a good thing, right? Where are you headed today?" He hands me a paper bag containing two chicken sandwiches with lettuce, tomato, bacon, and a little avocado spread, wrapped in foil, along with two bags of chips and two bottles of water. There aren't many customers who don't love this sandwich, so I figured I'd be safe in my selection.

"Headed out to Sculptured Falls for the day. Thanks, man." I walk away, trying to get out of there before someone else grills me.

I wave to Shannon in the kitchen helping Diane with the sandwich assembly. Of course, she's working. She never stops. Even when she doesn't have to be here, she finds work to do. I have to tell her to knock it off next time I see her.

Before taking off to Solia's, I place our lunch into the cooler in the back of my truck. It suddenly dawns on me I forgot ice. I return inside, using the rear staff entrance—it will be quicker, and hopefully, I can go unnoticed.

This door leads to the back of the kitchen where we have three chest freezers. I lift two bags of ice as quietly as I can and move to the door. I almost make it out, but Shannon appears from the other direction. "What am I hearing, Jackson? Date? Spill it."

"Shannon, I'm going to be late. I'm going out with Solia—you met her at the orchard the other day."

"Yeah, Grandpa and Grandma already told me. I wanted to see if you'd fess up. I'm thrilled you're going out. Her energy is infectious." She gives me a suffocating hug. "Have fun. Call me later."

"Of course. Hey, you look different. Why?"

"Different?"

"Yeah—your hair? New shirt?"

"Not sure, Jackson. I have a whole new outlook on life. I'm almost single and ready to mingle."

"What the hell does that mean? Who did you meet? Who? *You* have to spill it."

"Relax with the intensity, little brother. I haven't met anyone, I'm just ready to get out of my sweatpants and see what this summer brings. Take it easy. Everyone knows me around here, but you can never predict when a summertime hottie might walk through the door. I figure I'll put a little more effort into my appearance, just in case."

My sister is beautiful; no one would deny that. So much time has passed since her dating years, it's difficult to imagine her dating again, never mind having a boyfriend. "I get it. You look great! Bye, sis." Thinking I could get out of there unnoticed was naive. The whole town will know my plans by noon.

As excited as I am for this day, and as much as I can't wait to see Solia, I still question what the hell I'm doing. *Why am I starting something I can't finish? Why am I going down a path that leads nowhere?* I stop the spiral of doubt in its tracks and remember my grandfather's words: *You need love in your life.* Plus, it's just a date. I can handle this.

I arrive at the cabin, eager to be in Solia's presence and spend the day discovering more about her. Even though I saw her this morning, I'm excited for the uninterrupted time ahead.

"Hey there, Jackson," Solia says, lifting me from my thoughts. I look up to see her walking down the deck steps toward me. Her beauty throws me off balance every time. She looks irresistible each time I run into her, but today, she takes my breath away. Her light brown, beachy waves cascade around her shoulders, framing her mile-high cheekbones, sexy pink lips, and blue eyes that resemble tide pools you can get lost in. She has tied two little sections of hair from each side back into a loose braid. A lacy, white V-neck cover-up hangs on one shoulder and loosely falls off the other, revealing a thin, baby blue strap of her bikini underneath, the V-neck low enough to tease me with a glimpse of her full, desirable breasts. The cover-up flows around her seductive curves, giving me the urge to peel the dress right over her head. She's wearing tan flip-flops, displaying her pink-painted toenails.

She walks toward me with a beach tote swinging over her shoulder. Sure, I've seen her before today—many parts of her. But at this moment, we are discovering each other in a way we will never forget. She's seeping into my soul, steering me onto a new road I never intended to travel. I'm not convinced I'm ready for what comes next, but my heart isn't giving me a choice in the matter.

"Don't worry, I have sneakers in my bag and a change of clothes because I wasn't sure what you had planned. It's so hot, I figured water might be involved."

"Good thinking." I wrap my arms around and embrace her, and she softens into my body like a glove. As any gentleman would, I reach out for her bag and open the truck door to help her in. Solia steps onto the running boards and slides into the passenger's seat without having a clue she reveals her baby blue, cheeky bottoms. If she hears the groan I emit upon seeing her toned, silken cheek that is now sitting on my truck seat, she pretends not to. It takes everything in me not to lift her right out of the seat, slide myself underneath her, and wrap my arms around her tight from behind … and then find my way around her body to give her the pleasure I am imagining.

I force myself to take a deep breath and then three more, adjust my trunks, jog around the truck, and climb into the driver's seat.

Solia has me completely unwound, my nerves frayed. My infatuation and want are undeniable. I need to get it together. Fortunately, she can't see or hear my inside thoughts because she'd see I'm already in way too deep, and there's a dead end ahead.

# 12

*Sofia*

Unbeknownst to Jackson, I'm watching in the mirror as he walks around the truck. Either he is nervous or excited. His chest rises and falls at a rapid pace. It would be any woman's dream to render Jackson breathless, but I can't get ahead of myself. I need to focus on enjoying the day and not on getting in his pants.

Glad I chose to wear my bathing suit because he's wearing his. I travel from the waistband of his shorts to his chest, and I want to lift his T-shirt over his head and climb onto his lap and let him have his way with me. Seems Jackson isn't the only one who needs to inhale and count to three.

He gets into the truck, and once again I forget my filter. "Everything OK? I saw you take a few deep breaths."

"You noticed that, huh? Well, if I must tell you, you are easily the most beautiful woman I have ever seen. And if I am going to behave myself, I need those."

Holy shit, I'm stunned by his honesty and don't want him to behave. His comment has my mind racing. "I see." That's the best I can muster, and I twirl the gold stud in my ear.

"Are you ready for an adventure?"

"Always. Where are we headed?"

"I was thinking we could check out Sculptured Falls. Have you ever been there?"

My mind floods with childhood memories, of exploring this magical place. Sculptured Falls is otherworldly. "Yes, wow, I haven't been there since I was a kid. It's just outside Meriden, on the other side of the lake, right?"

"That's the one. Still hidden by a dirt road, it's technically part of the New Hampshire State Park system."

Years ago, my wannabe historian father would spout facts at every opportunity. I vaguely remember him saying the Sculptured Falls area spans over two hundred acres. Dating back to when the last Ice Age ended, the Slippery Rock River carved a narrow canyon into the rock as it pushed its way to Newfound Lake. When this happened, the river sculpted artistic and eye-popping creations into the rock and sand throughout the area. Fresh river water still flows through the deep canyon, attracting locals to a sight only Mother Nature could create. As a kid, I remember thinking that the waterfall was beautiful and the bridge over the canyon was so high.

"I am excited you're taking me. It's been decades. Every time Meriden and summer are mentioned in the same sentence, Sculptured Falls is one place that comes to mind."

"How's it going at the cabin? Summer is the best, but winter is the season to keep in the back of your mind."

"Yeah, you don't need to remind me. And my mother will call every other day to make sure I don't forget. I have most things in order. I really needed this change, though, and when I set my mind on a goal, I see it through. When my parents told my brother and me they planned to sell the cabin, it was a sign. I figured, now or never. My teaching job fell through, so leaving wasn't difficult. I did a little research and found the local schools might need teachers, or at least substitutes, so I'm hoping for an opening close by. With the cabin up for grabs, I couldn't think of a better place to start over. I'd be lying if I said winter doesn't have me a little nervous, more the loneliness than anything. The other stuff, I can figure out."

"Wait, you don't have a job yet?"

"No, I am hoping Meriden Elementary will hire me, but if not, there's a possibility of a building substitute position. Fingers crossed, because I have massive bills to pay."

"What school?"

"You are quick with the questions."

"Yeah, sorry. It's just, my sister teaches second grade at Meriden Elementary. I thought you meant the school in our town because what are the chances of that happening?"

"I'd say pretty damn good because that is exactly the school I'm hoping for. Your sister, Shannon, the one I met the other day?"

"The one and only. This is crazy. Well, I guess you can at least say you've met a potential coworker. Seriously, she's great. She'll help you with anything you need. She'll be shocked to find this out. What a coincidence."

This is fantastic because Shannon and I hit it off. Hopefully, it won't complicate things, since I'm on a date with her brother, but I'll press the brakes on those thoughts and not worry about things that haven't happened.

Jackson parks in the dirt lot on the left side of the road. The lot isn't much of a lot—small patch of dirt would be more accurate. Five cars can squeeze in at most. Jackson comes around to my side and helps me off the running boards. Points for being a gentleman!

"Let me get the cooler and bag I packed from the truck bed. I don't think you'll need anything, but you should change into sneakers. The rocks can be slippery, depending on how many people have been here today."

I walk to the back of the truck, and Jackson unlatches the

tailgate to get into the bed. "Come here. I'll lift you onto the gate."

"Sure."

I almost melt when I turn to face Jackson. He smells of pine, and his pure muscle excites me. He places his hands on my waist and lifts me in one swoop onto the tailgate. My flip-flops fall to the ground, and he removes his hands from my body. I desperately want them to stay right where they were. He motions toward my bag, and I pull out my sneakers. He takes them, slides them onto my feet, and ties them. Such a simple thing. I'm not sure how Jackson makes putting on sneakers passionate, but he does. His hands return to my waist, and he places me back on my feet.

We walk across the street and spot the trail to Sculptured Falls. I hear the falls before I see them. In the still of nature, I hear the pitter-patter of little critters, the calling of summer birds, the crashing of the waterfall, and the ripple of the water as it travels through the canyon. As we approach the wood line, Jackson puts the other strap of his backpack on his right shoulder, switches the cooler to his left, and gently reaches for my left hand.

"It can be slippery, so watch your step."

My pulse increases as our fingers intertwine. This guy may be too good to be true. We cross the wood line, come to the beginning of the trail, and spot a wooden suspension bridge ahead. The distance between us and the bridge shortens and we have an up-close view of the falls. The cascading water, the sun shining through the tree canopy, and this beautiful man by my side are more than I could've ever dreamed of, a scene out of a movie.

Jackson stops on the bridge. "Come on, you are safe."

I peek over the rail. "Wow, we are so high. This is even more breathtaking than I remember." Giant pine trees edge the entire length of the chasm, each leaning toward the water in synchronicity, as if they are protecting a secret. Enormous rocks jut out from the channel, carved in the most exquisite and intricate patterns. The water flows from under the bridge, diverts away from us, and funnels into a shallow area pebbled with stones that resemble jewels newly tumbled from a treasure chest. The sun glistening through the trees makes each stone shine and glimmer. The water bubbles and gurgles through the stones, streams around the corner to the left, and disappears into the depths of the woods. We take in the view and the surrounding stillness.

Mixed in with the delicate forest sounds, quiet voices murmur from below toward the other side of the bridge.

"Did you hear that?"

We look left and walk to the other side. I spot another couple hiking through the woods. They glance toward us and offer a friendly wave. As I wave back, I take in this equally beautiful side of the chasm. Fast-moving water gushes over the edge of a picturesque waterfall and then continues under the bridge below us.

Jackson steps closer behind me, and heat rushes through my body when his hand touches mine. "Nice, huh?"

"Nice doesn't do it justice. It's better than any memory I have. Thank you for bringing me here. This place is exactly why I love this area. It's unassumingly beautiful. Simple, yet so complex, beyond what man could ever recreate." I release his firm hand and turn to face him.

His expression is hard to describe—he looks as though he is contemplating or reliving a memory. He's frozen for a second and then opens his mouth to speak. "Yes, it is. Let's go and get a better view. I figure we can explore and go swimming."

I've been so distracted by Jackson's presence and the natural beauty around me, I didn't notice how hot I am. "That sounds amazing."

I follow him off the bridge and walk a narrow path to the

right. There is no marking for the trail, but travelers have worn it so thin, it's easy to spot. I stay close to Jackson because the path is tricky in spots due to tree roots and small rocks. At the end of the path, a huge, flat stone slab appears before us. Jackson grabs hold of my hand, allowing me to step safely onto the rock. "Careful. Walk sideways."

We shimmy onto the platform, which has to be thirty feet wide and twenty feet long. I look left and right; we are standing almost directly under the bridge. Jackson places the cooler and his bag toward the back of the rock, near the tree line. I'm not sure what he has in mind, so I follow him.

"I'm going to grab the towels in case we're brave enough to get in," Jackson says with a mischievous grin as he spreads the towels and sits. He pats the one adjacent and I join him. I unlace my sneakers and pull my cover-up over my head. It's too hot to keep any extra clothing on. Jackson takes my lead this time and pulls off his T-shirt to reveal a muscle playground I'm dying to explore. I think back to him stacking wood at the cabin, sweat glistening between his abs and forming a trail to his waistline. He is too hot to resist.

He reclines on his towel, looking at me as the sun highlights the stubble that thinly covers his cheeks and jawline. "So, tell me everything. Ready, set, go!" He laughs and seems quite captivated by his own humor. Pushing away images of his rough stubble brushing against my more sensitive spots, I laugh at the ridiculousness of my intrusive thoughts.

"Well, if I had to write a bio for a dating app, I guess I'd say: Libra, small-town girl, loves the outdoors, sports fanatic, excited to learn new things, watches trashy reality dating shows, believes in true love but is ultimately tired of being burned. So, would you swipe right?"

"Wow, trashy reality shows? That isn't what I expected." Jackson leans on his side toward me and rests on his right elbow.

I playfully push his left shoulder to return him to his previous position. "Seriously? That's what stood out the most?"

Pulling himself back up, Jackson hovers closer. "Yes, Solia, I would definitely swipe right. We have a lot in common."

"Well, your turn. Bio, please?"

Jackson's laugh melts me. The level of comfort and ease this man exudes is completely mind-boggling.

He repositions himself on his back and closes his eyes. I take this opportunity to lean on my side, facing him to get a closer look. God, he is beautiful.

"My birthday is August 27. What sign does that make me?"

"Jackson, you don't have to copy mine!" I laugh so hard, my stomach hurts. I can tell he is thinking this through.

"I'll just pull up my current profile and you can read it." Jackson grabs his phone out of his pocket.

The balloon holding my hopes that Jackson is one of the good ones pops. *Great, a prolific dater. What am I thinking? This isn't just sitting in the woods waiting for me. He probably has dates lined up every weekend. My past has taught me better than this.*

I shift on my towel and look at the passing clouds. Jackson seems to notice my change in demeanor because the next second, instead of admiring the sky, I'm mere inches from his lips as he planks over me, muscles bulging. He rises and places one knee on each side of my thighs, his hands on either side of my head as he holds himself over me.

Although none of our body parts are touching, his muscular frame blocks the sun, and heat washes over me from my head all the way between my legs. The tingling sensation is almost too much to bear. Seemingly reading my mind again, he flashes me a playful grin and I completely forget what I was worried about.

"If you think for a second that I have a bio out there, I do not. Not that I have anything against dating apps, but I'm just not of this decade, I guess. I wouldn't even know where to begin, nor am I interested. But if I had a bio, I guess mine would say Virgo, right? Farmer, loves nature, eats fairly healthy —most of the time. If I watch TV, it's sports. I've had the same three, four, best friends my whole life. Also, a devout grandson. Would that be sexy to add?"

"Oh, definitely. I am definitely swiping right. What about—"

Before I can say another word, Jackson's soft, full lips are on mine. He lowers himself closer to my body while his tongue explores my mouth. He lets out a small groan, and it takes everything in me not to come completely undone. Can he sense how desperate I am for his touch? He gently pulls back and grazes his teeth on my bottom lip before lifting and returning himself to his towel.

We lie in silence for a few moments. I try to regain a normal breathing pattern and take in the private, natural oasis surrounding me and this beautiful man. This is more than I'd bargained for and certainly not why I moved here, but the magnetic pull toward Jackson is indescribable. I can hear Mia in my mind saying *Enjoy it, Solia, don't overthink, take it one breath at a time.* I don't often tell Mia when she's right, but this time, she is.

"What do you say we get in the water and cool off?" He reaches for my hands and helps me to my feet.

"Absolutely." I watch as he walks to the edge of the rock platform. "Where are you going? Don't we get in there?" I point, cautiously step forward, lean, and look over the ledge.

"Well, that's the easy way. If you want to be a local, you need to get in this way."

His finger extends over the rock, pointing over the cliff toward the water below. He's implying we should jump.

"Are you serious? How deep is that water? How can you be sure it's safe?" I rattle off questions faster than the water flows through the chasm.

"First, yes, I'm serious. Second, the water is over forty feet deep. Third, it's safe because I've jumped countless times before. See that rock across the way?" Jackson points to a rock half underwater. "Most of the time, the water level is below that rock. The water level varies from season to season, depending on rain- and snowfall, and because the water is covering half of that rock, it tells me it's even deeper than usual. Are you game?"

My nerves are frayed and my mind reels. Jumping off cliffs is not a recreational activity of mine. Never mind jumping into a chasm with rock walls on both sides! I'll swim, paddleboard, hike, ski, but cliff jumping? Yikes.

"Do you trust me?"

*How do I answer that? Yes, I trust him. Why? I don't know, I just do. My gut is always right. I can trust him.* "Yes." I gaze up at Jackson.

He extends his hand back for me to hold, and I walk directly behind him, not wanting too much space between us. "See that circular pool directly below? That is where we jump. It appears higher than it is, but it's not too bad. From experience, the most shocking part is usually how cold the water is. There's no way around that other than to test the water first, but that tends to backfire and people chicken out."

Jackson strokes the back of my hand with his thumb, making soft circles that calm my nerves. Without a word, I lean over and see the spot he's referring to. *I can do this.*

"You don't have to. No pressure. But if you decide to jump, you might love it. I'll go first so you can see where I land. Watch when I come up—I'll swim to the left and rest on the rock right over there. See the one that's partially above the water? I'll stay right there so when you jump, you can swim to me."

Taking a deep breath, I center my emotions by looking at my surroundings and summon the courage to experience a moment I've been seeking—spontaneous and exciting, the opposite of the usual events in my life. Without hesitating or giving myself the chance to back out, I tilt my head. "Let's do it!"

"Now we're talking!" Jackson gives me a gentle squeeze of reassurance and releases my hand. He takes two steps forward and stands at the edge of the rock jutting out over the chasm. Running his hands through his hair, he looks back at me and winks. "Ready? Three! Two! One!" Leaping into the air, showcasing his sexy, defined back muscles, he drops over the edge.

Frantically stepping to the ledge, I look. "Yeah, baby! Woo-hoo!" His voice rings throughout and echoes off the rock walls, and he disappears under the water. Within seconds he resurfaces and looks straight at me, grinning from ear to ear. "Your turn. You ready?"

*Ready as I'll ever be.*

"I got you! You can do this. I'll be right here. It's cold, but you'll love it. You'll thank me after."

"Promise?"

"Yes, Solia, trust me."

His aura transfixes and convinces me to be braver than I am. "I'm ready." I am ready to take this leap with him, to trust he'll be there, to be fearless enough to release control.

Jackson yells and the sound again reverberates off the rocks, allowing every living being around the woods to hear. "Three, two, one!"

I hold my nose with my right hand, keep my left by my side, let out the loudest scream ever, and jump. Time stops for a moment, and there's so much space between me and the water, but then I hit the icy chill and it envelops my entire body, encasing me in a frozen layer of skin. As soon as I submerge, I bob back to the surface.

"Swim, swim to me." Jackson is holding on to the rock with

one arm and reaching for me with the other. I push my hair off my forehead and swim toward him. "You did it! You OK?"

My teeth chatter, but I'm OK. Better than OK—I'm terrific! "Yes! That was such a rush." I smile as I look at Jackson. He wraps his arm around my waist, just as the sun peaks and shines between the trees. The warmth of the sun and the heat between our skin makes me forget we are submerged in freezing water.

"I'm proud of you for jumping."

"I trusted you." I lean closer to him so the space between his body and mine disappears.

"Girl, you are brave. Look at you taking the leap. Solia, I consider myself a tough guy, and you have me feeling so much right now."

Jackson pulls me tighter, and my goose bumps melt as excitement and heat flow through my body. I push my chest against his, and he glides us around several rocks. "Here, over here. It's not as deep." We're standing in knee-height water, soft, gel-like sand under our feet. He slides his wet hands along the sides of my body and lifts me onto a flat rock sitting at the water level. He kneels in the sand in front, waist-deep in the water, leans forward, and places his mouth on my neck, kissing a path from my ear to my collarbone.

Soft, wet, kisses delicately and strategically placed cause my body to ache with pleasure. His lips find mine, and Jackson kisses me with a passion I've never experienced. His body, his emotion, and his want for me can be felt in every groan and touch, connecting us on a deeper level. His soft lips travel the back of my neck. He gently bites the strap of my bikini and teases it further down my arm.

With the strap lying near my elbow, the breeze warms my breast, and I watch as Jackson takes in the sight of me. He lifts his mouth to my breast and caresses every square inch with his strong, pulsating tongue.

There is simply no restraint strong enough to hold in my want. I groan in pleasure and whisper "Jackson" into the air. He lifts his face, focuses his gaze on mine, and makes his way to my neck, across my chest, to my other bikini strap. I arch my back and place my hands behind me. The icy water, the privacy of our surroundings, and the heat between us are almost too much to bear.

I spread my legs wide, allowing Jackson to crawl toward me. He places his hands on the rock while his mouth licks and caresses the path from my chest to the edge of my bikini bottom. My heartbeat thumps between my legs but no longer from the icy temperature of the water. He teases me by guiding his tongue along the edge of my bathing suit bottom; the heat radiates through the fabric and spreads to my insides.

*Is this happening?* I suddenly understand the meaning of primal urge.

Reading my mind, Jackson raises his tongue off the edge of my bottoms, bends low, and leads himself where I need it. He presses urgently against the fabric with his tongue and continues to lick until he reaches my navel. *This has been missing my whole life?* I moan louder than before and pant his name. Just as Jackson pulls his body against mine, a scream and a splash startle us out of the moment.

"Holy shit, someone else jumped." Jackson stands, revealing he is just as excited as I am. I wrap my arms around my breasts, stand in the shallow water, and run to the back side of the rock. I shove my breasts back into my bikini and adjust the straps. I can't contain my laughter—this situation is completely ridiculous.

*Did we honestly think no one else would show up here?*

During those few moments, the outside world didn't exist. It was him and me, heat and friction, and I'd do anything to rewind the clock and freeze time.

Jackson joins me, wide-eyed and grinning. With my back

against the rock, Jackson presses into me, places his chiseled arms by my face, and leans in. He bends his head to reach my mouth and whispers, "Solia, you drive me wild."

He pushes himself off, grabs my hand, and glances back at me. "Let's jump again."

All I can do, all I want to do, is leap again.

# 13

Jackson

I should've expected people would walk over and catch us.
What was I thinking? For once, I'm one hundred percent
living in the moment. When I'm around Solia, she appears in
portrait mode and everything fades into the background. She
makes me smile and laugh and turns me hot as hell.

The later afternoon has gone as well as the first half. We
make small talk with our party crashers for a little while, but
they eventually head out into the trail system. With the place
to ourselves again, we jump and climb the rocks over a dozen
times. Our energy and playful screams seem to put a force
field around the area, encasing us in a bubble where time
stands still. I manage to keep the rest of the afternoon PG but
would be lying if I didn't say I enjoy watching every inch of
Solia's body climb over the rocks. Her bikini bottoms are
much appreciated, but it makes stifling my erection more
difficult.

With towels wrapped around our waists, I unpack lunch
from the cooler.

"I'm impressed. You picked this breathtaking location *and*
brought lunch?"

"I don't mess around. A girl like you doesn't walk into town and not get my full effort."

"This sandwich is delicious," she says as she wipes her lips clean, leans over, and gives me several quick kisses. I'll take what I can get because I am certain I will never get enough of this sexy siren.

"I'm glad you like it. Greg is the chicken sandwich master of Newfound. The store is lucky to have him."

"Has he worked for your family for a long time?"

"Yes, he's a lifer. Our employees become family, and he's one of them."

"I love that."

"Most of our staff have been with us forever. There are a few newbies, but usually people stick around."

"Employees stick around when they are happy and treated well. Loving where you work makes an enormous difference."

We towel off and head back to the truck. The sun is farther west, so the air has cooled and it's a bit more comfortable. Opening the windows on the ride home allows the air to whip through the cab and dry the remaining moisture off our bodies and suits.

As we travel the winding road back around Newfound Lake, I glance at Solia gazing out her window, shoulders relaxed with her hands in her lap. I can tell by looking at her silhouette she is smiling at the scene unfolding around us. Seeing the scenery through her eyes reminds me just how beautiful it is around here.

*Can I leave this place behind?*

"I wish there weren't so many lawn signs. They're scattered everywhere along the road and in everyone's front yards. They look terrible. Don't you think so?" Solia asks, breaking the comfortable silence.

"You mean the political signs?"

"Yeah."

"I agree. It certainly does litter the area, but thankfully, it's only because it's an election year. As soon as that's over, they'll be removed." I've avoided looking at the water for almost a year now.

We continue around the lake and the signs persist: Bob for School Committee, Smith for Town Council, Susan for Town Administrator, Meriden Youth Soccer, sponsored by Green Breeze Enterprises ...

*Wait, what the hell is Green Breeze Enterprises?*

∾

I put the truck in park and take her hand as I walk her to the front door. We stand a foot apart. I could kiss her goodbye and walk away, but I don't want the date to end. Her presence is intoxicating. I look into her sultry, deep, blue eyes and wrap my arms around her. "Solia, I don't want this day to end. Can I take you to dinner?"

With each second that ticks by, my muscles tense and I search her face for a sign.

"I'd love that," she says, squeezing me tighter.

I slide my hand under her chin to lift her face toward mine. I lower my lips so they graze hers. "How's seven o'clock?"

A soft "mmm" vibrates on my lips when she pushes onto mine. I have to back away before it's too late. It's taking everything in my power not to scoop her into my arms and sprawl her out on this front porch. I want to slide off those baby blue bikini bottoms and explore her. I want to hear her moan, scream my name breathlessly into the wild, and make her shake until I exhaust her.

*Why am I picturing this right now?*

I back away from her because my hands desperately want to roam. She looks at me seductively and smiles.

*Does she realize what she's doing to me? Does she have the same level of attraction? This is just crazy.*

"Should I wear sneakers for this too?"

"What?"

"To dinner? Do I need sneakers for this adventure too?"

"Oh, no, not tonight. Go crazy, wear those flip-flops. We don't get too fancy in these parts."

A sweet smile spreads across her face, and it takes a force of epic proportions to pull me away and down the cabin steps. "I'll see you in a bit."

Solia crosses her ankles and leans against the front porch railing with a look that has me wanting more. I wink and reluctantly walk to my truck.

∾

I follow West Shore Road around the lake, unaccustomed to my newfound happiness. Spending the day with Solia has flipped my world upside down. Because of her, a little part of me that I thought was buried too deep is beginning to surface.

Once parked, I rest my head against the steering wheel and tap out for a minute. I won't let myself spiral. I force my doubt to the back of my head, enter my condo, and get ready for dinner.

The area around Meriden doesn't have many fancy restaurants. People here are simple and enjoy casual dinners. Fire Hearth is a four-season restaurant off Main Street. In the summer, the owners set up patio tables and chairs on the deck and string white lights to create a warm and inviting atmosphere.

"I've never been here." Solia reaches for my hand. She looks beautiful in her short yellow sundress and white sneakers. She has her hair tied into a high ponytail, accentuating her long, slender neck, and a delicate infinity gold necklace draped along her collarbone. My thoughts wander back to earlier, hoping tonight's conversation is as easy as today's. She makes me relax, so at home.

"The menu is extensive, so everyone finds at least a few options they like. The head chef has been here for as long as I can remember, and the owners are amazing."

The hostess seats us at an outside table, and we order two pints of the local IPA. As the waitress walks away, I see the owner, Gary, walking toward us. A sudden shift of unease settles in my stomach, and I wish I could disappear into thin air. Gary watched me grow up, practically family, so he's no stranger to what I've been through.

"Hey there, Jackson, how are you? It's great to see you here tonight." He looks from me to Solia, unapologetically obvious he is waiting for an introduction to my stunning date.

"Great. Thanks for asking. This is Solia—she's new to town."

Gary extends a welcome to Solia. She smiles sweetly and shakes his hand. "It's great to meet you. Have you lived here long?"

He lets out a hearty chuckle. "Sweetie, I've been here my whole life. Just like my parents and their parents. Once you fall in love with a place the way we did, you become a thread in the fabric. You can't leave. It'll destroy you—nothing will ever compare to these streets." Gary looks from Solia to me. "Jackson, I sure am happy to see you here. Sharon and I have missed you. Don't be a stranger." He winks and walks through the summer crowd and into the restaurant through the patio doors.

I shouldn't be surprised. Chances are always high I'll run into a familiar face. Analyzing Solia's expression, I see uncertainty rear its ugly head. Sensing her question before she speaks, I lean back in my chair and stroke my chin. "I guess it's been awhile since I've been here. That orchard keeps me busy, and busy is good. I'm better off keeping my mind focused."

"Oh. He seemed surprised to see you."

"Yeah, I guess it's been a long time." A waitress arrives at our table, not our waitress, but a waitress, and at this point I don't care. I'm just thankful for the interruption. Nicole sets two drinks on the table.

"Here you are, two Manhattans." She looks at me and then Solia. "Oh goodness, I am so sorry. I'm at the wrong table. I'm sure your waitress will be right with you." She gathers the small glasses filled with vermouth and a cherry and heads to the table behind us where an elderly couple sits smiling in her direction.

"Those were definitely not IPAs." Looking over at Solia, I'm stunned to see tears. I stretch past the flickering candle in the middle of our table and reach for her. "What's wrong, Solia?" I wait patiently to see if she'll respond. A single tear flows down her cheek, illuminated by the candlelight. I squeeze her hand a little tighter.

She pulls away and wipes the stream of tears. "I'm fine, I'm sorry. I can't believe I'm crying. You're going to think I'm a basket case if I tell you why."

"Try me. I'm pretty sure anything you say won't change my impression of you. Unless you don't want to share … I can pretend this didn't happen."

Surprising me, Solia speaks. "Growing up, I was extremely close to my mother's parents. They were amazing, not only separately but as a couple. Their stories were legendary, as was their commitment to family, and they shared an everlasting love people search for their whole lives." She pauses and shifts in her seat. "Married for seventy-six years, they loved life and each other until the very end. That side of my family is large, and they were our glue, our North Star. Losing them"—the tears continue, but she allows them to flow—"was awful. My grandfather passed first in November, at home, surrounded by his family. It was beautiful and just the way he wanted it. He insisted everyone pour a Manhattan and cheer for a life well lived. Not even four months later, my grandmother passed from a broken heart."

I caress her skin, hoping to reassure her I'm listening to her every word.

"After they passed, my family changed drastically. Instead of having Sunday dinners together and filling their home with laughter and music, each family started slowly distancing themselves to begin their own traditions. No one fought or argued—it was simply a new beginning, a different way of existing. I'm not sure my grandparents would be proud of this, but they're no longer here to hold us together. My life continued as planned and naturally, I missed them.

"It was later that I came across a book a friend had recommended. I love to read different genres, so I'm always willing to try new books. Her recommendation had to do with life after death, souls, energy, light, and so on. I never gave any of those things much thought. My parents took me to church when I was little, and I believe in heaven, but that's pretty much where my thoughts and beliefs end." She pauses. "I'm dragging this out. Sorry. You must be ready to pull your hair out."

She couldn't be further from the truth. I am so invested in her words, every single one. I stare at her, hoping she will continue, and reach across to wipe the smooth skin beneath her eyes. I take her hand back in mine and nod.

With a gentle smile and tilt of her chin, she proceeds. "After I read the book, my grandparents entered my thoughts often, and I began to contemplate life after death. If they could hear me, then maybe it would be possible to connect with loved ones who've passed, and I figured, why not try? You'd have to read the book to fully understand, but anyway, I started to talk to them aloud when I was alone in my car or before I went to bed. I found it comforting, and it brought me peace thinking they could sense my love.

"I read that for those who are open to the possibility of connecting to loved ones who have crossed, you should ask for a sign. A sign you can see, a specific sign, an object you wouldn't normally see in everyday life. I knew I was open. I never say never. So, I tried it.

"One day while driving, I was telling my grandparents about an event that happened in my life, that I was unsure if I was doing the right thing. I told them I needed guidance. I asked them to show me a sign of a Manhattan if I was on the right path since it was their favorite drink. Every day at five p.m., we would find them at their counter toasting a Manhattan.

"Days later, they sent me the sign and haven't stopped since. When that waitress came over with the wrong drinks, that was them. This move to New Hampshire is drastic, and I doubt myself at times, wondering if I can handle this and figure it out. Now, I'm reassured they agree with my decision." She lifts her chin and gently smiles.

Every word she speaks reaches the deep trenches of my soul. I work hard, I love my family, but I mainly see in black-and-white. Solia's story and emotion resonate in a way that startles and almost frightens me. Her story of family, love, and want for connection makes her more beautiful.

"Honestly, Solia, I'm at a loss for words. They clearly had a profound impact on you, and they had a beautiful love story. I admire how you see things most people wouldn't try to imagine. I never question the afterlife. Having them send you signs must be comforting."

"Very. Everybody questions themselves in life. We want to make the right decisions, don't we? Having them reach me from the other side is transformative, especially when I need a little reassurance. I've allowed myself to heal and still have them in my life." She smiles as I lean around the table and gently kiss her cheek.

"Do you think anybody can ask for a sign from a lost loved one?" I ask, looking at my lap.

"Yeah, totally. As long as you are open, anything is possible. It can't hurt to ask." Solia bends her head low, trying to catch my eye.

I can't help but think of Trinity. I'm desperate to escape the pain and thought I had exhausted all possibilities. Is there a way to heal without running?

# 14

*Sofia*

Dinner did not go as I'd imagined it would—it was better. Jackson is so supportive, the kind of man who usually lives in the pages of a romance novel. Our physical connection was off the charts this afternoon, and tonight, our emotional connection truly deepened. I would never have foreshadowed discussing my belief in life after death, my grandparents, and crying on a first date, but it made for an intense conversation. Jackson handled it effortlessly and accepted my vulnerability. No one has ever seen me, truly seen me.

Not only does Jackson drive me wild, he's sweet, reassuring, and he makes me comfortable enough to say things I've never spoken aloud.

As we're driving home, rain splatters the windshield, and the wind begins to whip. "Glad this held off. I enjoyed dinner on the patio."

"I couldn't agree more. So, what do you have planned for this week? Job searching? Dancing on the deck?"

"Hilarious. Certainly job hunting—I need to get my mother off my back—but I want to enjoy the summer the way it's meant to be enjoyed. I need to get to the lake. It's so beautiful. The way I see it, the more time spent there, the better. I love to paddleboard, but I'm always up for kayaking, swimming, or reading a book on the beach. I've always been a lake girl—the cool sand, the cleanest water anywhere, the mountains in the distance, and no crowds! You must be on the lake every free minute."

"It is beautiful. I have a boat at Gray Ledge Marina. Are any friends coming to visit during the summer?" Jackson changes the topic so abruptly, I angle my head toward him, wondering if I said the wrong thing. His voice and tone have completely changed.

However, when I look at him, he appears fine and smiles. Certainly, it's my imagination; assuming I can already read his body language would be presumptuous.

*Why does he seem so familiar?*

"My friend Mia is visiting the weekend after the Fourth. I'm excited to have her here. She and I met in college and have been inseparable ever since. She's the best."

"Those guys you met earlier have been my buddies forever as well. We laugh our asses off every time we're together." He jabs the steering wheel with his fist.

Suddenly, we are pitched into a black hole. The sky darkens, rain pours from the clouds, and the truck weaves in the wind. "Holy shit, hold on." Jackson yanks to the right, steering us to the side of the road. I feel the tires jut from the concrete onto the dirt shoulder.

I remember microbursts at the lake during summers with my family when we'd have to run as fast as we could to take cover. Everyone grabbed what they could—umbrellas, chairs, and towels, then ran to throw themselves and everything into the car. We'd laugh and watch the storm. Luckily, nothing serious ever occurred. Vacationers would be terrified and pack up for the day, not to return, but we knew the drill. We'd wait it out, unload, and enjoy the rest of the day.

These storms don't happen frequently, but enough that everyone here has their reaction time down pat. When you're in these parts, it's best to be informed and understand the impact they can have.

Jackson and I huddle together on the roadside as pounding rain pours over the truck. He scooches closer and wraps himself around my shoulders. Every inch of his arm leaning on my skin sends goose bumps across my body. Being this close in complete darkness with only the rain and wind echoing through the cab, I focus on the breaths between us and attempt to keep my excitement on simmer.

"We haven't had one of these in a while. Don't worry, it'll be quick," Jackson says, turning to me.

"These, I remember. Once you get caught in one, you never forget. My dad used to love these storms." The rain continues, beating the hood of the truck, and the wind whips around us. A sudden chill vibrates through me. I shudder slightly, and Jackson notices.

He reaches into the back seat and grabs a green zip-up hoodie and motions for me to lean forward. He then wraps it around my back and over my shoulders. "Does this help?"

"Yes, thank you. I'm still a little cold. Could you come closer?" Without hesitating, Jackson moves as far as he can in his seat. I take his face in my hands and pull him toward me. I crave more and my interest shifts into overdrive, no chance of putting it under lock and key.

He lets me lead, and I kiss him with urgency and passion. My heartbeat matches the rhythm of the rain. Our kiss becomes frantic and desperate, making me want to crawl out of my seat and straddle Jackson right here on the side of the road. Heat rises between my legs, and I'm ready to give him all of me.

However, we simultaneously start laughing because we're stunned into silence when twilight fills the cab. Once again, we're two kids getting caught making out. This time it isn't people but the weather.

We separate, my stomach aching from yet another intimate encounter cut short.

If Jackson had any idea what he's doing to me, he'd assume I'd never been with a man before. Every touch, even his stroking my hand, turns me on. I don't think I've grabbed a man's face and kissed him as intensely as I kissed Jackson. No one has made me fall apart at the seams so effortlessly.

Our conversation flows on the way home, but the sexual tension between us is palpable. Jackson walks me to the door. Thankfully, I forgot to turn on the outside light. Otherwise, we'd be swarmed by a zillion mosquitoes. The glow of the lamppost at the bottom of the lengthy staircase is just enough to light our path. We stand on the slightly crooked landing by the front door, and I'm unsure what to do next.

*Do I ask him to come in? Is it too soon?*

"I don't think we've exchanged numbers."

He's right. We seem to be doing everything backward. We trade phones and enter our contact information.

"I had a great time tonight."

"Me too. Sorry things got a little deep at dinner."

"The conversation was my favorite part. That, and making out in my truck." Jackson smirks.

His sweetness and humor are climbing the list of things I love about him.

"I'll agree with that. Are you working tomorrow?"

"Yeah. Earl and Sylvia need as much help as they can get these days. Have fun tomorrow. It should be beautiful." Jackson leans in and gives me a full, soft kiss, turns, and walks into the darkness below. I desperately want him to slip under the covers with me.

I could have asked him to stay or at least come inside for a drink. That would have seemed too eager. Right? I don't want to come on too strong.

Leaning against the screen door, I watch his headlights illuminate the dirt driveway and disappear into the night. I open the door to the cabin and the scent of pine and vanilla fills my nose. The table lamp illuminates the walls and pictures I brought from home. I admire the new items I've purchased— the cozy couch pillows, the small bookshelf showcasing my favorite reads, and the plants sitting on almost every flat surface. It fills me with warmth and pride. This cabin will be my safe haven, filled with items and people I love most, and I'm more confident than ever moving here was the correct decision.

And I don't want to get ahead of myself, but Jackson has invaded every cell in my mind and body since that day at the hardware store.

I cover a yawn and let the tiredness from today sink in. I wouldn't give back one minute of it, though. This day was by far the best date of my life. My phone beeps as I attempt to muster the energy to shower.

MOM:
Did you have fun tonight?

I quickly scan the empty living room and the vacant driveway outside. Seriously, did they install security cameras in this place?

Ummmmm? Yes???

That's great! Any other news?

Seriously, Mom, how did you know I was out?

Don't be mad. Your father and I were talking to your brother. He knows how much your father worries. He reminded Dad we installed the "find family" feature that shows us your location. Remember, when you were a teenager, we would keep tabs on you guys? I guess we never deleted it.

Is she serious? I'm twenty-six years old, and my parents are still tracking me. Fantastic.

I'm not mad but . . .

So, what did you do? I mean, I have the location of where you were, but who were you with? Meet anyone special?

There is no sense trying to pull one over on my intrusive mother. Even one hundred and fifty miles apart, she is still invading my personal space. It's never going to be any other way. I'm not sure if all moms act this way, but when she's wrong, she's right. Her unsolicited advice is always spot-on. She's pushy but supportive-ish. So, if she wants to track me, I guess I'll have to let her.

His name is Jackson.

Nice name. Is he a nice boy?

Man, Mom. He's a man.

Right.

Yes, he's very nice. Cute too.

That's fantastic, honey. Just be careful. Does he have any connections?

Mom, it was one date and no. Drop it. I'll figure
this out on my own.

Take it slow, Solia. Remember what you went
through. Getting dragged through the mud is
not in your best interests. Take it one day at a
time.

Once again, my mother has me second-guessing and
wondering if I spoke too soon. Being vulnerable and open to
love in the past has not ended well. I've already let Jackson in.
Yet I can't afford to make the same mistakes and move too fast.
Jackson hasn't shown any warning signs, but then again,
neither did the others. I don't want to construct a brick wall
before a second date. If it even happens.

Don't worry, Mom. I'll be careful.

What's his last name?

I'm no fool. I'm fully aware of exactly where this is going. I
could earn big money by betting that if I give her his last
name, within one hour she'd have a list of his ex-girlfriends
and his extended family with their addresses and annual
incomes.

Good night, Mom.

OK, Solia. Good night. Lock the doors. So, no
job yet, sweetie? Love you.

Love you too. They're locked 😊 And no
job yet.

Lying in bed, I see a full moon shining above the mountain
ridge in the east, illuminating the land. Billions of stars

decorate the night sky, and the only thing I wish for is Jackson lying by my side, sharing this moment.

Oh, and a damn job.

# 15

Jackson

The sun beaming through my window blinds me. I fell asleep on my leather couch. The last thing I remember is the five steps I took from my door to here. I'm wearing the same clothes from dinner and the TV is still on.

I have a busy day ahead at the farm. Vegetables need to be harvested, crates need to be sorted, labeled, and shipped, and hay has to be baled. The forecast indicates the heat wave won't be letting up anytime soon, so today may be a three-shower kind of day.

Still groggy and half-asleep with visions of Solia, I shuffle to the kitchen to make my first cup of coffee. One hot coffee in the morning is mandatory. The iced coffee that follows is optional, but today it'll be essential. My steaming mug is coming into the bathroom with me.

I lather the soap and let the warm water wash it away, my mind wandering to Solia, to her arched back on the slippery, cool rocks, her voluminous breasts front and center. I have to see her again. The connection forged between us in such a short time is undeniable. But showing up for work takes precedence right now.

I arrive on time, the temperature already above eighty at only seven a.m. Like clockwork, my dedicated grandfather is rocking on the front porch, iced coffee in hand, a second glass waiting for me on the table by his side. With a slight tilt of his hat, he yells, "Good morning, farmer."

"Hey, Grandpa."

"You lookin' a little sluggish this morning, or is it me?"

"It's not you. I'm dragging my boots a little more than usual."

"It wouldn't be because of your date with the beauty on the tractor? Your grandmother and I were watching you two lovebirds take a tour around the grounds. It sure was nice to see you smiling again."

"Thanks, Grandpa. She's beautiful, smart, funny. She's a catch."

"Good enough to reconsider leaving town? Because nothing is set in stone, Jackson. Your grandmother and I want nothing more than to leave this farm to you, our family. We aren't getting any younger."

"Grandpa, we've been through this. I made up my mind. I can't stay here. It's just not the same after everything ... I don't think it ever can be."

"Things are meant to change, Jackson. If they didn't, life wouldn't be what it's meant to be. People change, adapt, learn, and grow. You'll come around."

"Grandpa, I don't doubt you mean well, but I'm going to New York at the end of the summer. Dad is already setting things up at the cider facility for me. I'll come back all the time and visit."

"Jackson, you'll do what's right, and your grandma and I support you. Did you tell Solia about this?"

"No, I didn't." I wipe the sweat forming on my brow. "We just met. I haven't been on a date in almost a year, so it seemed a little forward to walk that path and pour out my soul. Right?"

I look over to my grandpa. He's staring off into the distance, rocking slowly. I'm so lucky to be able to see this man almost every day, and just now I'm noticing the deep lines creased into his face. He looks exhausted.

"You OK, Grandpa?"

"Sure am, son. Life has a way of working itself out. You'll see. Now, get to work." He laughs and shoos me off the porch.

"Yeah, yeah, I'm going." I keep my iced coffee, head to my tractor, and remember I have a question I wanted to ask him. I jog back to the porch. "Hey, Grandpa, do you know anything about Green Breeze Enterprises? Driving around the lake the other day, I saw a sign with that company on it. Any idea what that's about?"

My grandpa looks at me above the rim of his glasses. "Sure do, son. Ain't nothing you need to be worried about. You just take care of the farm and leave town stuff to me."

His answer makes me hesitate, and a wave of worry washes through me. I'm fairly certain my grandfather would confide in me if there was something I should be informed of, but his words aren't sitting right in my stomach. I'll try to take his response at face value and shove any worry aside.

Sitting high on my tractor, I survey the fields and get to work harvesting. I have a few hours until the orchard opens to the public, so the more harvesting I accomplish before the crowds arrive, the better. I peel my T-shirt over my head. Working in jeans and boots is a hell of a lot cooler, and besides, there's no one else around.

As I take one bushel after another, my thoughts find their way back to Solia. A reel plays of the best moments we've had since I first checked her out in the parking lot. Those ice-blue eyes, the bootie shorts, the baby blue bottoms, and the way she laid a heavy, sensual kiss on me as we sat on the side of the road. I want more. She has the wires wrapped around my hesitations loosening their grip. My chest feels roomier, more open, and it's easier to breathe.

I need to see her again. Another date may prove this is just a blip on the radar, nothing more than a couple magical dates. It isn't practical to establish a genuine connection without more time. One more date might be what I need to get my headspace back, to forge ahead with my move out of this town, to put everything behind me once and for all.

JACKSON

Hi, Solia. I had a great time and was wondering if you were free on Friday? It's the Fourth, so you may have plans.

SOLIA

I was just thinking about you. I had a great time too. I'm the new girl in town, remember? No plans here. I'd love to hang out.

Awesome. The town is having its annual fireworks display at the high school. We could do that?

That used to be one of my favorite parts of the summer. I could make dinner here before. Do they still have the boat parade during the day?

They do, but I can't be there for that. Anyway, I'm in. What time?

Seven?

See you then.

Terrific! Hope you have a great day. 😊

You too, Solia.

Perfect. With our next (and probably final) date in the books, I'll attempt to stop stressing about understanding these sudden emotions. If this next date is a disaster, so be it. If the date goes well, I need to come clean with Solia and tell her I plan on moving. I don't want to lead her on if I'm not staying.

My bones ache from only stopping for a quick lunch. I'm beat but proud of the day's work. My muscles are sore and sweat covers every inch of me, but I'm done and the farm is in tiptop shape.

I retire the tractor behind the barn and walk to the front porch where I predict I'll find my grandparents rocking away. Trudging through the tall green grass that desperately needs to be cut, I hear their predictable banter. As I approach, they stop midsentence and smile lovingly in my direction. "Based on all that dirt you're caked in, it appears you got a workout today, boy."

"Always, Grandpa."

"Don't you think you're going to miss this place when you leave?" My grandmother looks at me with an abundance of hope that would make any grandson sick with guilt.

"You can't be serious Grandma. Of course I will, especially the two of you, but it's for the best. You don't want me moping around here every freaking day. That kind of energy isn't good for anybody."

"Seems to me you've been pretty upbeat the last couple times I've seen you. Something, or should I say someone, has recently given you a reason to smile." Grandma Sylvia always has a way of noticing the slightest emotional changes.

I feel my cheeks flush, and my grandparents laugh and shake their heads. There's no saving myself. I adjust my baseball hat, smile at the two people I love most in the world, and head for my truck.

≈

The rest of the week flows in the predictable pattern of sleep, work, and shower. Thursday rolls around and instead of driving home after work, I have the urge to swing by the Binn to see if the guys are doing the usual Thursday night dinner.

Lo and behold, I spot their trucks in the parking lot. "Whoa, man, two times in the last two weeks? Awesome! Pull up a stool. Get this man a drink," Tyler calls out to Cindy.

"Coming right up, gentlemen."

"So, what's up, man? Great to see you." Tyler turns and looks at me expectantly.

"Just figured I'd swing by and see if you guys were here."

"We were just bitching about the balls of this green energy company bullshit that's going around town." Jay slams his pint glass on the table and looks angry as hell.

"What are you talking about?"

"Come on, man, don't tell me you haven't heard about it. This piece-of-shit green energy company, Green Breeze Enterprises, is trying to march in and plant those big-ass wind turbines everywhere."

"Green Breeze Enterprises? Huh. Nobody told me anything. But then again, I've had my head up my ass for the better part of a year. Wait—I did see a sign next to the political ones by the lake. I asked Earl if he knew anything, but he didn't seem concerned. Said he would handle it."

"He probably assumed there was no point in explaining since you are ditching this place at the end of the summer."

I stare at Ryan. His words cut sharp, and for the first time, it dawns on me he might be pissed I'm leaving. There isn't much I can say that will make his words less true, so I ignore his passive-aggressive comment. "Fill me in, Tyler. What's the deal?"

"Apparently, a whole mess of property owners received

letters informing them Green Breeze Enterprises is interested in purchasing and/or leasing their land and installing wind farms on the property. We're talking dozens of massive wind turbines in town. They'll look terrible, never mind what these monsters will do to the wildlife around here."

Jay, who still seems heated, pounces back into the conversation. "I don't know who these jackasses think they are, but I don't think people will go down without a fight. Sure, people will make money off the sale or lease of the land, but the integrity of this place has to be kept intact. Seriously, man, Green Breeze will destroy everything around here. Next thing you know, we'll have a strip mall on the side of the lake. My family will never sell to these tycoons."

"Unfortunately, it only takes one family to fold and the rest will too." Ryan has a good point.

A pit opens in my stomach. "Do we have a list of who was mailed a letter?"

"Sure do, man. Stable Farm is on their list—over my dead body." Ryan slams his fist on the table. "But, we aren't the only property they're after." Suddenly, their attention diverts to me and there is more meaning behind Ryan's words. "What? He has a right to know, guys."

"Shit, Ryan. Seriously?" Tyler stands and walks to the bathroom.

"What's he talking about? Guys, what the hell?"

"Sorry, man. I'm not a hundred percent sure, but with you leaving … It's public knowledge your family owns one of the biggest pieces of private land in this town. How could the orchard not be on the list? I know you don't want to hear it, but your grandparents aren't going to be around forever, man." Jay's brutal honesty cuts deep. I'm seeing a side of him I don't think I've ever seen. Anger? Frustration? Revenge?

Thoughts flood my head in an uncontrollable flurry. Earl would've told me he received a letter. They would never sell to green energy assholes. Right? What will this mean for the orchard? For the family? Shit. I've been living with my head in the sand, dwelling on my own problems for so long, ignoring the everyday things, and now it's backfiring big-time. I've been so focused on myself, on my bubble of a world. Bile rises in my throat.

"Guys, I had no idea. What now? Tell me everything. Spill it—let's go." I may be late to the party, but I can still fix this. This town is everything to my family. To see it taken over by massive turbines is serious bullshit.

Tyler returns from the bathroom and seems to be reading the group to see if we're civil or ready to beat the crap out of each other. We've had our share of bar brawls over the years. I can't blame him for wondering if that's next on the docket.

He takes in the scene, waits a minute, and says, "There's a town forum coming up toward the end of July for residents. Green Breeze Enterprises is going to send in their big shots from headquarters to tell us why allowing them to come in and destroy our land is a great idea. No one will decide anything then, but we can certainly voice our opinions loud and clear."

Upsetting doesn't begin to describe the anger building. Was it everyone's intention to treat me as a complete outsider in my hometown? The one solid, positive piece of information I hear is that no decisions have been made. This means there's still time to save Meriden, but I'm going to have to wait until Monday to speak to my grandfather. They always have plans with friends the weekend of the Fourth.

We change the subject to tomorrow's festivities. Our posse always parties on the Fourth. Tyler's family hosts a big get-together at their place, followed by tailgating at the high school for the town fireworks show. I've never missed a year, but I have to work it into the conversation that I have alternate plans tomorrow.

"So, speaking of the Fourth, I can't make it to the party, guys. I'll catch up with you at the fireworks."

The conversation silences and the three guys look at me wide-eyed, waiting for me to continue. "Yeah, well, um, I have plans with Solia tomorrow night. Remember the woman whose wood we stacked?"

The three of them break into laughter, and they fist bump across the table. "I knew it, man. I knew the log cabin hottie got to you. That's great, buddy. But what I want to know is, does she have any hot friends because this dump truck has a load that needs to be delivered. I could use action right about now," Tyler says. "You aren't stacking more wood, so how about you mention her bringing friends our way? Just saying." Tyler is forever a ladies' man whose key priority is getting into as many girls' panties as possible.

The other two knuckleheads cheer him on and high-five.

"Guys, it's just a date. We barely know each other. I don't want to crash the party and overwhelm her with a bunch of people. That's way too much, but we're planning on going to the fireworks. And as far as the friends go, she's new to town, remember?"

"I'm just busting your ass, man. Have a good time. Seriously, I'm happy for you. And if I can't get any, I'm happy for you if you do," Tyler says.

"You're hopeless, but she is freaking hot." The guys nod in agreement. I glance at the rustic analog clock on the wall and see it's already midnight. Things never change. Whenever I'm here with the guys, time flies right out the window. It's good to be back at the Binn.

# 16

*Solia*

More than any past Fourth of July, this one is different. Not only am I away from family and friends, but I'll be cooking dinner for a man I just met. I pace between the bedroom and kitchen, accomplishing nothing, so I grab my phone off my nightstand.

SOLIA

Hey, guess who has a hot date tonight?

MIA

I'm guessing you??? The sexy wood stacker?

Bingo! Just dinner and fireworks.

Nice, I like where this is going. Already planning for fireworks! Go get it!

No, actual fireworks. It's the Fourth of July.

Hahaha . . . right . . . well, you can have other fireworks too.

Can't wait to see you next weekend.

Me too!!! Have fun! I'm in a man drought over here. Get sexy for both of us.

Freaking Mia. The woman has sex on her mind more than any guy I've ever met. I'm not judging because she seems to have it figured out. She is always the heartbreaker, never the one left by the wayside. I'm not sure how she does it, but the men keep flocking to her. I mean, she's amazing, beautiful, and funny, but no part of her wants to be held down.

Guys might have a sixth sense and appreciate she's out for a good time and won't be much work, but then cascade like dominoes. They each fall harder in love than the last. She moves on to the next without looking back. I wish I could be less emotional with relationships, but it's just not in my DNA.

I spend most of the day doing chores, including a deep scrub of the kitchen. Keeping this cabin clean is proving more of a challenge than my small apartment back home. I remind myself the extra dusting and scrubbing is worth the million-dollar view I get to wake up to every morning. Convinced my mother installed cameras, I don't cut any corners. I wouldn't put anything past her.

Several hours later, I take my latest novel out to the porch and promise to only read for one hour tops, then I'll get ready.

It shouldn't surprise me when I suddenly wake in the comfortable lounge chair inside the screened-in porch. My book has dropped onto the wooden deck next to my chair, and the sun is receding behind the tree line, indicating more time has passed than I thought.

*What time is it?*

I look at my phone lying on the side table: six p.m. *Holy shit.* I need to shower, find an outfit, and do the prep work for dinner. Shit. Shit. Shit!

I run into my bedroom, grab two bath towels, frantically rip off my clothes, and throw them into the laundry basket inside the bathroom. I run back through the bedroom, into the kitchen, and out the screen door to the outdoor shower. I'm lucky I don't have neighbors.

It takes me three minutes to wash, shampoo, condition, shave, and towel off. I'm fairly certain I've never moved so quickly. My parents would laugh if I told them. I can't count the number of times when I was a teenager and one of them would yell at me to get my butt out of the shower or they'd turn off the hot water. One day soon, I'll apologize for those hot water bills.

I fly back into the cabin. The towels are tossed in with the rest of the laundry, and I rifle through my underwear drawer. It doesn't matter what I choose, but I'm certain any woman would agree, the sexier the underwear, the sexier you feel, even if no one ever sees them. Women love holding on to this little hidden secret, like, *You don't know what I'm wearing under here, but if you did, you'd love it.* After quickly narrowing the selection, I decide on a matching hot pink thong and bra.

Shimmying my way into both, I run into the bathroom to see how they look. A full-length mirror would come in handy. I'll add that to my shopping list. On tiptoes, I can at least see the bottom of my ass in the mirror. I rotate left, right, center, adjust my breasts for optimal cleavage, and tug my underwear a little higher on my hips. I'm confident I look hot, even though Jackson won't be seeing this.

I choose a royal blue sleeveless, fitted summer dress with wide straps and a pair of tan sandals. Taking a quick peek in the mirror, the outfit strikes me as too dressy or trying too hard. This option gets tossed to the floor. After three more attempts, I settle for a flowy pink tank and white cut-offs.

I tighten my hair behind my shoulders with a clip and head to the fridge. I pull out the potatoes to prep. Just as I begin chopping veggies for a fresh salad, I hear truck tires kicking up the pebbles from my driveway. Shit, I thought I had more time!

I run to the side porch and uncover the grill, throw a grilling spatula next to it, and light a beachy scented candle on the kitchen counter. I didn't anticipate being this nervous. It's one thing to go on a date, but this is on my turf, more personal, more intimate. But if things don't go well, at least we have the fireworks to break up the night.

I go over to the screen door, and as expected, Jackson is climbing the stairs, looking fine. He is wearing khaki shorts that are on the shorter side and show off his lean leg muscles, and a clean, white T-shirt that hugs his chest in all the right places. It screams "I tried to look nice for you," and it's sexy.

"Hey, Solia."

"Hi, Jackson. Come on in."

"You look amazing. And it smells great in here. This cabin is solid! Looks well built. I saw it from the outside before, but the inside showcases the craftsmanship." He runs his palm along the length of one of the logs by the front door.

"Thanks, but I certainly can't take credit for any of that."

"Well, I'm sure you chose everything that's inside, which looks great too."

"I grabbed a few IPAs and wine—which would you prefer? Come have a seat at the table. I just have to finish cutting the salad stuff and then we can grill."

"Sounds great. I'll have a beer," Jackson says. I hand him a chilled bottle and a clean pint glass and pour myself white wine. I put the salad veggies on the small island so I can chop while focusing on him.

"So, what do your Fourth of July's usually entail around these parts?" I ask, chopping a red onion. Jackson stands, leans against the wooden post across from me, and crosses one foot over the other. He watches me slice, and I swear he's undressing me while he assesses my body.

"My buddy, Tyler, one of the guys you met the other day, usually has an enormous party on the Fourth. It's a lot of fun, but sometimes it gets out of hand. Everyone ends up at the fireworks together and then heads back to Tyler's. It's kind of a tradition."

I put the knife on the counter and turn my attention to Jackson. "I hope you didn't skip the party because of me. They might miss you."

"I asked you out, remember?"

"True. So, Jackson from Meriden, tell me everything about yourself." Even though I'm obsessed with his body, it wouldn't hurt to learn what makes him tick, so I test out my sarcasm. Cucumber in hand, I wait to see how he'll answer.

Jackson clears his throat and laughs, evidence he seems to appreciate the joke. "Wow, shit. Let's get right into it. Well, I enjoy working hard, playing harder. Family is super important to me. And eventually, I want to get married to the right person. I don't know, maybe start a family. Sorry." Beer in hand, he paces into the living room. He has his back toward me as he looks at a framed picture of the mountains hanging on the wall behind the woodstove.

"Why are you apologizing? Those things are goals many of us long for."

"Yeah, yeah, sure. I don't think I've ever said that aloud, and I'm not exactly sure why it came flying out of my mouth."

My cheeks warm. I'm flattered he's comfortable enough to tell me what he's looking for in life. It makes me smile, convincing me not all guys suck.

"Shit! Ouch!" As I'm paying too much attention to Jackson and not enough to the knife, I nick my finger while chopping the cucumber. Jackson places his half-empty pint glass on the island and reaches across for my finger, and our faces are pulled closer together.

"You got lucky. I don't think you cut the skin. Let's run it under the faucet." He walks around the island and leads me to the sink. I love his attentiveness over a silly cut. He takes my hand so naturally and gently spins me around so my waist is against the kitchen counter. I sense him moving closer and closer until his body presses against mine. He turns on the faucet, pumps a bit of soap from the dispenser, and lathers my skin. "Does it sting?"

"No, not at all. Amazing." *Did I actually just say that out loud? The man is washing my hands, for god's sake.* I should seriously smack myself. How is it possible I am so turned on by this?

"Amazing, you say?" Jackson smirks.

I muster a gentle "mm-hmm." That sound gives him permission to position my hands on the edge of the counter. He trails his warm, wet fingertips along my chilled arms, then dips his mouth close to my ear and kisses my neck with his lips and tongue. I grip the counter firmly, growing weak in the knees. I am well aware of Jackson's excitement, his hardness pressing into me.

To stay vertical, I tilt my head back, and Jackson's mouth moves slightly below my neckline. I want to be bent over the sink so Jackson can have his way with me from behind.

I try to hold back my urge to bend over for this man, but it's becoming increasingly difficult. I have to force myself to calm down. "Do you think we should eat first?" I whisper, and immediately he pulls away from me.

"I'm sorry, Solia. I don't know what got into me. Of course, we should eat dinner. I didn't mean to get ahead of myself. Seriously, I apologize."

I turn to face him, and we're eye to eye. I grab the dish towel and wrap it around our hands and wipe them dry. "No need to apologize. It's crazy to say because we just met, but I am comfortable and extremely attracted to you. Maybe we should eat first, though." I laugh, hoping that frees him from any worry he may have done something wrong.

"I'm glad you said that, Solia. I feel the same—you've surprised the hell out of me. But I promise to be a gentleman … most of the time."

A gentleman with a side of spice is just what I want.

"I'll go start the grill. I don't mind grilling. What are we making?"

"Steak, and I have foil-wrapped potatoes to roast too. But you don't have to grill unless you want to?"

"It'd be my pleasure." He winks, and I melt.

I hand him the potatoes. "Let me grab the steak." I turn to the counter. *Shit!* With my hands on my hips, I dip my chin to my chest and take a deep breath. I open the freezer and stare at the solid block of steak marinating in a Ziploc bag on the shelf. I drop it on the counter. Jackson hears the clunk and throws his head back in laughter.

"We have a change in plans, Chef." Jackson taps the ice block with his fist.

I cover my face with my hands. "I'm so embarrassed. I marinated it and everything. See what happens when I move too fast? I put the damn bag in the freezer. Great."

"No big deal." Jackson opens the freezer and pulls out a package of frozen hamburger patties. "We can just throw these babies on. Do you have any rolls?"

"Why would I have rolls? That would make sense. Normal people have rolls when they have patties. I prepare food for dinner and freeze it." I throw my hands in the air and laugh.

"It's all good, we'll skip the bread. We've got hamburger patties, potatoes, and salad. Perfect. Come on. Can't sweat the small stuff."

While I admire Jackson at the grill, I haphazardly throw everything into the salad bowl. "I figured we could eat on the screened porch? It's beautiful out, and the bugs won't bother us." I walk behind him, close enough to inhale his scent and admire his biceps as he flips the burgers. With plates and utensils situated, I then add the salad and condiments to the table and turn on a playlist of today's hits, loud enough to hear through the screens.

"Food is ready. Can you grab the door for me?" he asks.

I open the porch door, and he carries in the plate of juicy burgers. "This looks amazing. Thanks for cooking. I knew you'd be the grilling kind of guy."

"What exactly does that mean?"

"Mmm, sexy, muscular, good with his hands, can handle fire …" I wink. He smiles with enchanting charm, sets the platter on the table, and walks over to where I'm standing.

"Well, thank you. I'm flattered you think I'm a grilling kind of guy." He grabs my hips, pulls me closer, and whispers in my ear, "I'm having a very hard time staying away from you."

My forehead rests against his chest, and I take a deep breath, slurping the drool that is escaping. "Oh, really?"

"Really." He plays with the fringe on my shorts and slides his hands into my back pockets, leaving no space between our bodies. "But we said we'd eat dinner first." He traces the sides of my stomach, my arms, my neck, to the back of my head. He kisses my forehead, and the space widens between us. "Let's eat."

I'm left frozen and breathless, paralyzed by his touch. I slowly regain my composure and take a seat, acutely aware that he's glued to my every move.

"How's it going up here? Are you enjoying living in Meriden?"

"I am, actually. I mean, I'm used to having more people around, but I don't mind the quiet. I'm discovering I might prefer it. Summer is my favorite season for a multitude of reasons, and being by the lake this time of year is perfect. Being able to rise to a silent, beautiful sunrise each morning, walk to the lake if I want, or take an outdoor shower in the fresh mountain air is amazing. This place isn't everyone's cup of tea, but I love it."

"It is beautiful. Some people think we're crazy for living out here in the 'boonies,' that we drive fifteen minutes to a store, or the fact we only have a handful of bars or restaurants. But we think it's crazy to live on top of each other, crammed in like sardines, with malls and skyscrapers and never-ending traffic. Out here, the beauty of the countryside is invaluable. There's nothing better …" He trails off, clearly in a daze. Then he shakes his head and looks toward the mountain range off to the east.

I think he loves this place as much as I do, and that is icing on the cake.

*Where did this guy come from?*

The rest of our conversation flows and before we know it, it's time to head to the school for the fireworks show.

As we pull into the parking lot, the atmosphere holds everything you'd expect to see at a hometown football game and a high school reunion mixed together. Rows of pickup trucks line the parking lot, athletic fields, and around the back of the school, facing the baseball diamond. Everyone sits in their truck beds on inflatable mattresses or perched on camping chairs. Speakers blast mostly country music every few rows, and girls dance and throw their hair around, enjoying life and celebrating the freedom of the holiday and what it stands for. Kids run around their parents who stand talking with friends and family.

Small towns provide comfort, ease, and laid-back vibes you can't get anywhere else. I'm loving every minute of this, thinking to myself this could be the first of many traditions I start here in Meriden. I may be an outsider, but this is a community I want to be a member of.

We drive through rows of vehicles, and people honk and shout at Jackson. It seems everyone knows him. A sense of warmth surrounds me, and my excitement for Meriden grows with Jackson at my side.

Jackson reverses his truck into an open spot far in the back. Luckily, the fireworks are visible from anywhere, so there isn't a bad spot in the lot.

"I've got a couple chairs in the back and a blanket if you're cold. And there's a beer tent if you want a drink."

"I'm good for now. Fireworks are enough for me."

Jackson opens the tailgate and pulls me into the bed of the truck. He pops two green camping chairs side by side and unfolds a soft blue blanket with fish on it and hands it to me.

"Fish? Unique."

"It's a Grandma Sylvia special, and it's clean. I'm not sure you can get better than that."

Teasing him is too much fun. "Oh, here we go! We got here just in time."

The first fireworks blast into the sky, displaying every color of the rainbow. The music silences as people settle into their space and clap in approval. Jackson reaches over and holds my hand. Although there are hundreds of people among us, the atmosphere exudes romance, and I can't stop smiling. I am incredibly lucky.

For a small town, Meriden's pyrotechnic display is impressive. Fireworks are pricey, and it's obvious the town invested to give the residents a show they'll remember. I startle each time a giant boom echoes into the sky, and Jackson squeezes my hand. The crowd oohs and aahs with every sparkle and shower of light. My soul is bursting with happiness —I am exactly where I want to be.

When the show finishes, I turn to Jackson, longing for this night to go on forever.

"Do you want to come back to my place for a fire? I have s'mores, if that entices you."

"As long as you have s'mores, I'm in." Jackson smiles and

squeezes my hand. "Let's go before we get stuck in a line a mile long."

Similar to our arrival, we hear the hoots and hollers ring out in every direction from people wishing each other a happy Fourth, no doubt headed to after-parties. Jackson honks and hollers right back at them. I enjoy seeing him in this environment. He is so happy and full of life, smiling ear to ear.

It doesn't take us long to make it back to the cabin. Jackson pulls out a pair of gray sweatpants and a hooded UNH sweatshirt from his back seat. "I'm always prepared," he says with a sexy wink.

We walk to the house, and there's a chill in the air. A quarter moon hangs high in the sky, not a cloud to be seen. Stars blaze in every direction. It is completely serene and beautiful.

Jackson follows me up the stairs, and I'm slightly self-conscious because he's walking a few steps behind, and my shorts are riding higher on my thighs. When we get inside, he asks me to show him where the bathroom is so he can change. While he runs upstairs, I throw on a pair of navy blue sweats and a white, cropped sweatshirt over my hot pink ensemble.

"The firepit is off the side porch. I'll grab the s'mores stuff and a few blankets and meet you out there," I yell. I hear nothing and figure he's still upstairs. I head out the screen door with a stack of blankets and an armload of graham crackers, more chocolate than the two of us can eat, and a bag of marshmallows.

I instantly understand why the house was silent. Jackson kneels by the firepit, arranging the kindling and logs around a growing blaze. I stand back and watch the fire light his face and the sparks rise into the air.

"You're quick!"

"I don't mess around. If there is one thing I have a talent for, it's fire."

*You're telling me,* I almost blurt. I've fanned more flames inside my body since meeting him than throughout all my other relationships.

"I appreciate you getting it going. You obviously located the wood you so expertly stacked."

We settle into the wooden Adirondack chairs that have been in the yard for longer than I can remember. Thankfully, I washed them during one of my cleaning-spree days.

We sit in silence for a few minutes and listen to the pop and crackle of the fire. While I appreciate the warmth of the flames, I desire the heat from Jackson's body.

"What do you know about the stars?" Jackson's face tilts to the sky.

"Honestly, not much. I can recite the names of a few constellations, the different birth signs, but I can't look up there and point them out. Can you?"

"Not exactly, but I'm good at spotting the North Star, Little Dipper, Big Dipper, and Orion on a clear night. There are so many constellations that can be seen with the naked eye."

"Very impressive."

He looks at me and then back to the sky and points toward the left. "Right there, find that bright star. Follow it to the right and then south. You can kind of see how it forms into a miniature spoon. See it?"

Squinting and roaming the sky, I try but as much as I want to pretend that I can see it, I can't. "My father has tried to point these things out to me for years. There are very few times I can honestly say I've connected the stars to see the constellations. I appreciate you trying, though."

"Come here." He stands, reaches for my hand, and pulls me to my feet. "Let me see the five hundred blankets you brought out." Laughing, he takes several from the back of my chair, and I watch as he spreads them neatly on the ground. He meticulously lays them out a few feet from the fire to equate to the size of a queen bed. He takes the rest and bunches them up into makeshift pillows. "I'm not giving up. Let's try this again."

He gestures for me to join him. As I lie on top of the fuzzy stack, Jackson pulls a few blankets up and over our bodies to keep the chill out. He rolls another and puts it under his neck. "Come lie your head on me." He loops his left arm under my neck. He certainly doesn't need to ask twice; I wiggle to my right side so I can snuggle against him. He pulls me in tighter as I rest my head on his chest. "OK, let's try this again. Look right over there." He points to the left as he did before.

I'd say I'm concentrating, but I'd be lying. I want him naked and on top of me. Instead, I nod and move my left hand to his chest and wrap my left foot up and around his leg. I must have caught his attention because he stops talking and pointing. It's not that I don't want to see the stars, but there is just so much more I want to see of him. I've never been so turned on by a man. Lying by the fire with his body against mine is almost more than I can handle.

As if reading my mind, he turns his head and stares with intensity. For a few moments, there are no words, no movements, just stillness and the sound of the crackling fire and the breaths between us. At this very moment, I'm convinced I can't give up on love. I'm going to split at the seams between my longing and the sexual tension I'm sensing from Jackson. It's worth walking through fire for.

I've experienced what it's like to be in love and have him leave you without giving it a second thought, and maybe, just maybe if I hadn't been pulled through the wringer, I wouldn't be here now. This moment is meant to be.

Jackson leans in and kisses me passionately. Keeping the blankets around us, he rolls me to my back without breaking the fervor of his kiss. I pull his face closer and he slides his body over mine. He is against me, rock hard and ready. He trails kisses along my neck and whispers, "I want to kiss every square inch of you." I wrestle him onto his back and pull my sweatshirt off, signaling I am primed and ready. Thankful for my choice of clothing underneath, I again lie down and guide him back to me.

He kneels on either side of my hips and caresses my breasts, running his tongue along the curve of my neck. My back arches in pleasure. Jackson lifts up and pulls off his sweatshirt and T-shirt to reveal his sculpted, solid body, and begins exploring my stomach. His hands are everywhere—my breasts, my back, my waistline. The steam from his mouth pours onto me, and the coolness from the air meeting the moisture his kisses leave behind is magic.

He follows his trail back until his face meets mine, his body tightly pressed against me, his hardness evident between our layers of clothing. He adjusts and presses into me, sending me reeling. I'm starting to think I haven't experienced true ecstasy with any man in my past. I am putty in his hands. His kisses continue as deeply and passionately as the first while he thrusts against me.

My words float into the night air. "I want you."

He hears me, and he responds. His tongue licks my body until he reaches my waistline. Once there, he kneels and grabs hold of my sweatpants, pulls them to my feet, stands, and tosses them into the yard. Without the blanket or his body, I lie there visible by the firelight, on display for him. He takes me in hungrily.

He settles between my legs, frees my thong with his teeth, tosses it in the grass, and covers his back with the blanket to keep me warm. The combination of the fire he ignites in me and the one we are lying beside forces me to throw the blankets aside. I reach behind my back and release the bra clasp, letting myself loose into the night air. Jackson smiles at the sight of me, taking in the view, obviously liking what he sees.

He then dips between my legs, pushes my knees back, and

spreads me wide open. I am panting and moaning at every swipe of his tongue. When he hits the right spot, he senses it; I tilt my head back to the stars, the fire blazing on my skin, and shudder and pulsate in complete and utter ecstasy. As my body shakes in release, Jackson reaches his hand to my breasts and continues to drain every last ounce of passion from me. He doesn't stop as I moan and yell his name into the night. I am floating. Jackson kisses his way up my body and reclines by my side.

"You … you are amazing," he purrs in my ear.

I turn my face toward his, admiring the way the fire glow flickers on his skin and lights up his chest. "Where did you come from?"

I tuck in close to his magnificent form and wonder how I got so lucky.

# 17

Jackson

She is asleep on my chest, and I gently sift through her hair. I don't think I've ever met a woman who makes me excited for tomorrow before the sun has risen. Her presence calms my soul. The sound of her crying out my name and witnessing her body react to the pleasure was more than I could have asked for. Every touch, every move was a perfectly played note.

I lie perfectly still under the blanket, her warm body wrapped around me. I never thought I'd be in this situation this summer. Our worlds have collided, and the connection that's forming is undeniable.

The cloudless night glows with the burn of countless, distant galaxies. Mountain ridges across the land paint the sky with their shadowed peaks, perfectly curated brushstrokes from an artist's hand. The air is still, the only sound the faint crackle of the dwindling fire and soft breaths leaving Solia's lips. The warmth of her exhales tickles the side of my neck. I pull the blanket higher to keep the chill at bay.

As I lie holding her, I look to the sky and ask what the fuck I'm supposed to do now. Solia is not going to jump in my pickup and hightail it out of Meriden. Before meeting Solia, leaving seemed best, and I promised myself I would come clean if this date went well. But lying here with this woman in my arms, it physically pains me to think of telling her what happened last summer. Leaving Meriden and everything behind has to be the right thing to do. I made up my mind, and everything is already arranged. There are too many people counting on me to start second-guessing myself now. *Right?*

The day Solia drove into town, the fog I'd been living in started to lift. My thoughts are clearer, and I once again see the beauty of the hometown I've loved my whole life. I'm falling in love with this woman. She's already taking up space in my heart. I need to go before this gets deeper so I can leave assured my heart is the only one breaking.

The fire is almost out, and the temperature is dropping. I gently pull my arm from under her neck, throw my shirt over my head, crouch low, and scoop her from the ground, trying to keep the blankets wrapped around her cradled in my arms. I walk to the house as she tucks herself tighter into my embrace and peeks from under her sleepy lids.

"Jackson?"

"Hey there, sleepyhead. I'm taking you inside. It's late and getting cold."

"I'm so embarrassed. I never intended to fall asleep."

"I guess I must have tired you out." I pull open the sliding screen door using my foot and carefully walk into her bedroom. There is nothing I want more than to lie her down and make love to her. For better or worse, my head shows up to stop my emotions. She deserves better; she deserves the truth. I lower her into her bed and gently tuck the blankets around her.

"Thank you, Jackson," she says, low and enticing. I want to hear my name on her lips again, but louder. I haven't begun to pleasure her in all the ways I'm capable of. I'm rethinking my decision to leave her alone in bed.

"You're welcome, Solia." I softly place my lips on her cheek and refrain from moving any further. "I'm going to make sure the fire is out, and I'll lock the door."

"Mmm, OK."

I walk outside and see only dark red ash in the firepit with little smoke swirling into the air, so I pour water from the bucket nearby to extinguish it completely. Using the flashlight from my phone, I collect the rest of the blankets and Solia's belongings. I tiptoe into the cabin through the screen door to find Solia leaning against the wooden post wearing a short, pink bathrobe, looking seductive. I'm not sure my self-control is strong enough for this.

Without breaking my stare, I walk to the couch and drop everything. In my peripheral vision, I spot her pink thong on top of the pile and wish I could eat those off her body again. But since her panties are on the couch, that means she isn't wearing them under her bathrobe. I want to rip the bathrobe off, toss her over my shoulder, and carry her back into the bedroom. I'll get her wet and ready and open her wide. I want my name reverberating off these log walls.

"Thank you for taking care of everything outside. I had an amazing time tonight, Jackson."

"I did too." I close the gap between us and wrap my arms around her waist. She embraces me in return. I gently kiss the top of her head and hold my breath. "Get a good night's sleep." If I stay one more second, there will be no turning back, so I force my feet to the door and convince myself not to turn around.

I'm exhausted but still hard as a rock when I get home. The last thing I want is to lie in bed and beat myself up for not being truthful with Solia. I want to hold on to the magic of tonight for as long as I can. In the darkness, I envision lying with her by the fire, her skin brushing against mine.

~

The work week goes by much the same as last week. The weather is beautiful, and the vacationers fill the streets and the shoreline. Each day that passes, more and more out-of-state plates drive into town. Seeing the trucks and SUVs filled with children and boats being towed to the shores of Newfound Lake reminds me, once again, that this place is a slice of paradise.

The increase in visitors results in the orchard being busier. We try to give our staff rotating time off, but it gets tough with the demands of the farm. The harvest this season is the best it's been in years, and the business side of things has never been so profitable. It goes to show that when people love their town and the surrounding businesses, the success of the farm and the happiness of the people go hand in hand. Word of our farm and cozy corner of the world has traveled far and wide, and it never gets old welcoming new folks to the farm and showing them around.

Throughout the week, I replay the moments Solia and I shared. I picture the very first time I saw her in the hardware parking lot, how perfectly she fits in with our lakeside town, and then her on my lap during the tractor ride. This thought leads to the next, which leads to another, and the next thing I know, my pulse is racing and I don't want the chain of memories to end.

I head out to the store for my last delivery, and a text comes through from Solia.

SOLIA

Hey, stranger. Plans tomorrow night? Mia is in town, and we were thinking of going out.

JACKSON

> Let me text the guys. They usually go to the Binn. We could get a group together—might be fun.

I need to tell her, not make plans. Damn it, I want to see her.

JACKSON

> Hey, man, are you guys getting together tomorrow night?

TYLER

The usual. The BINN. You in?

> Solia's friend Mia is in town for the weekend and she asked if we want to hang out.

My man Jackson, coming in clutch. Sweet. See you around eight?

> Sounds good.

I text Solia to confirm the time.

SOLIA

Sounds great!

Now I just have to get through the next twenty-six hours. But who's counting?

～

Thursday night around quarter to eight, I pull into the Binn. My tires kick up clouds of dust as they spin through the parking lot. The place is tight, but I find a spot toward the back. Must be vacationers mixed in with the locals for this kind of crowd.

Walking toward the bar, I'm glad I chose jeans and a hoodie. It's cool for a summer night, the temperature hovering a little under fifty degrees. Gravel crunches behind me, and I turn to see Greg. I reach for the door and hold it open.

"What's up, stranger?" Greg says, giving me a friendly slap on the back. I'm glad to see him in a place other than the store.

"Not much, stopping in for a beer." Greg walks to the bar where he joins a group of guys I've seen around town. I'll make a point to check in with him later. The country store is as busy as the orchard, if not busier, this time of year. I never see anyone outside of work these days.

The blackboard easel next to the door lists the specials, and I learn it's Ladies' Night, featuring musical guest Brice Hawkins. I'm not sure when the Binn started having theme nights, but I guess if it means keeping more business in town, then why not?

Cindy has the music turned up a little louder and the lights a little lower than usual. Each table has a tea light candle in a mason jar. Cindy, lover of anything twinkly, is still at it. A few more sparkly strings have been added to the overhead beam, emitting a warm stream of light from above.

The guys are at a round-top in the far left corner. I wave hello to Cindy and give a quick nod to friends sitting at the bar. Before I make it to the guys, I stop by to check out the rickety entertainment platform on the opposite side of the room. Three guitars lean on their stands in front of the platform, and a folding table is pushed to the side with stickers containing Brice's logo and social media details. I glance through the information, and a man who I assume is Brice walks toward me.

"Hey, man, thanks for coming out tonight."

"Oh yeah, sure. Are you from around here?" I don't recognize his name.

"Well, I've been here once a month for—let me think—the past six months?"

This shouldn't shock me because it's me who hasn't been around. "Oh, cool. Good luck tonight. You've got a great crowd."

"Sure thing. Enjoy." Brice tilts his hat and turns to finish setting up his stage. I grab one of his stickers and figure if this guy is any good, I'll search him later. I'm always into supporting local musicians.

"Do my eyes deceive me, or is Jackson out on the town again, and this time he's bringing the girls." Tyler's comment is anything but quiet and receives a few cheers from the regulars at the bar. Several of them raise a glass to me. "Cheers!"

Cindy appears by my side sporting her bar apron and holding the drink I have yet to order. "Here you go, Jackson. You're going to need it with this crew." She places the pint on the table, winks, tosses her ponytail behind her, and heads back toward the bar.

"Cheers to another hometown night with our boy Jackson." Jay lifts his pint for a toast.

"Cheers." The sound of the door opening collides with the clink of our glasses and in walks Solia and her friend, Mia.

A kick dents my shin. I look over at Tyler and see him panting and staring in the girls' direction. Every head in the place swivels to witness these two stunning women walk through the door. If you told me they were sisters, I'd take your word for it. While Mia is taller than Solia, they share enough features to make you assume they're related.

Despite everyone staring at them, I see Solia's baby blues searching for me, and everything else instantly fades. Another kick to the shin refocuses me.

"Hey, ladies." Tyler cuts directly in front of me, always the ladies' man, making sure he's the first to greet them.

"Hi. Tyler, right?" Solia asks. "This is my best friend, Mia."
I may be mistaken, but Mia seems to smile flirtatiously at Tyler.
"These are Jackson's friends—Tyler, Jay, and Ryan." Solia's
fingers weave between mine as I extend my other hand to
shake Mia's.

"Nice to meet everyone. I wish I would've gotten here
sooner, but at least it's still July. Let's get drinks!"

"Right on!" Tyler puts his arm around Mia's shoulders and
leads her to the bar.

"Tyler, always so shy," I say.

"Oh, he's met his match," Solia replies with an ear-to-ear
smile.

"What can I get you to drink?"

"I'll have whatever you're having. But I'm sticking to one
drink tonight. It's Mia's first night and I'm driving."

I look toward the bar and grab Cindy's attention while she
helps customers. I hold a finger in the air, and she nods. Even
though I haven't been around much lately, certain things never
change. Within minutes, we have our drinks, jokes are flying,
and the world is right.

The melody of Brice's voice fills the Binn around nine,
stunning the place into silence with his deep country vocals. He
starts with classics to get the crowd's attention, and it works.
After a few songs, people are out of their seats and on the
dance floor. Patrons turn their stools for a better view. The
atmosphere is nostalgic, the crowd sings along, and even the
regulars at the bar tap their fingers to the beat.

Mia and Solia sway arm in arm to the music, blending in with
the crowd as if they've been in town their whole lives. Both girls let
loose when Brice starts the next song on his set list, "Pour a Pint for
Me." Mia grabs Solia's hand and raises it in the air. I'm fixated on
Solia, and she looks over, motioning for me to join. I'm not much
of a dancer, but if she wants me out there, I won't think twice.

Tyler follows my lead, including himself in the invitation. He takes full advantage and gets Mia's attention by demonstrating his ridiculous dance moves. Solia immediately catches on, and the two of us laugh our asses off. Tyler can't dance to save his life, but Mia seems to be enjoying every minute of it.

Breathless, Solia and I leave the dance floor, fanning ourselves as we head back to the table where Greg is chatting it up with Jay and Ryan. Tyler and Mia maneuver to the bar, and within minutes are toasting Irish slammers. I remember the first time I drank one of those—the taste of Guinness, whiskey, and Bailey's will live forever in my gut. Way too heavy for me, but it's Tyler's favorite. And by the looks of it, Mia is holding her own.

Brice Hawkins switches it up with a slow Southern country rock song, reminding me of Stapleton. A few couples congregate on the dance floor accompanied by whistles and hoots from the locals. Solia looks in my direction, and I'm certain she wants to dance. *Why not?*

Wrapping my arm around her waist, I pull her in for a squeeze and lead her to the floor. It's been a long time since I've slow danced, and it takes me back to my high school days. With my arms wrapped around Solia, she rests her arms around my neck and is close enough to kiss.

*Is it my imagination, or is everyone in the room focused on us?*

Solia leans her head against my chest. I don't care who's staring. As we move in slow circles, Brice's voice takes over and I'm lost in the moment.

When the music begins to fade, I spot Tyler and Mia downing slammer number two in a dimly lit alcove. Tyler's arm slides around Mia's shoulders and he pulls her in for a kiss. Leave it to Tyler. I'll be driving his ass home.

"They found a cozy spot." Solia motions to where Tyler

and Mia are huddled, looking immersed in each other. I excuse myself and head over.

"Hey, guys, it'll be last call soon." I stick my hand in Tyler's pocket and lift the keys. We've run this drill more times than he'd like to admit, and he simply nods.

"Sure thing, boss. I'll meet you at the truck."

"Great meeting you, Mia. Solia's good to drive." She looks in my direction with a stone-cold stare, nods, but says nothing. Her lack of response sends a chill through me, but I'll chalk it up to the Irish slammers.

I arrive back at the table, admiring the glow surrounding Solia and the warmth of her smile. She's been here little under a month, and this is the first time she's had a piece of home with her. Her shoulders are relaxed as she sways to the beat, and I dig the laid-back vibe she's giving off. Being in her presence puts me at ease.

She checks me out from head to toe as the lights dim for last call.

"Thanks for coming out tonight, guys. Sorry you didn't get more time with Mia. Tyler seems to have hogged it all. I had fun hanging out with you, though, and Jackson, as always, I had a great night." She grabs my hand and rises on tiptoes, reaching for a kiss. I place my lips on hers and hope this isn't the last time I see her glow the way she is tonight.

A few minutes later, Cindy walks around collecting empties, saying good night and passing out the rest of Brice's promo items. The music was great, seriously entertaining. I can see why they invite him back. The best talent starts out playing in hole-in-the-wall places, local dive bars, waiting to be discovered. We'll see him selling out venues one day.

We head to the parking lot, Mia and Tyler in tow. I spot Solia's truck. The guys and I wait until their doors close before heading to ours. Jay has to coerce Tyler to say good night to Mia and move along. The guy is a sucker for a beautiful woman, but he can be a sloppy drunk. Luckily, he's never mean. He just needs a babysitter from time to time.

"We should invite them back to your place, Jackson. Come on, a little after-party," Tyler says, his speech slurred.

"We're going to call it a night, Tyler, but did you at least get her number?"

"Sure thing, buddy. It blows she doesn't live around here. But not as much as it sucks you haven't told Solia about Trinity because you're going to screw this up for me."

I immediately stop from taking one more step. "What did you just say?"

"Oh, shit." Ryan clasps my shoulder. "Take a deep breath."

"Say it again, Tyler. What the hell did you just say?"

"Sorry, man, it's just—um—I was talking with Mia, and she said Solia is into you."

"And?" I urge him to keep talking.

"Not sure, but something like, you've been better since you met her, the happiest we've seen you since the accident."

"What the fuck?" I slam my hands against my head.

"You haven't told her anything?" Ryan asks.

"Fuck!" I storm in the direction of my truck.

"Man! I'm sorry! I didn't know. I figured everyone in this goddamn town knows what happened. I figured the girl you're sleeping with would too."

I'm not the guy to react with a punch, but it takes everything I have not to knock his teeth out. "Not that it's any of your fucking business, man, but I'm not sleeping with her. I'm not a dirtbag. I think shit through first, something you don't seem capable of. You should drink less and shut the fuck up."

"Cool it, man. Listen, he had no way of knowing you hadn't told Solia." Jay's words have zero impact on the tension in the air.

Adrenaline surges through me, causing my ears to ring. I

get in my truck and slam the door, leaving the guys standing in the dirt staring at me. I open the window and toss Tyler's keys out. "Take his ass home." I step on the gas, letting the dirt spin out from under my tires, and leave.

*Go fucking figure. Why did I agree to this get-together? I never thought one of them would mention Trinity.*

I park in my driveway and throw my head back into the headrest. I'm such a dick. In an effort to keep Solia separate from the tragedy, I've managed to lose it on one of my best friends and hide the truth from Solia. They both deserve better than that. Keeping this a secret doesn't make it vanish. I have to tell her, and it'll destroy everything.

I snap out of my spiral when my phone vibrates in my pocket. Reaching for it, I use my other hand to push open my truck door, and do a double take at a text from an unknown number.

MIA

Hey, Jackson. Solia is already asleep, so I got your number from her phone. If you don't tell her, I will. Soon.

Understood. I never meant to hurt her.

Neither of us need to elaborate. I get the message loud and clear.

I drop my head into my hands as tears burn the corners of my eyes. I don't think it's possible to have made a worse first impression on Solia's best friend. I subconsciously convinced myself I was protecting Solia, but in reality, the only person I'm protecting is myself.

I push open my front door, already dreading walking through it tomorrow.

～

I rise before the sun has even peeked over the horizon, exhausted from tossing and turning, seeing every hour on the clock, rehearsing a hundred different ways to come clean with Solia. There are no words that make this any less awful. People around here know I'm leaving. This isn't the hard thing to say; I can force those words out of my mouth. It's the reason why I'm leaving I've never had to explain to anyone. Everyone already knows.

Everyone except Solia.

It's too early to text or call her, so I get dressed, head out for a coffee, and figure I'll take this time to visit my grandfather. Lying around any longer will lead to insanity. My stomach is in knots, my head banging from the inside out. If there is anyone who can guide me, it's Grandpa.

With enough caffeine to make it, I pull into the orchard expecting the two of them ready for the day, since they wake with the roosters.

With a gentle knock, I twist the unlocked doorknob and walk into their kitchen. This place hasn't changed since I was a kid. Red wooden cabinets hang on the wall with farm décor in every nook and cranny. The wooden counter juts out where three wooden swivel stools sit. Earl is there in his morning bathrobe and slippers, coffee in hand already, just as I knew he would be.

"Look what the cat dragged in."

"Hey, Grandpa."

"You OK, son? This is an early visit. Not that I don't enjoy seeing you. Just a surprise is all."

"Yeah," I say, slumping onto the stool next to him. I don't know where to begin. The weight from last night's events are suffocating, and I want to make the sensation disappear. "I'm in a bit of a mess, Grandpa."

"Well, let's start from the beginning and clean it up. I assume this has to do with the girl?"

I slowly nod. "Where's Grandma?"

"Oh, she's still in bed. She's exhausted lately, so I figured I'd come out here and let her rest."

"She's always awake by now." I peer around the corner at the bedroom door.

"We aren't exactly spring chickens any longer. Listen, take it from an old-timer like me—your grandmother and I have been married longer than most people get to enjoy this thing we call life. If you think times have always been easy, you are mistaken. Without the hard times and hard conversations, the good times don't rise to the top as they should. It's not that you have to earn the good times, but realizing life isn't always easy is part of the game.

"The best thing any of us can do is live with love in our hearts, and let the rest take care of itself. Your grandmother and I were separated by time, country, and war, and we survived raising five children. Trust me, raising five kids proved more difficult than being in separate countries." He pauses and lets out a spirited laugh. "Those were the good ol' days. I guess what I'm getting at is—chase love, speak the truth, and everything else will fall into place."

"How did you know what I was going to say?"

"I didn't. But you'll figure it out. What you've been through isn't easy—you'll always have to grapple with this. Whoever loves you will need to understand that. You think you have everything figured out, but there are times when a person walks into your life and tosses your so-called plans out the window. Our path isn't always ours to decide, Jackson."

"Thanks, Grandpa. I'm going to talk to her today. I can be honest, but I shouldn't have waited this long to tell her. Solia is …" I stumble for words. "I don't want to hurt her. And I've already decided I'm leaving, Grandpa. It's the right thing to do. I can't back out now or I'll disappoint my father."

"If she's as special as it sounds, she'll know your intent was never to hurt her. It isn't fair to her, but she will understand the pain you're going through."

I lift my head and notice deep lines that crinkle around his mouth, the tiredness set into his face. "Thanks for everything, Grandpa. And speaking of plans, the guys told me about Green Breeze Enterprises. Please tell me you didn't get a letter."

After my plea, my grandfather sits back in his stool, crosses his arms, and lets out a deep sigh. "Sure did, Jackson. I'm taking care of it. Things happen for a reason—you heard me last time. We're at a crossroads with the farm, and I'm not going to live forever."

"You and Grandma aren't considering selling the orchard, are you? We can fight these bastards. How much are they offering you? Whatever it is, it isn't worth it!"

"Jackson, you've decided that you're moving on. You have every right to do that—my children did the same. But that means your grandma and I have to decide what's best."

"I told you I'd continue to oversee things from New York, and Shannon is here in case you need her."

"Son, you are no stranger to how much work goes into running this place. Be practical. When we aren't here anymore, it'll be too much responsibility for you to run from afar. We can't expect your sister to do it. She wants to keep teaching. We'd never ask her to retire."

"So, what? You're just going to sell it without talking to us?"

"I have yet to decide. Your grandmother and I are leaving our options on the table. But yes, we are considering selling. Times are changing, and the money from the sale would benefit our children and grandchildren more than apples ever could."

"Grandpa, this place has been in our family for decades. How could you ever sell it?"

"Jackson, you are asking how could we ever sell? How can we *not* sell when no one wants to stay?"

"Grandpa, it's not that I don't want to stay. I just can't handle it."

"I said, it's not your decision. What you've been through, none of us can understand. That's why I haven't brought you into the conversation. I wasn't planning on it until the proposed deal was explained in detail. Shannon thought that'd be best."

"Shannon! Shannon knows? Seriously?" This is getting out of control. I rub my temples. Everything is shattering around me. Everyone has put me in a protective bubble, trying to keep me out of harm's way. To save me from greater hurt and devastation, they've sheltered me from truths they thought I couldn't handle. No one can erase the accident, but I need to know what's going on with my family, and to do so, I need them to see I can handle the truth.

"Yes, yes, she does, and she understands."

Standing, I put my hands on the counter, turn to my grandfather, and embrace him in a hug that I hope conveys how much I appreciate his wisdom and love. His frail bones and weak frame cause tears to infiltrate my vision. "I love you, Grandpa. I'm going to talk to Solia. We can discuss the wind farm later, OK?"

"Sure thing. Good luck. You know where to find me." And with that, I walk out of the kitchen with just a pinch more strength than I had when I walked in.

Before putting my truck in drive, I take out my phone and text Shannon.

JACKSON

> Seriously, Shannon, a wind farm? Kind of big news. We need to talk. I'm going to see Solia for a bit this afternoon. Let me know if you're around tonight or tomorrow.

My fingers hover over the screen, trying to formulate the words to send to Solia. Selfishly, I want to talk to her as soon as possible, but Mia is still in town.

Here goes nothing.

JACKSON

> Hi, Solia, are you around today? I was hoping to swing by and talk.

I press Send and hold my breath.

# 18

*Sofia*

Having Mia here in New Hampshire is like that first sip of coffee in the morning. She's the yin to my yang, my grounding force. Everything is better with her around.

And with each repair I make to the cabin, whether it's righting the crooked stair rail or hammering the nail back into the deck board, I mold this place into my own, and pride fills my heart. Being here is what I dreamed it would be. The stillness and quiet mountain air are so freeing. With Mia here, even just for these few days, I am happier than I've been in forever.

Once the school year starts, I know I'll meet more people and I won't feel Mia's absence so acutely. But meeting Jackson, as unexpected as it was, might ease my loneliness. Love is something I thought I ditched in the potholes outside the Meriden town limits. Except it's found its way back on its own, and I know I'm falling hard.

Jackson seems like a man worth taking my chances on.

Being able to enjoy the weather, the lake, and campfires at night without the stress of work the next day is fantastic—and

Mia and I took full advantage of this last night. Despite our late bedtime, we rise with the sun. She thinks it's the quiet causing her to wake up early—it's interesting how people become accustomed to their surroundings. Traffic, honking, and streetlights lull big-city residents to sleep, but out here, there's nothing but stillness. The cabin isn't just small-town quiet; it is silent, which I'll take any day, but Mia's not a fan.

The morning dawns warm, and since Mia is leaving tomorrow, we want to play during the time we have left. I have two paddleboards, paddles, and jackets in the garage in hopes I'd have someone to enjoy the water with this summer. Throwing the boards and paddles into the truck bed is the easy part; finding a place by the small craft launch at the beach on a Sunday morning will be the challenge.

To my surprise, only a few cars are parked along the shore. We secure a spot next to the launch and float the boards right into the water. Newfound Lake is magnificent, no matter the time of day, but there's something special that happens in the early-morning hours. The sun rising in the east over the mountains uses the sky as its canvas and reflects shapes of yellow and orange on the lake. In a word, it is awesome. On a morning like this, there isn't a breeze to be felt; the water appears glass-like.

As our paddles dip into the water, I can tell by the expression on Mia's face the view has her speechless. Looking across the lake on all sides, we seem to be the only ones around, the only ripples the wake left behind from our paddle strokes.

"I see why you love this place. It's a little magical right now." Mia turns to me, balancing well enough to stay on her feet.

"It does, doesn't it? Summer allows Newfound to shine. As a kid, I came with my family over break. My only goals were to meet other kids, and I lived for ice cream nights. Now, I see much more. I don't want to get sappy, but I'm eager to see this place in each of the four seasons and for longer than a weekend."

"Well, give it some time. It's still early. You may miss home."

She always has my best interests at heart. I know she wants me to be happy.

We reach the swim line and follow the shore bordered by gorgeous lake homes with views to die for and impressive mountain ranges as their backdrop. "I'd say these people have it made. Their morning view is stunning! Sometimes I wonder if my parents would've traded the privacy of their cabin for a water view. I'm not sure which I prefer."

Mia keeps her focus on balancing. "I don't think you can lose either way."

"Yeah ... soooo, last night was fun. You seemed into Tyler. Tell me ..."

Mia's head swivels. "He is a hottie. Did you know he has a tattoo of a mountain range on his shoulder? Freaking hot. I'm not sure if I could hack it out in the country, but the muscles that guy has from living around here and being outdoorsy—ugh. So sexy. You didn't tell me that his family owned Bear Farm. Have you seen his triceps? He looks like he wrestles bears. If it hadn't been so long since I'd seen you, I would've jumped in that truck and gone home with him." Confidence oozes from her as she tosses her hair behind her shoulders.

She always has a way of making me laugh. *Carefree* should be her middle name. Her attitude is admirable—she does what she wants, never overthinks things, just goes for it. "I'm glad you didn't go home with him. He was a little too sloshed. Maybe next time you come to visit."

"Well, he texted me a minute ago. I haven't responded, but it popped up on my watch."

I'm not surprised. I can't blame a guy for trying to keep Mia's attention. There is nothing not to love. If you don't laugh your ass off when you're with her, the problem is you and not her. And she is as beautiful as she is kind. "This early, huh? Impressive. You haven't lost your touch. Not even here in the mountains."

"Did you doubt me, Solia? I think he wants to grab dinner. I haven't answered him, but I'll say no. I'm here to spend time with you."

"Whatever you want to do, Mia. You know I understand. Let's head back and get some breakfast. Or we could go to Basic Ingredients for their famous sticky buns."

"Isn't that on the other side of the lake?"

"Yeah, but we can make it. We'll cut across."

"Girl, if you think I have the strength for that this morning, you're mistaken. How about we drive there?"

"OK, OK."

We paddle back to the shore, my arms a little sore. With the boards in the truck, I get into the driver's seat and check my phone. It surprises me to see a text from Jackson this early.

JACKSON

Hi, Solia, are you around today? I was hoping to swing by and talk.

My stomach tightens from the urgency of his message. I read it to Mia as she buckles in. She stares at me blankly, waiting for my reaction.

"I get butterflies every time I think about him. It's pathetic. Even a text message excites me. I'll tell him I can't today, though."

"No, no, you should see him. It'll be fine. I'll tell Tyler I can grab lunch instead, if he's around, and you can tell Jackson to come over. You and I can eat dinner together and then we'll hang. It's all good."

"Are you sure? I can make plans with Jackson another day. You traveled hours to be here. I'd rather hang out with you."

"I'm not going anywhere. It'll just be a couple hours. Of course. Tell him eleven."

"Do you want to check with Tyler first?"

"No, if he wants to see me, he'll make it work." Of course he will. Sometimes I wish I had Mia's conviction.

With our laughter filling the truck, I text Jackson back.

SOLIA

Sure, how's eleven? Mia and I are just getting off the lake now, but I'll be home and cleaned up by then.

Great, I'll bring sandwiches from the orchard store.

Sounds great. Those were amazing last time. See you soon.

~

Luckily, Tyler shows up after Mia helps me pick an outfit —navy blue shorts and my favorite white tank. Mia never needs fashion advice, and even though she is limited to her suitcase this weekend, she looks fabulous in her white cotton sundress. The little I've learned about Tyler is enough to know he'll love her look today.

I figure I'll put lemonade on the porch with two glasses since Jackson is bringing lunch. Thankfully, my parents had a ceiling fan installed in the screened-in porch. Before that, this area was an open deck and felt like an absolute oven under the midday sun. There was no way you could enjoy sitting out in the afternoon without sizzling like an egg in a frying pan.

Trying to relax and not read too deeply into Jackson's text,

I lie on the lounge outside to read until he arrives. I need to take advantage of the time I have because when the school year begins, if I land a job, my reading time will be replaced by correcting papers.

Jackson pulls in minutes after eleven, sandwiches in hand, wearing another hat backward with light blue swim trunks and a white T-shirt, looking sexy as hell. Every ounce of my common sense floats away on the breeze.

*He's here to talk. I have to focus.*

"Hey there, beautiful." He sets a brown bag on the table and gathers me in for a hug. His skin meets mine, spreading an electrical current through my body.

*How is that possible? Does everyone experience this with someone?*

"Hi, Jackson." I hold on to him and tilt my head, willing his lips on mine. Instead, he places a soft kiss on my cheek. *Always a gentleman.*

He loosens his grip around my waist, pulls a chair from the table, and sits. Following his lead, I sit across from him. The brown bag blocks our view of each other. He hesitates and then pushes the bag over to the end of the table. He slouches a little in his seat and briefly closes his eyes. In an instant, I know something's not right. Usually Jackson's energy is warm, embracing, and light. Right now, the air sits heavy, almost too heavy to breathe.

"Are you hungry now?" He talks in the direction of the bag instead of looking at me.

Now I'm certain he has something to say, and I'm sensing he doesn't want to say it. "No, it's OK. I can wait."

He finally turns to look at me. Seriousness falls over us, and I dread whatever he is seconds away from revealing. He takes a deep inhale and folds his arms behind his head, puffing out his chest to reveal a soft trail of hair past his belly button, disappearing under the waistband of his shorts. It takes everything in me to focus anywhere else.

Keeping his arms behind his head, he begins to speak. "I've played this conversation over and over in my head, and I can't find the right words." He opens his eyes, and a cloud of apprehension creeps in.

*Here we go. The "I'm just not that into you" conversation.* Once again, I read the situation completely wrong.

"Jackson. It's fine, whatever you need to say." I don't mean for my words to cut so sharp, but I've been through this conversation one too many times. I'm ready to stack those bricks and rebuild my wall of protection.

His eyes widen and sadness settles into the creases of his expression. "Solia, listen. When I met you, I wasn't looking for love or even a date. You simply appeared before me at the hardware store. I shouldn't have brought your card back to you because while I convinced myself I was just being a good guy, I should've been honest about the pull I felt toward you at that moment. We hadn't even talked, but something powerful drew me to you." He stops, refocuses his breath, and closes his eyes again. I concentrate on his every word, trying not to anticipate the next sentence. It's obvious he's struggling.

The silence is deafening, and then the floodgates open ...

"Almost one year ago, there was an accident. Trinity. She grew up in Meriden with us. She was part of our crew, like one of the guys. Our families were friends—cookouts, on the playground at school, sporting events—you name it, we were together. You ever see the movie *The Sandlot*? It was like that— we were those kids. When we grew older and one of us didn't have a homecoming date, we'd call dibs and beg her to go. There were so many great times.

"We were never anything but friends until last summer. Something changed. At first, I thought it was a mistake, risking our friendship. We both did, but emotions shifted and we saw each other from different angles. Things were good. We'd only been together a few months."

He pauses and returns his hands to his knees and sits straight, his gaze off in the distance. "She wanted to go tubing, something she never got to do. Our families owned boats but never purchased extra accessories like that. They thought it was a waste of money. I, on the other hand, couldn't wait to purchase the toys. It was a beautiful day on Labor Day weekend, so I knew it'd be busy, but we grew up here and knew every square inch of this lake. So Jay, Tyler, Ryan, and I packed the cooler and met Trinity and her friend Sara at the marina. Trinity was all smiles, her energy contagious. She and Sara cracked jokes, and everyone laughed and was having a great time.

"After cruising the lake, the girls wanted to go on the new tube I'd bought. We decided Jay would drive and the rest of us, me especially, would co-captain to let him know if one or both girls fell off. We went around and around, more times than I could count. The girls took turns going together and then separately. The yellow tube sailed through the wake from our boat and other vessels, sending the riders flying into the air, hair whipping in the breeze, their blue life jackets bouncing against the tube as they crashed into the water. Their laughs and shrieks echoed off the mountains and around the lake.

"They climbed back into the boat for a bit because their hands were sore from gripping the tube handles, so we pulled up along the sandbar on the west side. It's a popular spot for boats to drop anchor and then boaters blast their speakers, swim, and just chill. We stayed for an hour, and before we headed back around the lake, Trinity asked to take one more ride on the tube. At first glance, I knew there were more boats out than when we'd first left the marina. But Trinity was convincing, and seeing her have so much fun made it hard to say no.

"She jumped on the tube for one last ride. I remember Tyler pulled the anchor from the sandbar and Ryan refastened the tube rope to the boat. I drove to make sure my engine didn't scrape the bottom—there are some exceptionally shallow parts around the sandbar area.

"Once we got to the middle of the lake, out to the deep water, I handed Jay the wheel and I headed to the back to watch Trinity and signal if we needed to stop. Just like the rides before, I could hear Trinity's squeals of joy and her smile never left her face. Jay was doing an awesome job driving with just enough speed to send her sailing over a wave, and the tube would come sailing back. Jay took a quick left turn, which he had done many times that day, sending the tube as far as the tow rope would allow to the right side of the boat. Trinity waved to us, letting us know she wanted more. Just as her hand went into the air, the tube hit a hard wake from another boat or Jet Ski, and it sent Trinity flying."

Jackson rests his elbows on the table and digs his palms into his eye sockets. Tears begin to fall.

I sit frozen, sensing the pain take over his body, my breath held.

He doesn't lift his head but continues, "I threw my hand in the air and yelled to Jay to slow the engine. Trinity was off the tube, and we needed to swing around and get her back to the boat, just as we had done several times that day. Jay did what I asked—he slowed to almost a complete stop and circled left to pick up Trinity. The bright yellow empty tube bounced in the water as it followed the boat, and Trinity bobbed in the distance, waving at us to pick her up.

"Then, between the two islands on the lake, I caught a glimpse of this orange speedboat. I heard it before I saw it. The music was blasting, and they were flying." Jackson lifts his tear-stained face and looks directly at me. "I felt like my eyes were deceiving me because one minute I saw her and the next, she was gone. I remember screaming and turning in circles, thinking I lost where she was or maybe she swam a little or maybe she dipped her hair back into the water. The speedboat had flown by us from the direction where we last spotted Trinity.

"The rest is a complete blur. Our boat idled, but none of us could find her. The speedboat had stopped and pulled into the dock up ahead. The next thing I remember is being in the water, screaming and swimming to where I had last seen her. There were so many people in the water—I had no idea where they'd come from. Tyler threw me a life jacket. Someone next to me helped me into it. I couldn't breathe. Everyone was screaming her name. I desperately wanted her to appear from somewhere, yell back at me, tell me she was OK.

"I honestly don't know how long we were in the water. It felt like hours. Time froze. Our boat's engine must have been off at that point because I remember Jay screaming and choking out water, saying he had her.

"At that point, the Lake Coast Guard was there. Someone called 911 because we could hear the sirens from every direction. I was far from where Jay was, but as soon as I looked at him, even with the distance between us, I knew she was gone. I hadn't yelled quick enough when she fell into the water.

"Somehow I made it back to the boat and then to the hospital where paramedics transported Trinity. We were all there—my friends, family, her family—and then a doctor came out to deliver the news. She was gone ... a split second is all it took. The speed, force, and direction in which that boat had hit killed her instantly. There was nothing anyone could do. My heart sank 183 feet to the bottom of the lake." Jackson's voice cuts, his words interrupted by deep sobs.

"In the weeks that followed, we found out the kids on the speedboat were here vacationing and had been drinking nonstop throughout the morning. They were drunk on the lake that day and never even spotted Trinity in the water. She didn't stand a chance.

"We all blamed ourselves during those first few months. Jay tried to claim responsibility because he was driving. I blamed myself for even being out there that day, knowing the traffic would be heavy. I caved when she wanted to go out again on the tube because I saw how happy she was, so I was the one to say yes. Sara had egged her on to go again, and I'm sure she'll forever wish she hadn't.

"The months after were awful. Everyone was supportive. We had people checking on us, but I was numb. All I could think about was her family. The loss I had experienced was nothing compared to the pain they were going through. Despite their loss and anger, they still found it in their hearts to show kindness to me and the others. They never once blamed us. We grieved alongside them. For that, I will forever be grateful.

"They held the drivers of the speedboat responsible, but that changed nothing. She was gone, and the tragedy has forever connected us. We each have tried to move forward through the grief. Jay has had an extremely tough time.

"I … just kept replaying that moment in my head over and over again. She was right there, waiting for our boat to swing around to get her. She was smiling. Then she was just … gone. Everything was gone. The beauty of this place was gone. After that day, I avoided driving by the lake and looking at boats. I distanced myself from everyone and couldn't handle being around the guys without thinking about the accident. It's not like we talk about it because no one brings it up. It's just there, this unspeakable sadness. I can't shake it. I continue to work and go through the motions, but this place lost its magic. Every time someone sees me, their eyes sink. There's no way to escape it. It became too much to handle.

"I decided I needed to get away from here, same as Trinity's family, start over, not be reminded every single day of the accident. A couple months ago, I decided to move to

New York where my parents are. I'll still work in the family business but at the cider production end of things. My grandparents are supportive but would prefer I stay to run the orchard. I'm leaving Meriden at the end of August." He wipes his eyes, dries his hands on his shorts, and reaches for me.

I choke back my tears and hold on tight. A million thoughts flood my head as I try to comprehend everything Jackson has shared. He looks into my eyes and more tears fall, like drops of rain I never saw forecasted.

"Solia, these last couple weeks with you have been amazing. I haven't smiled or laughed like this in so long. Even though it seems crazy, given the amount of time we've known each other, it scares me to admit how I feel about you. I never intended to hide this or hurt you. Part of me figured if I held back, you'd be sick of me soon enough and I could spare myself having to tell you. I'm so sorry." He pulls away and closes his eyes.

We sit without talking as the sounds of nature surround us. I know he's waiting for me to say something. My heart aches for Jackson and what he's been through. Never in a million years did I foresee this conversation. But Jackson has known the entire time that this road would lead to a dead end.

I can't even begin to understand what he's going through, but the bricks are stacking. Despite my connection with Jackson, he's severing the tie that binds us. He's leaving. There's no avoiding it.

I push my chair back and walk over to Jackson. He meets me halfway, and I pull him into me, hoping to transfer every ounce of love I have for him. He is a good man, and what happened to him is tragic. The last thing he deserves is added guilt. I can easily rise above that; what Jackson needs is love and support.

"Thank you for telling me. I'm so sorry this happened to

you and your friends and that Trinity passed. I understand what you are saying."

The rigidity of Jackson's embrace loosens as he hangs his head and his tears soak into the fabric of my shirt. "I'm so sorry," he whispers in my ear.

Those are the last words I hear before his arms set me free and I'm looking at his back as he walks through the screen door. I'm glued to the deck, my chest empty while he walks away with my heart. I hear the gravel under his tires, and I collapse into the lounge chair, curling into the fetal position.

*Poor Jackson. The weight of the world has been on his shoulders since the day I met him.*

I lie crying and replay Jackson's words in my head. The sun moves past high noon and is in the western sky when the tires rumble over the dirt and rocks.

*He's back. He can't live without me.*

I jump from the chair and run to the top of the stairs. Tyler's truck rounds the corner, and the remaining pieces of my heart crumble.

I watch Mia lean over to Tyler, whisper something in his ear, and kiss his cheek. The truck door slams and Tyler looks at me, sadness in his eyes as he nods in understanding. Through my blurred vision, I see the outline of Mia climbing the stairs toward me. I want to collapse in her arms and rid myself of this pain.

Mia takes hold of me and leads me inside. With a box of tissues on my lap and my head on her shoulder, I share the entire conversation. She sits in silence, running her fingers through my hair, wiping her own tears. I'm so thankful she's here. I'm not sure how I would've handled this without her. A text or video call would never have sufficed.

"Solia, what Jackson's been through is more than either of us can imagine. I'm glad he told you before you fell in love with him because you are just getting your life started here. I want you to live out your dream here without heartache." She lowers her head to mine for reassurance, and her expression indicates she knows it's too late. "You're already in love, aren't you?"

I cover my face and lie back on the couch and sob. "I know I just met the guy. It's ridiculous to think I'm in love with Jackson. It's absurd, but it's true. I've never felt this way. Every time I see him, I liquefy. He's everything I didn't know I was looking for. So yeah, I'm in love with him, and he's leaving."

Mia always has something to say, and this is the first time I can remember her looking at me without offering a word. I leave Mia on the couch and go to the bathroom to grab towels for the outdoor shower. Maybe a little fresh air and water will clear my mind.

Walking back through the kitchen, towels in hand, I find Mia kneeling near the refrigerator.

"What are you doing?"

"I was filling a glass with ice water, and a cube fell on the floor. I reached and grabbed this. Did you know you have mail that fell underneath the refrigerator?" She stands, holding two envelopes.

"Let me see those."

She hands them over and I flash back to the day I went to the post office and threw my mail on the counter. I forgot these were delivered, and somehow they made it under the fridge. I look at both and remember seeing the one from Meriden Elementary, but I don't recall seeing the one addressed to my parents from Green Breeze Enterprises.

I rip open the envelope from the school to find an invitation to a Midsummer Teacher Meet-Up next week, along with a letter from the principal stating there is an anticipated grade three opening she'd like me to interview for at my convenience. Good thing Mia found these. I stick the invitation on the fridge with a magnet I made as a kid that's been hanging there for twenty years. *I need to get rid of that.*

The next letter I open slowly. It is addressed to my parents:

*Dear Mr. and Mrs. Anderson,*

*Allow me to introduce myself. My name is Nick Ford, CEO of Green Breeze Enterprises. Our company is expanding into the Lakes Region of New Hampshire. As I'm sure you are aware, green energy is the future, and the residents of Meriden, New Hampshire, can join the green energy revolution.*

*Green Breeze has selected your property, among many others, as an area of interest for the installation of a wind turbine farm. It is our sincere hope that with the help of Meriden town officials, the zoning board, and residents like you, we can put Meriden on the map in the coming year.*

*I'm sure you'll have a great deal of questions, which we hope to address at a special town hall meeting at 11 a.m. on July 24. We look forward to educating you and the public regarding the outstanding benefits of wind power and how you can play a role in this sustainable and renewable form of energy.*

*Sincerely,*
*Nick Ford*
*CEO, Green Breeze Enterprises*

"What the fuck? You've got to be kidding me. If this jackass thinks he is going to walk in here and turn this place into a metal factory, he is sadly mistaken. Where the hell is his phone number?" I frantically scan the letter and turn the envelope every which way in hopes of locating his contact information. There's nothing. Convenient.

Mia takes the letter from me and reads in silence while I pace the kitchen floor. With each step, my feet smash the remnants of my heart as my dreams for this cabin slip away.

My best friend places the document on the counter and

firmly grips my shoulders. "Listen, this is insane. Every fucking word of it is nuts. This is what you are going to do. Go take a shower and breathe. I'm going to town to grab a pizza and wine, and we are going to talk this through. I got you. Everything is going to be OK. Look at me, Solia. Look at me."

I stop and listen. "OK." And I walk toward the shower.

# 19

Jackson

Several days have passed since telling Solia, and the deep, nagging pit in my stomach remains. As terrible as it was to walk away from her, my decision to leave can't change now. It's not lost on me that baring my soul to Solia was the first time I've allowed myself to cry since Trinity's passing. And once I started, I cried more in those twenty-four hours than ever in my life.

I could tell by the look in Solia's eyes she's heartbroken. She understands my pain, but the shock in her expression couldn't be ignored. For this, I'm a complete asshole. I should never have started something with her, knowing the position I'm in. But I'm noticeably lighter. Solia is the first person I've told about what happened. Everyone in my life already knows, was there, or learned of the details elsewhere. To say the words, to start from the beginning and speak it aloud—it was as if someone removed the cinder blocks from my exhausted shoulders. I've been carrying this story with me and have replayed it every single day since the accident. Being able to cry released a tension rod filled with pain.

I know it's over between Solia and me, but I can't help

thinking about her, wondering if she is doing OK. She must be angry with me for waiting so long to tell her. But mostly, I rewind every moment I've been lucky enough to spend with her.

I won't text or call her. That isn't playing fair. With four weeks left before I leave for New York, the last thing I want to do is confuse Solia. She deserves better, and I will not let myself hurt her for a second time.

~

On my way to work on Wednesday, my phone blows up with text messages from my father. I talk to him often enough, but with the approaching deadline of my big move, I'm hearing from him more often.

DAD

Jackson, just checking in. I've got your office set up, and people are looking forward to having you on board. You ready?

JACKSON

Thanks, Dad. I'll be ready.

You sure? Grandpa might have mentioned something about a special someone.

It's set in stone, Dad. I'll be there. I'm heading to work. I'll text you later. Say hi to Mom.

Love you, son. Oh, Grandpa told me he talked to you about the wind farm thing. There'll be a lot of paperwork if this goes through. Be prepared to take care of that before you leave. I've been in talks with several orchards in upstate NY who've been wanting to partner with us for a while. We'll know more soon.

Has everyone lost their minds? I can't believe my father is OK with this. Is everyone going to just sit back and let this company destroy a town that took centuries to build? He's already planning for a freaking orchard replacement! My head spins.

~

After work, I sit in a rocking chair next to my grandmother. Neither of us says much. The sun is sinking, there is a slight breeze in the air, and being here with her is just what I need after a long day on the farm. Sometimes saying nothing can be so comforting.

"So, Jackson, it seems to me you've been around more these past couple days. It wouldn't have anything to do with that beauty you were taking out around town?"

I love how my grandmother thinks she's beating around the bush. Without a second thought, I tell her exactly what she wants to know and spare her the battle of trying to squeeze it out of me.

"Yes, it does, Grandma. Her name is Solia, remember? You know I'm leaving at the end of the summer, and I know you and Grandpa think it's the wrong decision. I was dragging my feet, but I told Solia everything. I shouldn't have waited. I regret that. I had to end it, even though we barely began. Seeing her again will also make it harder. It can't continue if I'm leaving."

"Jackson, why didn't you tell her sooner?"

"I'm not sure. I guess I got caught up in the moment. She's magnetic, and I didn't want it to end. I know how selfish that sounds."

"Honey, love makes us do crazy things. But listen to me. This is coming from an old lady who has seen a thing or two in this lifetime. There is nothing more important than love.

Everything else doesn't mean a damn thing. The only thing we take with us when we leave is love. Now, I know you haven't known this girl long, but what I know is, I haven't seen you smile and laugh like this in a very long time. And if you ask me, the reason you didn't tell her is that you're doubting your damn decision. But you didn't ask me, so I'll stay quiet." And with that unsolicited advice, a smile appears on her face.

"Thanks for your advice, Grandma. Even if I didn't ask for it." I take her hand in mine and laugh. Even in the toughest times, she has the perfect words.

"Will you be going to the town hall meeting on Saturday morning? Should be interesting, don't you think?"

"I'll be there, Grandma. This wind farm bullshit is alarm-level disturbing. There is no way in hell the people of Meriden are going to let this happen."

"Watch your mouth, Jackson. Be a gentleman. I guess we'll have to wait and see, won't we?"

"Sorry about that."

Before the meeting, I have a few things I need to do. I'll have to try to forget what happened between Solia and me long enough to focus. I want to research and understand the regulations involved in the sale of land and the development of wind farms using wind turbines.

I'll speak to my dad and ask him about zoning regulations and the laws around the destruction of habitats and wildlife. I know he supports my grandparents selling, but that doesn't mean he can't feed me some information.

∽

On the day of the town hall meeting, I arrive early, thinking I'll be among the first. I couldn't be further from the truth. People are searching for places to park.

Meriden Town Hall is a small building; I'm not sure anyone gave the potential size of the crowd much thought.

The building has been in the central downtown area since 1849 and the original single-story wood-frame structure remains, but improvements to the building have been made over the years. An addition was added in the late 1800s to incorporate an indoor stage. A wide recess in front provides a large entrance, and slender sash windows around the building allow light to enter from all angles. It still has its old-world charm while remaining functional for today's purposes. I've only ever stepped foot inside to vote. And before that, a play in elementary school.

But today, I'm walking into town hall with a whole new purpose. Through the crowd, I spot Greg.

"Hey, man. Glad to see you here. I guess the old man finally filled you in. What a load of horseshit, right?"

"Seriously, Greg. I'm not a snowflake. I should've known from the beginning. But whatever, I'm here now."

"I hear you, man, but it was Earl's call. If he says not to say something, I'll be damned if I'm the one who crosses him."

"I get it. Just can't believe these pricks think they can waltz in here and buy our land from under us. There are so many people here to support whoever's on the property list."

"For sure. But I'm not so sure everyone is on the same side of this thing. There's a lot of talk around town. Some people are dead set against it, some are willing to listen because raking in some money sounds appealing, and some don't know what the hell to think."

"Where do you stand on the issue?"

"Well, I'm not the one who owns any of the land they want. I don't know shit about wind farms, but the landscape around here is going to look a hell of a lot different with these monsters in the sky. And shit, I've been working for your family since I was a kid. To think of that place being sold to some big-city boys looking for a fat paycheck makes me sick. So if you ask me, I'm against it. But unfortunately, I'll be an audience member for this one. No one is looking to buy my little postage stand on the other side of the lake."

"I'm with you on all accounts. I don't understand the process and what rights the property owners have. It pisses me off."

We walk around the side of the building. I can tell by the vehicles filling the spots we're dealing with people who are certainly not from these parts. Two black SUVs with faded windows bear the Green Breeze Enterprises logo on their side. Several luxury vehicles are parked side by side, each one sticking out among the family SUVs and pickup trucks.

We walk inside and I spot Shannon, Lucas, and a few other orchard workers. Sharon and Gary from the Fire Hearth sit by the door. Most of the people we pass I either know personally or recognize from around town. Greg points to several empty seats toward the back, perfect as I prefer to stay away from the stage. I sit beside Greg and try to relax in my chair, nodding to Shannon when she turns and waves at me.

I twiddle my thumbs and look around the hall. This company has tacked twenty or more posters along the walls with information about wind farms and their benefits. From where I'm sitting, very few people seem interested in reading how the turbines will reduce the use of fossil fuels or energy imports. I certainly don't care about how wind farms will increase revenue in the area.

This is absolute bullshit—these guys are out to make a buck and will destroy a community to get it. I cross my arms against my chest and stare straight ahead.

People of all ages fill the room, from older couples up front holding hands to young mothers bouncing babies on their laps. Toddlers run circles around their parents who are trying to keep their cool. The sun beams through the glass of the floor-to-ceiling windows on both sides of the stage, illuminating everything inside. Between the windows, center stage, sits a large wooden conference table and three office chairs. The stage looks like a setup from a catalog.

*These fucking guys brought their own furniture.*

Each seat has a folded, upright nameplate with bold block lettering: **NICK FORD, CEO**, **MARK HOGAN, CFO**, and **TIM LAMBERT, COO**.

A hush falls over the crowd, parents hand out snacks to quiet the kids, and the energy in the room shifts to a higher level of discomfort. Several men in suits walk through the front side entrance, the door slamming behind them. The three men march in a single line toward the stage without a glance at the audience and then take their seats.

Everyone is facing forward and silent when, all of a sudden, the back door creaks open and slams shut. As if on cue, everyone looks. I force my eyes to refocus because I'm stunned to see Solia walking through. Her cheeks burst into a shade of hot pink and her eyes cast to the floor. The sight of her takes my breath away.

It's only been a week, but it might as well have been an eternity since I last laid eyes on her. Her thick hair hangs in a long braid over her left shoulder and her beautiful face shines. A short, flowy skirt blows to the side from the wind of the door and settles mid-thigh. A tight white tank is tucked into her shirt, revealing her firm, bronzed cleavage. She's absolutely edible and kissed by the sun.

My insides tighten, and I find it hard to breathe.

She follows the walkway, my eyes glued to her body as she scans for a seat. She approaches my aisle and her eyes meet mine for an extra half a beat, long enough for me to see the sadness and defeat in them. She gives me a soft smile and continues looking for an open chair. I follow her as she chooses a seat twenty rows in front of me, right behind my grandparents and Shannon.

She disappears from my view, and someone nudges my leg. Greg pushes his knee into mine, sporting a grin that tells me he watched me watch her. I don't have the energy to respond; I simply shrug and smile. There's no way I'm going to deny or even pretend I'm not undressing Solia with my eyes. She is the sexiest woman who's ever walked into my life.

Once the men settle onstage, I stop envisioning Solia's body for two minutes and make sense of the fact that if she's at this meeting, she received a letter from Green Breeze Enterprises. My heart sinks. Not only did I let her down, but now her dream of starting over in a place that means so much to her is at risk.

I try my best to focus on the presentation. Nick Ford will be the first to speak. I recognize his name—my grandfather mentioned it at one point. Mr. Ford introduces himself as the CEO. He stares at the paper in his hand and begins, robotically rattling off the fiscal advantages of wind farms and how Meriden will benefit as a community.

The tone and arrogance coming off this guy is unbearable. Audience members are shaking their heads, but Mr. Ford continues to read as if a teleprompter is feeding him the words. It's clear there will be no attempts to connect with the community. His voice is condescending and unlikable.

He rambles on about the excellent offers and packages the company will put together for each property owner. People murmur and shift in their seats. The mention of offers causes a definite stir in the crowd. Someone yells out, "How much? We want to know!"

In response, another community member speaks out. "There is nothing I want from you people. It's my land."

The meeting is at a fork in the road, and the energy of the

crowd shifts from interested to angry. The second man sitting at the table joins Mr. Ford at the microphone. "Now, folks, let's not get ahead of ourselves. Many things need to happen prior to the installation of any wind turbines. We are here to give you facts and information regarding the benefits of green energy and how your town will prosper. We want you to understand the excellent offer you're getting ready to accept, a decision that will better life for you and your fellow residents. In addition, we plan to work with your town officials and your zoning board to ensure that we abide by state and town laws. With everyone's effort, we will move Meriden into the green energy future."

Listen to this guy. "The excellent offer you're getting ready to accept." No one has decided anything yet. These guys are so presumptuous. They don't know who they're dealing with.

The crowd grows louder and people begin to shout out questions. Waving his hand, the third company official joins the other two at the microphone and whispers something to both of them. Ford and Hogan sit back, and Lambert takes the mic.

"The purpose of today is to give you, the residents of Meriden, the opportunity to come together and meet the company behind the letters you received. We want this to be a cordial exchange between our company and the residents of this town. Understanding that this decision is personal is at the forefront of our minds. We plan to meet with your town representatives later this week, as well as with the zoning board.

"If you are a property owner who received a letter from us, we encourage you to read the resources we have provided here today. Understanding the benefits and financial advantage that you'll receive by accepting this offer is extremely important. We'll be walking around the room to answer as many individual questions as we can. The next time we meet will be at the town council meeting in approximately two weeks to discuss the project's progress, and we will continue to treat you as partners in this endeavor."

Upon the conclusion of Mr. Lambert's attempt to satisfy the crowd and calm the negativity, the room buzzes. By the looks on everyone's faces, people seem overwhelmed and eager to learn and discuss the aspects of this project with one another and the company.

I'm not impressed with anything they've presented and have zero interest in speaking with any of them. My opinion on the matter hasn't changed from before I entered this meeting; these men are out for a buck. Based on their demeanor, they don't give a shit about this town. Aside from the orchard and not wanting to see it destroyed, I'm now concerned for Solia and the possibility of her losing the cabin.

*What are her parents' thoughts regarding this? Is she nervous? Is she devastated? What is she going to do?*

I know I have no right to involve myself in Solia's life. I know she's a strong woman and can figure this out, but I desperately want to help her. She has tremendous pride regarding her decision to move here, and every time I'm in her presence she has a new item she completed checked off her list. She's hoping to secure a position at Meriden Elementary, making the fact that this company wants to take it out from under her feet devastating. I have to help her.

Everyone is leaving their seats and inching forward to speak to the representatives. Squeezing through the aisles, I scan the room, looking for Solia. I rush past my grandparents and Shannon, standing with a group of locals. Reaching the row Solia was in, I frantically look right, left, behind me. She's nowhere to be found.

I spin one more time, searching in every direction and then spot the floral print of her dress as she heads out the back door. My heart sinks. There's no way I'll get to her in time. The crowd is too thick, and she has already exited. I throw myself into a chair and clasp my hands against the back of my head. The chaos of questions and the noise in the room reaches a crescendo as people's emotions rise.

The only question I have is, how can I fix this?

I put my head in my hands just as someone grasps my shoulder. I turn to find good ol' Gerry standing behind me.

"You got it bad, son." Gerry lets out a laugh and nods toward the back door. "I know love when I see it. I've got a plan—follow me."

Too stunned to speak, I follow Gerry out the door and toward his truck. "Hop in. Let's get lunch at Billy's and figure this out." Without questioning him, I climb in, and we head to the restaurant. My grandparents and Gerry go way back, so I know whatever he has in mind, he has good intentions.

Billy's is a little on the slow side, only a few trucks parked out front. Most of the regulars are likely still at the meeting. Susan greets us at the door—I'm not sure this woman ever sleeps. Every time I eat here, Susan is front and center. They originally named the restaurant after Billy Senior, but anyone will tell you Susan runs the show.

"Hey there, gentlemen. Table for two?" She smiles brightly and pulls out two folded menus from her red-checkered apron. Before we even answer, she turns and heads to a small booth across from the breakfast bar, motioning us to follow.

Billy's is Meriden's version of Cheers in Boston. Everybody knows your name and the menu never changes. At Billy's, you watch your pancakes get flipped via the peep-through that looks into the kitchen, behind the coffee pots with the brown and black handles distinguishing regular from decaf. The place smells of grease and coffee grounds, and to most of us, it's home.

Gerry and I settle into our booth. As Susan slides two waters onto the table, Gerry orders.

I guess I won't need my menu. Gerry clearly wants to get

down to business. Fine by me. I'm dying to know what Gerry has up his sleeve.

"OK, so I gather you are upset Solia was in attendance today."

"Yes. I had no idea her property was on the list. It's awful. She is trying to start a new life here. This company has some serious nerve."

"Cheers to that, Jackson. Listen, my property may not be on the line, but I've been in the town longer than anybody, and I'll be damned if I see it destroyed by some rich pricks from New York. People assume because I'm old as dirt, I don't know what's going on, but I'll tell you what, I've got connections."

"I don't doubt you for one second, Gerry. What are you thinking?"

"First thing I know is almost every property owner who received a letter of interest from these guys is either old or doesn't live here full time. I've seen the first list of properties, and they're playing dirty. If you ask me, they're preying on the weak for round one. There will be a second list and then a third—they'll keep going until the damn wind has blown away the whole town!"

"How did you see the complete list?"

"Don't you worry about that. We have two weeks until the next meeting, and we need to pull together and strategize. The people on the list don't deserve this, and most of them are against it. I'm afraid Green Breeze will bulldoze the ones on the fence into selling or make the payout too difficult to turn down.

"So, the first thing we need to do is gather the property owners and get on the same page. We can't have everyone all over the place. They'll take advantage of that. I think we need to print signs of opposition and place them around Meriden and surrounding towns. If they're coming for us, the neighboring towns are next. It'll be in their best interests to be educated and help support us."

"That's a good point, Gerry. You've given this a lot of thought."

"I've got the time. Might as well use it."

"These guys want to plaster the benefits of their wind farms around town. We're going to advertise the negatives! You may be too young to remember, but another old-timer, Mike Kelley, is a retired real estate attorney. Your grandfather Earl, Mike, and I go way back. We've lived through a great number of ugly cases involving the land in this town. Mike's a real shark. Anyway, I reached out to him. I know he wants to stay out of the spotlight since he's retired, but I got him fired up. He knows the ins and outs of zoning laws in these parts, and if there was ever an expert on real estate law, he's the guy."

"Meaning?"

"Right to the chase, huh? Mike agreed to help the property owners pro bono to preserve the integrity of the town. He may be a real ass to the opposition, but he's the guy you want on your side. You'll quickly see how valuable he is. Mike also knows Ben and Jenna, which I figure is especially interesting to you."

Susan delivers our lunch plates. "Anything else for now?"

"We're all set, hon. Thanks."

Running those names through my mind, I come up shorthanded. I tear through my burger, suddenly realizing how famished I am. "Who exactly are Ben and Jenna?"

"Solia's parents. Ben and I have known each other for years, which is why he asked me to keep an eye on Solia. And, by the way you look at Solia, you want to keep an eye on her as well."

"Wow, look at you, Gerry. I didn't know you had inside info on Solia's family. So, what do you know? How are they handling this? Not that I have a right to know, but I don't want to stand by and watch her lose that place."

"Listen, Jackson, I know you've been through hell and back, and I won't give you a lecture listing the reasons you're making a mistake here, but—you're making a mistake, plain and simple. Regardless, I'm hell-bent on saving the land. I haven't spoken to Ben yet. That's where you come in. I don't want to stick my nose where I don't belong. See, I figured you knew about the Andersons' situation until you were sitting alone at the meeting, drooling when Solia walked in and then looking like a lost puppy when she left. I assume you don't have any information about what's going on at the Anderson cabin."

"Gerry, I didn't have a clue her cabin was on the list. Things were great between us, but I had to tell her the truth about Trinity and me leaving. It's shitty no matter how you dice it, and now that I've found out she might lose the cabin, it's worse. This woman came here to start over and begin a new journey, and she's getting let down left and right. I'll do whatever I can to help her."

Gerry's eyes widen, and he stops chewing for a moment at the mention of Trinity's name. "Help her, and the orchard, is what you mean."

"Yeah, I hear you about the farm, but that might be an uphill battle. My grandfather is considering the deal. He broke the news to me the other day. I've been racking my brain for a solution ever since, but with me in New York and Shannon teaching, what choice do I have? I can't believe he's considering selling."

"That's some facts right there, Jackson. You've got a lot to figure out, boy, but let's start at step one. You reach out to Solia and see where her family stands. I'll get an idea of which property owners are willing to fight these jackasses and which we need to convince not to sell. Then we need to get a group together before the next town hall meeting and strategize.

Since Mike is retired, he'll make himself available as long as we let him know when. How does that sound?"

"I'm not sure if she'll speak with me, but I'm certainly willing to give it a shot. You want me to call you after? I can talk to Ryan too. I know his parents received a letter. Should we pick a time and location to meet?"

"You just convince her to come to our meet-up before the scheduled town council session. That's all you have to do. How does assembling at town hall, Saturday at ten a.m. sound? Most people came out today, so maybe if we do a good job spreading the word, people will show up. I'll have some flyers made and get the word out through the store. Most people are in and out during the week. Sound like a plan?"

"Sounds good to me," I say, ignoring the knot in my stomach as I plan what I'll text Solia in the hopes of not upsetting her. I'm thankful to have already finished my meal.

"Let's go. I'll give you a ride back to town hall." Gerry throws two twenties on the table and stands.

"Thanks, Gerry, but I'll walk. I appreciate your help. You think we can pull this off?"

"Sure do. People around here look out for one another. No one should ever underestimate the pride of a small town. No one."

"Thanks again, Gerry. See you Saturday."

∼

I wipe the sweat from my forehead and slide my truck into reverse just as a message pings in my pocket. I shift back into park.

DAD

Hey! How'd the meeting go?

JACKSON

I'll call you later. Too many details. It's a shit show. People are going to work together to fight this.

Green Breeze can't force people to sell. But Jackson, you need to get your ass to New York. You won't make a fool out of me, right? They are expecting you here.

Yes, I'll be there. Just need to see a few things through and tie up some loose ends. There's got to be a better way to handle the family orchard than to sell it.

That's up to my parents. It's not your call.

Talk later, Dad.

# 20

*Sofia*

It's been a week. Thank God Mia was with me last weekend. Between Jackson telling me he is leaving town at the end of summer and a potential wind farm erupting in my backyard, I am a total wreck. Mia did a great job talking me off the ledge and reminding me why I came to the cabin in the first place—romance wasn't it.

Just because the hottest farmer I've ever seen walked into my life and all I can picture is jumping his bones, the reality of the situation still hits hard. Jackson is everything I've ever dreamed of. The connection between us was like spider silk, strong, almost invisible. With Jackson, the stars were aligning, and I couldn't get him out of my mind.

I lie in bed at night and crave his gentle kisses on every inch of my body. My thoughts fly back to when I was lying on the rock under the warm sun, the breeze across my bare chest, Jackson between my thighs. The moments we had were the hottest, most sensual I've ever experienced. Heat spreads through my body every time his name is spoken.

*Am I selfish for feeling this way? For replaying every touch and wanting things to be different?*

195 Reasons · 195

I want him, I can't have him, and it's as simple as that.

Not hearing from him since that night has been torture. I've thought about driving to his place on more than one occasion, to lie next to him and tell him everything will be OK. I'm sure everyone has told him countless times the accident wasn't his fault, but grieving is a personal journey. Jackson isn't ready to allow love back in. Mia's advice, which I can't say I follow often, is to concentrate on the cabin, manifest this potential job at the elementary school, and save this damn place from turning into a wildlife death trap.

The first town hall meeting was packed, and it was difficult to find a seat. Awkwardly enough, I found an empty spot directly behind Jackson's sister and grandparents. Thankfully, they were focused on the presentation and didn't notice me. However, I was aware the CEO spent half the time undressing Shannon with his eyes. The nerve of that guy to stand there in his fancy black suit and tie and spout reasons people should sell their land. Unbelievable.

I'll be the first to admit—Nick Ford is drop-dead gorgeous. Tall, dark, and handsome, he has an edge to him that screams "I can control things." And while he may have been addressing the entire room, his focus was glued to Shannon.

I don't blame him. She's striking. I'm confident if their orchard is on the "most wanted" property list, she wants to kick in his teeth instead of allow him into her pants. The guy doesn't stand a chance.

I left the meeting as concerned as I was when I'd arrived. I must find a way out of this mess.

Just as I'm heading out the door for the Midsummer Teacher Meet-Up, a text message comes through.

JACKSON

Hi, Solia. I promised myself I wouldn't text or call you. I don't want to hurt you any more than I have, but I saw you at the town hall meeting. I'm distraught you received a letter. A lot of the property owners are making a plan, and I want you to be part of it. Some of the information I have will be helpful. Are you willing to meet? I can fill you in. I'll go wherever you want, just to talk, I promise.

Holy shit, my breath catches in my throat and my fingers tingle. The phone almost slips out of my hand. I'm trying to formulate a response but continue to draw a blank. There can't be a future between us, but Jackson is offering to help me save the cabin.

I've been putting off calling my parents, hoping to gather more information first to propose a solution to them since I'm trying to prove I can handle the cabin myself. Until now, I've had nothing but sleepless nights, scouring the internet for a way out. If Jackson has information that could rectify the problem, I'm all ears.

My heart softens now that I am certain I will be next to Jackson again—and I'm afraid I can't trust myself around him. The fact he wants to help me deepens my affection. I doubt he will change his mind about leaving because he made it clear that he needs to head out of town to heal.

Screw it. If he wants to help, I'll take it and try my damnedest to keep my hands and lips off him.

SOLIA

I am surprised to hear from you, but I could certainly use the help. Are you free tomorrow after work? I have a school meet-up today.

I'm making a delivery to the store around five
and then I'm done for the day. Did you land
a job?

> Not yet, but my fingers are crossed. I'm talking
> to the principal today. There may be an
> opening. I'll meet you around five. I'm going
> paddleboarding and will head over right after.

Sounds good. Good luck!

I don't have time to reflect on what this means or what I'm getting myself into. I need to get to the school.

Butterflies flutter in my stomach. I get so nervous meeting people in large crowds, especially potential colleagues, wondering if they will like me, if we'll get along. The older I get, the harder it is to make real connections and new friends.

I agonize over my outfit, not too casual and not too dressy. I decide on a jean skirt with buttons that fasten in front, mid-thigh length, conservative but not too uptight. I figure a plain yellow vintage tee and my white laced sneakers are cute, yet comfortable. I've been playing phone tag with the principal, and she asked if she could give me some insight into the opening at the meet-up.

I'm glad I drove by the school when I first got to town. I hate not knowing where to go. I pull up and see a group of teachers setting a few tents, tables, and chairs in the grass. They look to be wearing mostly shorts and T-shirts. Comfortable that I made a wise choice, I park at the back of the school and head to the playground where everyone seems to be gathering.

I count approximately fifteen to twenty teachers here already. Many are hugging and chatting. I assume this is the first time in a month or more they've seen each other. I can sympathize—when you work with children every single day, the other teachers keep your sanity in check. Watching the scene unfold makes me miss home for the first time. I'll never miss my old job, but I do miss my fellow teachers.

Before I enter the gate surrounding the playground, a woman pops up next to me and scares me half to death.

"Hi! I'm Brooke. I can tell by the look on your face you're new. Are you? Because I am. Just got a job here—my first. I'm so nervous, but I'm hoping everything is great. Is everything great at this school?"

Holy shit. This chick talks a million miles an hour. She catches me so off guard, I cover my mouth to stifle a laugh and smile. "Actually, yeah, I am new. Well, maybe new. There's an opening, and I've got my fingers crossed. I can't believe you could tell. Apparently, it's obvious. My name is Solia. Nice to meet you." I extend my hand, but she jumps up and down and embraces me.

*I guess we're hugging.*

"I love your name. Solia. Like the sun. I get it. Well, I'm happy you're here. This means I'm not the only newbie. What grade is the opening? I'm third. I'm going to love third grade. The kids will be sweet and love school, but I don't think they will be fresh."

This girl's energy is unlike any I've witnessed. Brooke and I are the same height, but she is a complete bombshell with blue eyes and the whitest teeth I've ever seen. I'd guess she's twenty-two if this is her first position. I'm hoping the overwhelming energy is just her nerves getting the best of her because she is going to take a lot of getting used to.

"The opening is for grade three as well."

A high-pitched screech pierces my ears, and Brooke engulfs me in another hug. I guess I can count on one thing—this potential team won't be short on energy or personality.

Linking her arm with mine, we make our way into the playground. The butterflies dissipate once I sense the chill vibe.

A few tables sit scattered under the tent. On one side are four coolers filled with water and sodas, and a small table is lined with trays of sandwiches, chips, and cookies. There appears to be no folder waiting for me on the table, no agenda being passed around. It's casual and social. I can handle this.

"I'll catch up with you in a bit. I'm going to get something to drink and introduce myself to some other teachers."

"Sure thing! I'll find you later!" Brooke tosses her hair and skips across the playground. *Wow, she's got a ton of spunk.*

Bending into the cooler, I hear a familiar voice behind me.

"Anything good in there? No adult drinks, I assume."

I laugh out loud. "Unfortunately, it's water or soda." I grab one of each and turn to offer it to the teacher behind me. As I spin around, my jaw drops. "Shannon ... Hi! We met the other day."

Shannon stands there for a minute in silence, as if deciding if she remembers me. "Solia, hi. Oh, jeez, sorry. When you said you were new to town, I never asked whether you were working. I guess Jackson and I never discussed it either. This is crazy."

"Don't worry about it."

Shannon takes a step back and pulls her jet-black hair together between her shoulders and stands perfectly straight. "OK, let's start over. Hi, Solia, remember me? I'm Jackson's sister and also a second-grade teacher at Meriden Elementary. You must be a new teacher here?"

I appreciate her making light of the moment and restarting on the right foot because there is the possibility of this getting awkward. I laugh and respond with as much wit as I can muster. "Hi, Shannon, I remember you. I am the woman who rode on your brother's tractor and am also hoping to be hired as a teacher here at Meriden Elementary. I'm supposed to talk to the principal today about a potential opening."

Shannon giggles and her friendly green eyes flicker in the

sunlight, reminding me so much of Jackson's. "No way. That's amazing. Yeah, I heard there was a last-minute retirement in grade three. You'll fit right in, Solia. The principal, teachers, and kids are great. I'm not just saying that. This is going to be my seventh year, and every year seems to top the last."

"That's awesome. I'm looking forward to a fresh start. This is a great idea getting everyone together."

"Right? I thought so too. We've never done anything like this before, but we have a few new hires, so I guess they figured it would help break the ice. And it's always great to see one another without students."

"Yes, makes perfect sense."

I follow Shannon as she heads toward a group of women standing together on the other side of the tent. "Have you met Madison?"

"No, I haven't."

"Well, she is amazing. If you get hired, you'll love the team. If I didn't love second grade so much, I would switch just to work with her. She's a total team player, an awesome teacher, and she doesn't take herself too seriously."

Music to my ears. Teaching is definitely a team sport. I'm proud of the great job I do for my students, but to survive the year, you need to connect with other teachers to laugh, scream, and talk through the struggles.

As we reach the group, Shannon stops in front of a tall, slender brunette who has her hair tied back in a sleek ponytail. "Hey, Madison, I want to make sure I introduce you to your potential new team member. This is Solia. She just moved here."

Madison immediately turns toward me, and I'm greeted by the warmest, most inviting smile. "Hey, Solia, what a beautiful name. I'm so glad you're here. I met the other new team member, Brooke. The two of you probably think I scared away the rest of my teaching team. But don't worry, I didn't. They both decided to retire together—one took a little longer to make her decision final."

"That's amazing, and don't worry. I wasn't thinking that. I'm thrilled to be here."

"This upcoming year is going to be great. And hey, if you're hired and we run out of energy, Brooke has enough for all of us. But before we start the year, we have to enjoy what's left of summer," she says with a wink. I can already tell I like this girl. "Let's go find Christine, our principal. Have you met?"

"I did, briefly, when I stopped by a few weeks ago. She seems nice, certainly welcoming."

"Wait here, I'll be right back." Madison leaves me standing under the tent. I watch her walk up to Mrs. Smith. They engage in a short conversation and then both turn their heads to look at me. Madison waves me over.

"Solia! I'm so glad you came."

"Thanks so much for having me. This is great!"

Madison reaches for my hand and squeezes it, leaving me alone with the principal.

"So, I looked over your résumé, called a few references, and it looks as though you may be the perfect fit. Are you interested in coming in for an interview for the third-grade position?"

"Yes, oh my goodness, yes. That would be amazing. Thank you." I reach to shake her hand, confident my excitement is felt on her end.

"HR will schedule it, and I have a folder from them on my desk. Have fun. Go meet the staff."

Every teacher is as nice as the next. My nerves calm as the meet-up progresses—this school would be a perfect fit. The only potential hiccup would be working with Jackson's sister. Being in a small town, the odds are good I'd bump into a relative or two, but it's still awkward to be colleagues with one.

I'm not sure how close she and her brother are, but I'm thankful she doesn't mention Jackson and me. It's hard enough not thinking about him every minute of the day, but working with her will be a constant reminder. I could always ask her how he's doing, and stopping myself will be torture. I'll have to work on separating them in my mind.

When the event draws to a close, I'm ready for a nap and know I'll forget half the names I've just learned. I make it a point to say goodbye to Shannon, Brooke, and Madison and exchange numbers with all three. We discuss the possibility of getting together again before the end of summer. I may not have Jackson, but a few friends are a step forward.

∼

After the fun of the teacher meet-up yesterday, I received a call about an interview for later this week. Today I'm determined to keep busy and not think of Jackson. I remind myself that our scheduled meeting is about the wind farm, not us. Regardless, all I can concentrate on is what we started together, and my body and soul ache for him.

The morning is beautiful, a comfortable eighty degrees, so I go for a paddle around the lake. Weekdays are where it's at—quiet, undisturbed, and peaceful. The water is perfectly still, providing a mirror for Mother Nature. As I glide along the shore, a pair of loons congregate to catch fish for their morning meal. Loons are very territorial, so each lake, unless exceptionally large, is home to only one pair of loons. These must be ours. I don't blame them. This lake is too beautiful to share.

I stop and glimpse at the lakeside homes. Over the years, many owners have remodeled and added on, reminding me of the mansions in Newport, Rhode Island, lining Bellevue Avenue. Years ago, most lake homes were similar to my family's quaint cabin, but now the boat houses are comparable to the cabin.

Because of this, the price of homes on Newfound Lake has skyrocketed. For those of us who love a small town and low commercialism, the less land for sale around Meriden, the better. Keeping the population stable allows for gradual change, if any. I see very few For Sale signs around the lake.

The midmorning sun warms my skin. I place my paddle under the bungee cord at the front of my board and lie back, taking a moment for myself. I allow my paddleboard to drift slightly with the calm breeze. I watch as the clouds pass overhead toward the peaks in the distance. And of course, my thoughts drift back to Jackson, wishing I could share this moment with him today, tomorrow, and every day going forward.

No matter how hard I try to push him out of my mind, he resurfaces. Every lakeside fantasy scrolls on a nonstop feed. It would be a dream to have him sitting across from me, floating on the water with my legs wrapped around his waist. I want his strong, muscular hands to rake my back with my chest pressed against him, to look into his eyes and tell him how badly he needs to stay. I can help him heal and believe in love again.

To ignore everything he told me would be insensitive, but having him to myself for three weeks was better than nothing. This is the opposite of what my head tells me, but my heart is set on him.

Receiving Jackson's text yesterday knocked me off my feet, and my excitement is palpable. I've typed and deleted countless texts to him since he told me where he stood on things. Even though his circumstances are the same, the fact he texted me means he wants to see me, and no matter the reason, I'll take it.

Every physical need I have for Jackson is balanced with an emotional one. No man has ever put my needs first. Reaching out to help save my property when he has no obligation to do so tells me he's a genuine guy, not an ass like the other men I've had the displeasure of experiencing.

But I want to know him inside and out. We could be stronger together than apart. However, I'm not a fool. I know full well that no matter how badly I long for Jackson, he is not mine. I'll embrace any time I can get with him, so if that means seeing him in a parking lot to discuss wind turbines, so be it.

A sliver of hope sits at the bottom of my heart, holding on to the chance he'll reconsider, somehow, some way. It's awful to admit, but if he thinks for a second that I won't try to make him stay, he's mistaken. I plan to run a few errands and leave enough time to choose the right outfit for what I hope isn't the last time I see Jackson.

Storing the board in my garage takes a little maneuvering, and my clothes stick to my skin, making the task more difficult. I love my outdoor shower, but it would be nice to have a working showerhead that doesn't drip like a leaky hose, so I head into town to grab a few items. Something slightly more powerful and luxurious for my outdoor oasis would be nice.

Raubuchon's is the place to go when you need random stuff—they have everything from toilet paper to sheetrock. There aren't any large chain stores around this area, only homegrown businesses. Now that I have a shot at a predictable income, I select a pretty soap dish, shower gel, and my favorite shampoo and conditioner. Passing by the lumber aisle, I mentally add building some sort of shelving unit to keep my towels dry.

*Maybe I can even put up an outdoor speaker. Then I may never get out.*

If everything works out with this teaching position, I'll be one step closer to keeping the cabin at the end of the year— and keeping my mother's nagging at bay.

Despite beginning to understand the severity of this wind farm issue, I still haven't told my parents about the Green Breeze letter. I promise myself that I'll listen to the information Jackson has to share and let them know. While this may be my cabin after our deal expires, my parents are still the legal owners. They have the right to know; I'm stunned they don't already. Small-town news travels similar to wildfire, and while they may not visit much anymore, they still have a connection to some of Meriden's residents.

"Hey, Solia!"

I whip my head around at the sound of my name to see Madison, whom I met the other day at the school.

"Hey, Madison. How are you?"

"Great, thanks! I was going to text you, Shannon, and Brooke to see if you guys were free tonight. Maybe we could get together at Caitlyn's next door."

"Sure. I could use a girls' night. Send it out. Looking forward to it!"

"Say, seven o'clock?"

"Perfect, see you then."

"Enjoy the day. It's beautiful," Madison says and heads in the opposite direction.

Having a group of friends here makes a difference. I know Mia will visit when she can, but the distance between us is difficult.

I'm excited to go to Caitlyn's tonight. It's connected to Raubuchon's—the two are housed in the same enormous old red barn. The hardware store occupies the main section, and the owners of Caitlyn's remodeled the overhang and opened a restaurant. It's been years since I've gone inside, but I remember its coziness, with an old wooden bar and a small concrete patio with a few tables and chairs. Only in New England can you find this combination of businesses.

As clueless as a plumber teaching third grade, I aimlessly

search up and down the aisles for a new showerhead. There are so many sizes, speeds, and connection options. I'm in the middle of reading my third package and am contemplating that this may be a lost cause when I see Gerry walk toward me with a tilted grin. He can tell I'm in unfamiliar territory.

"Finding everything you need, young lady?" Gerry takes the box out of my hand.

"Hilarious. You know I'm treading water here. I need a new showerhead for my outdoor shower. Why are there so many options?"

"Here, you need to be over in this section." I follow him toward the end of the aisle like a baby duck.

"Let's see, we have a ten-speed, one that has several illumination options, and a few basic models with a variety of sprays."

"Since I'm not having any disco parties in the shower yet, I don't need the different light-up options. The idea of different sprays and the ability to adjust the pressure sounds appealing. I want something with more pressure. The one I have now is pathetic. It's basically drizzling when I have it on."

"You'll want to pick one of these here." Gerry holds two boxes, one in each hand, and faces me.

"Eeny, meeny, miny, moe," I say, ultimately landing on the one in his left hand.

"Very educated decision, Solia."

"Very funny, Gerry. Thanks for your help. Now, thanks to the virtual world, I'll search up a video and install this baby."

Gerry holds his stomach with both arms to contain his amusement. "No offense, Solia. I'm sure you'll do just fine, but aren't you seeing Jackson today? I'm sure he'd be happy to give you a hand."

Seems my plans are public knowledge. I shouldn't be surprised. "Jeez, Gerry. You're taking this job of looking after me to a whole new level."

"Well, now you're just making me sound as if I'm a creepy old man, Solia. Jackson and I go way back. No better guy around these parts than him. But I do know you both are meeting today to discuss the wind farm. We're going to fix this, Solia. Nobody is going to walk into this town and tell us what to do with our land. I'll let Jackson fill you in, though."

"I'm relieved to hear that, Gerry. I've been in a bit of denial. I came to Meriden to prove to my parents I could handle living here and take care of the cabin on my own. My plate was crowded before Green Breeze and now it seems overflowing. I appreciate Jackson reaching out." At the mere mention of his name, my cheeks warm and I speak quickly. "I'll take any help I can get. I haven't even told my parents yet, so if you talk to them, give me a chance to break the news. I was planning on calling them after meeting with Jackson. Would you mind holding off mentioning it for now?"

"Sure thing, love. These guys are steamrollers, and your folks need to be in the loop as soon as possible. The more people crawling up these guys' asses, the better. And remember, there are many properties on the list. Did you see how many people piled into town hall the other day? You can count on never being alone with this headache. You talk to Jackson. I'm sure he'll fill you in on everything we're planning, but if you need me, you know where to find me. Oh, and if you don't have any luck with the showerhead, call me. I can always swing by the cabin, but I'm sure Jackson's muscles are better suited for the job."

I'm as transparent as lake water; Gerry is clearly aware of my interest in Jackson. My cheeks are still heated, so it's obvious the mention of Jackson excites me. Thankfully, Gerry rolls with it, and I don't mind him reading me like a book.

I arrive home with enough time to eat and get dressed to meet Jackson. This is the most anxious I've ever been before spending time with him, or with any man, for that matter. I'll have Jackson alone, all to myself, and I need to tell him exactly what's on my mind. The last time we spoke, he opened up and told me what happened to Trinity, and I never saw it coming. I was unprepared. His days here are numbered, but I'm not ready to begin the countdown.

A little before five o'clock, I back my truck into a parking spot behind the country store. The sun is dipping lower in the sky, casting a golden glow over my skin. Today has been beautiful. The temperature is a comfortable seventy-five degrees, not a drop of humidity.

Unable to contain my excitement, I unlock my tailgate and hoist myself up on the ledge. I toss my hair behind my shoulders and adjust the spaghetti straps of my white baby-doll sundress. I may appear to be trying a little too hard, but I don't care. My dress allows for a healthy dose of cleavage to pour out the top, and I cross my legs to reveal considerable thigh. I let my tan flip-flops dangle off my toes as I scan for Jackson's black pickup. If this is the last time he checks me out, I want it to be memorable.

A few customers look my way as they exit the store. I'll admit I look a little out of place, but it'll be worth the second glances. I'm sure they're wondering what in the hell I'm doing, but no one says anything. Everyone just smiles and goes on their way. Except for one couple who politely say hello as they walk past me to the SUV alongside my truck.

Then I see Jackson. He's wearing that damn backward hat, and his deep green eyes pierce through me as he pulls into the adjacent empty spot. His work boots hit the dirt and the distance between us shortens. He stands directly in front of me, looking every bit the farmer from head to toe, sexy as hell, and not saying a word.

I know he just came from work, but I didn't expect the dirt and grass stains to be such a turn-on. He has on a fitted T-shirt with a slight rip in the shoulder, allowing me a peek at his defined delts. He tucks the shirt into the side of his jeans, but it hangs loose around the rest of his waist, and he appears to have gotten a workout from the tractor.

The intensity of his stare gives me hope that he's still thinking of me. If he's feeling even half of what I am, I don't know how we can end here. He takes several steps forward and places both hands on the tailgate beside my legs, leaning forward so he's level with my chest, and hangs his head.

The seconds slip by, and I wonder what thoughts are going through his mind. My pulse quickens and my heart pounds. I want him to tell me he wants me, that he won't leave. I stay silent, desperately hoping he'll make the first move.

"Solia, I'm sorry, but you look so fucking edible, I'm not sure how I'm going to get through this conversation. I hope you know you're the most beautiful, sexiest woman I've ever met. If I'm being totally honest with you, it's taking everything in my power not to lay you back into this pickup, toss your dress aside, and show you how hot I am for you." He leans closer so his mouth touches my neck. He inhales the scent of my skin and moans deeply. A fire blazes between my thighs, my body responding to his frustration.

"Jackson, I—"

His lips hover over my neck. He then places one finger against my lips, and in a deep, sexy voice, he pleads, "I am trying hard to resist you. I don't want to hurt you, Solia. I'm leaving, but …"

I grasp his finger from my lips, move it to my chin, lower it to my chest, to the front of my dress, and stop. It takes every ounce of willpower to stop guiding his finger up along the inside of my thigh and to the center of my panties. "Jackson, I've never wanted someone as much as I want you. You've told me you're leaving, but I want you." I reach for his other hand, searching his face for the slightest sign of weakness.

"I can't imagine what you've gone through. It's awful,

and no one should have to experience such loss. I'm not going to sit here and tell you I don't want you to leave because I understand you need to. But I don't want you to leave without you knowing the truth. And, while I may wish you'd throw me in the back of this pickup and have your way with me, I also need you to understand what we have is deeper. It's as though I've known you forever—our paths crossed for a reason. This may sound ridiculous, but even when you leave, I won't regret the short time we had together."

"Hey, man!" comes a holler from the back of the store. I'm laser-focused on Jackson and honestly forgot we're in broad daylight in the middle of a parking lot.

Jackson spins around as a store employee tosses trash into a dumpster.

"Didn't see you there."

"Yeah, I didn't think so. You must be Solia?"

I wave back. "Sure am." The young man turns and walks back into the store.

"I kind of forgot we're in public." Jackson lets go of my hands and jumps on my tailgate to sit beside me. His jeans brush against my thigh and I look at his hand sitting on his leg, wishing it would make its way to mine.

"Solia, I don't want to hurt you. You can do so much better. This place has been my whole life, and I've been moping around for almost a year. I'm tired of being the town sob story and everyone walking on eggshells around me. My father is up my ass, making sure I'm holding up my end of the bargain. He has my position lined up, an office ready. There's no going back on this. I need to figure out this situation with the wind farm before I leave. I have to know your cabin and my family's orchard are safe."

The conversation takes a major shift, and my world tilts on its axis. He places his muscular hand on my leg, his effort to comfort me exciting me instead, sending tingles up my thighs. "Back to the wind farm, I have news to share with you."

"Of course." I keep my cool and try not to appear completely undone by his hand.

"After the town hall meeting, everyone understands this isn't a joke. These guys are out for our land. Gerry is up in arms and ready to tackle this head-on. He has an old buddy from town who is a retired real estate lawyer, Mike Kelley. I hear he's a real asshole in the best possible ways. He and Gerry spoke a few days back, and Mike wants to represent the property owners opposed to this deal. Most of us can't navigate the legality of it or even determine what our rights are. Having Mike on our side will be invaluable." Jackson searches my face. "Isn't that great?"

"Yes, that's amazing. In all seriousness, though, when I first found the letter, I underestimated the situation. It wasn't until the town hall meeting that a bolt of lightning struck me. I haven't even told my parents."

"Oh, Solia, you need to tell them. Listen, we can fight this, but everyone has to be invested. There are laws and regulations and zoning issues. Past precedent plays a role, plus things that I never would've thought of. We need Mike, but there is strength in numbers. Gerry thinks it's necessary to organize ourselves before the town council meeting."

"That makes sense. Tell me when and where and I will help however I can. I certainly don't want to lose the cabin. That's why I'm here, but I'll need to strap on my boots because it'll be an uphill battle for sure. My parents are already interested in selling. With a hefty offer from this company, I'm afraid they may toss our deal out the window." I have to tell my parents, and since my name isn't on the deed, it's ultimately up to them what happens to the cabin.

"Even though I'm leaving, I don't want to see my family's land destroyed. My grandparents are getting up there in age, and the other day Earl expressed to me he is considering selling. I never thought there'd be a day he and my grandmother would give such an idea any thought. I understand everyone's time here is temporary, but I figured we would keep the land in the family. But here we are—I'm heading to New York, and Shannon is dedicated to her career, so we can't expect her to run the farm. She and I are the only family left here. I'm trying to develop a plan that'll allow the family to keep rights to the land, but somehow have the orchard run privately. I'm not sure. My thoughts are scrambled. First, I need to get the orchard and cabin out of their claws, and then I can figure out the rest."

"I guess we have more in common than we realized. You and I are both working toward a fresh start with one foot stuck in the past. But this isn't entirely your responsibility to fix. We can each do our part. Leave the cabin to me—you have enough to worry about." I pause and reflect on the enormity of the situation and the countless puzzle pieces needing to line up for this town to remain unscathed. "So, when are we meeting?"

"This Saturday at ten a.m. at town hall. Can you be there? Gerry is working on the rest of the property owners. I was in charge of you."

I tilt my chin and look at Jackson, liking the idea of him being in charge of me. "I'll be there. I'm thankful you're keeping me in the loop."

"Me too, and we will." Jackson takes my left hand and kisses the back of it, pausing for a moment.

"I guess I'll see you on Saturday?" I ask.

He hops off the tailgate.

"Sure will. I'm not gone yet." He uncrosses my legs, lifts me by my waist, and puts my feet on the ground. He holds me long enough for me to feel him harden behind the fabric of his jeans. I take full advantage of the moment, stand on my tiptoes, and wrap my arms around his neck.

Just as I'd hoped, he slides his arms around my lower back and embraces me, knowing full well my dress is short enough to allow my white lace panties to peek out. As he places his chin on my shoulder, he stiffens and deeply inhales, leaving me to hope he'll be thinking of me later tonight.

∼

After, I pop by the cabin, change into something more casual, and head to Caitlyn's where I'll meet up with the girls. With one foot in the dirt and one on the bottom step, I hear a rustling of leaves and the snap of a branch. I hold my breath and freeze, keys dangling in my hands, and peer into the surrounding woods. The sun is behind the trees casting shadows, making it difficult to see past the tree line. I'd be a fool to think large animals aren't living in these woods. Knowing this and actually encountering them are two different things.

My father used to have a wildlife camera attached to one of the trees at the beginning of the driveway. My brother and I would ask relentlessly for him to take out the SIM card and show us if any animals had been spotted. We'd be wide-eyed upon seeing a photo of a massive black bear sauntering past in the early-morning hours or a mama bear and her cubs strolling through the forest. I recall being intrigued but terrified.

I'm not naive to the fact that creatures roam around while we're away or sleeping, but it spooks me out. My parents did an excellent job of keeping our fears in check and reminding us never to leave food or trash outside. Back then, when we walked down our street to the lake, we'd always have a bear bell on one of our bags and we'd make as much noise as we could to inform the bears of our presence. Black bears can be dangerous but will usually retreat at the sound of humans. Most of the time, a bear moves on without a human ever realizing they were there.

I stay frozen and hear another stick break off in the distance. My truck is ten yards away; I calculate how fast I can run to the door. I remind myself there is nothing to be afraid of —just make my presence known and go!

"Hey, bear! I hear you! I'm coming down from these stairs and heading to my truck," I yell into the woods. "Did you hear me? You should stay where you are because I'm pretty dangerous. We can be friends as long as you stay put and I get to my truck. OK?"

My fists clench by my sides, my shoulders hike near my ears, and I figure it's now or never. "I'm running to my truck. I hope we understand each other." Here goes nothing.

I clap wildly and hit the ground running. "I'm going. Almost there. Don't you move!" I yank the handle, jump into the front seat, and slam the door, almost smashing my foot in the process. Crossing my arms over the steering wheel, I peer out into the woods and slow my breathing.

A slight movement catches my eye, and I concentrate on the tree to my left. I sit in complete silence as a white-tailed doe and two fawns scamper across the path and into the adjacent woods.

*Bambi! And his family!*

My relieved laugh dissolves when I think about the reality of this situation—I'll bet Green Breeze wouldn't give a shit about killing Bambi a second time.

∿

As I pull into Caitlyn's, it doesn't appear crowded. The front light mounted near the entrance is on and the open sign hangs on the windowless door. The glow of table lamps illuminates each window and strings of twinkly lights hang from the patio umbrellas. I open the creaky wooden door and am transported into a traditional Irish pub.

The owners have outdone themselves. Black-and-white vintage photos of various Irish landmarks hang on the dark brown walls; old street signs and Guinness pint glasses decorate a long rail mounted around the pub's perimeter. A well-stocked mahogany bar sits along the back wall with six or seven high-tops in the center of the room, each with a dim light, and several booths along the wall are crowded with customers sitting on dark green cushions. Caitlyn's exudes warmth and coziness.

Madison beckons me from one of the center high-top tables.

"Hey! How are you girls? I'm so excited we decided to do this," I say, choosing the stool to my right.

"Oh my gosh, me too! I was so thrilled to meet both of you the other day. Having fun peeps will make this job fun. Don't you think? I mean, kids are great, but working with friends is what gets you through the day." Brooke finally stops to take in air and smiles, looking from Madison to me and back. Maybe it's our expression or lack of response, but either way, she continues, "I know, I know what you're thinking. I'm a lot. I'm sorry, I've always been this way. I get even chattier when I'm nervous."

Madison stifles her laugh and says, "Brooke, you're good. Just remember to breathe. I don't want you to pass out and fall off your stool."

Brooke's nose crinkles and she covers her mouth to contain her giggle.

"I'm just happy you guys invited me. Having a few friends around here is awesome. I love this town, but everyone is so spread out. It makes it difficult to meet people. Where's Shannon?"

Madison speaks up. "She canceled last minute. Not something she usually does, but given the circumstances, I'll let it slide."

"You don't think it's because I'm here, do you?" I ask Madison.

"No! Definitely not. Why would you ever think that?"

*Open mouth, insert foot. I need to think before I speak.*

"Oh, I met her brother the other day, and I thought maybe she was uneasy or something."

"No way! You're dating Shannon's brother? That's amazing. You've been here for such a short time and you've already got yourself a man. Impressive."

"Brooke, slow down." I shake my head and smile. "I'm not dating Jackson. I mean, I would, but things are complicated."

"Whatever you say, Solia. But if you ever need a wingwoman, I'm your girl."

"I'll keep that in mind. Thanks."

The waitress comes over with menus and takes our drink order. I scan the selection and we decide on several appetizers.

One of the wooden stools at the bar turns around and a bearded man wearing a Harley-Davidson T-shirt, arms covered in tattoos, stumbles to our table with a beer in his hand. "Ladies! Where's Shannon?"

I don't have the slightest clue who this man is or how he knows Shannon. I scan Brooke's and Madison's expressions hoping they do.

"Shannon's not here, Richard." Madison stands from her stool, crosses her arms, and stares directly at the man who is now leaning his elbow on the table.

"You're spilling your beer," I say, pointing at the wet spots absorbing into the tips of his work boots.

"And what of it? Who the hell are you?" He looks at me, righting his glass and slamming it down.

I slide my stool closer to Brooke as the energy shifts.

"Take a hike, Richard. She's not here, and we have nothing to say to you," Madison says while she searches the restaurant behind us. I turn around just as the bartender sets the drinks in his hands on the counter. He lifts the bar flap and heads over.

"All right, Richard, let's get something to eat." Smiling apologetically, the bartender puts his arm around Richard and attempts to move him.

"I ain't doing nothing wrong. Just chatting with these ladies, trying to figure out where my wife is." The barman rolls his eyes and guides Richard away from us.

Madison returns to her seat. "Unfreakingbelievable. That guy needs to learn when it's time to quit. Sorry, that was an unpleasant, unexpected scene."

"I thought Shannon was going through a divorce?" I ask.

"She is, and now you see why. Richard is a piece of shit. Shannon tried so hard to straighten him out, but he's hopeless. They were high school sweethearts, and everyone in town thought they'd make it. It's so sad what booze can do to someone. But this is her story to tell. I shouldn't have spewed all those details. You guys will get to know Shannon soon enough. She deserves better. I wish he would let her go. He's hanging on for dear life. It's kind of scary," Madison says, picking at her nails.

"Oh my goodness, that is so sad. I love high school sweethearts. They're so cute. I always thought I'd marry mine. Shannon will find someone. She's so nice and so pretty. Do you think she's ready to date? How is she handling this?" Brooke asks, her hands placed over her heart.

"She's fine, Brooke. Seriously. She's ready to move on. She wants to put this behind her. And no, she's not ready to get out there yet."

"Wow, that's heavy. I'm not gonna lie—Richard gives me scary vibes. They should stop serving him." As if on cue,

Richard stands alongside another man in a biker jacket, and the muscles in my chest tighten watching them get closer.

"Nothing but a bunch of bitches. I'll go make sure she's OK, seeing you three couldn't give a shit where she is."

They head to the exit, rendering us speechless. Seconds later, we hear the revving of their bikes in the parking lot as our waitress arrives with a tray of steaming food. The smell snaps our focus away from the door and to one another.

"I don't like the sound of that." Brooke's eyes cloud with tears.

"I'll take care of this." Madison storms to the exit faster than I can get my thoughts together.

I leave the table and run after Madison. Whatever is about to unfold was not part of tonight's plans.

# 21

*Jackson*

Leaving Solia behind in that parking lot felt like slowly ripping off a Band-Aid. Her legs crossed on the tailgate drove me wild. I don't know if she's aware how insane her body appears in that white dress. Her sexy shoulders held nothing but a thin white strap, forcing her cleavage front and center.

It didn't go unnoticed how her dress rose just enough when she hugged me to reveal irresistible white lace panties. I'm a fraud, pretending to be strong enough to keep my sexual urges at bay. I want to avoid hurting her at all costs, but I'd be lying if I didn't want to say "Fuck it, let me have you for three weeks. I'll show you exactly how much I want you." But I need to lead with my head, the one resting on my shoulders.

Later in the week, I'm driving down Main Street, annoyed to see Green Breeze Enterprises making their presence known. Two of their trucks pass me going in the opposite direction. This company doesn't plan on leaving anytime soon. At the corner of Main and Summer, I spot several land surveyors with the GB logo on their chests. They're assembling their tripods and measuring equipment. My blood boils. The audacity of these guys thinking they're going to pull this off.

I stop to get an update from Gerry and let him know I spoke to Solia. Leaving the store as I'm entering is my vacation-mode sister.

"Hey, little brother," she calls out, running over. "Where have you been hiding?"

"You know where to find me. My usual triangle—home, work, store, repeat."

"Speaking of work, I had a teacher meet-up. You didn't tell me Solia is under consideration for a job at Meriden Elementary. It surprised me to see her. She's great, by the way. She hit it off with Madison and their new team member Brooke."

"I don't know how I missed telling you that. These past few weeks have been a blur. Did she get the job?"

"I'll be shocked if she doesn't. Everyone loves her. Come on, Jackson. You need to stay on top of this info."

I'm a complete asshole for not asking how the event went. My sister knows me better than anyone, but what I don't want to get into is what's going on between Solia and me.

"She's pretty, huh? Have you noticed?" she teases, blatantly searching for more than I'm willing to offer.

"Oh, she's pretty, all right. And smart and funny. You name it, she's got it."

"There's a noticeable difference in you. And I'm not the only one who can tell. Several people around town have commented. You know how it works around here, everyone in everybody's business. Of course, they mean well. People love seeing you smile again."

"OK, Shannon, you got me. She makes me smile, and yes, I'm in a better place than I have been in a long time. But it's complicated, and I don't want to drag her into my mess. Months ago, I asked Dad to make room for me in New York. I poured my damn heart out, so he understands how important it is for me to get out of this town. I can't continue to let the accident define who I am. I can't bring Solia down with me. But what I can do is help her keep her family's land safe."

"That's honorable of you, Jackson. And I'm sure she will appreciate any help you and the rest of the town give her. But is it just the cabin you're trying to save?"

I pause at Shannon's words. Of course I care for Solia. Seeing her happy and fulfilling her dreams is something I want to be a part of. Maybe deep down, I'm trying to stay connected in any way I can. "I'm being a good guy, believe it or not. If I can't be with her, I can at least help her live the life she's seeking."

"Oh, I know you're a good guy. I've never questioned that for a second. When you're alone tonight, I want you to identify what or who is stopping you from being happy."

"Yes, old wise one. I will do as you say." I give her a gentle shove as I head into the store to catch up with Gerry.

Like clockwork, Gerry is at the end of a register line, bagging for a customer who appears to have bought more birdseed than the store can hold on the shelves. Gerry is breaking a sweat trying to squeeze the birdseed into the bags. No task is ever beneath this store owner. He is an all-hands-on-deck kind of guy, which is why everyone loves to work here. Some people started at Raubuchon's as teenagers, then found careers outside the store, but still work a shift or two because they love being around Gerry.

"Hey, Gerry, do you have time for a break?"

"Sure do, my friend. Let me just finish bagging this for Mrs. Jones, and I'm all yours."

"Sounds good. I'll meet you outside."

After a few minutes, Gerry exits following Mrs. Jones, carrying her bags of birdseed. Ever the ladies' man, he loads her car and meanders back in my direction.

"What's the good word, Jackson?"

"I met with Solia."

"I heard."

"Seriously, Gerry. You are the goddamn mayor around here. Of course, you already know. Do I need to fill you in on our conversation, or do you already know that too?"

Gerry is all smiles, knowing full well I'm messing with him. "Right, I see what you're getting at. I don't go around seeking other people's business—it finds me. What can I say?"

"Sure, sure. Well, Solia was all ears. She wants to save her place as badly as I want to save the orchard. It's ironic the two of us have found ourselves in similar situations. She's thrilled we have a lawyer on board. I told her he would be here on Saturday. The only thing she needs to do, which she said she'd get on right away, is inform her parents."

"Yeah, I do know that part."

"Of course you do, Gerry."

"What's new on your end?"

"Let's see ... every single property owner I've talked to wants to fight. No one is even considering selling to these bastards, except Earl and possibly the two others I haven't gotten to yet."

"Your grandpa has it in his head that he'd rather leave a fortune than a field of apples to his family. He figures you can do what you want with the money, but the apples will be nothing but a headache. Getting older is difficult—wouldn't I know? And part of him wants this chapter to end on his terms. Which, I've got to admit, I understand, but it's not the right call."

"This is my fault, Gerry. I can't get my head on straight. Ever since the accident, my world here hasn't been the same. I need to start a new chapter. I guess I've always known Grandpa wanted me to take over the orchard, and I hate letting him down. But now my father is counting on me, and

I'm not going to disappoint him. He went out on a limb to get me into the fold at the cider company. I can't screw up."

"I hear you. You're a good man, Jackson. Just remember, either way you slice it, you are going to disappoint someone. The one person you shouldn't cut short is yourself. Remember that. And while you're at it, ask yourself why you need a new zip code to write a new chapter."

Exhaustion washes over me. I've done more deep thinking in the past month than I have in my entire life. "OK, Gerry. Got it. What's my therapy copay today?" I jab his ribs.

"You need to pay in poster board and Sharpie markers."

"What the hell are you talking about?"

"You are to bring at least fifty poster boards and enough markers for everyone at the meeting this Saturday. We don't have enough in stock and another shipment doesn't arrive in time."

"Ahh, clever. OK, I can do that."

"Excellent. Oh, and Mike met with some members of our zoning board the other day. You need to get your girl, Solia, to obtain a copy of her plat map from the town clerk. I don't want to tip off these bigwigs that we are up to something. Have her grab a copy and bring it to the meeting on Saturday. Mike thinks her family's cabin abuts acres of conservation land, and there's no way in hell Green Breeze will fight the state for the rights to that. Every bit helps. We want to get all our ducks in a row before we reveal our hand."

"I can manage that. But are you sure you don't want to tell her yourself? Seeing that you seem to know what's going on with her, anyway." I smile knowingly at Gerry.

"Nah, I'll let you handle that, pretty boy. Oh, and by the way. You hear your brother-in-law got picked up again last night?"

"Richard?" My nails dig into my skin in my tightly rolled fists.

"Drunk again, causing a scene. Luckily, Nate was parked in the middle school parking lot when Madison called him from Caitlyn's. That guy needs to get himself straightened out quick before he ends up behind bars." And with that, Gerry turns and shuffles back into the store.

As if we don't have enough to deal with right now. Fucking Richard.

Before pulling out of the parking lot, I notice an incoming text from my father.

DAD

All good there?

JACKSON

Yeah. I'm working with Gerry to figure out this wind farm mess.

Good. It's a bunch of bullshit. Hey, I need you here for a few days to check some things out before you move. This won't be a problem, will it?

His message gives me pause. Asking me to leave Meriden early is a reality check. I have so much to do here—the meeting on Saturday, then the town council meeting, and I want to meet up with the guys again. I haven't honestly admitted to myself how great it was to hang out, just like old times. And Greg has become a trusted friend—not seeing him every day will be strange. I've been meaning to get out with him for a beer too.

I'm being split down the middle.

Traveling to New York for a few days won't be plausible. I have way too much going on here. I need to wrap things up so I can start fresh in New York.

Sorry, Dad, too many loose ends to fit in a trip.
I'll be there soon enough.

. . .

No other reply. My father can be a hothead; I don't want this plan going sideways before I even get there. However, it isn't lost on me that I said no to turning the first page of my new chapter in New York for the unfinished chapter I'm writing here in Meriden.

~

I struggle to fall asleep. The air is comfortable and quiet, but all I can hear are the conflicting arguments bouncing around in my head. After listening to Shannon and Gerry today, my brain is foggier than ever. I'm a hundred percent certain they want what's best for me, but I've thoroughly considered the decision to leave.

*Haven't I?*

Pushing those thoughts out of my mind is next to impossible, so I start adding more to exhaust myself. Finally, when enough wind turbines have rotated in my head, my tired eyes grow heavy and sleep is upon me.

~

The farm is busy throughout the week. My grandparents stay inside more than usual because of the sweltering heat. I make it a point to check on them each day after I've completed the farm work. Filling them in on the real estate lawyer and the meeting with the property owners is a little uninspiring. As always, they listen intently, and they seem enthusiastic at the prospect of property owners maintaining the right to their land, but their reaction didn't convince me I was swaying them in the direction I need.

As Thursday comes to a close, I run into Lucas as I pull the tractor into the barn. "Hey, how's the corn looking?" Corn is a new addition to our fields this year. We planted a small plot to see how it would work out.

"The sweet corn is looking good. I'm keeping an eye out for insect infestation, but so far, so good. I'm not sure we'll want to go much bigger next year, but we'll see what happens. Assuming we're still here next year."

Hearing these words from Lucas, someone who's been with us for years and relies on us for his livelihood, is a crushing blow. "Listen, I don't know what's going to happen. I know I'm leaving, but I don't want to see this place left to wind developers, that's for sure. I'm working real hard to fight this. I won't sit by on the sidelines."

"I wasn't expecting anything different, Jackson, but Earl's been dropping hints here and there. So, I'm keeping it real."

"Sure, I get it. I'll keep you in the loop."

As I retreat to the house to check on my grandparents, I spot a soccer ball rolling down the drive in my peripheral view. Breaking into a jog, I stop it before it ends up all the way down the hill. I hold the heavily worn ball, turn in the direction from which it came, and spot a woman running toward me in an electric-pink tank top. She looks to be in her late twenties and is coming toward me at a full sprint. As she approaches, her eyes meet the soccer ball, and she stops and bends in half, hands on her knees, back heaving with deep breaths.

"Hey, thanks so much. We live up the road there," she says between gasps, standing slowly and pointing at the steep incline, "and my kids can't seem to keep the ball in our yard. Sorry about that."

"You bought the O'Briens' old place, huh? Sorry I haven't had a chance to introduce myself." I smile and hand her the ball. "Glad I could grab it. You would've had quite a run if it had kept rolling."

"Thanks so much. We lived in the town over, but we're loving Meriden. The closer we can get to the lake, the better. Is this your land here?"

"Sure is. Well, it's my family's land. I'm Jackson. Nice to meet you."

She gives me a firm handshake. "Katie. Nice to meet you. Do you have any children?"

Somewhat surprised by her question, I squint in response. "No, I don't."

"Oh, just curious. I joined the Meriden Youth Soccer Board. Trying to jump right in and they seemed desperate for help. And they've got that wind company, Green Breeze Enterprise, partnering with them. It's not a terrible thing. We made out in the deal, but I'm curious if you know anything. They offered a thousand dollars to print their logo on the back of a team jersey from each division. On top of sponsorship, we're one of the property owners considering the deal they're offering."

"Didn't you just buy the place? Why would you ever do that?" I pause. "Sorry. I didn't mean to sound so rude. We received a letter, too, but there's no way in hell I'm letting this happen here."

"Trust me, it's not what we want either. We've only just settled in and love it. The only reason we deal with northern winters is because the beauty is unparalleled. But as luck would have it, my husband lost his job a month to the day after we had our closing, and we've got three young children." She looks at the beat-up soccer ball. "Leaving is the last thing we want and wind turbines on our land sounds awful, but land is something we have. And money is something we don't. This company is offering a lifeline, one I'm not sure we can turn down." She looks desperate and my heart breaks. This company is pulling on the heartstrings of good people. It just isn't right.

"I understand why you are considering it, but it'll destroy this area, plain and simple."

"It's an unfortunate predicament to be in. I heard there's supposed to be an update at the next town council meeting. See you there?"

"Yeah, I'll be there. Good luck." I dip my head and walk to my truck. I decide to skip talking with my grandparents. I know we have a problem on our hands if some property owners are considering the deal.

# 22

*Solia*

It's not going to happen, Mia.

MIA

Another one bites the dust. 🙁

When are you coming back to visit? I could use a little more Mia time.

Actually . . . I've been messaging with Tyler and was hoping to see you both soon.

Why am I not surprised?

I have a few vacation days I still need to take this summer. How's this Sunday night till Tuesday?

I'll be here.

K, I'll let Ty know.

Seriously? Ty? You already have nicknames ...

Never too soon. TTYL!

Nothing should surprise me when it comes to Mia. But I guess I'd rather her be in New Hampshire dating one of Jackson's friends than swiping right on another weirdo stranger. Having her come for a couple days is just what I need.

~

Looking at my watch, I figure I have some time to head out on the water for a quick go-round. One of my goals this summer is to try launching my board at different spots on the lake to see it in its entirety. Newfound isn't large in comparison to others in the area, but on a paddleboard, it takes quite a bit longer to circumnavigate. There are only so many miles I can paddle before my arms grow too exhausted, so launching from different places allows me to see new sections.

Today I figure I'll try Gray Lodge Marina. I have an hour to ride out and back to make it in time to the meeting Gerry called with the Meriden residents who are fighting the turbine farm. When I arrive, numerous trucks are lined up to back their boats down the launch. It's a small marina, but a popular one. Not only are the regulars here, but lots of day trippers are also launching or filling with gas.

The marina also rents boats for day use. This got hugely popular a few years back when everyone became more interested in the great outdoors. The lucky ones find a spot in the lot and hop onto their boat already in the slip. They turn the key and go. For a beautiful Saturday on Newfound Lake, crowds are to be expected. Fortunately for me, there is never a wait to launch a small watercraft.

I lift my board from my truck bed and pass by the people who are loading their boats. Kids run around with Popsicles, moms wrangle babies, and dads sling coolers over their shoulders, ready to enjoy this beautiful day. I'm exhausted watching as I pass by.

I glide my board straight into the cool lake water, tighten my life jacket around my chest, and kneel. I dip my paddle in and with small, gentle strokes, I steer through the channel between the boats lining the marina. A group of young guys are loading a speedboat with coolers, and I reflect on Jackson's story about Trinity's accident. One of these boats sitting here is his. I wonder if he bothered to shrink-wrap and winterize it.

My heart breaks all over again at the thought of what they endured that day. They experienced more than anyone should have to bear, and it seems Jackson can no longer see the beauty of this lake. It has affected Jackson and his family's ties to this community. He's running as a way of coping, but it's at the risk of his family losing their orchard.

Holding on to the board with both hands, I inch my feet forward, stand, and continue into the open water. I wish Jackson could experience the beauty of this place the way I do. Maybe then he could remember.

I quicken my pace and try to make this a workout, hoping to get my mind off Jackson. I push myself toward the east into one cove after another, paddling around the perimeter and working up a sweat. The coves are quiet, except for a few boats leaving their docks for the day. Passengers wave as they slowly pass by, mindful of the no-wake zone. Families and couples dot the shoreline, setting chairs and coolers in semicircles. All seems well around Newfound Lake.

It wasn't long ago  my father taught me how to fish over the edge of a kayak. I always envisioned passing on this knowledge to my own children.

Retracing my strokes back to the marina, I notice how crowded the shoreline and water are. As I've gotten older and hopefully wiser, I now believe the best time to be out on the lake is when everyone else is sleeping. There's nothing more satisfying than being the first one to launch as the sun rises.

Upon entering the channel surrounding the marina, I notice most of the boat slips are vacant. Mindful of the time, I hurry back to the cabin. I can't be late for the meeting. This town is offering to help us, and I will not keep them waiting.

My truck bumps along Main Street, and I'm astounded at the traffic. People should be heading toward the lake on a day this gorgeous, not away from it. *What's going on?*

I finally reach town hall and am confused by the number of people ahead of me waiting to turn into the same lot. Maybe something else is going on that I don't know about?

If I wait in this line, there's no way I'll make it in time. I signal to the right and pull into the full-service gas station. Swinging around to the last spot, I park and jog across to town hall.

A huge crowd has gathered in the parking lot. I stand corrected—I thought they mailed only a few owners letters of interest. There are at least a hundred and fifty people here. As I walk up the concrete steps, an older gentleman tips his head and holds the door for me.

"Thank you, sir."

"You are very welcome, my dear. Anyone here to fight this is a friend of mine," he says with a kind smile and sincere expression.

I scan the crowded room and see people ages five to ninety. Only a few rows of wooden chairs have been positioned in front of the small stage. A group has formed an assembly line next to a hallway leading to a closet that stores the remaining chairs. One by one, chairs are passed down the line and set up, creating row after row.

I quickly fix my pocketbook across my body and join the back of the assembly line. As I take the tenth or eleventh chair and form a new row, I turn to the stage to find both Gerry and Jackson looking my way. As if caught committing a crime, Jackson startles and Gerry throws his arm up and waves.

I can't help but laugh and walk back to rejoin the line.

Soon, the rickety chairs are out of the closet, and people find seats. Those without one line the wood-paneled walls. Most people talk passionately about the wind farm, at least those conversations I overhear. I walk toward the back and lean against the wall, spotting Gerry on the stage. I discreetly search for Jackson, but he's nowhere to be found.

Gerry typically dresses casually in a T-shirt and jeans with a store apron, but today he has on a short-sleeve button-down shirt tucked into a pair of loose slacks, held up by a wide, brown leather belt.

*Impressive, Gerry. Quite professional.*

Next to Gerry is another older gentleman I've never seen before. He has to be in his midseventies, guessing by his thick white hair and deep wrinkles. The intensity this man exudes suffuses the gathering to the back wall. I figure this must be the lawyer Jackson mentioned. He looks like he can handle himself in a courtroom. Broad shoulders, a wide jaw, powerful, but there's also a kindness in the energy around him. There must be, though. If this is indeed the lawyer, he came out of retirement to help a bunch of strangers save their land.

As I'm sizing up this guy, Gerry steps to the podium.

"Good morning, everyone! Can I have your attention?" Despite the volume of the microphone, the chatter continues. "Ladies and gentlemen, we have a lot to discuss. Let's get quiet and organize ourselves." The heated conversations simmer to a murmur while Gerry stands idle waiting for the room to be quiet enough for him to talk again. "Thank you, everyone, for coming out today. As you know, we are here because of Green Breeze Enterprises. For those of you who were not in attendance at the town hall meeting last week, these folks have their sights set on purchasing multiple properties in town upon which to build large wind farms."

In response, a bearded man from the front stands and yells, "Bullshit." His anger permeates the whole room.

"Who do these assholes think they are?" someone shouts from the back.

"OK, OK, I hear you and share your frustration on the matter, so much so, I organized this meeting to see what we can accomplish together. So, hear me out. First thing is, most of you who are here today are not property owners of lots that interest Green Breeze—yet. After speaking to many of you at the store and throughout town, I understand your frustration and can empathize with you wanting to keep Meriden in its current state. I listened to the facts proving there'd be an increase in traffic, commercialism, and the devastating effects this could have on wildlife."

"Damn right!" an audience member shouts from somewhere along the wall. Gerry continues.

"This week, we have an opportunity to have our voices heard. A council meeting is scheduled to happen right here in town hall. Most of us don't bother with those meetings until they matter to us, and this one must matter to us. A representative from Green Breeze is on the agenda this week. I'm hearing they're going to provide an update on the project. Typically, the meetings start with the listening of public comments. Anyone can take a minute or two to express their concerns about the proposed wind farms. After talking to Mike —shoot, Mike, come on over here."

The older gentleman I spotted earlier approaches Gerry from a seat behind him. "Folks, I am getting carried away. I've been planning what to say for weeks, but after seeing how many of you turned out today, I got a little ahead of myself. My apologies, Mike. This is my good friend, Mike Kelley. You old-timers like me will remember the days people feared this shark in a courtroom. Well, word traveled about Green Breeze and what they are trying to do to Meriden, and he wants to help. He's lived here his whole life, and, well, let me allow him to speak for himself." Gerry gestures toward the podium, backing up as Mike steps forward.

"Thanks, old buddy. Hello, everyone. Gerry is correct. There isn't anything I thought could drag me out of retirement until I heard this windblown bullshit."

"Hell yeah!" a younger resident yells.

"That's right, my friend. Roots run deep in these parts, and we don't want our land turned into a metal-monster factory. To my knowledge, six property owners were mailed letters from this green energy company. It's the company's understanding these key properties are the most advantageous for them to buy or lease to generate the electricity they are seeking. I'm going to assume many of you attended the town hall meeting where they listed the benefits of green energy and wind turbines. Regardless of how strongly you oppose this project, it'll be a fight.

"As of today, it's my understanding we have four property owners in obvious objection to the project, one very much undecided, and one, unfortunately, is leaning toward accepting the Green Breeze deal as it will be in the best interests of their family. What we will not do, folks, is turn on each other. This will not become a battle of property owners. I'll support those four owners and their commitment to save their land. I cannot represent the owners who are considering the deal, but I ask you to respect your fellow neighbors and trust they're doing what they believe is right for their families. We'll work together with what we can control.

"After speaking with Gerry, most of us aren't interested in hearing any more about this deal. You all just want them to keep their hands off your land. And it's also my understanding you want Meriden to stay untouched and beautiful. I'm with you on that, and I'm here to help make that happen."

The room erupts with applause.

Mike waits, hands raised to quiet the crowd. "So, here is what I need you to do." He clears his throat, and the room seems to sit on the edge of their seats. "I need everyone willing to speak during the public comment section to write up a few talking points beforehand and be confident with what you're going to say. We don't want yelling or obscenities—we want to be professional, to make it clear why we don't want this company coming into Meriden. Also, there is strength in numbers. Talk to your family, your friends, your neighbors, anyone who will listen and see if they will come to support us at the town council meeting on Tuesday at four p.m.

"I'll be working on the legal side of things in the meantime. For those of you who received the first round of letters, I'll be in contact in the coming weeks. If there is anything I should be informed of regarding your property specifically, please contact me. I'll run a property search on each parcel, but the more information I have collected, the better. We want to find as many reasons as possible to send this company packing.

"When Gerry wraps up today, I'll walk around with my card for those who received the letter and anyone else who has questions for me. Be sure you don't leave without it. Let's stay positive, folks. We are stronger together than we would ever be apart."

"Right on!" says a man from somewhere in the crowd.

The energy in the room shifts from angry to hopeful. Mr. Kelley seems to be the real deal, a guy we can depend on. I'm so thankful Gerry was able to organize this.

Gerry is back behind the podium. "Thanks, Mike. I can speak for all of us when I say we are extremely grateful for your time and expertise. While many of us love Meriden, we don't have a clue how to interpret the legality or the land rights involved in these types of situations. So, thank you for being here." He turns around and gives Mike a nod. It's clear they have years of memories and experiences between them from growing up on the land.

"Besides giving Mike anything and everything you find or learn relevant to your property in the coming weeks, I hope you'll stay and make signs to post around town and outside the meeting. Everyone should arrive around five to protest outside next week's meeting. Nothing crazy, totally civil, a show of support for the landowners who oppose the proposed wind project. We can hold signs and people may stop and ask questions, but the point is to state our presence and make it clear that we will not let this company come here and ruin our small town. So, let's make some signs and get the word out, folks." Applause, hooting, and hollering follow as Gerry steps away.

I stand a little taller, clap feverishly, and eat up the enthusiasm Gerry conjures from the crowd. I'm so thankful for Mike's time and talent, and most of all for the community support. Tears sting the corner of my eyes. I grab a tissue from my pocket and spot a pair of work boots I wouldn't forget anywhere.

I look and find myself in a soundproof space. I'm not sure how long we stand frozen, but our trance is broken when I hear footsteps walking up behind Jackson. Having no luck locating a tissue, I quickly wipe my face with my palms. I sense the worry in Jackson's expression and try to reassure him with a smile and a slight tilt of my head.

"Guys, that was amazing. I can't believe how many people are here!" I say to Gerry and Mr. Kelley, sneaking another glance at Jackson. "Hi, Gerry. Mr. Kelley, it's a pleasure to meet you. I'm Solia Anderson."

"Ah, Ms. Anderson of the Anderson cabin. The pleasure is mine. I hear you returned to the family cabin with the intent to make this your permanent home."

"Yes, sir, I sure have. I never would've imagined this as one of the hurdles I'd have to jump, though."

"We can agree on that. I'll do my best to help Meriden stay as it should. I'm going to bet no one ever told you this, but I was a friend of your grandparents some time ago. They were good people, but I'm sure I don't have to tell you that."

"No, sir, you don't. No one better than them. It would devastate them to know that a wind farm might surround the cabin, so whatever you can do to help eliminate that threat, I am so thankful."

"You bet, Solia. Here's my card. Call me if you need or think of anything." He and Gerry turn to walk away, leaving Jackson and me alone.

Just as Jackson and I look at each other, Gerry turns back around and says, "Sorry, Solia—any luck with that showerhead?" He winks and off he goes.

*Are you serious, Gerry? This guy doesn't miss a beat.*

I can't help but laugh and smile in response. This old man knows exactly what he's doing.

Jackson leans toward me, so close I inhale his intoxicating scent. As the noise seems to grow louder, he leans in. "Do you need help with something?"

"The outdoor showerhead is acting up. Nothing urgent. I'm sure I can figure it out. That's what Google is for." I am breathless trying to articulate a complete sentence while standing next to Jackson.

"Let me help, seriously. It'll take me ten minutes. Honestly, it's no bother. Maybe I can swing by later in the week before the town council meeting." He flashes white teeth as he flips his freshly washed hair out of his dreamy eyes.

I can fix the damn showerhead myself, but watching him fix it would be a hell of a lot more enjoyable. "If you don't mind, that would be awesome." I stare at him and hope he'll come soon.

"Sure thing."

Unable to hide my excitement, I zigzag through the crowd, smiling at my neighbors as I exit. Thankfully, polite drivers from both directions stop to allow me to cross Main Street. I can't remember ever seeing downtown this busy. More traffic means more business for the local shops and restaurants, and for a small town that relies on summer tourism, this is sensational.

Hopping onto my truck's running board, I slide into the driver's seat. I promised myself I'd call my parents as soon as the residents' meeting was over. Knowing this will be a tough conversation, I figure I won't even wait until I'm back at the cabin. I'll sit right here and get it over with.

I slip the key into the ignition and the engine roars to life. A cool, calming breeze pushes the stale, musty air out as I lower the windows. I shut the car off when the windows open and tilt my seat back slightly to get comfy.

I figure my mom will answer the quickest, so I call her. My assumptions are correct when her cheery voice blares through the speaker, "Solia, hi!"

"Hi, Mom. Am I catching you at a good time?"

"Anytime is a good time, honey. What's up?"

"Is Dad there?"

"Oh boy. Should I get him? Are you OK? Did something happen? Do you need us to get in the car, because we can … damn, I knew this was the wrong decision."

"Mom! I'm fine. Nothing is wrong. I figure it'll be easier to speak to both of you rather than having you relay the story to Dad. If he's there, you can just put it on speaker."

"Well, that's a relief. Hold on, let me find the button. Solia? Are you still there? Ben, Solia is on the phone and wants to talk to us. No, no, she's fine. What? Just come here and have a seat. Can you hear us, dear?"

The two of them are just too much, making a simple task harder than it needs to be. "Yes, Mom. I can hear you. Hi, Dad."

"Hi, honey. It's so good to hear your voice. Are you doing well? How's the cabin?"

"I'm doing well, and the cabin is still standing, if that's what you mean." I hear a snicker from my mother.

"I'm sure we would've heard if the place burned to the ground, Solia."

"Right, well, anyway, there is something pretty important I need to talk to you guys about. A few weeks ago, I received a letter from this company—"

My dad cuts in. "Honey, instead of torturing yourself, I'll stop you and let you know we already have the facts. We understand what Green Breeze wants."

Stunned, I sit back in my seat and try to find the words, but my father continues.

"Solia, we've known for a week. You've got to remember that even though we aren't up there anymore, we still have quite a few connections. And these phones make it easy to find things out."

"Why didn't you say anything to me?" I ask, more confused than ever.

"Honey, your father and I know how strongly you believe you can survive there on your own. An old friend gave us a call. I wanted to see how long it would take for you to fill us in. This is a big deal, Solia. Your father and I were ready to sell, so this isn't a battle we are willing to fight. It might be perfect timing and even more money than we were planning on."

*Go figure. Just when I'm one step ahead, I step into quicksand.*

My father speaks next. "We certainly had hoped if we were to sell the cabin, another family would spend years there making memories. To have a wind farm installed is not what we ever would've imagined. When we received the call enlisting our help and asking our opinions, your mother and I told the Green Breeze people that this is now your fight. We'll hold up our end of our original bargain, but that's the only thing we can promise. Most of this will be out of our control."

Tears fill my eyes listening to my father's words. I want the cabin. I want a new life here, but this wind project has me completely rattled. I guess I'd planned on them being in my corner to help me figure this out. I never actually considered the possibility of standing alone, taking charge of this situation.

Listening to myself, I sound ridiculous. I came here to be independent, to start fresh. I'm a fucking twenty-six-year-old woman, for god's sake. I can't expect my parents to dig me out of every difficult problem that comes my way, especially if I want to be a homeowner.

"Honey?"

"I'm here, and I don't know why I didn't think of the possibility of someone telling you. Sorry you didn't hear the news from me. I should've told you sooner."

"Maybe, but like I said, this is up to you now. We've added your name to the property deed, so you can decide what's going to happen with Green Breeze. Either way, we will discuss the financial aspects, but the decision is ultimately yours."

"Dad, I will not let this happen. There is no way I'm going for this deal, and you shouldn't either."

"Solia, Dad just told you, we are not dealing with this—you are. You may have to come to terms with the fact that it may not work out. Dad and I decided it is time to move on to another chapter in our lives, too, so this is your battle to fight. Do you even have a job yet?"

My mother's words cut like a knife. "Actually, I interviewed and was hired for a third-grade position in the fall. So, yes, Mom, I do have a job. Maybe you could back off a little and have faith in me for once."

"Solia, watch your tone." She clears her throat. "That's wonderful news. It seems you've checked one necessary box. Good job. I'll let you speak with your father now. I hope you're planning ahead for the winter weather too."

My dad takes it off speaker, so it's just the two of us talking. "It's great to hear Mike Kelley is stepping up. He's a good man, Solia. He's Meriden born and bred, like your grandparents. If there is anyone you want on your side, he's the guy. If it were us fighting this, he's the lawyer I'd call. Let Mike and Gerry take the lead. You're in expert hands over there. Just keep us in the loop. There may be some property owners who are out to make a buck and won't think twice about leasing their land, or worse yet, selling it. It wouldn't surprise me."

I'm glad my father is confident enough to allow me to take this on. "Thanks. I know you weren't sure I should come here and handle everything, never mind adding this to the picture. But I'm doing the right thing, Dad. I'll do whatever I can to get this company out of Meriden. We had a resident meeting and ..."

"Honey ..."

"Let me guess. You already know."

"Sure do. I haven't heard how it went, but I knew Gerry scheduled it. Did it go well?"

"Ask Gerry."

"Don't you be picking on my buddy, Solia. If you ever need anything that we can't get there fast enough for, you call him. OK?"

"Yes, Dad. He's been great, even if you told him to check on me."

"Can you blame me?"

"Sounds like you're figuring it out, Solia," my father says, clearing his throat as his voice dips a little lower.

"Love you guys. I'll text or call soon."

"Here's your mom." Dad hands her the phone.

"One more thing, honey—I'm sure he's a catch, but remember your track record. Be careful."

*Jeez, is anything off-limits?*

"Mom, he's great but unavailable. He's leaving town at the end of the summer. It's just another dead end."

"Oh, Solia. Don't be so dramatic. Have fun. You never know how things will turn out. Enjoy the weather and be safe. Don't forget the trash."

"Thanks, Mom. I won't forget the trash."

*Wait until I see Gerry next.*

I laugh out loud as I put the truck in reverse and head back to my peaceful paradise in the woods.

# 23

*Jackson*

The meeting couldn't have gone better, thanks to the majority of town residents who showed. I have such a sense of pride watching the lengths people will go to for their neighbors and to preserve the integrity of this town we love. Having Mike Kelley on our team is certainly the cherry on top. I'm trusting this man to stop us from falling into the deep trench Green Breeze is digging.

I also have complete faith that more than enough people will prepare words for the public comment portion of the meeting. I need to brainstorm what I'm going to say.

Gerry's done such a great job of informing the public, despite the fact he has zero knowledge of social media. He uses every opportunity to spread the word. I'm fairly convinced the residents of Meriden either spoke to Gerry directly or someone relayed his message to them. "Get to the next town hall meeting to save Meriden" has been echoing along the mountainside ever since the first Green Breeze meeting, thanks to Gerry.

I, too, have been so focused on getting the word out and focusing on how I can help Solia that the summer is slipping through my fingers like beach sand. In a mere few weeks, I'll be leaving Meriden behind, but not before we release the grip Green Breeze is trying to secure. The reality of leaving is hitting home and missing this place wasn't supposed to inflict this level of discomfort.

Solia continues to infiltrate my thoughts. I can't avoid her and frankly, I don't want to. We've shared many intimate stories and experiences in the little time we've had. That, combined with this burning sexual desire I have for her, means I can't get her off my mind. I wake up thinking of her being by my side and close my eyes at night with her silhouette outlined in my dreams.

I know I've made a promise to my father, and I would never want to break that. Maybe this is an example of that saying, "You want what you can't have." When I see her next, I'll try to remember that and maybe I won't picture her naked or dream how amazing it would be to make love to her. It's worth a try.

JACKSON

Hey, you guys free tonight?

TYLER

Sure. The Binn?

RYAN

I'm in.

JAY

What time are you guys thinking?

JACKSON

How's eight?

RYAN

K.

JAY

Works for me.

TYLER

I can finish by then.

RYAN

Who you got in your bed this time?

TYLER

A true gentleman never tells.

JAY

You are so full of shit. A true gentleman.

TYLER

What are you saying, Jay? I'm a man whore.

RYAN

You said it.

TYLER

Jealous bitches.

JACKSON

See you at 8.

Man, I've missed bullshitting with the guys. Sure, they're crude and offensive, but that's what I love. Since the accident, these guys have put up with a one-sided friendship, and not one among them has called me out. They've hung back and waited for me to be ready. There were months I went without even calling or texting, never mind going out.

My phone never went silent for more than a few days. One of the guys would always check in. I should thank them. I hope they know I appreciate them, but we don't talk about emotional shit. In reality, I'm an asshole. They were there that day too. We were all friends with Trinity. But since she and I had taken things to another level, I've held myself responsible this whole time.

Truth is, they experienced the horror unfold as much as I did. Each of us dealt with it in our own ways, but I never considered how much they might be suffering. I was too suffocated by my own emotions to worry about how they were handling everything. They deserve more than that, and I'm not ashamed to admit it.

I'm the first to arrive at the Binn. Cindy is behind the bar as usual and has four pints of beer balancing in her hands as I walk through the door. The wobbling of the glasses doesn't stop her from shouting hello across the room. I don't see a sign showing entertainment tonight. Part of me was hoping Brice Hawkins might be playing again. That guy is pure talent. Most of the high-tops and other tables are empty. I forget eight o'clock is early for a night out.

"Hey, Cindy, I'm going to grab a table for the guys." I sit at an empty high-top and face the television hanging over the bar.

"Sure thing, sweetheart, be right over," Cindy says in her usual cheerful tone.

The Binn is an extension of home, filled with familiar faces and recognizable laughter. I'm mad at myself for how long I stayed away, locked in my own personal hell.

As I'm checking the score of the Red Sox game, an elderly man spins around on his wooden bar stool to face me. "You Earl's grandson?"

"Sure am. John, right? Good to see you." I stand and shake his frail, weathered hand.

"I haven't seen you around in a few years, but I knew it had to be you. You're looking more and more like the old man."

I chuckle. "Thanks."

"Now, I ain't gonna bad-mouth Earl, but I hear he's thinking of selling his land. That true?"

"Well, it's a little more complicated than that, but let's just say a decision hasn't been made yet. If it were up to me, that would never happen."

"Ain't it up to you, boy? Damn Earl has to have one foot in the grave by now. Trust me, I'm right behind him. Makes little sense for someone our age to make such big decisions. It's a shame. What do you plan to do?"

I take a second to compose myself after absorbing his harsh words. I know my grandfather is aging, but being reminded so bluntly is a stab to the heart. "I can tell you that Earl still has his wits about him. As for agreeing with him, I don't, and I haven't given up yet."

"You shouldn't, that's for damn sure. Only a fool would leave land here. An old friend used to say that the only thing that you can buy for certain is dirt. Once it's yours, you keep it. You dig deep and put your roots down. Don't let your grandpa be a fool."

Struck by the rawness of his words, I simply nod in agreement. John turns his stool back toward the bar and signals for another drink. The old man is correct, though—you can't buy anything for sure, other than dirt. Whether it be Green Breeze or my grandfather, there is no way in hell I'm going to let our land turn into a turbine farm.

A gust of wind blows into the tavern as the door swings open, and in walk the guys. "What's up, homie?" Tyler approaches and slaps my shoulder blade. "This is becoming a regular occurrence. I love it, man."

"I wouldn't call it a regular thing when I'm leaving town in a couple weeks, but yeah, I'm glad I'm here." I was about to mention my appreciation for them, but talking about serious shit doesn't come easy with these guys. I decide to buy a round for the table, a thank-you they understand.

"I'll be back." I head to the bar and squeeze behind two women in their forties. They've visited the country store a few times. I get the sense they must recognize me because they elbow each other and smile. "Hello, ladies, sorry to crowd you. I'm going to place a quick order and be out of your way."

"No problem. You can squeeze in wherever you'd like," the woman to the left says. Her friend gives her a hard jab.

"I'm sorry about her. She's had quite a day, and apparently, we've had a few too many drinks. I'll watch her while you get what you need," she says with a laugh and wraps her arm around her friend, whispering something in her ear.

Cindy finishes serving a customer at the end of the bar and makes her way over to me. "What'll it be, Jackson? Pick your poison."

"Oh, we're not getting crazy tonight, Cindy. Just three IPA drafts and one soda water."

"Coming right up. Your boy, Ryan, is still on the wagon, huh? Good for him."

"For sure. I don't see that changing soon. When he puts his mind to something, there's no changing it. And it seems to work, so more power to him, right?"

"As long as you boys keep coming around, I'll pour you whatever you need."

"Thanks, Cindy." I take the drinks but avoid her eyes because I know what she's hinting at. Cindy's been serving me since the day I turned twenty-one. She also knows I plan on leaving. Cindy will be someone else I leave behind.

Knowing soon I won't be able to stop in for a beer and to shoot the shit knots my stomach. Will there be bars similar to the Binn in New York, or will they be stuffy and cramped? I'll be starting over from scratch, knowing no one other than my parents.

I head back to the table, trying to shake the uncertainty building in my chest.

"Here we go, guys." I pass the drinks around. "A toast, to us."

"A toast? Dude? What?"

"Shut up and listen. Raise your damn glass."

The guys side-eye each other as if I've lost my mind. I clear my throat to get their attention. When I leave, I don't want any regrets.

"Seriously, guys, I want to say thanks. Thanks for sticking by me this last year, even though I've been MIA and not the greatest friend at times. Cheers."

Short and sweet. Looking at one another in silence, they hold their glasses and drink. I breathe a sigh of relief.

"OK, enough sappy shit," Tyler says. "I hear your girl's friend is driving north tomorrow night. Mia. I've got to say, man, I'm looking forward to seeing her."

"Actually, I didn't know, and you shouldn't be calling her 'my girl.' She knows I'm leaving."

"Dude, your loss. That girl is hot, and from the looks of it, she's into you. Why not take her for a ride and then cut your losses?"

He can be such an ass sometimes. The thing is, though, Tyler is a lot of hot air. He riffles through women as fast as underwear. They never stick around, and if you ask me why, I'd say it's because he keeps himself emotionally unavailable. He's a deep guy, a great guy, but he won't let a woman in. Like, really in. And he has no filter. Anyone who overheard him would assume Tyler is a total asshole.

"Ty, don't say shit like that. I'm not into her for the sex, and I'm leaving. That'd be a real dick move. Solia is an amazing girl."

"You're right, man, I'm sorry. She seems great. I'm sure she'll have no trouble finding someone around these parts. Those eyes are enough to melt ice," Tyler says, nudging Jay, proud of his retort.

I've got to admit, his words sting. But I know he's right. Solia is the total package. Girls like her don't show up every day. Of course I want her to be happy, but I want to be the one who's part of her happiness. Leaving her in the arms of another man makes my stomach sick.

I steer the conversation in a different direction. "So, Mia, huh? You've been keeping in touch?"

"Sure have. Have you seen her? She's sexy as hell, and she's got her shit together. I'm assuming once we kick these green assholes out of Meriden and Solia stays, Mia will visit often. I have no problem entertaining her when she's in town, if you know what I mean."

Jay shakes his head in laughter. "Tyler, you never cease to amaze me. Good for you, man."

"It's genius. There won't be any major strings attached. I'll just make sure she's warm at night while she's here. But in all seriousness, I'm going to take her to dinner tomorrow."

"Dinner?" He made plans other than to undress her? I'm shocked. "Isn't she here to see Solia?"

"They're hanging out tomorrow for most of the day, but I asked if she was free tomorrow night. I'm not sure what Solia is up to, but Mia agreed. I'm picking her up at six."

My mind drifts to thoughts of Solia alone in her cabin at sunset. She'll probably be wrapped in blankets, sitting out on the front porch watching the sky turn brilliant shades of red. I shouldn't let myself go there, but I can't stop the thoughts.

*Wait—she needs help with the showerhead. It'd be rude to not follow up on that, right? Maybe I'll text her later to see if I can swing by.*

"Speaking of these green assholes." Ryan pulls his chair closer to the table, and I sense the conversation is about to get a lot more serious. "What's the latest? Have we heard anything? How is the first town council meeting going to go?"

"Well, based on the turnout from the resident meeting yesterday, it seems we've got a lot of people on our side." I sip my beer and check the Sox score.

Jay pushes his pint forward and crosses his arms over the

table. "We can have the whole town on our side, but it's up to the individual property owners to decide. And unfortunately, if someone takes the deal, it'll cause a domino effect. More will follow."

I sit straighter, knowing my grandfather is one of those still undecided. "Out of all the owners, we know there are only two for sure who are taking the deal. I can't even be pissed at them. It seems this company went around and sought out the most vulnerable people with the biggest land."

"How can you even question it? Of course that's what they did," Tyler says, slamming his fist into the table. "Do you consider it a coincidence?"

"What are you guys talking about?" Jay asks.

I lean back and shift in my seat. "The two property owners taking the deal are a young family in which the husband recently lost his job, and they are hard up for money. I met his wife, Katie, the other day. She's very nice, and their situation is unfortunate.

"The other property owner's name is Mary something. She's in her seventies and a widow. She lost her husband to cancer last year and is struggling to maintain her land. They don't have any children, so there isn't much family to assist her. Both of these families see this proposal as a blessing."

"Man, that's messed up, preying on the weak. That's low," Jay says, shaking his head.

"No shit. Solia's family doesn't vacation up here anymore, so Green Breeze is preying on a young woman who's trying to make it on her own. They've got Earl and Sylvia whose grandson is leaving town and can't possibly keep the orchard going." Tyler turns to me. "Sorry, dude, but it's true. And you've got that Ted Folger guy who lives on Bear Mountain Road who's as old as dirt and had his blueberry fields destroyed a few years back because of insect infestation. The last family is Ryan's, which I guess is the oddball of the group."

"Thanks, Tyler, for your positive outlook," Ryan says.

"For real, guys. These corporate suits aren't idiots. They know exactly what they're doing." Tyler shrugs, pushes his stool back, and walks toward the bar.

"It's bullshit, and hearing it laid out pisses me off," Ryan says.

"I know. It is bullshit. But we have to trust that Mr. Kelley will figure something out. He's the real deal."

"It's going to be tough, Jackson. These guys aren't new to this. There's no way they haven't been scoping out this area for a long time. I'm sure they figure owners want to make money. They've done their research. The zoning board zones every piece of land a certain way. I was talking to my father the other night—there's no way Green Breeze sent those letters without being one hundred percent certain a wind farm could be built on the specific land. My parents are prepared to fight this until the end, but they aren't naive to the situation. As long as Green Breeze has a few willing owners, they may drag the others into taking the deal. Look at you—your own family is considering selling. I'm sure no one in Meriden ever thought your family's land would be anything but an orchard, but now look where we are. Time changes and things happen, and no offense, man, but you are skipping town," Ryan says, holding both palms in the air.

An unease settles in my stomach. "I guess we'll have to place our bets on Mike Kelley."

Tyler returns to the table while I try to recover from Ryan's gut punch. "Yeah, sounds like it. Listen, guys, I'm going to head out. I've got a lot going on in the next couple of days. I'll see you at the meeting Tuesday?" I say.

"Jackson. Sorry, man. You aren't leaving because of what I said, are you?"

"Nah, don't worry. You're only speaking the truth. I wish

things worked out differently. Shit is getting real. Time is slipping away."

"You're the one deciding to let it slip away. Remember that. You are letting something we all experienced define the rest of your life," Tyler says, and the four of us sit in silence for a few minutes, avoiding eye contact.

"Yeah, I know," I respond. Standing, I head for the door. As much as Tyler can be an ass, he's honest.

Without processing what I'm doing, I turn left out of the parking lot and drive home via the east side of the lake. I haven't followed this route since the accident. Taking a right out of the parking lot shields me from getting a glimpse of Newfound Lake. The water's edge is enclosed by giant family retreats with enormous pine and evergreen trees.

Since the accident, it's been safe turning right because I couldn't bring myself to look at the water or Trinity's childhood home. Seeing it will drop me right back into that moment when I lost her, the moment when I should've been able to save her. It's been more than I can bear, so avoiding it has been the easiest thing to do.

The road along this side is spotted with older homes, much more modest, granting the lake visibility between the lots. Maybe it's time for me to stop sheltering myself. Maybe it's time to stop hiding. Thinking back to Solia remembering her memories growing up here and how she would be heartbroken if her family put the cabin up for sale reminds me of the love I once had for this area. The accident changed my outlook, and not for the better.

This town shines through Solia's eyes and has allowed tiny shards of light to penetrate my darkness.

As I follow the road around the lake, heading east, tears threaten to cloud my vision. I take in the view of the water shimmering in the moonlight. There are no other cars on the road, so I slow to a crawl and luxuriate in the gentle breeze blowing through the cab. A slight ripple in the water forms as it flows toward the shore and over the sand. Campfires flicker on the water's edge, sending sparks into the air as families laugh and enjoy the night.

These sights and sounds remind me of old times, when life was easy, so free. I wish I could erase that day, travel back in time and prevent it. Trinity should still be here, but she's not, and I am.

I'm dwelling on an event I cannot change or control. I won't allow the past to follow me like a dark cloud, muddying my judgment and stealing my happiness.

Tonight, for whatever reason, a fraction of the guilt I've been carrying around dissipates with the breeze. In its place, I allow a memory of the love and happiness these waters have provided me over the years. I hold on to this moment of clarity and vow to never let it go. It's time for me to move on and be honest with myself about what I truly want out of life. I can't keep running from the tough stuff.

~

I'm tired but restless, kicking the sheets off my legs. I replay the conversation I had tonight with the guys at the Binn, and the truth stings. I am more determined than ever to fight before I leave Meriden. My friends and part of my family will still be here, and when I come back to visit, I don't want to see that our town has been erased by this company's big plans.

A sudden urge to text Solia overcomes me, and without regard to the time, I pick up my phone from the nightstand.

JACKSON

> Hey, sorry it's so late. Are you around tomorrow night? I thought I could swing by and take care of that showerhead for you.

SOLIA

It's OK, I'm still awake. Sure, I'll be here. Mia is coming to town tomorrow, but she'll be out with Tyler tomorrow night. She mentioned dinner. Either way, I'll be here.

Sounds good. I'll text you before I come to make sure your plans haven't changed. That's cool about Mia. You must be looking forward to her visiting again.

It's great she's coming. Tyler has a lot to do with it too. But I'll take it. 😊

I'm sure. Everything else OK with you?

Yes, everything is fine. But . . .

What's the matter?

I just miss you. I'm sorry, I shouldn't say that, but I do.

I bite my tongue and stare at the ceiling. What I wouldn't give to drive to the cabin right now and comfort her. I'm not sure how to handle this, or what the right thing to say is. *Fuck it, I want her to know.*

JACKSON

I miss you too. Good night, Solia.

SOLIA

Night.

More confused than ever, I rest my head on my pillow and look out into the starry night. My head is lighter, but my heart is torn.

～

A round five o'clock the next evening, I text Solia to see if she still wants me to fix the shower. She says yes, so I head out.

Even though it's painfully obvious I'm not in the position to start a relationship, I can't ignore the fact I took a shower to go fix a shower. It's ridiculous, but I can't stop thinking about her, wanting to impress her, longing to hold her close. The weather is cooler than usual, so I have on jeans and a blue Henley long-sleeve. I'm not sure why I'm torturing us both, but the idea of seeing Solia again sends testosterone flowing through me.

I pull up to see her on the front porch reaching to water one of her giant hanging plants. She's balanced on her tiptoes and her white crop top rises, revealing her torso. Even from where I am in my truck, I practically start drooling at the sight of her toned waist and low-rise jean shorts.

I honk to let her know I am here, and it's louder than expected, which startles her and she jumps, spilling water down the front of herself. I couldn't ask for a better mishap.

She busts out laughing as she inspects her top. Although my intention wasn't to initiate a wet T-shirt contest, I'm happy as hell I did. I park and head up the stairs. As I get closer, I'm pleased her top is more sheer than it appeared from a distance, revealing a perfect silhouette of her breasts, which are clearly chilled by the cool evening breeze. I'm not sure if she picks up on how much she is turning me on, or if she simply doesn't care, when she leans against the porch post and smiles seductively.

"Nice going, farmer," she says in a sexy, sweet tone with a glimmer in her eyes.

"Hi, Solia, I didn't mean to scare you. I never thought you'd spill a watering can on yourself, but I must admit that I'm not sorry you did." I stop on the step just below the one she's standing on. She smells of warm vanilla and is covered in goose bumps, making me want to wrap my arms around her to keep her warm. The sexual tension between us could be cut with a knife.

When I see this woman, the scene fades and there is nothing I can think of or want besides her. Standing here face-to-face, she inches a bit closer, her breasts lightly brushing against my chest. I stiffen from the heat between our bodies.

"Solia," I say breathlessly into the night air.

"Jackson, you don't have to tell me again. You're leaving. And you're just here to fix my shower." She takes two slow steps backward, keeping her gaze locked on me.

I want to reach out and pull her back and run my hands along her body. But the moment is lost, and I take the last step to the landing. "Lead the way." I gesture.

I follow her around the house, onto the covered porch, to the outdoor shower. As we approach, we pass by the firepit, intense memories of the night we spent there racing to the fore. I pause, and snapshots appear in my mind of lying on the blankets by the fire getting lost in her. I hear her clear her throat as she looks at me staring at the firepit. I snap out of it. "OK, let's see what's wrong with this thing."

Solia unlatches the shower door, secured shut with a deer antler. *Very rustic.* Upon entry, it has a changing stall with a narrow wooden wall that separates the shower so users can dry off in privacy. The shower section is roomy and well-constructed. A small wooden shelf runs along the edge of the shower a few feet above the ground for bathing accessories. It's impressive.

"Here, let me show you." Solia squeezes behind me, close enough for me to inhale her alluring scent once again. She reaches for the nozzle and turns it to hot.

The showerhead sputters, and more water sprays from around the cracked seal where it attaches to the pipe.

"It was fine at first, but lately, it's been doing this, so you can imagine how long it takes to wash everything. I love this shower, but I'd love it more if it worked properly."

*She has no idea what I could do to her in this shower. I envision lathering her up under the stars, steam rising to the clouds, and then gently wrapping her in a towel and carrying her into the cabin.*

"Well, after this quick switch, it will be the best outdoor shower around." I wink, take off my hat, and pull my shirt over my head. "Do you mind holding this? I'm bound to get wet."

Solia takes the shirt from me, and I can't help but notice she's focused on my chest. I clear my throat, and she looks up, blushing. She's even sexy when she's shy. God, this woman drives me crazy.

"OK, I'll let you be. I don't want to be in your way. I left the toolbox and the new showerhead. If there's anything you need, I'll be inside. Just yell."

"You got it. It shouldn't take me long." Admiring her from behind, I let out a sigh of frustration and get to work.

It's a simple switch and takes me less than fifteen minutes. I test my handiwork, confident she'll love the improvement.

I don't see Solia anywhere but hear music playing from inside. For a fraction of a second, I wonder if this is going to be a repeat of our first porch encounter. Part of me wants to walk in and see if I'm lucky enough to be right, but I can't just waltz into her house. I give a loud, firm knock, and through the screen door, I see Solia come twirling around the corner and into the living room.

*So I was correct. She is dancing, just not naked this time. Damn!*

"You're done already? Wow, you work fast! That would've taken me a bit longer. Thank you so much. Let me get you something to drink."

I sit in one of the green wooden rocking chairs that adorn the front porch, and she comes out a few moments later holding two glasses of lemonade. She is no longer wearing the wet, white top from before but has changed into a royal blue sports bra, black running shorts, and workout sneakers, looking equally hot. She hands me a glass and sits beside me on the other rocker. She notices me checking her out.

"I know. I look like I'm going to the gym. My goal today was to clean the second floor and stay out of your way. There is so much old junk up there, and most of it is garbage and needs to be tossed, and I cringe at the thought of more trash bags. I'll be at it for hours." She lets out a sigh and stares straight ahead.

"I could take the trash to the dump for you."

"Absolutely not. The waste facility, as I've been informed it's properly called, is a place I need to get used to. But thanks for the offer."

I join her in silence and follow her gaze into the distance. The view is out of this world. Her dirt driveway curves around the side of the house, and beyond is a thin tree line comprised of pine and birch. Because the cabin sits on a hill, you can easily see above and beyond the trees and into the marshland that stretches for a mile until it meets the edge of the forest. From there, the forest extends for miles to and up the mountain range. A view this beautiful could never get old.

"I could sit here for hours."

"Sometimes I do. As a kid, I didn't fully appreciate the beauty of this place like I do now. I remember my parents sitting out here for hours with their blankets, stargazing. I thought it was lame back then, but now it's amazing, peaceful. Can you imagine letting them sell this?"

I know she isn't only referring to her parents and the decision to sell. She is concerned Green Breeze will win this battle. "We will figure this out, Solia. I have complete faith in Gerry and Mike. There has to be a way. People are going to come out in big numbers."

"Don't I know it? People around here fight for each other.

When I was at the last meeting, I thought to myself, most of these people haven't even met me, yet they showed up to support my piece of property. It's amazing. I mean, ultimately they are protecting the town they love, but I'm a part of this town now too. If everything works out the way I hope, I will forever be indebted to these residents—especially you."

She lingers for a moment and then looks from the mountains back to me. Her eyes drift from my face to my chest. "I should give you your shirt back, huh? I forgot." She puts her glass on the deck and heads back inside.

Upon returning, she places the shirt in my lap. "Here you are." I set my glass on the porch railing, remove my hat, and pull my shirt over my head. She watches my every move. I know if I stay another minute, I'll be removing more than my shirt.

"Well, I'm sure you have a lot of cleaning to do. What time are you expecting Mia back?"

"She said eight, but I won't be surprised if I see her later than that, if you know what I mean."

"Oh, yes, I know exactly what you mean. I've known Tyler my whole life."

"He's a good guy, right? I mean, Mia is Mia. She's a man magnet, but she's my best friend."

"Well, they have that in common. I can honestly say Tyler is a chick magnet. But he's a decent guy. He loves his family and has been one of my best friends since I was little. We've been through hell this past year, and he has never left my side. So, that says a lot. But does he love women? Definitely."

"Two peas in a pod. Thank you. Now I can stop worrying."

"Mia is lucky to have you looking out for her," I say and retreat down the steps, turning back to take one last long look, trying to imprint the image of her body in my mind for later. "I'll see you tomorrow night."

"You sure will. See you then. And Jackson, thank you again."

Every time I leave this cabin, I'm reminded that it could be for the last time. I want to hold on to the delicate string that ties me to Solia.

Sitting at the stop sign at the bottom of her road, I have the urge to drive east around the lake again. I flip my blinker on and take a right. Every little step toward healing is another piece chipping off the boulder sitting on my shoulder, weighing me down a little less than before.

~

I walk through the front door, pull out my phone, and see several messages.

SHANNON

Where are you? I drove by your place earlier, and you weren't there. You're always home around this time.

SHANNON

Jackson? Call me when you get this.

DAD

Hey, Jackson. Just wanted to wish you good luck at the meeting tomorrow. I talked to your grandfather earlier. I thought it went well, but I guess we'll have to wait and see.

DAD

I know it's going to be tough leaving, but we're looking forward to you being here with us. Your mother is very excited. You'll never have to cook again, so that's a plus.

DAD

Call me when you can.

I text them both back and tell them everything is good here on my end, but my father insists on a phone call. I certainly won't tell either of them I was at Solia's—Dad will think I'm a jerk for leading her on, and I'm sure Shannon will be hopeful I've changed my mind. I already know she is holding on to hope for Solia and me. They clearly hit it off. Solia has seamlessly woven herself into the fabric of Meriden, and she'll be on my mind regardless of where I rest my head.

I call Dad from my driveway a few minutes later. He spoke to my grandmother earlier and she had trouble recalling Shannon's name. Grandpa insisted she was tired from a long day, but it raised an alarm. My father then called Shannon because I was unreachable. Everyone has their panties in a bunch, worried that Sylvia might be showing early signs of dementia.

Like the saying goes, when it rains, it pours.

I promise to pay closer attention and inquire about a doctor's visit. But the conversation and the worry in my father's voice plants yet another seed of doubt. Meriden seems reluctant to release her grip on my future.

# 24

*Solia*

T he knots in my stomach harden to stone around two
o'clock. Even though I know no decisions will be made
at this meeting, I'm nervous as hell. The summer is flying by,
and I want this whole debacle to be over and Green Breeze
Enterprises to leave so I can keep my cabin and move on.

I arrive at town hall early as promised, along with what
seems like the entire town. I drive to the crowded entrance of
the parking lot, realizing I will have to park up the way and
walk. Residents already line the road in front of town hall.
Most people are holding protest signs, and trucks roll past
honking in support. Guilt sinks in as I hightail it half a mile up
the road and run back to the meeting. Thank goodness I wore
sneakers!

With my sign in hand, I approach the building. Unsure of
what to do or where to stand, I scan the growing throng in
search of a familiar face. Sure enough, to my relief, Gerry
appears.

"Solia!" he yells through the crowd. I tuck my poster under
my arm and squeeze through the mob.

When I reach Gerry, he loops his arm around mine and

leads me to the end of the line of protestors. "Here, there is a little more space to breathe. You've got your sign, so hold it high!"

I tossed and turned for nights over what to write on this freaking sign but finally went with "Blow your wind somewhere else! Don't touch my cabin!" I cringe at the decision, but whatever.

I hold the sign, my arms locked in position, and put on my *don't mess with me* face. Cars and trucks continue to honk as they drive by, the protestors getting louder as the crowd grows. I wish Mia had come with me, but she finds crowds overwhelming, and my attending the meeting was a convenient excuse for her to see Tyler again. I know she's into this guy, but he's taking an awful lot of her time.

Everyone waves their signs in the air. After a while, my arms ache. Around five forty-five, a murmur spreads through the crowd that it's time to head in. I pull my sign to my side and turn when I hear a man in the crowd yell, "Stop!"

Everyone turns to glare at the Green Breeze corporate vehicle cruising to the last reserved spot in the parking lot. I'm not exactly sure why they receive front-row parking, but I guess that's beside the point. I immediately recognize the two men through the windshield of the blacked-out SUV. The driver is the sexy CEO asshole, Nick Ford, and Mark Hogan is in the passenger's seat.

To get through the crowd, they have to drive at a snail's pace. People start yelling, "Get out of our town." "Take your wind turbines and get out!" "You can't buy us out of here." "This is our town!" The gathering borders on aggressive.

My hands sweat, and I see worried looks on residents' faces. I breathe easier when the crowd moves toward the building entrance.

The two Green Breeze reps finally make it into their parking spot, but they remain in the vehicle. I watch them as I wait at the back of the group of protestors. Ford and Hogan must figure it'll be safer for them to join the meeting once everyone is inside. I can't say I blame them; I'd do the same thing. The size of the group is rather intimidating and emotions are on edge.

Being new to town makes it difficult to blend in. People continuously stare my way and smile unknowingly. I prepared a statement, but other than that, I plan to hide in the back. Gerry nods when I walk through the door. He's holding a clipboard and pen, directing traffic to keep the line moving.

There are definitely more people than chairs. At least forty rows have been set up and are filled. People congregate on both sides of the room, allowing a tiny, narrow aisle to walk through. People lean against their spouse or friend, creating groups of two or three people deep. The room is not large enough to accommodate everyone comfortably. This has to be some sort of fire code violation.

Residents continue to squeeze in wherever they can, and the noise level rises as people try to talk over one another's conversations. They've organized the stage in what I assume is the regular town council setup. The same small podium with the microphone sits at the front with a large boardroom table and seven chairs in the middle.

Gerry loops his arm around mine, passes the clipboard to the man at his side, and says, "There you are. You're the last one. Everyone else is here. Oh, and don't worry, I already put your name at the top of the list."

Without another word, Gerry leads me to the front of the audience. As we walk by each row, people shift in their seats, and I see them whispering. I cross my arms over my chest and concentrate on moving forward. "Gerry, what are you doing? I'd rather be in the back. I don't need to sit in front."

"Solia, all the property owners are sitting in front." Gerry points to the hanging rope holding a Reserved sign at the end of the second row. There is one seat left I assume to be mine. Even though Gerry and Mr. Kelley informed me of who the other property owners were, I haven't met them all.

I nervously sit on the cold metal chair. I look to my right and spot Earl and Sylvia alongside Jackson and Shannon. Jackson looks hotter than ever. Gone is his hat and dirty jeans. His hair is styled back and out of his face, making his eyes stand out more than usual. He has on a dark green polo shirt, which is snug on his biceps.

*What I would give to have those arms around me.*

From the looks of it, he tucked his shirt into his khakis, and instead of work boots, he's wearing brown dress shoes. This guy is hot no matter what he's wearing, making it almost impossible to focus on anything else, including this meeting. I look at the seat between us and am thankful for the distance. I would've had a difficult time keeping my hands to myself.

Next to them, I recognize Janice, Ryan's mom, from Stable Farm with a man I assume is her husband. An elderly man and two women sit next to the Stables, which has to be Ted Folger and his wife from Bear Mountain Road, and then Mary, the widow I'm told is taking the deal. Sitting on the opposite side of me is a young couple Jackson met the other day. He said the wife's name is Katie, but I can't recall the husband's name. As I scan the aisle, everyone glances my way, and they either wave or nod in my direction.

I secretly wish I were at the other end of the aisle near the Christiansons, but I guess that's what happens when you walk in late. Another reserved sign hangs in the row in front of us, and the seats are still empty.

There's a commotion onstage as the town council members walk up the side steps and select their seats. One man in the group hangs back at the top of the stairs as Mr. Ford and Mr. Hogan enter the room via the side door. As if a fire alarm sounds, everyone goes silent and stares at the two men. The energy in the room shifts, the tension suffocating.

The two executives stare straight ahead, never once looking at the residents, and confidently strut to the front row. They keep their eyes trained on their seats and don't give any indication of concern. They swagger through the row and sit directly in front of the Christiansons. Both men are in tailored suits that fit as perfectly as one would expect.

While Mr. Hogan is a bit rougher around the edges and not so easy on the eyes, Mr. Ford makes up for it. I can tell Mr. Ford is the type who leads with his looks. His body fills his suit well. He's muscular and tall, and it's obvious he's meticulous about his grooming. He sits with his right ankle resting on his left thigh and hangs his left elbow on the folding chair next to him.

Mr. Hogan leans to whisper in Nick's ear, causing him to turn around and look at Earl. They are too far away for me to make out what Nick says to Jackson's grandfather. Earl responds to whatever he says with a firm handshake. Then Nick turns to the left and looks directly at Shannon and again says something I can't hear. Shannon smiles nervously in return and looks directly at Jackson, who's readying missiles and shooting directly at Nick.

Nick maintains his cocky smile and returns to face the stage. This guy is a piece of work. I can only imagine how pissed Jackson must be. I've never witnessed Jackson angry, but I sense the temperature rising inside him from my seat despite the distance between us. I share in his anger and want more than anything for this to be over. Not only is Jackson fighting for his family's land, he's sitting among a family divided. I hope for Jackson's sake his grandfather hasn't made a final decision yet. If he decides to take the deal, Jackson will be crushed.

"I call this meeting to order." A man stands behind the podium who I assume is the council president, Sal Morgan.

I've never met him, but Gerry mentioned him once or twice. He's been around forever, a Meriden favorite. "We have a lot on today's agenda, so let's get started."

Mr. Morgan clears his throat and adjusts the volume on the microphone. A piercing shriek emanates from the sound system; the crowd groans and people cover their ears.

"My apologies, folks. The first order of business is public comment. Each person will be called from the list generated. Because of the size of the crowd, we will limit the speakers' comments to three minutes. I will notify you when your time has ended. Understood? Great."

People shift in their seats, and everyone is glued to our row. Talk about not being able to blend in.

Janice Stable is the first to speak. She walks tall and holds her head high as she approaches the podium. She faces the stage, states her name and address, and is told to continue. She clears her throat and places her arms by her side. I am nervous for her but relieved she's going first.

"I was born and raised in this town. My parents founded Stable Farm, and my family still runs it to this day. We will not be signing any kind of agreement with Green Breeze today or any day. While I understand that our collective future will require innovation to meet the growing demand for energy solutions, including from wind-powered turbines, Meriden is not the place to do this. I suggest this company find another town to smother because the people of Meriden will not stand for it." Her voice is strong and confident to the very end. She even goes so far as to stamp her right foot on the floor before she turns on her heel and hurries back to her seat.

Ted Folger is next. I step out of the row to allow him enough space to move through the aisle and head to the microphone. He is steady but slow. "Ladies and gentlemen of the Meriden town council, I've lived in Meriden longer than any of you council members have walked the earth. People stay here for a reason. There aren't many places that compare. Over my dead body will your turbines cross town lines." He turns his attention toward the two men in the front row. "Pack it up because I'm not planning on going anywhere anytime soon." The crowd cheers in response.

Jackson's turn. I hold my breath and watch his every step. How is it that a little more than a month ago, I didn't even know this man existed but now I have an irresistible urge to stand by his side? He has shown me how pure his intentions are, and I know how badly he wants this deal to fall through. It breaks me he's leaving a place he is fiercely trying to save.

I look at Earl and Sylvia as Jackson states his name and address and notice their hands gripping each other's tight.

"My family's orchard has been here for over a century. I, like most of the people here today, stand firmly against the development of wind farms in Meriden. We are the protectors of this land, and allowing this company to come in here and destroy it is completely unacceptable. I've done my research, gentlemen." Jackson now turns and searches the front row. "I've done my due diligence researching your company. You walk into our little town and promise the world to my family and five of my neighbors. You spout about the financial benefits, how you'll protect the wildlife, how this will bring business to the area, and so on. Well, guess what, folks? This company, which now calls itself Green Breeze Enterprises, was once Wind Incorporated. And before that, it was something else. In fact, this is the fourth company name they are working under because the other three have gone bankrupt.

"I'm sure you have a bullshit story about why and how that isn't your fault, but I'd love to ask the residents of Stonehill what their opinion is. That's right, folks. For those of you who aren't familiar, Stonehill is two hours north of here. This company, under the name Wind Incorporated, successfully secured properties up there to do exactly what they have proposed here.

"And guess what? It seems their plan flopped and those metal monsters sit abandoned on those properties. They leased people's land, destroyed it, and left town. Is this what we want happening here?"

"Mr. Christianson, your time has ended."

Jackson shakes his head in disgust, but stops and returns to his seat, not without sending a smile my way. I'm filled with pride—he handled himself like a pro. No matter what his grandparents decide, they have to be proud.

Lost in my thoughts of Jackson and I against the rock at Sculptured Falls, I flinch when my name is called.

My entire body shakes as I walk to the podium. I count to three and take a deep breath, but my chest pounds uncontrollably and the thumping reaches my ears.

"Many of you may not know me, but my name is Solia Anderson. I spent my summers as a child in Meriden. Recently, I made the big decision to move here full time and settle into my family's cabin. For the same reasons many of you have mentioned, I fell in love with this place a long time ago. This small town clings to your soul and leaves its imprint. My cabin is my home. There is nothing that would destroy my peace and that of the wilderness more than this proposed wind farm. This company says they will do everything in their power to protect our wildlife. These are empty words. There is absolutely nothing they can tell me that will convince me they can provide any protection. They are here for one reason only: financial gain.

"Once those turbines are installed, they won't be taken out. For those of you who may not be familiar with the term *shadow flicker*, you need to research this. Green Breeze knows there is nothing they can do to avoid the effects of a shadow flicker. This is produced by wind turbines and can endanger wildlife in the area but is also associated with nausea, vertigo, and headaches in people living in proximity to the turbines. I will not be signing any kind of agreement with Green Breeze, and I urge each property owner to do the same."

When I finish, I am overwhelmed with relief. I'm not sure anyone understood what I said because I couldn't even hear myself over the waves of nerves crashing through my body. However, as I return to my seat, I hear clapping, and a few residents shout words of support.

I look over and see Jackson gazing directly at me with a huge smile on his face. He winks and returns his stare to the stage.

*I guess I did OK.*

I become lost in my thoughts as resident after resident take the microphone. Everyone speaks out against the proposed deal. There must be some who sit on the other side of the fence, but maybe they are nervous to voice their opposition, given the sentiment of the crowd. It doesn't go unnoticed two of the property owners sitting among us did not say a word the entire time.

The last person to speak is our lawyer, Mike Kelley. Because he's a resident, he is allowed to speak during the public comment portion. "For those of you I haven't had the pleasure of meeting, I was also, like many of you, born from a long line of ancestors who built this town. I've been fortunate enough to raise my children here and will soon have my grandchildren playing on the shores of Newfound Lake.

"Spending the better part of my life working as a real estate attorney, retirement was an incredibly difficult decision. But it was the right time. What wasn't difficult was coming out of retirement to support the property owners who are against the proposed project. I will work harder than ever to ensure that their properties remain intact and the integrity of Meriden is untouched. This company underestimates the power of the people in a small town. We come together when it matters most. And that, folks, is today."

Mike receives a standing ovation. I jump out of my chair, beaming with pride, thankful to have Mr. Kelley on our side.

The crowd stays on their feet until the town council president calls the meeting back to order. It takes a few minutes, but eventually, everyone sits and a hush falls over the crowd.

Mr. Morgan remains at the podium and waits. "Our second item on the agenda is hearing from the representatives of Green Breeze. Gentlemen."

Mr. Ford saunters to the podium as Mr. Hogan places an easel at each end of the stage. The poster boards have diagrams and layout designs on them. Mr. Hogan remains standing next to the easel on the left. Both men look calm, cool, and collected. Based on their smug expressions, I assume our words had zero impact.

"Greetings, town council members and residents. Thank you for having us here today. We'd like to take this opportunity to update you on the progress of our proposed project. As discussed at our last town hall meeting, we intend to secure properties in Meriden, either through lease or purchase agreements. We have identified six properties that will be the best fit for the wind farm installation. Letters have gone out to these property owners. We selected each property for its size and elevation.

"On the stage, we have a digital rendering of what you can expect the wind farm to look like. It is our intention to have our wind turbines blend into the natural beauty of the area. We plan to be mindful of local wildlife and will do everything possible to protect every species of animal.

"Beyond the wind farm, we will construct a substation to serve as the primary source to transfer the energy generated from the wind turbine farm into the electrical grid system.

Based on size, characteristics, and elevation, we have yet to determine the best place to house this substation and will share this information with the intended property owner.

"We also hope to integrate ourselves into the folds of the community and have contacted the boards for many of the town's sports groups, as we have an interest in supporting and sponsoring the youth of this community. We look forward to working with the members of this town. Thank you." And with that, Mr. Ford turns and walks with perfect posture back to his seat.

I, for one, am stunned silent. The tone and texture of Mr. Ford's condescending voice make my skin crawl. Not only do they want to dig up our land for these monster turbines, but they also want to dump a substation on one of our properties. Unbelievable.

Mr. Morgan steps toward the microphone again to announce there will be a brief five-minute recess after which the meeting will continue to address the rest of the agenda. The attendees burst into commotion. A Meriden police officer appears and escorts the two men from Green Breeze out the side door. A second officer appears beside me and motions for our row to follow him out if we want to leave.

I am thankful for the direction and fresh air. Inside town hall was stifling—it had to be ninety degrees. I have to let my parents know how the meeting went, and I want to get home before Mia is back. But I'm dragging my feet, hoping to catch Jackson.

Thankfully, he is walking out the door, his hand on his grandmother's elbow to balance her, and he spots me right away. He settles his grandmother onto Shannon's arm while saying something, and Shannon scans and spots me. She gives me a friendly wave and leads her grandparents in the opposite direction. Watching Shannon guide them to their car makes me think of my grandparents and how much I miss them.

While Shannon opens the passenger door for Sylvia, the driver's door of the corporate SUV two spots over opens and out walks Nick Ford. *You've got to be kidding me.* With Sylvia and Earl both safely in the car, Shannon faces Nick and walks in his direction. I can tell by her body language that Shannon isn't telling him off. In fact, I'm fairly certain Nick is hitting on her. *What a piece of crap this asshole is!*

"Hey, you," Jackson says breathlessly. "How do you think it went? You were amazing."

He looks and smells even better up close. "So were you. I can't believe you were able to dig up the history on their company. It went well. Long. Hot. But well. Those guys were unfazed by what we said or the size of the crowd, though."

"They are accustomed to pissing people off. It goes with the territory. Like the others said, money is their focus. Neither of them lives in Meriden. They aren't invested in preserving this town," he says.

"You're right. I've got my money on Kelley."

"He seems in it to win it, for sure. We're lucky to have him."

"Are you heading home?"

"Yeah, Mia should be back, and she's leaving tomorrow. I want to spend the rest of the time with her. I'm not sure when she'll visit again," I say, depressed at the thought of not yet having a future trip on the calendar.

"Well, if Tyler has anything to say, it won't be too long. Let's go. I'll walk you to your truck."

Giddy for the extra few minutes I'll get with Jackson, we follow the sidewalk toward my truck. Most of the residents have dispersed and proceeded toward their cars. The sidewalks bustle with people who carry their homemade signs by their sides. My shoulder rubs against Jackson's arm, like we're just an everyday couple taking a walk. Being with Jackson is easy, natural. I resist the urge to reach for his hand.

"Are you aware Nick approached Shannon outside after the meeting?"

"Sure am. Don't get me started."

"What's up with that? Friends with the enemy?"

"That prick has been making passes at her since day one. Shannon hasn't been single for a long time, so she's eating up the attention. I tried talking to her, but she stopped listening before I even started."

"Oh, I see. Yeah, she must be going through so many emotions right now. I hate that the guy giving her attention is the CEO of this company, though. I had the pleasure of meeting her ex when I was out the other night."

"I heard. He doesn't learn. It's sad how booze can destroy relationships. Sorry you had to meet him."

"He is a scary guy. It seems Shannon made the right call."

"It's not a matter of *if* something bad will happen, it's when. I'm glad Madison called Nate. If Richard ever hurts Shannon …"

"Sorry, I didn't mean to upset you."

"No, you're good. For his sake, I better never run into him. As for that CEO, I tried, trust me. But apparently, I'm the last person she wants dating advice from right now."

"Fair enough." I drop the conversation as we approach my truck. I lean against the passenger door, Jackson in front of me, and spin through the same carousel of emotions I do every time Jackson and I separate. I don't want him to go, but I understand why he is. Wrapping my arms around him will only make things harder. If he were to realize how often I think of him, practically all day, every day, I'm certain he'd think I'm pathetic, given he's told me "we" aren't possible.

We stand inches apart. The sun beats on us, and Jackson squints. "What are we doing, Solia?"

He places his hands on the truck beside me and leans forward so that the sun's glare disappears between us.

"I don't know, Jackson. What I do know is, every time I see you, I don't want it to be the last."

"Do you think two people can be destined to be together, but the timing is wrong? I wish I'd met you a year ago, two years ago, shit, anytime but now. But it doesn't change the fact I can't get you off my mind."

I can't hold back any longer. I take his hands into mine and press my lips against his knuckles. With a swift motion, he lets go of my hands and weaves his fingers through the back of my hair and gently leans me against the side of the truck. He kisses me with intensity and wraps his other arm around my waist. His body presses hard against mine as his tongue explores my mouth. I can't get enough of him. We're two teenagers, unaware of the world until a couple of cars honk.

Instead of releasing me, Jackson kisses me harder, a smile forming. After three more obnoxious honks, I can't help but laugh. We stand for a minute, laughing and shaking our heads. Every moment I spend with Jackson is another small treasure I tuck into my pocket to save for eternity. I want to create a life full of precious memories with him, but that isn't possible if he leaves Meriden.

"I guess we should stop making out on the street." Jackson laughs, taking a step back onto the sidewalk.

"Yeah, I guess so. I'll see you at the next meeting?" I ask, hoping he'll respond by saying he'll meet me at the cabin in five minutes.

"That's probably best. Bye, Solia."

Watching him walk away stings as intensely as the first time. Tears stream down my face as I try to block the pain. I return to the cabin, hoping to find Mia. She'll know just how to help. She always does.

"There she is!" Mia says, rocking on the front porch. "I was worried you weren't ever coming back. How'd it go?"

I wrap my arms around her in a desperately needed hug.

"It went well. So many residents spoke their minds and said powerful things. I'm not sure it's going to change anything, but I have hope. Completely unrelated to the meeting, I saw the CEO hitting on Jackson's sister. And Jackson kissed me again."

"Wait, what? Holy shit, sit and tell me everything."

In her Mia way, she listens. She interjects with advice and has me roaring in laughter by the end. She always makes everything better.

"You said you had cleaning left to do, right?"

"Sure, but it can wait," I say.

"No way. It'll be like old times. Let's crank the music, get drinks, and clean our asses off!"

So that is exactly what we do. Mia still has an old college playlist on her phone. She hooks it up to the speaker while I gather the cleaning supplies, and we head upstairs to clean the loft.

There are two old bureaus, a few shelves, and a bed that needs the sheets washed and returned. Mia gets to work on the bed, and I empty and dust the bureaus. Sweat covers us from head to toe in minutes from our hard-core dance moves and slow-paced cleaning. My mind is clear of conflicting thoughts, our feet are stomping, hair flying, and for a blissful little while, I don't have a freaking care in the world.

Thank god for the seclusion of the cabin. Otherwise, my neighbors would petition for a noise ordinance.

After two hours and five hundred burned calories, I'm dumping the contents of the last drawer into the trash bag when papers catch my eye. Several forms in the middle of the pile stick out, bearing the State of New Hampshire logo on the top. I pull them from the pile and toss the rest.

Upon first glance, I can tell these papers are old, crinkled and worn. The words looked typed using a typewriter. I know the papers have something to do with this property, but most of it is a bunch of legal jargon.

"Hey, Mia. Come look at this." I sit and lean against the bed.

Mia bends, looking closer. "These look a hundred years old."

"No kidding. I'll play it safe and put them aside. The lawyer working on the case asked us to show him anything we had regarding our properties. These papers are loaded with signatures—and look here, there's something about conservation land, and this address is listed." I remain still and try to make sense of the pages in front of me.

"Don't get your hopes up. Leave it to the lawyer—that's why he gets paid the big bucks." Mia takes the papers and folds them, placing them on top of the bureau.

"He's not getting paid." I shake my head and lower my chin.

"Whatever, come on. Let's go!" she yells, cranking the volume.

We're finished cleaning but our dance party continues until the two of us are out of breath and we throw ourselves onto the bed. "I needed that, Mia. I didn't think about a damn thing the whole time."

"That's exactly the point. Not only did we get a workout, we tossed that boy right out of your mind, and we have a clean loft to boot." She reaches over for a high five.

She's spot-on, except I'm convinced Jackson will never be an afterthought. Even when I don't think I'm thinking about him, I am. I can't help it.

I'm eternally screwed. I said I was done getting my heart broken, and look where I am now, falling in love with him.

# 25

*Jackson*

I promised myself I wouldn't make a move on Solia again, but damn it, I can't keep my hands off her. Just seeing her renders me helpless. I'm certain kissing another woman will never paralyze me the way she does, but I won't be another number on her list of jerks.

The only way I can avoid that is to stay out of her orbit. As hard as that is to do, I owe it to her. There have been so many moments when I've picked up the phone and almost sent a quick text, days I've almost driven out to her cabin to wrap my arms around her, but I've held strong. I cannot be that guy.

Keeping myself busy has proven fairly easy between the farm, the country store, and slowly packing my condo. Peak apple-picking season will be upon the orchard soon, so there are a lot of things to prepare before I leave. A few of the other farmers have plenty of seasons under their belts, and I'm confident in their ability to handle the volume we produce. But it saddens me to know I'll miss this fun, crazy time of year.

The store is busier than ever with summer tourism at its highest. It seems every guest has a visit to a local mom-and-pop shop in New Hampshire on their summer bucket list. It's amazing how things have changed over the years. Farms are now cool and local products are the hype. We are certainly not complaining over here at Christianson's—all business is good business.

Packing, on the other hand, sucks. With every screech of the packing tape over a box, I cringe. Each item I place in these boxes is one less item keeping me grounded in Meriden. And every box I stack is a forceful reminder of how soon things are about to change and how real this decision is. No matter how badly I want Solia, I know I have to do this. There's no turning back now.

I see Mike under the awning on the side of the barn as I park the tractor for the day. He's rocking away alongside my grandparents, and I hear him mention Solia's name. I catch little of the conversation, but I know September 1 is the deadline for property owners to give their final decision to Green Breeze. Headquarters will announce decisions and give an update at the town council meeting and lay out the rest of the timeline.

"Hey there, Jackson," my grandfather says as I duck my head, stepping closer to them.

"Hi, Grandpa. Mr. Kelley."

"Call me Mike, Jackson. How are you holding up? I know you're heading out soon."

"Yeah, I am. The summer has flown by. I wish I knew everything was going to be OK here. It would put my mind at ease."

Mike rubs his hand along his chin and looks at my grandfather. "I wish I could give you that peace of mind, Jackson. Unfortunately, I have other news."

I hold my breath and sit in the wicker chair across from them.

"Solia's property happens to be the largest of the properties on the list. And because of that, Green Breeze has slated that lot for the substation."

"You have to be kidding me. Does she know this?"

"She does. She's staying firm and not at all interested in the deal, even if they up the offer. This will get more complicated. For this wind farm to work, they need an electrical substation. But there isn't much you can do. Just hang tight—I'm working on my end of things. You have my word. I am working as hard as I can to fight this."

"I know you are, Mike. I don't doubt you for a second. It's terrible for everyone involved. We've all heard horror stories about states taking land from property owners. That story is an old one, and it better not happen here to anyone, especially Solia. She doesn't deserve any of this."

"You're right, son. Just be there for her," my grandfather says.

~

Two days until the next town council meeting, and god knows how many more after that one. The town is abuzz, wondering what news Green Breeze will have. I hear people chatting in the parking lot of the grocery store, in line to get coffee at the Brown Bean. Anywhere I go in town, wind turbines are part of every conversation. The plan is the same for meeting number two: show up early, have a sign, get ready to speak, and stay strong.

The only person not saying much lately is my grandfather. He's grown quieter by the day. I try to ask him what his plans are or where he stands on his decision, but he changes the subject, as though it is no longer my business what goes on here. It hurts.

Today is the first rainy day in a long time. It's coming down in a strong, steady drizzle, and while the temperature is comfortable, the sun hides the entire day. Puddles form on the roads. Driving home, I have to dodge a few to avoid splashing a waterfall over people walking to their cars. I don't think anyone would appreciate the extra shower.

My mind drifts off and I wonder what Solia is doing at her cabin. *Is she lonely? Does she think of me like I think of her? Is she having second thoughts about staying here?*

I torture myself late into the evening, despite trying to focus on packing the rest of my condo. The rain continues at a steady pace, and a larger storm seems to be developing as I hear claps of thunder echoing over the mountain ridges. Makes me remember the nights I'd sit on the front porch with my grandfather and count the seconds between the thunder and lightning strikes. He'd tell me every second in between was equal to how many miles away the storm was.

I don't know to this day whether that's true, but whatever my grandfather says is a fact in my book. So tonight, I reminisce about those nights, wondering if he remembers them, too, and the next thing I know, I'm counting the seconds.

In bed, I roll over and continue to listen to the hypnotic rain. Looking at the moon struggling to be seen between the bursts of clouds, I find it more and more difficult to get Solia out of my mind. *Is she listening to the same raindrops? Is she scared in the cabin alone?*

Screw it.

JACKSON

I know it's late, but I wanted to make sure you're OK. The storm is pretty intense.

SOLIA

I was thinking I wouldn't hear from you again. I'm OK. I love storms. It's magical to be surrounded by woods, hear the rain splash through the leaves. You should see the mountain ridge each time the lightning strikes. Unbelievable.

I wish I was there with you. It's been difficult not to text, but I'm trying to protect you.

Protect me?

Not protect. Maybe that isn't the correct word, but stop myself from falling for you any harder than I have, just to leave you in the end ...

Which means you've already fallen for me?!

Solia, you must realize that. It's just this place and the timing ...

I can't stop thinking about you.

You have no idea.

Trust me, I do.

You deserve a man better than me. You deserve an equal, someone who isn't weighed down.

Jackson, I wish you understood you are enough. I came here with love last on the list, and somehow you appeared. Maybe the sooner you realize things happen for a reason, the better. See you tomorrow at the meeting. Four?

Yes, four.

K, I'm going to squeeze in a paddle and then I'll be there.

Enjoy. Hopefully the skies clear for you. Good night, Solia.

Night. 😊

The storm rages on. I'm painfully aware of every rumble and flash because my eyes are pinned to the ceiling as I lose myself in thoughts of Solia and what could be between us. I'm in love with her, but my feet are walking away. This woman has shifted my world, and knowing she is lying in bed five minutes down the road constricts the vessels to my heart.

My lids grow heavy and I drift to sleep around four a.m.

∼

When I startle awake, it's still dark and the rain pours relentlessly. I tap my phone on my bedside table and the screen illuminates, displaying eight a.m. I haven't slept this late in as long as I can remember. I never set an alarm because my internal clock is usually foolproof. In the little time I slept, dreams of happiness filled my mind instead of my recurring nightmare ... thanks to Solia.

Rain boots and mud puddles complicate most of my work throughout the day on the farm. The sun finally breaks through around two. Heat sizzles the ground and shallow puddles evaporate. The air becomes thick and suffocating from the gradual rise in temperature and humidity, and I'm exhausted. The meeting is in one hour, and I'm so filthy, I could convince people I wrestled in a mud pit. A long shower is calling my name.

SHANNON

I'll get the lovebirds and bring them to the
meeting.

JACKSON

Great, thanks. Steer clear of Nick.

Relax, I'm a big girl. You've never even spoken
to him.

*What the hell is that supposed to mean?* The last thing I need to add to this gigantic clusterfuck is the CEO hooking up with my sister. No freaking way am I going to let that happen.

Heading into town, I'm surprised to find the cars bumper to bumper. Judging by the interest at the first meeting, this one will be busier as more people come out to support our little town.

I walk almost a mile, and while I'm thankful to be dry, the heat fries my skin. With every step I take toward town hall, I scan the trucks and people for any sign of Solia. I'm sure the property owners will have seats up front, but remembering the last time I saw her—and her body pressed between mine and her truck—I'm going to have a difficult time concentrating. She has seeped into my every cell.

After our back-and-forth texts last night, then my dreams of her, the thought of seeing her today makes me want her more than I ever have.

Solia is nowhere in sight. She may be already inside. A crowd has formed outside town hall with their signs, yelling shouts of opposition and vehicles honking in support. The crowd grows by the minute. It seems for every one person who was here last time, there are ten more this time. We may not all know each other, but we share a powerful love for this place, and it shows.

I stand among my neighbors and friends and hold my sign

high. There's no way I'll see Shannon and my grandparents in this crowd and heat—it would be too much for them. I'm certain Shannon will park in the back handicap spot and enter through the side door.

After small talk and a lot of shouting and beeping, the crowds assemble toward the front doors. Walking behind me are Ryan, his parents, and Cindy from the bar. Ryan's mom reaches out and squeezes my hand, and Cindy gently waves. Gerry greets us at the door with a clipboard in hand, collecting signatures of those who are interested in speaking. At a glance, there are over fifty names.

Gerry offers me the clipboard to sign. "This is a lot of fucking names, Gerry. We're going to be here all night. I'm not saying it's a bad thing, but …"

"Better too many than not enough."

"Sure. Is there a limit?"

"Not that I'm aware of. I believe they may limit the time from three minutes to two or maybe even one. I think it might be more impactful to have the property owners speak last this time. End on a power note. What do you think?"

"Whatever you think. You've been leading this and have done a great job, so I'd say you know best."

He nods in appreciation and takes the clipboard back. I'd do almost anything to have my property removed from the Green Breeze list, but I am thankful for the reserved seating. Residents are packed in like sardines, and we move at a glacial pace. Ahead are a few elderly residents being rolled to the front for priority seating. This, combined with the volume of attendees, is causing quite the backup.

I spot Shannon's long black hair, grateful she's here. I'm one of the last property owners to arrive. Katie, her husband, and Mary are together at the end of the aisle, clearly putting a divider between the properties that are on board with the wind farm and those that are not. Mr. Folger sits by my grandfather, and I spot two empty seats.

I go around the other side of the aisle so I don't step over Katie and crew. I squeeze past my grandparents and Shannon and take a seat next to my sister, leaving an empty chair on my other side.

Placing my hand on Shannon's knee, I ask, "All good getting in here? Any problems?" As I wait for her response, I search the room for Solia.

"Everything is fine. These two are safe and sound."

My grandparents smile in response, although I'm not sure if they even hear her with the noise surrounding them.

"Excellent." I sit taller and crane my neck for Solia.

"I haven't seen her yet," Shannon says, reading my mind.

I smile. There's no hiding who my heart is set on, especially from my sister. I slide back into my seat, the emptiness of the adjacent chair scattering my thoughts. I hope she arrives soon.

Onstage, the town council organizes themselves at their seats, shuffling stacks of papers and testing their microphones. The podium is in the same spot as last time to allow residents to speak.

The side door swings open and in walk the suits. With no observable emotion, they proceed to the reserved section and sit directly in front of us. How these guys pull off three-piece suits is impressive in this heat, but downright ridiculous. They must have special corporate bullshit deodorant.

They both sit, and jackass number one winks at Shannon. He doesn't even try to be slick, just blatantly winks and turns back around. The worst part is, Shannon smiles in return. Unfreakingbelievable! Now is not the time nor place for me to get into it with her, so I bite my tongue.

Lost in thought, I stare out the bay windows flanking both sides of the stage. Although both gigantic glass panes could use a good cleaning, the view from this room is beautiful. The weather has turned from the doom and gloom of last night to bright, glowing sunshine. It's only a matter of minutes until this room, filled way beyond capacity, bakes us like a sheet cake.

Gerry and I make eye contact from across the room, and he shrugs in what I believe means he, too, is unsure of her whereabouts.

The town council president, Mr. Morgan, takes the podium.

*Maybe she is stuck trying to find parking. Or maybe she's running late. It happens.*

"Residents of Meriden, we're going to call this meeting to order. I look back at the door to see if she's coming in, darting from wall to wall in hopes of spotting her, but she is nowhere.

"We will proceed with this meeting in the same fashion as the last, for those of you joining us again. I'm Sal Morgan, president of the town council. Thank you for joining us here today for what I'm sure will be a civil and respectful discussion. We will begin the meeting with public comment.

"I will turn the meeting over to our moderator. She will announce the name of the next person to speak. When you approach the microphone, please state your name and address for the town record. Because of the number of individuals on the list, we ask residents to limit their comments to one and a half minutes each. We apologize for shortening this, but many of us want to get home before midnight." Mr. Morgan laughs and heads back to his seat at the table.

Shannon taps me on the leg. "Where is Solia?"

"I have no idea. Maybe just running late. She'll be here. I texted her last night, and she said she would be here. I just tried texting her, but the service in here is shit."

The moderator continues with the meeting. "Can we please have Connie O'Reilly?"

A woman in her late seventies rises from one of the back rows. She embodies a sweet old aunt who knits sweaters in her recliner and bakes cookies for little kids. I've seen her in town before.

Connie stands sweetly with her hands crossed, appearing quite nervous to address the panel and a room stuffed with residents. "Thank you. I want to say it's a damn shame you walked into this town, you two." She points to the two suits. "Thought you could waltz in here with your fancy cars and high fashion. Well, you know what I think? I think you should get yourself a pair of damn work boots, roll your sleeves, and live in this town for ten minutes before you decide to destroy it." She nods her chin, points at the two men, then crosses her arms and stomps back to her seat. The crowd goes wild, most people standing and applauding. So much for the sweet old aunt!

The moderator gets back on the microphone. "Order!"

People settle and the next name is called. After ten residents, I've tuned out, the voices blending into one long monotonous sound, and I cannot stop worrying about why Solia hasn't walked through the door.

*Something isn't right. She should be here. She wouldn't miss this. The cabin is way too important to her.*

As if someone switched off the lights, the windows turn black. The rain cascades outside and wind whips around the building.

*Well, if we're going to have a microburst, at least we're inside.*

A light bulb pops in my head. I jump, trip over Shannon and then my grandparents. I rush to the aisle, frantically weaving in and out of people who are trying to see what's going on outside. The room is growing increasingly noisy, but I need to get the hell out of here.

*Solia! Solia is outside.*

She told me last night she was going paddleboarding today. She's on the lake!

At that moment, the thought of the lake transports me

back to last Labor Day weekend. I am over my head in the water of Newfound Lake, struggling to breathe, whipping my hands in every direction, holding my breath as long as I can to dive underneath the black surface, screaming her name until my throat aches. Hot tears stream down my face against the cool lake water. No matter how loud I scream, no matter how fast I swim, I can't save her. Trinity is gone, slipped right through my fingers, taken without permission. I'm right there. Why can't I find her? Where did she go? Why didn't they see her? The guys scream my name in the distance, but I ignore them. I won't stop. I have to find her.

She was just here. She was just here! She was smiling and riding on the tube, the sun in her hair. I told her she could go again. I wanted to see her happy. I couldn't find her.

It was my fault. They had to drag me kicking and screaming from the water. I wouldn't leave without her. I told her it was OK to go again; I needed her to be safe. I needed to return her to her parents. I couldn't let her stay in the water for eternity.

After that, I don't remember much.

These waters have haunted me every single day since the accident. But Solia began mending my wound. She's allowed me to see the beauty in this place as if for the first time. Now she is on the lake. In the very waters I swore I would never step foot in again.

Without turning back for a second, I run through the screaming wind and rain to my truck and hightail it to the marina. Every second of the drive, I hold my breath. I can't breathe; I won't breathe until she's safe. I can't let her slip away from me. She has to be out there. She told me she'd be out there.

My truck plows into the parking lot, and I frantically slam on my horn while I throw it in park. Thankfully, Joe pops out of the main building when he hears the horn and comes running out to the dock. He shields himself from the rain as I run toward him, hollering to be heard over the howling wind.

"I need my keys. I gave them to you. I need to get out there now!" I'm soaked to the bone but don't give a shit. All I can think of is Solia, alone and afraid out on the water.

"Jackson, you can't be serious. This microburst isn't done. Wait it out, man."

"Give me my fucking keys, now!"

Looking shocked and startled, he runs into the dock hut and comes running back with the keys in his hand. "It's in the same spot. I took the cover off hoping you'd be by this summer." His voice fades in the distance because I'm already halfway to my boat.

I throw the throttle in reverse, gun it, and slam forward. I raise the propeller out of the water until I'm clear of the lake bottom and then steam through the channel. She has to be out here. When I reach the lake, there are no boats to be seen. They must've made it to the shoreline.

Visibility is terrible, the rain won't let up, and the wind bruises my cheeks. I don't know what part of the lake she started at, and I'm not even sure she's out here. Driving as slow as possible for fear of missing her, I squint, scanning the water. Time stands still.

*I have to save her. She went out here on a board, not a boat. There is no one out here to help her. I have to save her.*

My heart races, pounding through my chest wall. I'm shaking from fear and anxiety and the thought of losing her.

*I can't lose her. I have to find her. She shouldn't have been out here alone. Where is she?*

I can't think straight. I can't even see straight. A hot stream of tears flows and clouds my vision even more than the rain. I inch toward the shore of the first of two islands in the center of Newfound Lake. Just ahead between them, I see something red in the water.

*Is that her?*

It's just a tiny flash of red. I push the throttle slightly and carefully cruise to the center of the channel between the two islands. Inching closer, the red image becomes clearer, bigger even. It's a life jacket. It's a person, but face down.

*No! No! No, Solia!*

I scream into the wind.

*I am too late. I wasn't here for her. She was alone. She needed me, and I wasn't here. I've been so focused on protecting her heart that I let her go and now she's gone. Oh my god.*

The rain relents enough so the image on the life jacket is visible through ripples in the wind-driven lake water. Brown hair—there's brown hair in the water and two arms overhead. *No! God, no!* It's impossible to get any closer with the boat. It won't be safe. I kill the engine, run to the bow of the boat, and throw myself into the water.

Swimming as fast as I can, the shape of a person comes into view. It is Solia.

"SOLIA! SOLIA!" My voice fights the power of the wind, my words slapping me in the face. Her hair floats on the water, her red vest surfaces, and her arms are laid out in front. I'm almost there. "SOLIA! SOLIA!" I choke out the water that I drink from swimming and screaming. There's movement!

Her head turns to the side, and what I couldn't see until now is the blue paddleboard lying on the surface, half hidden from the powerful push of the wind-driven water.

"SOLIA!"

She stretches her arm slowly in the air.

"Jackson!"

*She's alive. I'm not too late.*

I crush my last strokes as the wind slows and the storm clouds part, and I make it to her board.

"Solia, oh my god. Solia." I reach for her, and her tear-filled eyes meet mine.

"Jackson?" she whispers as she clings to the board.

A surge of adrenaline propels me forward, I tell her to hold on, and I swim to the opposite side of the board. "I'm going to hold on to your hands and pull you toward me. I want you to give it everything you've got. We're going to slide you on top and get you back to the boat. OK? Ready? On the count of three: one, two, three."

Pulling as hard as my muscles can bear, we get her on top of the board. She's coughing, exhausted, and shivering, but in one piece.

*We can do this. The boat is right there.*

"Good job. OK. Are you OK? Solia? Just lie right there, I'm going to get you back to the boat."

She's face down, extended across the length of the board. The boat is thirty feet away.

*We can do this. I've swum farther than this before.*

My whole body is on overdrive. I swim to the tail end of the paddleboard, and with my hands on the back, I push Solia to the boat. "Hang in there. It's going to be OK. I got you."

The microburst has passed, and the sun forces its way through the storm clouds. Seeing the rays hit Solia, I know the warmth will help.

We make it to the rear of the boat and I swim to the front of the board, not once letting it out of my grip.

*I will never let this woman go.*

My future is crystal clear—she did that.

"Solia, I'm going to release the ladder on the back. Do you have enough strength to climb?"

"Yes, I can do that," she says breathlessly but with conviction. When she looks at me, I have the answers my soul needs. She smashes every wall I've ever built, and I want to wake with her face next to mine every morning.

I hold on to her feet and guide them so she slides into the water. "Here, give me your hands." With her hands in mine, I put them on the ladder and hold it still while she slowly climbs the three metal rungs and steps into the boat. She throws herself onto the cushioned seat.

"Stay right there, I'm coming." Thinking quickly, I spot an old bungee cord hooked on a buoy. I secure the clip to the bungee cord Solia has attached to her board. With that connection, I hustle up the ladder. Collapsing next to Solia, I wrap her in my arms tight as if she might get carried away by the wind.

She lies back with her head against the side of the boat, the sun on her skin. Her breathing has finally slowed. I undo the buckles of her life jacket like a package marked Fragile and peel it off her shoulders. "Here, try to lean forward so I can take this off you."

Slowly, I grab hold of the jacket from behind, freeing her from it. I pull my drenched T-shirt over my head, throw it on top of the jacket, and move as close to her as I physically can, lifting her legs onto my lap and hugging her into my chest. Her skin warms against me. She nuzzles her head into the crook of my neck and presses her open palm to my chest.

With a gentle whisper, her breath on my skin, she asks, "How did you know?"

"Oh, Solia. You weren't there. At the meeting. I know you'd never miss it. I kept searching for you. As soon as the storm began, it hit me like a bolt of lightning. I remember you saying you were planning to go out on the lake. All I could think was you were out here alone. Nothing else crossed my mind other than finding you. The thought of losing you broke me.

"You have had my heart from the day I met you. And every day since, you've put me back together, piece by piece. Thinking I'd lost you forever shattered every piece all over again. Solia, leaving was the only solution that would allow me to forget the past, the hurt, and the loss, but leaving Meriden is not the answer. You are my answer."

She slowly pulls her head back to stare at me. Tears continue as she cups my face. "What are you saying, Jackson?"

"I'm saying, I don't give a shit what I thought my plans were. There is no future without you. This place, this lake, this town darkened for me—the lights have been out for too long. You turned them back on, and little by little, I've seen the beauty again.

"Because of you, I see the possibility of love, the forever kind of love that people spend a lifetime searching for. I was being a complete fool, thinking I had it figured out. I thought running away from here would solve my problems, but I had it wrong. My future is here, right in front of me. It's you, Solia. It's always been you. I don't want to live another day without you by my side."

I take her face into my hands and pull her lips to mine, kissing her with wild abandon. I want the passion that has been brewing within me on full display. I can't hold back for another second. Solia moans in response, driving me to want more.

My hands drift from her hair, down her back, caressing her skin and finding her bikini tie. I lift her onto my lap as she wraps her long, sexy legs around my waist. I pull her into my body and let my hands run wild. Solia kisses me back fiercely, allowing me in.

Before we get any further, Joe's boat comes into view around the island, and he's waving and honking from the cockpit. Solia doesn't move one inch. She stays right where she is and softly giggles against my neck, whispering, "Why is it every time things get good, we are interrupted?"

I laugh and turn my head toward the approaching boat.

"Hey there, Captain! I guess you found what you were looking for?"

"Sure did, Joe, and I'm never letting her out of my sight again. Solia, this is Joe, the owner of the marina."

Solia's legs are wrapped around my waist, and she tries to turn to face Joe. "I've seen you a time or two at the boat launch. Nice to meet you. Sorry it's under these conditions."

"I actually can't think of a better condition. I haven't seen my boy here smile this big in forever. And I've known him since he started walking. Whatever Jackson lost, he's found it with you." Joe chuckles. "I'm glad I didn't stop you, Jackson. When you're ready, head back in. The channel is empty. And people are gathering back at the marina."

"People? Why?"

"I'm not sure. As soon as the storm cleared, I flew out to open water. But you certainly don't need me here. You've got it covered." He turns the wheel and speeds off.

Solia beams and snuggles closer, undoing me all over again. I harden underneath her and try to stop my hands from moving further.

"What happened out here?"

Solia hops off my lap, sitting next to me. "I came out a few hours ago and went farther than usual. By the time I started back, the wind shifted and threw me off-balance. I hadn't fallen off my board in ages, but when I did, my paddle went flying. Seems I bought an aluminum one without thinking, and it's at the bottom of the lake for sure. I figured I could make it back lying on my board and paddling with my arms or kicking."

She takes a deep inhale, and I pull her closer. "I did that for a while, but the marina was an oasis. It was just too far, and then the storm came through. I figured it would pass, eventually." Solia's pain-stricken eyes water and I wipe away every drop as it falls.

"You're OK. You're safe. I've got you."

"I was exhausted. I tried, but the wind was too strong and the rain was unrelenting. Holding on was my only chance. I prayed while I laid there, and then ..." She turns and takes me in her arms. "And then you answered my prayers."

"You must have been so scared," I say, brushing her hair off her forehead.

"You're here now. I can't believe you came out onto the water."

"I can. These waters have haunted me for the past year, but I never gave it a thought. You were my only focus—nothing else mattered. In a moment of so much chaos, I've never experienced such clarity. You are all I want, all I need. Everything else in my life comes second and is better because of you. I can love this place again because I've completely fallen in love with you."

"Oh, Jackson." She crawls back onto my lap and holds me. "I've tried so hard to push you out of my mind, but from the moment I met you, my head wasn't going to win. You had my heart without my head's permission. I've given my heart hundreds of reasons why I needed to let you go, but I can't."

I hold her close, hoping I'll never have to live without her. "Let me get you back to shore. Shannon is probably wondering where the hell I went." I lift her onto the seat and hold her chin. "Everything is going to be OK. Whatever happens, I promise I'm not going anywhere."

"What about your father? What about New York? What if I lose the cabin?"

"Solia, look at me," I say, kneeling in front of her and taking her soft, loving hands into mine. "I'm not going anywhere. We can figure everything else out. I'm yours, assuming you want me?"

"That would be a hundred percent yes." She leans forward and kisses me with gentleness and love. "Let's go."

I drive without causing a wake to the mouth of the channel, realizing how much I've missed this water. And because of Solia, I can now let that love grow again.

183 Reasons · 299

As we turn through the channel, more than a few people are waiting at the marina. The closer we come to the docks, the bigger the mob grows. At first sight of us, people shout, wave, and yell out. The only people I see at first are Shannon and Gerry at the front of the crowd, nearing the boat as I pull in. Their faces relax.

I throw the buoys overboard and Gerry grabs the ropes midair. I smile at Shannon, reassuring her. "You found her. Thank god," I hear her say.

"Sure did." With the boat secured, I jet to the spot where Solia is sitting and carefully lift her from the cushion.

"It's OK, Jackson. I'm good, I promise. I can get out."

I set her on her feet and she steps onto the cushion, accepting Gerry's extended hand. With her solidly on the dock, I jump out of the boat and wrap my arm around her waist. Likely sensing we need space, people move back into the dirt parking lot and continue to watch from afar.

"What the hell happened?" Shannon asks. "One minute you are at the meeting and the next, you aren't. I didn't know where you ran off to. It wasn't until Gerry said Solia must be in trouble, and the only thing he could think of was paddleboarding."

"Leave it to Gerry," Solia says, giggling. She hugs Gerry. "Thank you."

"I remember you saying the one thing you enjoy best is boarding around the lake. Given Jackson's reaction, I put two and two together. I'm glad nothing happened out here."

"That makes two of us," says a voice from behind Shannon. Her eyebrows rise, her mouth half open.

Standing directly behind her is Nick Ford.

*What the actual fuck? Who does this guy think he is showing his face here?*

Shannon clenches her jaw and her face reddens. She looks at me in warning.

Solia wraps her arms around my waist. "Let's get you home," I say.

Looking at Shannon, then dead-eyeing Nick, I tilt my head to the crowd. "I am so sorry if I worried or scared anyone by leaving abruptly. Thankfully, she's OK." I kiss the top of Solia's head. "I assume the meeting is still going on? I need to get Solia to her cabin. Everyone must want to get back to business. Thank you for checking on us."

A man I can't see speaks with authority from the back. "Jackson, this is what small towns do. You know that, boy. The look on your face when you ran out of town hall said nothing but pure panic. We were right behind you."

"Thank you," Solia says, surprising even me. "I'm thankful Jackson found me. But I am sorry it took you away from the meeting. I know how important this is."

"Actually, kids, there isn't much to discuss after all," Gerry says. "These suits are going to pack their bags. Come on, let's get her home, and I'll fill you in on the details."

Solia's mouth drops, and I wonder if my ears are clogged with water.

Turning to Shannon, I see Nick the Prick hasn't moved an inch. I can't resist; I whisper into Solia's ear, "I'll be right back."

Walking next to Shannon but not in earshot of the others, I ask, "What the hell is going on?" I look from Shannon to Nick and back to Shannon. "The wind farm? The reason this asshole is behind you?"

"Whoa, Jackson, chill out. First, there are a lot of details, and second, Nick came to make sure everything was all right here."

"He came to make sure everything was all right? Do you hear yourself? This guy, along with the rest of his homies, was ready to destroy this town, and you think he's here to make sure everything is OK?"

"Jackson, not now."

Nick steps forward next to Shannon. "Listen, man. First, I'm happy to see your girl is OK. Second, the wind farm was just business. And business is business. It's never personal. I heard your man, Gerry, is going to fill you in on the details because I know you want to get out of here. But your sister ..."

"Nick, let's let them go," Shannon says, interrupting Nick midsentence.

There isn't enough room for the fury building in my core. "Shannon, I'll call you later." *She can't seriously entertain this piece of scum.*

I shake my head and walk to Solia. I wrap my arm around her and attempt to avoid the mud puddles pooling in the parking lot. "We can come for your truck later," I say. Most people are back in their vehicles and honk as they leave.

I open the passenger door and help her into her seat before walking to the other side, envisioning a dangling sign that reads Fragile, Handle with Care.

Gerry pushes off the driver's side door and puts his hand on my shoulder. "Your dad would be proud of you. You take your girl home, and I'll stop by in a bit to fill you in."

"Thanks, Gerry. I don't want to think what could've happened. Head over as soon as you can—I need the details."

"You got it. I'll be right there."

With one hand on the wheel, I can finally breathe. I place my other arm over the center console and slip my hand into Solia's. Without saying a word, we head to her cabin.

❧

"Wait—what? You're going to have to back way up," Solia says to Gerry who's sitting across from us on the screened-in porch. The temperature is cool enough for Solia to have a thin blanket wrapped around her. She's been on the edge of her seat since Gerry arrived. I'm equally interested and desperately curious to know what happened, but I'd be lying if I said my priority isn't making sure she is comfortable. My hand, tucked under the blanket, holds hers.

"When you ran out, a few people took notice, but another resident was called to the mic and the meeting continued. At some point soon after, Nick stood and asked special permission to address the town council. Sal agreed to the request. Remember that paper you found, Solia? Did you tell Jackson anything?"

"I didn't. I never gave it a second thought after I handed it over to you." She turns to me. "The other day, Mia and I were cleaning, and I came across several papers that were stuffed into an old bureau. I remembered Mike saying he wanted anything we had—forms, letters, whatever. I figured it might be important because it had the State of New Hampshire logo on it and this address. I called Mike but couldn't get a hold of him. I figured the next best person would be Gerry."

"So, after Solia gave me the papers, I left another message for Mike. He was out of town for the day, but when he returned, he picked them up from my place. I heard little until right before the meeting. And even then, I wasn't entirely sure what would happen."

"And?" I ask, wanting to hear the end of this story before the beginning.

"The letter Solia found was from the New Hampshire Conservation Commission in 1977. You were correct in thinking it was a bunch of legal jargon. Mike had to dig, but he learned that the state owns the development rights to the eighty acres surrounding your cabin. I'm assuming no one ever thought this would be important, considering the intent was to leave the land untouched. Not passing this information down the family line may be a simple oversight.

"While your family still owns the eighty acres surrounding

the cabin, the state owns the developmental rights to sixty of them. Under the United States Federal Open Space Preservation Act of 1977, they awarded New Hampshire federal money contingent upon locating open space that was in the best interest of the state to preserve for outlined reasons, such as wildlife and so on.

"The Open Space Preservation Act required the state to solidify agreements with the property owners of said interested land. The property owners would forgo their development rights for the proposed conservation land for a tax break.

"So, Solia's grandparents agreed to this deal. Green Breeze thought they did their due diligence researching the chain of title, but there was an oversight. Corporate lawyers thought the cabin was, in fact, zoned appropriately for the wind turbines. However, Mike discovered that once they deem land for conservation, they can only use it for agricultural and/or farm purposes."

"I'm following you. But isn't that exactly what Green Breeze intended to do with the property—create a wind farm?" Solia asks, looking from Gerry to me and back to Gerry.

"Here's the catch. Your property turns out to be the most important piece in the entire project because of its acreage and elevation. Due to these factors, Green Breeze intended to build the substation. Remember, they mentioned that there needed to be an electrical substation to transfer the energy from the wind turbines to the electrical grid? They were correct in determining a wind turbine farm was qualified to be built on conservation land. However, since the covenants of that deed for open space state they can only use the land for agriculture and/or farming, the substation doesn't fall within those parameters. So it's an obvious violation of the Open Space Act.

"I know I am dragging this out—sorry. The short version

is, it was going to cost them too much money to seek additional properties or figure out how to build it somewhere else. So they're pulling the plug on Meriden."

Solia and I look at each other in disbelief. "That's it? It's just over?"

"Sure is. Your girl here saved the day for herself, this cabin, and the rest of us here in Meriden. I'm sure thankful you found those papers."

"I had no idea they were that important. I can't believe it—and I don't think anyone in my family had any clue this deal existed. They're going to be as shocked as all of us."

"Well, there's a happy ending here in Meriden tonight," Gerry says, getting up from his rocker.

"Where are you going?" I ask.

"I'm leaving you two to it. You don't need an old geezer hanging around here. You need to celebrate."

"Thanks for everything, Gerry. Seriously. We could not have pulled this off without you getting things moving from the very beginning."

"It's a small town, Jackson. When many hands do a few little things, it adds up to a lot. I'm going to miss you around here."

"Oh, Gerry. I haven't told anyone, but I'm not going anywhere. No chance in hell," I say, kissing the top of Solia's head.

"Man, I am sure glad to hear that. And I won't lie. Earl and Sylvia experienced a wave of relief when the deal fell apart. It relieved them from having to make a decision they were torn about. By staying, you answered their prayers. I'm on my way there now to join them for a drink."

"Fill them in and keep a close eye on Grandma. I've heard rumblings she's been a bit forgetful lately. I won't get there tonight," I say, squeezing Solia a little tighter under the blanket.

"Will do. Oh, and Jackson, not that you need to worry, but word has it that Nick Ford is prowling around a few of the luxury lake homes that are for sale. So don't ring the alarm if he's spotted around these parts."

"You've got to be kidding me," I say, but the image of him standing behind Shannon at the marina floods my mind.

I shove that picture directly to the back of my skull. I only have space for one person in my head tonight. Solia.

"Thanks for the info, Gerry. I'll keep that in mind." I laugh to cover my frustration.

Nature's silence settles in as Gerry drives toward the road. I replay the crazy details on a reel in my mind, it's equally unbelievable and amazing. "Come on, you must be exhausted. Let's get you to bed," I say, pushing my chair back and standing to take Solia inside.

"Sorry to tell you, Jackson, but sleep is the last thing on my mind," she says deep and seductive.

# 26

*Sofia*

I pinch myself to make sure I haven't woken in an alternate universe. The walls I'd built around myself have crumbled. Jackson redefines the meaning of love, a soulmate. I had myself believing he was only renting space in my mind and could not possibly take up permanent residence. But he came for me when I needed him most.

Every single word he spoke when he found me, my soul needed to hear. With every point of contact his hands make with my skin, I know he is here to stay. He is staying for me. Now I know, without a doubt, this man is mine.

After Gerry leaves, we sit rocking in the chairs on the front porch, watching the sky turn from blue to pink to orange to yellow and then fade slowly into darkness. The events of the day will eventually settle in but for now, we can rejoice in the outcome. Jackson holds my hand, enjoying these moments of silence.

Snapshots from the past month flash in my mind of the times I longed for more, the times we held ourselves back, tried to cut the strings of attachment before we became too entangled. Kissing him on the hill, his body on mine in the water at Sculptured Falls, our connection by the fire—these times are mine to keep, and now there will be more.

I don't want to waste another moment fighting the urge to fully connect with Jackson.

"Today was more than I could've ever asked for. You came for me, the cabin is safe, and you've decided to stay. I—"

"Solia, I didn't decide to stay. I need to stay. Where you are is where I will be. You gave me 183 reasons and more to open my heart and love again. You are my forever."

I stand from the rocker and take Jackson's hands. "I can't wait another minute."

His stare sears into my body as he places both hands on my hips and pulls me into him. He kisses me with the force of a lifetime of love. His lips meet the crook of my neck, and he trails soft, sensual kisses up to my earlobe. I breathe in his sexy scent, and his warm exhale wafts into my ear. "I'm going to show you exactly how much I want every single inch of your body. I want to make every thought, every dream, and every fantasy I've had about you a reality. One lifetime won't be long enough to show you how much I love you."

He slides the straps of my loosely fitted tank down my arms, letting it fall to the deck, kissing every inch from my neck to the border of my linen shorts. As he stands, he pulls off his hat, tosses it, and shakes out his thick mop. He yanks his T-shirt up and over his head, revealing his muscled chest and glorious six-pack. He takes my face in his hands, and his tongue explores every crevice of my mouth with a passion I've never experienced. He uses one hand to untie my bikini, and my top falls. He cups my breasts, kneading and squeezing. I moan into his mouth.

Hands are everywhere, mapping every inch. He tugs my shorts and panties off in one slick move and scoops me into his arms. With my skin against his, I know I'd let him carry me anywhere.

His brawny arms cradle me against his fevered body. "Where are you taking me?"

"To the shower," he says firmly. My body reacts feverishly to the thought of him finally being mine.

He places my feet back on the ground and opens the shower door. With one of his hands squeezing each of my ass cheeks, he guides me to the shower stall and whispers in my ear, "I want every inch of you, inside and out."

I gasp in delight and shudder uncontrollably.

I turn on the shower so the warm, steamy water massages my body as Jackson removes his shorts and boxers and tosses them on the bench. Seeing him naked instantly rips a burning sensation through my core. While looking at what will be mine, I want more than anything to be explored.

He moves behind me while I face the shower and takes both my hands and places them on the shower wall, tilting me forward. His mouth is on my neck, his hands on my breasts, and he nudges my feet slightly apart. His touch moves down my stomach to between my legs. He parts my lips and circulates with just the right amount of pressure, sending my head back to his chest and eyes to the sky.

*Holy hell, this man knows how to turn me loose.*

His hands and fingers continue to slide up and down, touching every square inch. With my hands pressed firmly on the wall and my legs spread wide, I moan into the dark. I can hear Jackson's "mmm" in my ear, sending me further into heat. He rocks me back and forth … not yet, too soon … it's never been so easy to come undone.

I swiftly spin around to face this handsome god of a man. His ripped body, water flowing down, his hair dripping, his sexiness eating me alive. Wrapping my arms around his neck, I know that true love exists. I can't wait another second to devour him. I drop to my knees and take all of him until I can hear him grunt in satisfaction.

Bringing him almost to the point of release, I glide my tongue to his lips and we are pressed together in passion. He moves away with a devilish stare and heads to the changing area. I hear the rustle of a foil packet and am thankful he was prepared.

With no hesitation, he lifts me, my legs around his waist, and backs me into the shower wall. His powerful arms hold me tight, as if I were a feather in the wind. He then grabs my ass and gently pulls back just enough for him to slip inside. The thrust and force of his size send a rush of fire burning.

There is no way to hold anything back. I scream out his name into the night air. As he pushes deeper inside me, I lose total control and ride the waves of sensation that race through my every cell.

Jackson thrusts into me, my arms wrapped tightly around his neck. My breasts bouncing and slapping into his chest are almost more than I can take. As if reading my body, Jackson knows I'm reaching a climax that I won't return from. He whispers in my ear again, "Oh, no you don't. Not yet. I'm not done with you."

His words alone almost make me release. His thrusting ceases, but he remains inside me thick and strong. For a moment, just a split second, I ask myself, *Can I handle this man?* And then I whisper, "Show me everything you've got, Jackson. I want all of you, and I want you to have all of me."

Squeezing my ass in response, he lifts me to pull out, gathers my face, and kisses me with purpose and passion as he sets my feet on the ground. The water sluices off my body, leaving the wetness inside me, waiting for more.

"Turn around and hold on, Solia," he says as he places my hands on the wooden shelf under the showerhead. I obey, and he takes me by the waist and spreads my feet apart again. There is an element of anticipation because I can't see him.

Suddenly, his tongue is between my legs, from the front to the back.

*Holy shit, I'm going to explode.*

And just as quickly, his tongue disappears, and his mouth is near my ear. In his sex-driven voice, I hear, "I'm just making sure you're still ready for me."

"Jackson, I am so ready for you. Take me."

His body pushes against my back and he shifts slightly. I hold on tight and back myself right into the solid rock of pleasure. Filling me, he thrusts inside my body, grabbing my hips, and slamming me into him. I am screaming his name and gasping for air.

I've never experienced such an involuntary shatter of heat withering my body. Every thick inch of him delivers more ecstasy than I knew existed. Every thrust is deeper and stronger than the last. I am ready to release, and I have no choice. I lose total control of my body.

"Yes, yes, yes, yes, Jackson! Oh my god." My release washes over him inside, making the moment even more intense. This sends Jackson into overdrive. He has been ready and waiting for me because he goes wild. He shakes me, pulls me, and enters me stronger and stronger until his ultimate release.

Shivering and groaning in pleasure, he slowly leaves my body and turns me around. "If tonight is any sign of what's yet to come, Solia, we have a lifetime under these stars."

"After that performance, don't even think that crossing the town limit is an option. You belong to me."

∽

**Preorder book 2 in the Newfound Lake Series,**
*43° North,*
**releasing on April 16, 2024!**

BOOK 2 IN THE NEWFOUND LAKE SERIES

43° North

APRIL 16, 2024

PREORDER NOW!

# 43° north, coming april 16, 2024!

Dive into a captivating tale of love, choices, and second chances in this heart-stirring romance. Meet Shannon, a woman forever entangled with her high school sweetheart, Rich—a love story marred by his increasing devotion to the bottle over his wife. As their marriage teeters on the edge of collapse, Shannon makes a soul-wrenching decision to set herself free.

But freedom comes in the most unexpected form: Nick, the dashing outsider who's not just the town's green energy adversary, but a man who looks as if he's stepped straight out of a romance novel. His allure is irresistible, yet he is the one man everyone in their idyllic lakeside community loves to hate.

When whispers of their newfound passion ripple through the small town of Newfound, the locals are scandalized. Rich, unwilling to fade into the background, stirs up a storm of his own, while Nick turns up the temperature on their sizzling connection.

Will Shannon risk leaving the only love she's ever known for a tantalizing second chance with the town's most controversial figure? Get ready for a roller coaster of emotions that will leave you questioning what you would do for love— and how far you'd go to find it again.

### *Preorder 43° North today!*

# acknowledgments

Never in a million years did I think I'd chase this dream and achieve it. Deciding to become an author is one the best decisions of my life. I've met so many amazing and inspiring people so far, and each of you have helped this journey an unparalleled adventure.

Ruth, you set this show in motion when you told me to "write the damn book." Thank you for giving me the push I needed, advice along the way, and for reading my debut novel before anyone else did.

To Jenn Sommersby, my editor, sidekick, biggest cheerleader, and friend, the stars aligned and sent me on a path to you. Thank you for betting on me, for taking on way more than you intended to, and for helping me navigate these crazy, exciting waters. I appreciate you more than you'll ever know. I'll forever be your PITA.

To K.A. Tucker, you were on my dream board, and you graciously read *183 Reasons*. Pinch me because I still can't believe it.

To Chelsi Lombardo, Cerena, and Danielle, you are the best beta readers an author could ask for. Thank you a million times over.

My street team and ARC readers, thank you for every minute you've spent supporting me. Thank you for every post, email, text, and phone call. I never would've gotten to the finish line without you!

To Mia Sheridan, thank you for sharing my story with your readers. I am so grateful!

To all the BookTokers, Bookstagrammers, fellow authors, readers, and anyone who liked, commented, shared, and/or saved a post I've created, thank you. Marketing this book was an experience like no other. I've accomplished a lifelong goal with your help, and your support has been essential.

Fellow authors, you inspire me every day. You are out there writing, editing, promoting, and supporting each other, and you're some of the nicest people I've ever met. I'm blessed to be on this journey with you.

And lastly, thank you to my husband, my children, my parents, and my extended family. Your support, patience, and encouragement have made this all possible. I love you more than words.

# about the author

Alanna Grace's debut novel, *183 Reasons*, is the first in the Newfound Lake series. Alanna spent most of her summers falling in love with the Lakes Region of New Hampshire where her story begins. When not isn't writing, Alanna is an outdoors enthusiast. Skiing, hiking, and paddleboarding are among her favorites. She lives in New England with her husband, children, and two fur babies. Visit her website for the latest news and to sign up for her newsletter! https://alannagraceauthor.com/

Printed in the USA
CPSIA information can be obtained
at www.ICGtesting.com
JSHW021620130124
55291JS00002B/3